THE RAVEN IN THE GLASS

Gisela spoke softly, quickly, the words running clearly but continuously, flowing as though she were in a trance. "We are linked, you and I, and not only by this Hercules, this man we cannot share. It is a personal bond, but I see larger things at stake: war, nations overturned."

She pushed the cards together and returned the beryl to the table. Her hands echoed its shape in space, as if she caressed it without touching it. Suddenly she gave a little cry.

"The clouds are clearing away — it's so long since they moved! There's a room now — no, a hallway, green-and-white marble, circular, a great door — with glass, like a fan, at the top of it. I see light through the glass — gold, red, lemon-colored. Now I see a bird, like a raven, but I don't think it's a raven — ah — now I see the other, the —" Suddenly Gisela pushed the crystal from her, turning her head away from it. "No!" Her shuddering cry filled the room and she stood up, swayed, and fell to the floor.

THE RAVEN IN THE GLASS

Jill Downie

PaperJacks LTD.

TORONTO   NEW YORK

PaperJacks

THE RAVEN IN THE GLASS

PaperJacks LTD

330 STEELCASE RD. E., MARKHAM, ONT. L3R 2M1
210 FIFTH AVE., NEW YORK, N.Y. 10010

PaperJacks edition published October 1987

CAN. ISBN 0-7701-0747-8
U.S. ISBN 0-7701-0699-4
Copyright © 1987 by Jill Downie
Printed in the USA

To Ian.

Dein ist mein ganzes Herz
Wo du nicht bist
Kann ich nicht sein.

Book One

Matrix

Chapter One

New York

As the mist clears, one of the earliest memories that swims from its shrouded centre is of light through glass. Gold and scarlet, lemon and lime, the light falls warmly upon her. She realizes she is remembering the faceted glass above the front door of the house on the Hudson. The glass itself is untinted, but the trees beyond it change colour with the seasons and mark the passage of the year. Of Elizabeth LaPierre Holman's early years.

Mama and Papa were not often there with her, and she wondered if they had ever seen the lemon-lime colours of the early spring leaves as she had. At that time of the year, Papa would be at the office he still liked to keep on Wall Street, although he no longer

4

sat on the Stock Exchange, that seat he had so triumphantly bought with his first successful speculations in railroads and stocks. Railroads were his main preoccupation now. For a man who, at fourteen, had started as an office boy on Wall Street, he had come a long way.

A long way indeed. Not that it was far, as the crow flies, to the discreet prosperity of the brownstone on Fifth Avenue in the Murray Hill area, where he had moved from Washington Square as the millions began to roll in.

Mama would, of course, be in the Fifth Avenue house in early spring. For further explanation one had only to add that Mr. and Mrs. Holman were members of Mrs. Astor's Four Hundred, and this was the centre of Ada Holman's life. Oh, the joy of receiving the invitation that read: "Mrs. Astor requests the pleasure of the company of —". She would never miss a patriarch's ball, a gala night at the opera, or a chance to show off in Central Park each afternoon her new victoria and footmen in their matching corded livery.

Ada Holman had told her daughter that her birth had taken place "between Mrs. Astor's fancy-dress ball in the March of 1883 and the great Vanderbilt truce of January 1884. So advantageous, my dear Beth, because I could attend both events."

"Why did there have to be a truce, Mama? Are not the Vanderbilts on Fifth Avenue like us?"

"Well, yes, they are on Fifth Avenue — but no, they are not like us. Well, they are now, but they weren't then."

And because it was supremely important for Beth to understand such distinctions, Ada Holman tried to explain it to her.

The most interesting part was not what Beth learned

of the previous social unacceptability of Cornelius
Vanderbilt but of her own family's place in this
complex structure. For even though her father's family
had been in New York as long as the Phelps or the
Varicks, it had previously fallen on hard times. Her
mother, however, was descended from Huguenot stock
that had achieved fortune and position with a rice
planation in the Carolinas. Ada Holman was a
LaPierre of South Carolina, and as such was recommended for inclusion in the inner circle by Ward
McAllister, who at that time was the social arbiter
of the top society hostesses. His own family had social
and business links with the LaPierres, and if Ward
McAllister said they were all right, then they were.

Beth found it strange that it was her maternal
grandmother who had given them entrée into the elite.
Grandmama LaPierre still liked to "dip snuff" and
ate with her fingers instead of her fork, much to her
daughter Ada's mortification.

Beth's younger brother, Henry, had been born during another Vanderbilt stir, when Cornelius Vanderbilt became engaged to Grace Wilson, of whom the
Vanderbilts disapproved. Beth never grasped why,
except that this time there was no truce, but a split
in the Vanderbilt family itself.

When Ada Holman reminisced about this event, she
was most concerned with impressing on her daughter
the effect of unfortunate engagements and marriage
arrangements on a family. The point was not lost on
Beth, and she was content to accept her mother's word.

She knew her parents' marriage had been arranged,
and they seemed quite happy with one another, as
far as she could see, during the limited amount of
time they spent together. Her older brother, William,
Jr., had been born about a year after the wedding,

but Beth hadn't been told which social events had accompanied his birth. Generally, her mother talked of the brilliance of her wedding day, adding "and then William was born, eleven months to the day later," with the satisfaction of one who speaks of a job well done.

She had indeed done her duty well. As William Holman had once said in his daughter's presence, "Sons strengthen a fortune; daughters dissipate it." Beth had fled the room in tears.

Her grandmother LaPierre had come after her, finding her in the maids' sewing room where she had taken refuge. Stroking Beth's head, the familiar smell of parma violet and camphor wafting around her, she talked to Beth in her comforting soft drawl.

"Bethie, your papa never can say what he means, although he always means what he says. Don't you see, honey? Your pa really means that you've got to have sons in this world, because they're a necessity. Who else could take on the business if he didn't have William and Henry growing up to help him? But you, lambie — well, you have the best of everything. Daughters, Bethie, are a *luxury*, that's what he means to say. Why, honey, you're like the rubies and diamonds your papa gave your mama. You decorate his home, and when you get married it will be to an earl or a duke, or some such titled person. That's what your mama has in mind for you. Isn't that wonderful? Isn't it better than having to go to that stuffy old office like your papa does, and like poor William and Henry'll have to do?"

Poor William! Poor Henry! Poor Papa! The older Beth got, the wiser Grandmama seemed to be. It was hard to believe that boisterous William and dreamy, bookish Henry could turn into replicas of the severe ramrod figure their father presented as he left each morning for Wall Street in his frock coat, winged collar, and Ascot tie, square-topped derby in the winter and wide-brimmed panama in the summer. Would they too believe in the sanctity of property, vote the Republican ticket, serve on the board of a few carefully chosen charities? Would they too subscribe to the most conservative of newspapers, join the Union Club? Would they show emotion only when talking of certain Democratic politicians and all labour agitators? All the adult males in Beth's life fit this mould, so presumably some magic metamorphosis was expected to overtake William and Henry during their formative years.

All Beth wanted was to grow up like her mother, a jewelled star in the New York firmament, and illumine the Hudson Highlands, Bar Harbor, Newport, and Europe at the appropriate times of the year. Oh, to dress like Mama in black velvet and diamonds, white silk taffeta and rubies, swathed in chinchilla and ropes of rosy pearls bigger than sugared almonds! To laugh like Mama, smell of jasmine like Mama, and, like her, surround herself with Sèvres china, Gobelin tapestries, the deep pink of Gloire de Paris, and the dark crimson of Jacqueminot roses in rock crystal and lustre bowls everywhere!

It certainly seemed more fun to dissipate a fortune than to strengthen it.

Somewhere around the age of fourteen the mist clears. Beth knows who she is, where she is, and where her mother and father are most of the time, even though she is not always with them. In the fall, when the leaves along the Hudson are red and gold, Mama often goes to Paris to choose her wardrobe, principally from Worth. The family is together for Christmas. In January, Ada Holman may leave for St. Moritz, then go on to London to take in some of the season there before returning for the balls in New York. Together Beth and her mother go to the Hudson property for a while in June before leaving for Newport. There is an occasional variation in the theme, but it remains basically the same.

In a year's time, Mama will take Beth to Newport with her, instead of leaving her in the Highlands. Papa is succumbing to pressure and building a splendid marble mansion in Newport on Bellevue Avenue, although he would much rather remain on the Hudson. It is a compromise gesture, because he has so far resisted all his wife's attempts to get a new palace constructed farther up Fifth Avenue. He likes the brownstone, and he likes Murray Hill, and he will have none of it.

Ada pouts and sniffs prettily, but all she achieves is the mansion in Newport instead of having to use one of the cottages owned by Mrs. Amanda Meunchinger and rented only to a select few. Knowing her mother's skill at financial dissipation, Beth doesn't fancy her father's chances in the long run.

Yes, it was clearly more fun to dissipate than to strengthen, just as Grandmama LaPierre foretold. Elizabeth LaPierre Holman cannot wait to play her part in it all.

Chapter Two

Vienna

The light shifts and splinters between the plumes in Franzi's hat and the lilacs and laburnums of the terraced garden behind her. Franzi is laughing, her head thrown back, exposing the smooth column of her neck above the high, ruffled collar. Even while laughing, her eyes are wide open beneath the straight, strongly marked eyebrows. A blonde curl blows loose beneath the broad-brimmed hat and brushes against the curved, expressive mouth.

The gentleman sitting beside Franzi's daughter, Gisela, is her father, Leo Fischer, but he is not married to her mother. He also is laughing, his eyes on his mistress's bosom as it swells enticingly with the backward curve of her body, making her waist look smaller than it really is. *Mollert* is what the Viennese call women like Franzi Valeska. She is blonde, rounded, almost hefty, close to the ideal of the day. This is fortunate for Franzi, because she is an actress with the Vienna *Burgtheater*, an imperial and court actor — *Kaiserlicher und Königlicher Burgschauspieler* — and perfect in type for the popular light comedies favored by the Emperor Franz Josef and the nobility.

In front of them on the table is the new, young wine of Vienna, the *Heurige*, and Gisela is as intoxicated with its sparkle as the man and woman are tipsy with the wine.

That is how she remembers it, when the dappled light behind her mother grows black, the shadow shifts, and a man is standing there, face shadowed, knife curved against the smooth column of her mother's throat. She, Gisela, starts to scream and scream.

Consternation and commotion ensue as she is gathered to her mother's bosom and hastened from the scene. In the carriage, Gisela keeps sobbing, "I saw him — didn't you see him, Leo? He was there, threatening you, Mama! He was there!"

"Who was there? No one was near our table, Gisela!"

"Behind you — didn't you see him, Leo?" She turns beseechingly to her father, but he shakes his head and puts a hand on her forehead. "There was no one, Gisela, no one. You are hot. Perhaps you have a fever."

Yes, that was it, it must be her fevered imagination. Leo had seen no one, and there sat her mother, alive and well. Her father should know, for he was a respected doctor at the Krankenhaus, with the money

and position of an old, established Jewish banking
family of the Second Society of Vienna — the *Zweite
Gesellschaft* — behind him.

She was taken back to the elegant apartment on
the Asperngasse that Leo Fischer provided for her
mother and put to bed. The concerned whispers outside
her door soon faded away, and she could hear the
bubble of her mother's laughter again. It was not good
to be sad, as Franzi so often told Gisela. Men didn't
like it. They wanted everything to be light and laughter, for life to be pleasantly comfortable — *gemütlich*.

"But what if you really are sad, *Mutti*?"

"Then you must hide it, *Liebe*, and pretend that
all is well. It is part of the art of being a woman,
and the better you are at it, the more successful you
will be."

"At what, *Mutti*?"

"At anything, my darling! But most of all at getting
a lovely man like your father to look after you."

Franzi Valeska claimed to be descended from Russian nobility. She had made her way from Galicia to
Vienna to enrol in the Kirschner Academy and become
an actress. She had had protectors from the age of
fifteen, and at seventeen had met Leo Fischer at a wild
party in a studio on the Gusshausstrasse. There, among
the gilt mirrors, the rosewood furniture, with the
ostrich feathers of her fan held across her face in mock
surrender, she had been impregnated with Gisela.

Being a man of principle as well as a fool for the
theatre — *ein Theaternarr* — Leo Fischer had stood
by Franzi Valeska during the pregnancy and birth.
Afterward they had established an easygoing relation-

ship of some stability and much mutual pleasure. Franzi was skilled as a lover, moderately successful as an actress, and Leo was envied by many men. To see others eyeing his mistress did not in the least disturb him. On the contrary, it gave a zest to the relationship which had so far prevented him from becoming jaded.

And if Franzi occasionally obliged a court minister or some *Herr Baron* or other, Leo turned a blind eye. Why should he care when there were so many other oysters and so many other pearls? Besides, when he felt the approach of melancholy, he would persuade Franzi to recount the private peculiarities and penchants of some of the best-known men about town. She would do so with such delicious, gossipy wit that he would laugh until the tears ran down his cheeks. Tears of happiness were the only kind he wanted to feel against his well-tended skin. It was something he had learned early in clinical practice and now applied to everyday life: never let the emotions become involved.

By "emotions" Leo Fischer meant the black ones. There were many brightly coloured ones to indulge in during the golden Indian summer of the middle years of the reign of Franz Josef. And where better to enjoy them than in Vienna, the Imperial city? Its roots stretched back beyond the Romans, who called it Vindabona for its fabled vineyards, where the Turks were turned back eastward and Leopold, Margrave of Babenberg, lord of the Austrian March, built his castle and established himself. To the south lay the peaks of the Alps, across the plain where ancient roads led to Syria, Carinthia and Italy. The particular genius of these races flavoured the Viennese character, making it distinct from any other in Europe, even from the rest of Austro-Hungary.

Gisela looked more like her father than her mother, a little to Franzi's chagrin. Not that her father was not a fine-looking man, with his slender, strong build, thick, dark hair, and strong nose set in an oval face. He looked quite like the members of the Austrian nobility, with their long, lean bodies and small heads, like greyhounds, and he cultivated the resemblance. But rich and privileged though he was, he would never be more than tolerated by the nobility, in spite of the loans made by his banker father to various counts and barons. In Vienna, the nobility preferred to associate only with each other or the emperor. Leo's lack of title, the fact that he was not one of the "noble ones," *die Adeligen*, mattered quite as much as his Jewishness.

Franzi, however, was sharp enough to see that being Jewish could be a greater disadvantage than it appeared to be in the Vienna of the early 1880s, where anti-Semitism lay simmering like a boil beneath the surface of the city's skin. It had not yet erupted in full force, but since a Jew had to be baptised to get into the army or the court bureaucracy, the powers that be were certainly implying that being Jewish was not completely acceptable. When Leo Fischer offered to give Gisela his name, Franzi had declined charmingly, giving as her reason that she had chosen the name Gisela especially to go with Valeska and had set her heart on it.

"It will look so pretty on a theatre programme, darling."

"Supposing the child doesn't want to go into the theatre?"

"Of course she will, Leo! What else should she do? She will be her mother's daughter, you'll see. A performer!"

Gisela was accordingly enrolled in the ballet school of the Vienna Court Opera, where she was to train as a dancer and receive a certain amount of schooling until she could join the Kirschner Academy, as her mother had done.

Gisela found favour at the ballet school; her strong back and long, slender legs made her a natural for the dance. Here, no one sighed sadly because she was slender and dark instead of rounded and blonde, although Franzi was not at all sure she wanted her daughter to be a *coryphée* with the opera.

"There is more cachet, Gisela, in being an actress. Actresses receive better jewels, better furs, better attention than those little souls dancing in the crowd scenes. Now, if you could sing —"

Gisela's husky voice was charming, but it was not considered by the teachers at the school outstanding enough to show promise of achieving *Glanzrollen*, the star roles.

Yet Franzi was not too displeased with her daughter's prospects. She promised to be a talented dancer, with an attractive speaking voice. Her particular physique and personality did not accord with the current taste for curvaceous blondes of quicksilver mood and wide-eyed charm, but Franzi had watched the males in her circle eyeing her young daughter's graceful body. She had watched them react to the large dark eyes suddenly revealed as Gisela raised her curved eyelids beneath the strong line of eyebrow, and been well satisfied. For some men, only contrast and change were pleasing, and Gisela's looks certainly provided that.

When there were unpleasant anti-Semitic demonstrations in 1888, disturbing the accommodation between the nobility and the finance barons of the *haute juiverie*, Franzi thanked her stars that she had followed her instincts with regard to Gisela's name.

"I cannot see what a stock crash in 1873 should have to do with any of this, Leo — what *is* a stock crash, anyway? — no, no, don't tell me, darling, *das ist mir ganz wurst*, I couldn't care less! All I know is that my feminine instincts have not let me down. Gisela needs protecting — all women need protecting. You males, Jewish or not, will be all right, you'll see. It'll blow over, my love."

Blow over it did, for the time being, and things looked happy and comfortable, *gemutlich*, once more. A new *Burgtheater* was finished, and Forster, the new director, liked Franzi's work. The beautiful Ringstrasse, the new street of glorious palaces and public buildings encircling the heart of the city, was completed, setting the tone for a Vienna that waltzed to the music of Strauss toward carnival time, the *Fasching* of 1889, and the event that would alter the direction of Gisela's life.

The period leading to Lent was carnival time in Vienna, a time of parties, fancy-dress balls, and operettas. Gisela was to make her first stage appearance in a Strauss opera in which the great comedian Alexander Girardi was playing. Although not born in Vienna, he spoke to perfection the Viennese dialect with its French and Italian lightness, casual grammar, quaintly archaic expressions. Girardi so typified the Viennese self-image that he had become a legend in his lifetime. Young Viennese men affected the straw boater habitually worn by the comedian and called it a "girardi."

The cast had been invited to celebrate after the performance at a party given by Friederich Schley, a wealthy banker of the *haute juiverie*, at his Ringstrasse mansion, which was a centre of political, intellectual, and artistic life. The invitation included even the youngest members of the chorus.

Franzi was delighted. Gisela's costume was a particularly becoming one, white silk trimmed with gold ribbon and swan's-down, the skirt short enough to show her slender legs in white silk tights and her small feet in golden slippers. To be sure, Gisela was only eight years old, but, as Franzi knew, it was never too soon to start making people aware that there would soon be a new beauty in their midst. If Gisela's first protector were a good deal older, it would be a kindness to the child herself, after all, and there were only about seven more years until such a decision had to be made. Maybe even five or six — who knew? Franzi herself had waited until she was fifteen only because she had no intention of wasting herself on some rustic Galician boor. Gisela was much luckier, for she would not have to waste two precious years, which would bring a lot more furs, jewels, and security before the mid-twenties were reached and the struggle to hold on to one's appeal began.

Gisela herself was looking forward to the party. There would be Rothschilds there, her mother had told her, and a baron or two, drawn by the prospect of meeting Girardi and a bevy of beautiful actresses.

Outside the *Palais* the snow sparkled beneath the great illuminated windows as the carriages carrying the guests drew up. Some were elaborately painted coaches, some had the Austrian double eagle on their doors; all had liveried coachmen and lackeys. The women's dazzling ensembles were matched only by the gorgeous uniforms of the Imperial army — more splendid, surely, than any others on the face of the globe. Laughing, chattering, singing, they entered the *Palais*.

The mansion itself was a lavish extravaganza of marble, stucco, and gold in a romantic neo-Gothic style. The imposing staircase up which they ascended was decorated with brilliant frescos, and chandeliers glistened over their heads like thousands upon thousands of stars.

During the evening, Girardi sang some of his *Fiak-erlied*, the witty, comic songs of the Viennese man in the street; two of the young actresses sang together; and Gisela and the other dancers performed for the distinguished assembly. Afterward, everyone ate, drank, danced to that springtime-summertime music of Strauss, the man who had captured the spirit of the city, as had Girardi and the inspired architects of the Ringstrasse.

Wien, Wien, nur du allein,
Sollst stets die Stadt meiner Träume sein.
Vienna — only you — city of my dreams...

The evening was a dream to Gisela, drifting by in a kaleidoscope of colour and sound. Close to her mother's side, she shyly received the compliments showered upon them both.

"Delightful — a gem, Franzi, pretty as you — an original, a gazelle!"

The compliments scented the air quite as deliciously as lily of the valley, and Gisela felt intoxicated by their heady perfume.

There was, of course, plenty of gossip, and the favourite topic was the current affair of the emperor's son and heir, Rudolph. The crown prince's affairs were legion, but this one had attracted attention because the girl, May Vetséra, was only seventeen, and rumour had it that her mother had engineered the romance. Her uncles, the rich Baltazzi brothers, were close acquaintances of many of those present and of the emperor's own *chère amie*, Kathi Schratt, an actress with the *Burgtheater* whom Franzi Valeska knew slightly. Everyone was anxious to appear to have inside knowledge of the matter, and the remarks flew thick and fast around Gisela, where she sat close to her mother.

"They say he is addicted to morphine and alcohol — that he has syphilis — no, no, it isn't syphilis, it's the madness of his Wittelsbach inheritance — mad Ludwig of Bavaria, uncle to the empress, you know — the girl is blind to all this, madly infatuated — "

Franzi's silvery laugh bubbled above Gisela's head.

"Ah, you're all so unromantic! It's all so beautiful — a handsome prince, heir to the Hapsburgs, and a lovely seventeen-year-old girl of good family! How many would not envy her and long to be in her shoes? And if her mother encouraged her, what a wise woman!"

"She can never hope to marry him. It would not be an *ebenburtige* marriage, blood issue of a ruling dynasty," objected a male voice.

"Ah, pooh! Marriage is not everything. Happiness is all, my darlings, happiness is all — and what has marriage to do with happiness?"

Amid the ensuing laughter, the child's voice rang out, clear as her mother's laugh.

"I see a raven, *Mutti*. A raven in the glass."

There was an intake of breath, a shocked silence. Franzi jerked her daughter's hand, started to remonstrate with her. "Gisela, hush!"

Even as Franzi stood up to remove her daughter from the group, someone knelt down beside Gisela and took her hand. It was the great Girardi himself, his face gentle, his voice quiet.

"Where do you see the raven, little one?"

Gisela pointed. "There, in the glass." She was pointing at a large cut-crystal bowl on a table, in which floated lilies and orchids. Everyone present gazed at the bowl, but all that could be seen was the light reflecting on the crystal and the clear water within.

"Do you know that the raven is the Hapsburg bird of misfortune? Is that why you thought you saw it?"

Wordlessly, Gisela shook her head.

"What can you see now."

"Alexander, please!" Franzi's voice was agitated, but someone else said, "No, let her continue. This is amusing, Franzi. She has imagination." Girardi repeated, "What can you see now, Gisela?"

The child's voice was lower now, and the people around her had to bend close to hear what she was saying. Staring at the crystal, she continued. "The

raven is flying now, over a beautiful house — in the
country, for there are many trees. There's a girl inside
the house — so pretty she is, lying asleep on a big
bed. And there's a man writing a letter, only the man
is crying and crying, because the girl isn't sleeping.
She's dead. The man is sad — he is taking a gun
and he — he — the raven is flying away now."

Gisela started to shiver violently, and Alexander
Girardi put his arms around her. "All is well, little
one, all is well."

A chill had fallen over the group. Someone gasped
and said, "My God, what has she seen? How did she
see it?"

Girardi stood up and looked at his friends. "I don't
know, but that was not imagination. That was div-
ination." He turned to Franzi Valeska.

"Your daughter has a gift. Perhaps you should
encourage rather than discourage her. After all, it is
a gift almost as rare as my own."

He gave his humorous smile and twinkled at his
audience. The mood changed again, anxiety forgotten
as they all moved out of the shadows of the vision
into the glitter of the ballroom once more.

On 30 January 1889, Crown Prince Rudolph, heir to
the Hapsburg throne, shot his mistress, May Vetséra,
at a shooting lodge in Mayerling. Six or seven hours
later, having first written a suicide note which suggested that he and the unfortunate young woman had
made a pact, he shot himself. Forty-eight hours later,
the body of May Vetséra was smuggled out by her
two Baltazzi uncles and taken to the monastery at

Heiligenkreuz in an attempt to prevent the scandal breaking. It was all in vain. Count Hoyos, who had discovered the bodies, had to stop the Trieste-Vienna express to send the news back to the Imperial palace — and the station master was a loyal employee of the Sudbahn, whose principal shareholder was the Rothschild bank.

The rumours reached Vienna faster than the Trieste-Vienna express and soon spread like wildfire among the set who had heard a little girl speak of a raven in a crystal bowl and violent death. Although secret negotiations were held with the Vatican for a Christian burial, which took place at dead of night and at the height of a terrible storm, a dozen versions of the truth were abroad.

With Franz Josef shut away in the Hofburg or at Ischl, and the Empress wandering like a lost soul across the face of Europe, the members of Vienna's Second Society grew more brilliant and powerful. It suddenly became important to know a Rothschild or to speak with familiarity of Strauss, Brahms, or Mahler.

One of Franzi's admirers gave Gisela a crystal of pale green beryl on an ivory stand lettered in gold, and Franzi set about finding a teacher of the tarot for her daughter, the new performer in the Valeska household.

Chapter Three

New York

In 1897, Beth said farewell to Miss Lucy Green's exclusive girls' school at number one Fifth Avenue for the last time and went to Newport for the season. At the time she saw the two events as marking her passage from girlhood into womanhood.

Nearly as significant was her trip to that part of Sixth Avenue which was Manhattan's fashionable shopping centre, for some of her new wardrobe. Up to that moment she had been confined to strictly controlled areas around the Fifth Avenue brownstone. She was astounded by the crowds, the bustle, the tall buildings which seemed to be going up everywhere around them.

"Goodness, Beth, must you gape in that unladylike manner?"

"I'm sorry, Mama. It all looks so busy — so prosperous."

"I know, and it's not so long since your father had me so worried, foretelling gloom and doom with his talk of dwindling gold reserves and droughts and unemployment, as if all the plagues of Egypt were upon us. It's been so depressing without all the balls, and I was never so glad as when Mrs. Astor inaugurated her new château with that wonderful dance last year. Of course, the Bradley-Martins went too far, and their extravagance has driven them from the country, but there you have the difference, don't you see, between a true lady of society and — and, well, those who don't know how to do things. But with the Waldorf-Astoria going up thirteen stories, besides all the other improvements, he cannot tell me we can't afford to move uptown."

Beth knew her father was under renewed pressure for a marble mansion — "French Gothic, neo-Rennaissance, I don't care what. *You* choose," Ada had begged her husband, placatingly offering a confused architectural choice of styles "— anything but brownstone and Murray Hill, William, *anything*."

But brownstone and Murray Hill and William Holman were winning out so far.

In a fit of pique Ada had her parlour done up in Japanese bamboo studded with jeweled crickets and butterflies, and she ordered two more paintings by the Dutch masters and a set of gold dinner plates; all while William was in California attending to railroad business. When he came back, he didn't seem to notice.

He was far too preoccupied with teaching William, Jr., who was now seventeen, the tricks of his trade while trying to curb his fondness for the horses and his growing awareness of women. At the same time, he found Henry's "bookishness" disturbing.

"Read for a purpose, my boy, read for a purpose."

"I do, Father — to amuse myself."

"Amusement isn't a purpose — it's the fruit of hard work and determination."

Poor William! Poor Henry! For Beth, life seemed perfect. She appeared to be maturing into the kind of young girl a Holman daughter should be. She was perhaps too slim for perfection, a fraction too tall, but her mother was hoping she would round out in the next year or so. "That's what happened to your Aunt Medora. As for me, I developed early."

Ada Holman ran her hands over her ample figure and glanced complacently at her still-attractive face reflected in the carriage window.

It was at the beginning of July that Mrs. Holman left for Newport with Beth and Henry. Both William, Sr., and William, Jr., were overseeing the last details on the Holmans' new seagoing yacht, *Allegra*, and planned to join them at Newport, berthing at Hasards, the yacht club exclusive to the Four Hundred. Henry had opted to accompany his mother and sister, and Beth knew it was not entirely out of affection, although she and her brother got along well. He would be out of his father's steely gaze for a precious week or so, and as long as he accompanied his mother when duty dictated, she would not interfere with the way he spent his free time.

Not that there were many free hours, for the structure of Newport society was as rigidly preordained by the great hostesses as that of New York. Still, as long as Henry was present for the three o'clock ride down Bellevue Avenue, attended the formal dinners, and put in an appearance at the Casino Club, he could be forgiven the occasional late arrival at Bailey's Beach. None of the locals, who were known as "the foot-stools," were allowed on it, but the footman recognized Henry as one of the chosen few, and he was permitted to join his mother's party.

Wearing one of her eighty new dresses, shrouded by a matching parasol, the priceless lace ruffles of her skirts trailing in the dust of the Casino's Horseshoe Piazza, Beth blissfully followed her mother from function to function, only removing her white gloves for approved reasons, such as eating clams cooked among hot stones and brought to the table in a tin basin — one of the currently chic "peasant" things to do in Newport. Sometimes a lady went through five pairs of gloves in a day, and it was well known that one of the Newport set had returned her gloves to their Paris maker because they did not faultlessly follow the contour of her nails.

Mrs. Holman was upset at the absence of her husband and older son. Henry was still too young to open the cotillion with her when they held their own ball at Beausejour, the new marble mansion that Ada Holman liked to call her "cottage."

"Where can he be?" she complained to Beth. "He

has had plenty of time to get here, and I'm sure he has allowed himself to be sidetracked."

Beth was sure her mother was right. Apart from business, one of the greatest pleasures in her father's life was his yacht. It was one thing he had in common with his eldest son, and Beth imagined that William had easily persuaded his father into some oceangoing racing. However, the invitations to the ball had been sent, the replies received, and there could be no turning back.

The answer to Ada Holman's problem was unexpectedly solved on the tennis courts at the Casino Club. She was not to know that on that fateful day she had exchanged a temporary inconvenience for a problem of different proportions.

A few years previously tennis had been introduced from the continent to the younger Newport set. Since it seemed to be a suitable activity in which Beth could be introduced to her contemporaries, her mother had accordingly fitted her out with the appropriate clothing: white tennis shoes, black stockings, white silk blouses, and pleated skirts. The addition of bloomers and a large sailor hat with a double veil ensured her modesty. Henry had played tennis the previous year and could show his sister how to play the game.

Beth took to it quickly, enjoying the freedom of movement despite the layers of clothing and the veil before her eyes. Mrs. Holman sat in the dappled shade watching her children play, but much of her attention was elsewhere.

"My dear Mrs. Holman, how quickly your daughter has learned to play. She is quite charming!"

Ada Holman peered up distractedly through the

fringes of her parasol at the slim, fair-haired young man standing at her side.

"Why, thank you. It's Jonathan Shotover, is it not?"

"Correct, Mrs. Holman — at your service. May I join you?"

"Of course." Mrs. Holman indicated the lawn chair next to her, and the young man sank gracefully into it. He was impeccably dressed and gloved, skin shining with good health, every fair hair immaculately in place.

Mrs. Holman knew he was the scion of a very exclusive Bostonian family of Anglo-Saxon stock who now lived in New York. She did not know the family well, nor had she personally met Jonathan Shotover before — she had heard he had been abroad for a while — but various members of his family had married into the exclusive Four Hundred set. Because of his unerring taste and wit, Jonathan Shotover himself was considered quite a social leader and was in great demand at dinner parties where there were older family members or out-of-towners to impress and entertain. Conversation came easily to him, and he could charm the most stuffy dowager from Beacon Hill. Speculatively eyeing him, Ada Holman opened the conversation.

"Are you enjoying Newport, Mr. Shotover?"

Jonathan Shotover laughed delightedly with a gaiety that made Ada Holman's spirits suddenly lift. "Ah, who would not? It's the most marvellous place to be in the world, isn't it?"

"Certainly it is. Where else would one want to be in July?"

"Oh, I agree entirely. I hear that Mr. Holman is bringing his new yacht to Hasards. Will he be joining you soon?"

Ada Holman was unable to conceal her agitation when she replied. "I do so hope so, Mr. Shotover, but he seems to have been delayed, and I have this problem..."

Not quite knowing why, she found herself confiding in this charming young man who listened with such touching concern. When she had finished speaking, Jonathan Shotover sighed and said, "Mrs. Holman, I sympathize with you. Can there be any art, any profession more taxing than being a leader of society, I wonder?"

A flood of warmth filled Ada Holman. "Mr. Shotover, would it be presumptuous of me to ask *you* to open the cotillion? That is, if you have not promised to do so for anyone else. I would not want to offend anyone."

Jonathan Shotover's smooth, attractive features reflected unabashed delight. "Mrs. Holman, I cannot tell you what an honour it would be! If you like, I could give you a hand with the details. It must be very difficult without your husband here to help you."

"Oh it is," said Ada Holman earnestly, hardly able to believe her good fortune. "Perhaps you could come to Beausejour tomorrow and go over the arrangements with me. There's so much to think of."

"I understand," was the reply. "Every detail must be considered, for it is in the details that one makes an impression, that one builds up the memories that others will take back to New York with them in September." The candid blue eyes gazed earnestly at her.

Ada Holman knew exactly what he meant. Parties and dances were not a matter of fun; they were moves made in the battle for supremacy in New York society.

She sighed, relief flooding her. "I could not have expressed it better myself, Mr. Shotover."

"Jonty, please," said her saviour with his infectious smile. "I shall be at Beausejour tomorrow morning and can help you with the guest list, the menus, decorations, and so forth."

Jonty Shotover looked across at the tennis court and the two young Holmans. "What handsome children you have, Mrs. Holman! Would it be presumptuous of me to ask what you have chosen for your daughter to wear?"

"I could show you tomorrow the ensemble we have in mind."

"Wonderful!"

They were mutually delighted with each other as the conversation came to an end and Ada Holman removed her reluctant offspring from the tennis court to meet her new courtier. He was charming to them, complimenting them on their athletic skill and their energy and seeing them all to the foyer of the club and into the hands of their liveried footman.

With a last bow, Jonty Shotover turned back into the club and made his way to the Horseshoe Piazza. He was elated at his success. It had all gone so well! Ada Holman had actually asked him for help without his having had to engineer the request. The season stretched before him, filled with delights.

"Mr. Shotover."

So, he was there already, waiting in the Piazza. He saw the magnetic eyes beneath the hooded lids, heard the voice like brandy over ice, warm as velvet, yet with cold steel hidden beneath.

"Count von Schönstein."

"At your service. I think your interview went well?"

"Very well. I am going over the invitations for the ball with Mrs. Holman tomorrow, and I shall make certain your name is on the list."

"Wonderful, Mr. Shotover. I congratulate you."

"Not at all, Count von Schönstein. It is Mrs. Holman who should be congratulated. Your presence will bring her the cachet she so desperately seeks and which no other guest this year could bring her."

"You are too kind. I trust the cuff links from Black, Starr and Frost were to your taste?"

"Exquisite, sir, and it is you who are too kind."

"I hope you will also enjoy the addition to your wine cellar from George Kessler's when you return once more to New York."

With a sharp bow from the waist, the slim, graceful figure of Count Maximilian von Schönstein turned to leave, bringing the conversation to a close.

Jonty Shotover no longer felt merely elated; he felt positively euphoric. He would be able to walk into Beausejour the next day carrying the count's name like an offering before him. His conquest of Ada Holman would be complete, for the count was the catch of the season as far as foreign titles were concerned. He brought with him the romantic charm of Vienna and, above all, a title almost as ancient as the Hapsburg name itself.

For ornamentation, organisation, and pure panache, the Holman ball turned out to be one of the highlights of the Newport season. The grounds of Beausejour were illuminated, and the staff wore new livery of blue and gold. Cascades of roses and jasmine fell from the chandeliers, and orchids hung from the palm trees. The menu, prepared by the new French chef acquired with Jonty Shotover's help, was superb. From the bisque of crabs à la Norfolk to the parfait noisettes with the 1805 cognac, the meal was declared a symphony.

The *pièce de résistance* of the evening, however, was Elizabeth LaPierre Holman. When it came to decorating Ada Holman's daughter, Jonty Shotover's mastery of the external, his eye for the perfect detail, reached its apogee. He had counselled against the original ensemble, and Ada Holman had taken that decision with reasonable calm. When he made his next suggestion, however, she protested loudly.

"No jewels! Jonty, you've lost your mind! Of course Beth shall wear jewels — she shall be covered with jewels, thousands of dollars' worth of jewels!"

"No." Jonty leaned across the table and gazed earnestly into Ada Holman's eyes. "Not jewels — but thousands of dollars' worth, yes. Thousands of dollars' worth of *nature's* jewels and then —" with a careless gesture of his perfectly manicured hands "— you will throw them away!"

Beth Holman made her entrance into the ballroom of Beausejour wearing not a single precious stone, but a thousand dollars' worth of purple violets, their tender velvet petals fluttering against her white lace dress and the soft sheen of satin ribbons in purple, mauve, and white wrapped around her tiny waist. Her dark hair had been left to fall in heavy, shining waves around her face, and violets on ribbon cascaded over it. Ada Holman, blazing in enough diamonds for the two of them, saw that her daughter was a sensation and that she owed it to Jonty Shotover. He had perceived the delicate quality of her looks and youth and had taken advantage of it.

Glittering in her jewels and in triumph, Ada Holman watched Beth dance with the sons of her friends and the young men imported from the local naval training station to even up the numbers. There was always a shortage of men, for hers was not the only husband to be absent. After all, it would be difficult for such a lifestyle to exist if the men were not keeping their fingers on the financial pulse of the nation.

The sons of her friends were of only minor importance and the other young men were just so many extra bodies to dance with. Ada Holman was after bigger fish. She watched Count Maximilian von Schönstein dancing with her daughter and had difficulty restraining an audible whoop of triumph. He was exotically handsome, fluent in English — and his bloodlines were impeccable. And it was nice for Beth that he was young, although that wasn't, strictly speaking, necessary.

On the dance floor, in the middle of a hundred dancers or more, the hypnotic eyes, the mesmeric voice cast their spell on Beth. The smooth, lightly tanned skin was marked on the forehead and one cheekbone by tiny scars, small white threads against the olive complexion. Strangely, they only served to deepen the exotic nature of his looks rather than detracting from them. The young, inexperienced girl was overwhelmed by the seductive light in those melting dark eyes, the voice that licked around her like a flame.

"Miss Holman, you are so like someone I know

in Vienna — so very like. Have you relatives there, do you know?"

His voice seemed to shiver through her, making her own voice tremble. "I — I think not, Count von Schönstein."

"Ah. Do you know, Miss Elizabeth, that it is the custom on the first day of March for Viennese to give violets to our friends — and those we love?"

"No, I didn't, Count von Schönstein."

"Max, please."

"I am called Beth, usually, by my family."

"Beth — delightful! So simple, natural and charming, like its owner."

She could think of no reply, was incapable of even saying "thank you," all words sucked from her into the vortex of feelings that swirled inside her at the sound of his voice, the attentive gaze of his eyes, brooding and tender. Carefully protected from the opposite sex in the shape of young, unattached, unrelated males, she would have felt shy with any of the men in that ballroom. This Viennese count with his pretty compliments, his European sophistication, and his lilting accent, totally overwhelmed her.

That night, and in the nights that followed, Beth could not sleep for thinking of him. During her waking hours she spent most of her time dreaming about him. Her brother Henry had discovered that the marks on the count's face were duelling scars. When he had told her, Beth had felt a thrill so acute she could not have said whether it was of terror or delight, but it only added to his magic. When he called to pay his respects, and when they met again at other balls in other houses, she could not hide the adoration in her eyes. She was desolate when he left Newport at the end of July.

A week after his departure a package arrived for Beth. It contained a brooch of amethyst violets, a diamond at the heart of each flower. With it was a message: "For Beth, to remind you of our Viennese custom of giving violets to those we love."

Ada Holman, although shocked by the forwardness of such a gift and such a message, simmered with delight and advised caution. "Charming, my dear, but of course it will have to be returned."

"But Mama!" Beth cried. "He will think we disapprove of him!"

"Trust me, Beth, to do it in such a way that he will not take offense or misunderstand my feelings on the matter. You are only fifteen, and we don't want your father turned against — well, turned off any possibilities, do we?"

Beth moved as if in a dream through August to the last event of the season on the first Saturday of September, when Mrs. Stuyvesant Fish gave the Farewell Ball at Crossings. The orchestra played "Home Sweet Home," and everyone left to go to their houses on the Hudson or Long Island until the New York season started again.

This, then, was love. It was exactly as it had been described in the "True Love Stories" magazines that Else, her mother's personal maid, had smuggled into Beth's bedroom along with the marzipan candies from Germantown that they both loved so much. Beth knew that she was still too young to marry, or even to be engaged, but she also knew that her mother would not pass up this opportunity. Ada Holman stood a far better chance of talking her husband into Beth's marriage with a count than into a new palace on Fifth Avenue. Beth only wished Grandmama LaPierre was still alive to see it all, for she would have loved Count Maximilian von Schönstein.

Falling in love was as magical and intoxicating as she could ever have hoped, ever have dreamed. The future lay ahead of Beth, bright with promise.

Chapter Four

New York

Count Maximilian von Schönstein returned to America that winter, and visited the Holmans in New York.

"There, you see!" cried Ada to her husband. "We should have been out of here by now, William. I just hope he doesn't think we're only worth a million or something!" She had the main salon redone in red silk damask patterned with the arms of some noble Italian family from whose palace it had been ripped, and ordered new furniture the exact replica of that in le Petit Trianon at Versailles.

This time the count had a gift for Ada Holman which he brought over on the boat himself and drove

up Fifth Avenue across the newly fallen snow. It was
a sleigh, imported from Russia, with silver bells and
crimson pompons, piled with bearskins. Ada Holman
was ecstatic at the very public nature of the offering,
which could be displayed in Central Park in the
afternoons to the Astors, the Oelrichs, the Belmonts,
and anyone else who mattered. She decided to accept
it.

Beth looked delightful sitting among the furs,
accompanied by the count and her mother. Although
Beth had not yet done any of the filling out her mother
had envisaged, Count Maximilian seemed completely
enthralled by her. It was during the course of this
visit that he first spoke to the Holmans of his intentions
and his feelings.

"I realize Beth is much too young yet to be thinking
of marriage, but I am anxious you should know that
my intentions are honourable, and to give you, sir,
a chance to peruse my family background and ascertain
that I am as I present myself to be."

"Oh, my dear Count, we would never doubt your
word!" declared Ada Holman, clasping her hands
together in ecstacy. To have her prayers answered, and
before Beth had even reached the age of sixteen!

William Holman looked dourly at his prospective
son-in-law. Although they shared nearly the same
ethnic heritage, it made little difference. William
Holman thought of himself as American, not German,
and of this man as a foreigner, and he fully intended
to have him carefully checked out. He himself would
have preferred an alliance for Beth with the son of
one of his business associates, carefully chosen to

amalgamate such family interests as potentially competitive railroads or manufacturing companies. He knew, however, that his wife had set her heart on a title for Beth, and he had an aversion to the British nobility, which had been Ada's first choice.

"I'll do that, sir, for Beth's sake," was his steely reply as he gazed into the young Austrian's velvet eyes. Count von Schönstein suddenly appeared to become hesitant, almost shy.

"Mr. Holman, sir, if you will forgive me — I discovered from a mutual friend that we share a common interest, and I took the liberty of bringing you a small gift. May I ask your footman to bring it up?"

William Holman looked first taken aback, then uncomfortable. He could not think what he and this exotic creature could possibly have in common. Taking his confused and muttered rejoinder as consent, his wife summoned the servant, exclaiming excitedly, "Oh, William, isn't this thoughtful of the count! I wonder what it can be?"

The footman arrived carrying a fairly small wooden box with a glass lid. He handed it to the count, who held it out to his host with his usual deep bow.

"With my compliments, sir. As you undoubtedly know, they were just discovered in South America."

Mrs. Holman was disappointed when she peered into the box and saw a rather unattractive-looking plant lying on some moss. It didn't look too healthy, since it was mottled and gave off an offensive odour. Then she heard her husband's intake of breath and his exclamation.

"My God! *Restrepia cucatensis!*"

"Indeed, sir. Isn't it incredible?!"

Ada Holman saw to her amazement that her husband appeared close to tears. When they acquired paintings he usually asked, "What's it worth?" When they went to the Metropolitan Opera House on Mondays, he called it "caterwauling." To move him thus, she knew what the evil-smelling plant had to be.

"Oh," she said, "it's an orchid."

Making money was William Holman's avocation; sailing was his relaxation; orchids were his passion. He had a conservatory full of them attached to the Murray Hill house, and there he spent most of his spare time. It was the main reason he refused to move from the brownstone, even though his wife promised much more splendid greenhouses. He, like his orchids, had roots in the soil of his Murray Hill conservatory, and he wasn't going to be uprooted for anything or anybody. Let Ada redecorate around him and cultivate foreign nobility, as long as she left his orchids alone. The scales fell from William Holman's eyes, and he saw what a paragon stood before him.

"Sir, you — I don't know what to say."

"Please. It is enough to know it is in good hands."

"Oh, it is, it is, I assure you! You must see my collection — but, first, this should be removed from this box as soon as possible."

As William Holman hurried from the room, barely excusing himself, Count von Schönstein turned and smiled sweetly at Ada Holman, and she realized what a stroke of genius the gift had been. The count had managed to find something to give a multimillionaire, surely one of the more challenging tasks in the world. He was an even more remarkable young man than she had thought, since her husband was fairly secretive about his passion, and she wondered who the count's source of information had been. She would have been very surprised to know it had been her own son, William, Jr., and even more surprised at the circumstances surrounding the exchange of information.

Count Maximilian von Schönstein returned to Newport the following summer, 1898, and although no announcement had been made, his engagement to Beth was considered a foregone conclusion.

With the count as a prospective son-in-law, and Jonty Shotover organizing her social life, Ada Holman's stock had never been higher. True, William, Jr., had begun to spend far too much of his time with women, and Henry was still too bookish for his father's tastes, but even there the two new men in Mrs. Holman's life had made a difference. Count von Schönstein was spending some of his time with William and had somehow managed to persuade him that finding favour with his father through showing an interest in the business might not be a bad thing.

As for Jonty Shotover, he had worked wonders with Henry's self-confidence. He had taken the boy's wardrobe in hand and encouraged him to use his athletic skills in such pursuits as tennis and riding. In consequence, Henry appeared a much happier boy. As Jonty himself said to Ada Holman, "You see, if he feels better about himself, it will make him a different person — even if it's only so small a matter as being able to walk into a room with confidence. After all, you know what the great Barnum says, don't you?"

"No, I don't!" said Ada with amusement. Jonty's wide range of knowledge and acquaintances never failed to amaze her. "Oh, you mean that man with the circus at Madison Square Garden. What does he say, Jonty?"

" 'Cultivate the externals,' my dear Mrs. Holman, and I think he makes a lot of sense, don't you?"

Looking around at her Gobelin tapestries and the new gold-encrusted Florentine doors leading into the library, Ada Holman could not help but agree with him.

Chapter Five

New York

By the last year of the dying century all the stores were outlined in incandescent lamps and New York began to glitter in the night. There was yet another rift in one of the major families when a war for social supremacy broke out between two of the Mrs. Astors. William W. Astor left for England with his Mrs. Astor and became a Britisher.

But for Beth Holman all that mattered was that she became officially engaged. True, she had not yet had a genuinely private conversation with the man she was going to marry, and she knew little more about him than she had two years previously, but none of that had any importance. The effect he had on her was still the same — no, it was stronger, more compelling than it had ever been. She knew with absolute certainty that she was going to live happily ever after just as Grandmama LaPierre had told her. The count brought her jewels, paid her compliments, sent her tender little notes; therefore he loved her. Was that not what she had been taught?

In spite of being seduced by an orchid, William Holman had his lawyers draw up an elaborate marriage settlement involving cash, stocks, and shares to be given to his prospective son-in-law. One did not, after all, get a title for nothing.

As the century turned, Mrs. Astor ushered it in by granting a newspaper interview. Ada Holman was quite taken with the idea and discussed it with Jonty Shotover.

"It would seem like a good time for us to do the same thing, with Beth's wedding coming up. What do you think, Jonty?"

Jonty agreed. "But we must be careful to choose the right journal. I'll make some enquiries."

After some research and discussion, they settled on a paper that was well to the right, and as far away from the yellow journalism of Hearst's *Evening Journal* as possible. The editor was an old friend of the Shotover family in Boston and delighted to get an interview from the distaff side of the Holman empire.

"He feels you'll be very comfortable with this reporter. His father is a lawyer, I believe, and lives on London Terrace. It isn't Fifth Avenue, but it's most respectable."

"That sounds acceptable, Jonty. Arrange it for me, will you?"

Years later, every detail was still clear, standing out against the mists of her girlhood like a beacon. Strange, because she couldn't have known at the time the significance of what was happening to her. No warning bells sounded inside her. It wasn't love at first sight. How could it have been? She was already in love, wasn't she?

It was early afternoon — rather a gloomy one, as she recalled. She was just back from a visit to her Aunt Sadie's, and had decided not to go riding in Central Park that afternoon because it looked like rain. Instead, she went to the library to play the piano. It had been a while since she had practised, and she didn't want to let any of her skills get rusty. European women were so accomplished, she had heard; she wanted so much for Max to be proud of her.

When she opened the double Florentine doors, she gave a start of surprise. A young man was standing near the porcelain fireplace, his hands in his pockets, his back to her. He swung around as he heard the door open.

"Mrs. Holman? Oh, I'm so sorry."

"Are you here to see my mother?"

"Yes, I have an appointment, but there seems to be —"

"That's strange! My mother is out today. Are you sure she's expecting you?"

"I thought she was, but the maid seemed put out also. She's checking. I wonder if I've got it wrong?"

While this disjointed exchange was going on, the young man and woman were taking in each other's appearance. Beth saw a tall man in his mid-twenties, perhaps, with springy dark hair and the bluest eyes she had ever seen in her life. They were not china blue like Jonty Shotover's, but a clear azure, like her mother's turquoises. He was more solidly built than either of her brothers or her fiancé, craggier in feature, with a slight cleft in his square chin. There was a musical lilt to his deep voice, but she couldn't place it.

"Perhaps if you told me why she was expecting you?"

"I guess I got the dates mixed up. I was expecting to interview Mrs. Holman for the *New York Courier*. My name is Liam O'Connor."

Irish, of course — that's what the lilt was. Beth saw he had a dimple in his cheek as well as the one in his chin. The blue eyes danced, as if he couldn't help but be cheerful in spite of his blunder. Beth found herself smiling.

"I'm afraid you have made a mistake, Mr. O'Connor. I believe my mother is expecting you tomorrow, and since her secretary makes her appointments, she is unlikely to have made an error. Perhaps your paper —?"

"I must have misread my own handwriting. It isn't the first time. I'll take up no more of your time, Miss — Holman, I presume?"

"That's correct."

"How do you do?" He came forward with his hand outstretched, and since it would have seemed rude not to acknowledge it, Beth took his hand in hers. His hand was large and strong-looking, the handshake firm. She had taken off her gloves on entering the house, and the feel of a male hand in hers was unaccustomed, unexpected. She supposed that was why she had such a strange sensation when they touched. He himself seemed undisturbed by what he had done, so it was apparently accepted behaviour in his circle. The only male hand she had touched, except those in her family, was her fiancé's, and the effect on her had also been unaccustomed, extraordinary. But she had expected that — she was in love with him, wasn't she?

"May I wish you happiness, Miss Holman, on your engagement? I believe it is one of the topics I am to discuss with your mother — tomorrow."

"Tomorrow, yes."

Liam O'Connor shrugged his shoulders and smiled at her, and Beth found herself smiling again in response. Suddenly, out of nowhere it seemed, she heard herself saying, "This is most unfortunate for you, a wasted trip. Would you like some tea before you go?"

It was obvious from the expression on his face that the young Irishman was as surprised as she was by her unexpected invitation. There was a pause before he said, almost gruffly, "That would be nice — if it's not inconveniencing you."

"Not at all. I was going to ride in the park, but the weather isn't good, so I decided to stay at home."

"Perhaps — would you allow me to interview you while I'm here? It would make an interesting addition to my talk tomorrow with your mother."

Beth hesitated and the young man added quickly, "If you feel it would be indiscreet to show I had spoken to you privately, I could use some of your thoughts — your perspective, as you might say — without directly mentioning your name. It would make for a more interesting piece."

"Why, I think that would be fine, Mr. O'Connor."

The parlourmaid's face was a study when she arrived for her orders. It was an unheard-of thing for a young girl of good family to be alone with a man, and here sat Miss Elizabeth with a newspaper reporter! She couldn't wait until she had brought in the trolley and could get back to the pantry to tell the rest of the staff.

Liam O'Connor looked across the table at his hostess. He had heard she was seventeen, but she seemed older in some way. He supposed it was the self-possession bestowed by money and wealth. He could see the resemblance to both father and mother in the face: dark eyes and hair, determined chin, mobile mouth. Beneath the strongly marked eyebrows her eyes were intelligent, observant; straight and slender, she carried herself like a queen. Her skin was flawless, the light and shade playing over it as if it loved every pore. Steady, he told himself. She's not just any young girl, she's a multimillionaire's daughter and probably sees you as a minion.

An old familiar loathing of the privileged and the powerful rose inside him. He thought of the ball he had covered for his paper only a week ago — the two fountains in the ballroom had flowed with champagne. It had been hard to take when he had thought of the six-storey tenements in the Seventeenth Ward owned by the host. They could not even boast running water, only a shared tap in the tenement yard, the water flowing with typhus germs and God only knew what else. Now, when he looked at the girl, it was the silk blouse with the handmade lace and the perfectly matched pearl strands around the slender neck that caught his attention.

As he did so, a fleeting smile crossed her mobile mouth, and she suddenly said, "I sometimes have trouble with my handwriting, too. Grandmama La-Pierre used to say it looked like a three-legged scorpion had taken a walk in an inkwell after a touch too much old Charleston 'n Savannah Madeira.''

Liam O'Connor was completely disarmed. It wasn't that the remark was outstandingly clever or witty, but it was so unexpected, done with such a nice touch of her grandmother's accent, that he was charmed in spite of himself. He felt himself grinning. "Sounds just like mine, only in my case I guess it'd be a spider in Irish whiskey. Why don't we start by your telling me about your grandmother?''

The conversation between them flowed easily, interrupted only by the arrival of the trolley, the serving of the tea and cakes. Beth had never had a conversation like this with a man before. She had never talked about her life with her father or her brothers or her fiancé. Somehow, it would have seemed improper.

Why she should feel so comfortable sitting in Papa's library talking to a newspaper reporter about her grandmother, her mother and father, the house on the Hudson, she had no idea.

"You seem fond of your Hudson home."

"The trees are so beautiful, as if they really *belong*, you know — not placed, if you see what I mean.''

"I do. Have you ever been to the Adirondacks?''

"No, I haven't. Is that what the trees are like there?''

"Even more so!''

'Really?'' The straight, strong eyebrows were raised in delight, the dark eyes looked directly into his, sparkling with animation. This isn't what rich girls are supposed to be like, thought Liam O'Connor, not with the likes of me they're not. She's too good for that decadent Viennese she's going to marry. Does she know, I wonder. Does she care? How could she, shuttling between Newport and Millionaires' Row, not even diverging far enough from the Hudson Valley to know what the Adirondacks are like?

Did she even, he wondered, know what her older brother was like? She was almost certainly unaware that William Holman, Jr., and the count had first met in the Peacock Alley of the Waldorf-Astoria, eyeing the demimondaines, and had since spent a considerable amount of time in each other's company. These were pieces of information that had come to him when he was doing his research for the interview with her mother. At the time, he had laughed with his colleagues over the duplicity of the son, the deception of the father — and the protected little rich brat sold for a decayed title to an inbred Austrian decadent. He looked across the tea table at the little rich brat with her shining eyes and glowing cheeks and his next remark burst from him.

"You say you've never seen the Adirondacks. How much do you know about New York, Miss Holman?" He watched the surprise flare in her eyes.

"Why, I was born here, Mr. O'Connor. I'm not sure what you mean."

It was not so much the question itself as the tone in which it had been put to her that startled Beth. He was challenging her and she wasn't sure why.

"I mean places like Broadway, or Sixth Avenue, or Little Italy, or any of the Lower East Side."

"I have shopped on Sixth Avenue, and seen parts of Broadway — I believe Grace Church is close by. Why do you ask?"

Liam O'Connor ran his hands through his hair a couple of times in as uncontrolled a gesture as Beth had ever seen in an adult. She also noticed it made his hair seem even thicker and curlier.

"Because, Miss Holman, the Irish in me gets the better of me from time to time, and I speak before I think — please excuse me."

He had been trying to tell her something and she knew it. The same doggedness that had made a rich man of her father and a leading society matron of her mother drove her on now, when she should have put an end to such an unsatisfactory and improper interview and sent Liam O'Connor about his business. She looked straight into the brilliant blue eyes in a way that would have shattered her mother and continued grimly with her questions.

"Mr. O'Connor, I think you asked me the question for a reason. All your Irishness did was enable you to do so. Why?"

Damnit, he thought, I'll tell her — why not? If she tells her mama, I'll be in trouble with the chief, but it won't be the first time, nor the last.

"Because of how different those places I mentioned are from Fifth Avenue, and the places you seem to know, that's all, Miss Holman. If I could show you, you might understand. Just forget what I said, and thank you for the tea and cakes, and I'll see your mother tomorrow — if she still wants to see me by then."

No wonder Mama preferred not to have anyone Irish on the staff, thought Beth. They were rough, rude and untrustworthy, as she so often said — just like this curly haired, blue-eyed Liam O'Connor, with his dimples and his strong hands that had so firmly held hers.

Liam O'Connor stood up and started toward the Florentine doors without looking back.

"*Mister* O'Connor!"

When he turned back to look at her standing by

the china teacups, doilies, and monogrammed linen napkins, her eyes were blazing like a forest fire and the northern lights combined. For the first time he noticed the strength and depth of her voice.

"Show me. I challenge you to show me."

He couldn't believe his ears. "Show you? How? When?"

"Has your Irishness deserted you, Mr. O'Connor? You seem to be at a loss for words. Are you afraid I'll tell my mama and you'll lose your interview or your position?"

He felt like an eight-year-old in the street challenged to prove himself, and he replied indignantly, "I'm afraid of very little, Miss Holman, and I'll take the consequences. I've faced worse on this job — that's why I'm standing here now. For challenging a Tammany boss when I was on the police beat, they put me on this social trash — er, stuff — there, you'll have to excuse me again.

To his amazement, Elizabeth Holman was laughing. "I think your Irishness just returned. Very well, show me the New York I haven't seen."

"How? You're like a princess in a tower here. Okay, I'll show you, but you'll have to find a way out of all this." Liam O'Connor's gesture embraced the barrier of marble and tapestry and the formidable mother beyond it.

"Easy. I walk out, having ordered a carriage to take me to Sixth Avenue. I told you I'd been there, didn't I?"

"Not the Tenderloin, I'll wager."

"I don't know what you mean — as you very well know — but I'll meet you outside Siegel-Cooper's on the fifteenth of this month at two o'clock."

Holy Mother of God, what a woman! Girl, he reminded himself, and you're an idiot, O'Connor, but you're not going to resist this one, are you?

"Siegel-Cooper's it is, on the fifteenth, at two."

"I'll ring for the maid to see you out, Mr. O'Connor."

"Thank you. I guess I say nothing of this tomorrow, right?"

She didn't reply, and he kicked himself mentally for the cheap shot. It was one thing to do what she was doing, quite another to put into words the duplicity that would be necessary to do it.

"Thank you, Miss Holman. It's been a pleasure."

"Good-bye, Mr. O'Connor. *A bientôt.*"

He didn't know what she meant, but he guessed it meant she'd be there. Dazedly, he walked out of the brownstone on Fifth Avenue, leaving his gloves in the hall.

He had hoped he would see her when he arrived to interview her mother the next day, but she was nowhere in sight. Nor were his gloves, which he had remembered about on the way home and cursed himself for forgetting, since they were his only pair. The same footman and maid attended on him, and if looks could have killed he would have dropped dead beneath the Italian chandelier in the hall.

Mrs. Holman, however, evidently knew nothing of his unofficial interview with her daughter. She was exactly what he had expected: cool, formal, and condescendingly polite. Although there was some physical resemblance between mother and daughter, it was difficult to imagine how this woman could have produced the courageous spitfire he had encountered the previous day. Remember, he told himself, it takes guts and drive to be a robber baron, not forgetting intelligence or native wit, at the very least. He must not let his own prejudices blind him to what it took to build such a palace and fill it with European plunder.

It seemed, then, that the daughter had inherited a fair slice of all those characteristics from her papa. Fixing his attention with difficulty on the woman opposite him, sitting in the same chair in which her daughter had sat, Liam O'Connor continued with the interview until the time graciously allotted to him had run out.

The girl was still nowhere in sight when he left, and he felt the disappointment gnawing like hunger pangs inside him. Ah, O'Connor you fool, she'll not be there on the fifteenth and the feeling in your stomach probably is hunger pangs. Putting Elizabeth LaPierre Holman firmly out of his mind, he made his way to his own part of town, away from the rarefied atmosphere of Millionaires' Row to Brown's chop-house near Broadway, for the mutton chop he suddenly fancied, with a good baked potato on the side, and a mug of beer. Let the Holmans and their kind keep their caviar and their Chateau-Latour and their Moët et Chandon.

And their daughter. He'd not see her again, of that he felt sure.

Chapter Six

New York

There were children dancing to the music of a hurdy-gurdy in the street as Liam O'Connor turned onto Sixth Avenue, that part of New York Elizabeth Holman had never seen. A policeman in his grayish-blue uniform and gray felt helmet watched them benignly, smiling at their exuberance. For Liam, this part of Sixth Avenue seemed to embody the heart and soul of the workingman, with its permanent aroma of fish, cabbage, and cheap tobacco, the street stalls and beer saloons along its length, the clatter of carts, and the racket and smoke of the "el," the elevated railroad that ran above it.

But he liked it — God, he liked it. It wasn't Sixth Avenue that made him angry; it was Allan Street, and Hester, Mulberry Bend, and Broadway from Canal to Twenty-third Street. When Elizabeth Holman thought of Broadway, she thought of Grace Church with the carillon ringing out, and her Sixth Avenue consisted of Siegel-Cooper's and Crawford and Simpson, and probably ran from Eighteenth to Twenty-third streets.

Was he really meaning to show her McGurk's "suicide hall" or the brothels on Hester Street? Anyway, none of this mattered, because she wouldn't be there. He'd just go, wait a few minutes, and then return to the office.

He got to Siegel-Cooper's just before two o'clock. As he reached the door, he realized his heart was pounding in his chest. Hell, he hadn't walked that far! Had she said "outside"? He couldn't remember; perhaps she had meant by the fountain inside, with its Goddess of Liberty statue looming over it. It was *the* meeting place in this part of New York. Liam O'Connor pushed through the doors with the crowd and looked around the open area inside. There was no sign of her — but what had he expected?

He was coming out through the doors again when he saw the elegant carriage that had pulled up at the curb outside the store. A young woman was stepping out of it, heavily veiled.

Elizabeth LaPierre Holman, multimillionaire's daughter, a brownstone princess from an avenue paved with gold, had come to meet him as she had said she would. He sprinted across the sidewalk toward her, his hat in his hand, his heart in his mouth.

"Miss Holman!"

He could feel her relief, and in his anxiety to reassure her he grasped her hands. She didn't withdraw as he had felt her withdraw on their first meeting; he felt his pressure returned.

"Thank goodness!" She turned and made a gesture of dismissal toward the driver, who immediately pulled away. He could see she was smiling anxiously at him through the veil, and he felt an immense wave of protectiveness toward her. In that moment, he knew he wouldn't show her gambling saloons like Daly's or Charley's Place, the houses of assignation on Hester Street where he had seen her brother and fiancé. He didn't want to lecture or jibe or score points. He wanted to show her a good time, to pretend for an afternoon that she was his girl.

"Well," said Elizabeth Holman, "show me, Mr. O'Connor."

He could hear a tremor in her voice, but he didn't know if it was because of what she feared she might see, the enormity of what she had done, or both.

"May I change the plan a little, Miss Holman? Can I show you some of *my* city instead of — well, just instead, and let's leave it at that."

He had said the right thing. Through the veil her eyes were dancing, delighted. "Very well, Mr. O'Connor, I would like that."

"I'll get a cab."

The slender, square-chinned face looked up at him eagerly as she asked, "Do you think we could take a streetcar?"

He could feel himself grinning so hard he thought

his mouth would reach his ears. "We sure could. You've never been in one before? No, of course you haven't. We sure could!"

The old horsecar swayed like a ship at sea, and he put an arm under her elbow to steady her. She leaned firmly against it, and a breath of fragrance from her hair tickled his nostrils. He felt giddy, drunk with happiness.

"Anywhere in particular *you* want to go?"

"Germantown."

"We're heading in the right direction. Why Germantown?"

"Else — she's my mother's maid — that's where her family lives, and she used to tell me about it, bring me back things to eat that I didn't get at home. More than anything in the world I wanted to take a streetcar to Germantown, like Else. My father's family came from Germany, but you'd never know it now."

"I guess not." The streetcar was now very crowded, and he could sense she was intimidated by the press of people around her. This alone would be a new experience, being hemmed in by the noisy, smelly multitudes. He didn't suppose Else from Germantown had mentioned such things as the 330,000 people per square mile who now lived in the slums and the tenements on which her father and many of his friends had built much of their fortunes. He hesitated, and then put his arm around her, steadying her against his body.

"Thank you, Mr. O'Connor."

"Liam."

"I never knew anyone with that name before."

"Ah, then you'll not have known anyone Irish

before." She was so close he could feel her breath against his cheek.

"That's true." There was a moment's silence between them in the midst of the uproar, and then he heard her say, "Please call me Beth."

"Okay, Beth. Let's have a look at Germantown."

Although she had chosen one of the safer and better-organized ethnic communities, he could tell it was not at all what she had expected. He imagined that Else the maid came from a warm and close-knit immigrant family, and that it was their loving nature she had conveyed to Beth Holman rather than the narrow, filthy streets with the overcrowded houses on each side, the sweatshops among which they lived.

Liam made no comment on the shock he sensed she was feeling. As their excursion continued on beyond Germantown, he merely indicated to her what she could clearly see for herself. They were in the Jewish area of the city now, and he pointed out to her the Orthodox Jews in the community in their skullcaps and long caftans, the small parchment scrolls hanging on many of the doors. He spoke of the friction between the older, established Jewish community and these newer arrivals, how, in his opinion, a Jewish child had the better chance because he came from a tradition that prized learning and expected a child to attend school.

"You tell me that Chinatown comes next to this, and Little Italy is next to Chinatown. Where's Irishtown?"

"Nowhere, everywhere. We are the most trouble, more trouble than all the others put together."

"Are you? Why?"

Liam O'Connor shrugged his shoulders. "Because we're a race of fighters, brawlers. It's helped us survive, but it makes us a heap of trouble." He looked down at her and smiled. "Know what Irish confetti is?"

"No. Tell me."

"It's a shower of rocks and tin cans, usually on the heads and helmets of the law. That gives you some idea of our reputation."

She smiled, but he sensed she was now tired. She had had the good sense to wear neutral colours, and her clothes were not particularly stylish, so they had been given only the occasional glance by passers-by, but the shoes he glimpsed beneath the edge of her skirt didn't seem ideal for walking.

"That's enough for one day. This time I will get a cab. We'll find one back on the main thoroughfare — it's not too far."

How much time had she got, he wondered, and how was she planning to return? He had asked her none of these things.

"Miss Holman — Beth — I'd like to take you to dinner, although it's kind of early, before you go back. Have you got time?"

She answered composedly, expressing for the first time the need for duplicity inherent in the afternoon's outing. "Yes, I would like that. I have time. My mother is in Long Island and my father is in Buffalo. But it would be better if we didn't eat where we might see — well — anyone, you understand."

"Perfectly. Anyway, if you'd expected me to take you to Delmonico's or The Netherlands, you'd have taken my salary for the next month."

He had expected to get a laugh, but all she said
was "oh," in slight surprise, and when he saw that
it was something that would never have occurred to
her, he was reminded of the yawning gulf that lay
between them.

She sat down in the cab with an audible sigh of
relief.

"I'm sorry, I walked you too far."

"Only as far as I wanted, but these shoes weren't
designed for walking."

"It was sensible of you to wear something that didn't
draw attention to us. Fifth Avenue doesn't often visit
the Lower East Side."

"It was Else's idea. This is her Sunday best."

He was taken aback. "She knows?"

"Yes, but she'll not say anything, as much for her
sake as for mine. No, that's not fair. She wouldn't,
anyway. But the shoes were mine, and they alone let
me down."

The brief rest had restored her, and she leaned
forward to look out of the window. "Where are we
going?"

"To the Café Boulevard. We'll still be on the Lower
East Side, but it's quite respectable and I like the food.
You say you liked the things Else brought you to eat
from Germantown. Well, this isn't quite German
— more French, with a touch of Viennese about it."

In the yawning gulf that lay between them, the word
"Viennese" dropped like a stone, the ripples spreading
out around them. He saw her head snap back as if
she had come out of a trance.

Her lips parted as if she were about to say something,

but instead she turned again to the window and kept silent. Liam O'Connor watched the beautiful slow movement of her head, the slender column of her neck against the peeling upholstery of the cab, and cursed himself for getting involved, even for an afternoon, with this inaccessible, enchanting girl who had to borrow her maid's clothes to come on an outing with him.

"Would you like to change your mind? I can ask the cabbie to take you straight home."

"No. I'd really like to see what sort of food is French with a touch of Viennese."

The last word was said with a kind of deliberate defiance, as if she were trying it out on her tongue to see what effect it had on her. From where he sat he couldn't tell what the effect had been.

At the Café Boulevard they ate veal which seemed more French than Viennese, and a dessert that was more Viennese than French: dumplings filled with apricots which the waiter called *"Marillen-Knödel."* The restaurant was pleasant, respectable and friendly. Elizabeth Holman seemed quite relaxed, at peace with herself and her companion, the tension in the cab forgotten. They drank a Rhone wine with the meal, and Liam watched the colour mount in her cheeks, the sparkle that brightened her eyes. When she had turned up the veil across her face, the moment seemed as stunning, as revealing as if she had removed one of the garments loaned by Else.

In that moment it hit Liam afresh that his companion was the daughter of a man who owned railroads and banks and real estate. It hit him between the eyes and in the pit of his stomach; it made his heart beat again as it had when he'd wondered if she would keep their appointment. During the afternoon he had almost forgotten who she was, but with the sight of her face he was reminded of William and of Count Maximilian von Schönstein. All this raced through his mind as he answered her questions.

"If the Greeks, the Syrians, the Turks, and the Arabs are to the south and east of Chinatown, and Little Hungary is to the west of where we were, and the Irish are everywhere, where are the Negroes?"

"They were down and around Little Italy, but they got squeezed out and pushed up to the Upper East Side around Harlem."

"Did you write about all these people when you were a police reporter? Is that why you know so much about them?"

"Sure, but I really got interested when I read the stuff written by Jacob Riis, who was with the *New York Tribune* and the *Evening Sun.* It opened my eyes about this city, made me want to do something, anything. I thought I'd start with the politicians — see, if you control the immigrant vote, Beth, you've got it made, and Croker knows that."

"Croker?"

"Richard Croker, that's who! Never mind, it's too long a story for the time we've got. Anyway, it's too big for me — now. But I'm not going to forget it. I'm writing a series of articles in my spare time. My paper won't take them, but one of the magazines will, I'm sure, and that's what I've got in mind."

"Do you want to change the world?" The voice was teasing, but she was smiling at him.

"Sure I do! There's a description of this city I like:

'like a lady in a ball costume, with diamonds in her ears and her toes out at her boots.' That's you and me, Beth, and this city. But I can understand why you wouldn't want to change it. For you, the world must be pretty much as you would want it."

"It was."

She murmured it, looking down into her lap, and Liam O'Connor felt desolate, desperate to hold onto the moment.

"Does your mother go often to Long Island?"

"From time to time."

"I'd love to show you Greenwich Village. It's a great place — I live close by."

"Would the sixth of next month be convenient?"

He couldn't believe what he had heard. "Sure — fine, perfect," he stammered, feeling the blood rush into his face. "Same time, same place?"

The smile she gave him seemed as brilliant as the lights of Broadway. "Of course. Poor Else. I'll be wearing out her Sunday best."

"Wear something of your own — would you?"

She nodded, looking down at her lap again. "I must go now, I really must. Perhaps you would get me a cab? I told the driver who brought me that I was shopping at Siegel-Cooper's and meeting friends of the family there, and that they would bring me home."

All this subterfuge to be with him! Liam had the same feeling of disbelief he had experienced when she had offered him tea. "Of course," he replied, "but if you don't mind, I'll come with you. It's quite a distance and I don't want you to be on your own around here, not even in a cab."

It was a good reason, but not the real reason, and they both knew it. In the cab, as Beth started to pull the veil across her face, Liam said, "Please don't. Not until Fifth Avenue."

She looked up at him. He put his arm around her, as he had in the streetcar, and knew that she wanted him to kiss her as much as he wanted to. As his lips touched her mouth, he felt the tremor that passed through her slim body and then, to his delight, her arms go around him, her hand on the nape of his neck. Neither of them spoke. They kissed yearningly, bridging the gulf that lay between the diamond earrings of Millionaires' Row and the toeless boots of the Lower East Side of which Liam O'Connor had spoken. He took her upturned face between his hands.

"Ah, God, Beth, don't marry him. I can't even begin to think about being part of your life, but don't marry that — that —" She pulled away from him as he spoke, and he cursed himself inwardly. Why hurt her, and for what purpose?

"Don't talk about him. I don't know what to think, what to do. I'm not even sure what that has to do with this anymore."

He knew what she meant. This — whatever it was between them — had little to do with Count von Schönstein in a dive on Hester Street or negotiating for the favours of a lady in the Waldorf's Peacock Alley. This had to do with him, and with her, and was damn stupid of both of them, because it was pointless, hopeless. Besides, she was so young, and he must be mad, mad, mad.

"Do you still want to see me on the sixth?"

"Yes, I will. I can't — not —"

The cab jolted around a corner and there was Fifth Avenue and the Astors and the Vanderbilts and the Holmans and her reality staring Liam O'Connor in the face.

Chapter Seven

New York

Not love at first sight, perhaps. But at second sight, maybe. Yes, that was how she remembered it. Every moment she would remember, just as she remembered every moment of the first meeting, when she hadn't loved him, when she thought she still loved Max von Schönstein, when she had seen him standing against the porcelain mantel, and those bluest of blue eyes had looked across the room at her.

What was it, then, she had felt for the count? She couldn't answer that to herself, because she couldn't remember any of what she had felt. Desperately she told herself that all would be well when she saw the count once more.

Only she didn't want to see him, and it had every-thing to do with Liam O'Connor and how she felt about him. That much she knew.

Should she tell her mother that she suddenly felt the need of more reflection? No, she decided, best not to say anything yet, until she had seen Liam again. Her mother's antennae were fine-tuned to the slightest hint of evasive or devious behaviour; Beth's best chance was to go ahead for the time being as if everything was as it should be. All she could do was pray that some miraculous solution would appear over the horizon.

When Mrs. Holman returned from Long Island she did not find anything in Beth's behaviour to trouble her. She and Beth put in the required appearances in Central Park, at dances, and at the opera, and then Ada Holman departed once more for a short visit to her sister in Philadelphia.

Under normal circumstances Beth would have accompanied her mother, but she was not asked to come along this time because there was trouble in Philadelphia.

Beth knew the trouble had something to do with her aunt's marriage. From what she had picked up at the dinner table, she gathered that her Uncle Cecil had been caught out in an indiscretion and her Aunt Medora was threatening divorce. Ada was off hotfoot to Philadelphia to persuade her sister to calm down. In Ada Holman's book, and that of all her friends, divorce was a far more shocking business than the discovery of a mistress.

"Heaven knows, but it might affect Beth's eligibility!'' declared Mrs. Holman in horrified tones to her husband. Beth wondered desperately if her aunt might persevere, but she doubted it. Her mother was the older of the two sisters and the stronger in character. Beth didn't give Aunt Medora much chance.

The day before Ada Holman's departure, there were a few terrible moments when her mother toyed with the idea of taking her daughter with her. Beth sat holding her breath as Ada went through the pros and cons with her husband, who was giving her only half his attention over the top of the *New York Times*.

"It might be helpful for Medora to see Beth and be reminded of her brilliant prospects and then think of what her behaviour might do to her own Nancy's future. On the other hand, I don't want Beth to be in any way associated with the affair, if you see what I mean, William.''

"Then leave her,'' muttered her father, picking up on the final part of the remark.

"You think so? Then that's what I'll do. Your feeling for these things is so sound, my dear.''

She was to be left at home! She could have hugged and kissed her father for making it possible for her to meet again a man he would have despised with every fibre of his being.

Yet she did not feel safe until she had watched her mother's carriage disappear down Fifth Avenue and out of sight, heading for the train and Philadelphia. She did not feel safe until she herself was sitting in the same carriage the following day and heading for Sixth Avenue.

Wear something of your own, he had said, so she

had chosen an outfit she particularly liked, a tailored costume in deep blue with a white trim, a wide corselette belt that accentuated her narrow waist, and a bolero jacket. The blouse beneath the jacket was of white organza but without the ruffles and lace her mother so adored. The hat was the most sophisticated she had, in a natural straw with blue and white feathers on the crown, and a veil that pulled tight across her face. It might not be right for Greenwich Village, but she hoped it was right for Liam O'Connor.

This time she was early, but he was already there, twisting his hat round and round in his hands, long legs pacing the sidewalk. As her carriage moved away, he approached swiftly and Beth felt a shiver pass through her, like the breeze rushing through the trees by the Hudson River.

"The heavens opened, and an angel came down to Sixth Avenue."

His eyes were as blue as she remembered, bluer than her dress, bluer than the sky above springtime New York.

"That's the Irish in you speaking."

"That's Liam O'Connor speaking. We'll take a cab this time."

The kiss was as she remembered, and so were his arms around her, the feel of his springy hair against her hands, the strength of his neck beneath her fingers.

"God, Beth, I can't believe you're here! A million things could have happened — your mother could have changed her mind, you could have changed your mind!"

"A million things nearly happened, but I would never have changed my mind — never!"

"We'll only think of today, of the sixth of June 1901, and no further."

He was right. They must live for the present or the gift of the day would be spoiled. "Today then," she said, "today and Greenwich Village."

"Today and Greenwich Village, and you and me!" Liam O'Connor's natural gaiety and optimism had returned to him. He laughed down at her, and she laughed with him, with the resilience of youth that believes in miracles, and true love stories, and happy endings.

"Greenwich Village, Miss Holman, is on the Lower West Side — remember you were on the Lower East Side before? — and is bounded on the south by West Houston Street, on the east by Broadway, on the north by Fourteenth Street, and on the west by, logically enough, West Street."

"I could draw a map of it now, but I can't imagine the people. What are the people like?"

"Ah, the people! They are artists and anarchists, writers and philosophers, gypsies and gentlemen."

"No wonder you live there — you'd fit in so well."

"Why, which am I?"

"All of them, all of those things."

"What a perceptive girl I have fallen for!"

Finally, it was spoken between them. As Liam spoke, the cab came to a halt, and they dismounted with his words hanging in the air like diamonds.

He showed her the cafés, the bistros, the book shops: Polly Holliday's *salle à manger* with Bow's book shop above it, the Pen and Brush Club, the basements in which gypsy violinists played their wild sweet music as the tea leaves were read. Then he took her to eat at the Hotel Lafayette rather than one of the bistros he had first thought of. He didn't want to run into too many of his own acquaintances any more than she wanted to be seen by any of hers. At the Hotel Lafayette they were more likely to see golden Lillian Russell or Diamond Jim Brady than an Astor, a Vanderbilt, or a Belmont.

"Where do you live?"

"Off MacDougall Street." There was a slight pause, and then he asked, "Would you like to see it?"

"Yes, I would, very much."

They passed the cafés and the book shops once more, then through the little courtyard hidden behind the face of the street to the studio he rented on the second floor, above a writer and below an artist.

Beth was relieved when she saw his rooms. She did not want to have to imagine him living like Else, without colour and warmth in some narrow tenement with hordes of human beings heaped one upon the other. Here, there was space and light, although it bore no resemblance to her own home. The furnishings were spartan, but the place was clean, with drapes at the windows and paintings on the walls. Mostly, she was aware of the books and papers everywhere. Slowly, she removed her hat and placed it on a chair.

"Where do you work?"

"There." He pointed to a desk in one corner of the room. "I sleep here too, on the divan. The only other room is the kitchen, which is through here. But this is a big room and I like it."

From across the courtyard drifted the sound of a cello, and a man in the street started to sing in a trained tenor voice. There was a bowl of daffodils on the round oak table in the centre of the room, caught in a shaft of sunlight. Liam O'Connor followed the direction of her glance.

"I put them there for you."

The dark eyes looked straight into his. "You knew I would come?"

"No. But I hoped you would."

They hadn't touched since they had entered the room, and she felt the gulf between them yawning fathoms deep beneath the table and the daffodils he had placed there for her.

"I don't know when I will be free to come again."

He slammed his hand down on the table and the flowers trembled at the impact. "Goddamnit. I don't know why this happened, I never asked for it, but I'm in love with you."

She felt herself laughing and shaking uncontrollably at the same time. "What is 'in love,' then, Mr. O'Connor — what is 'in love'? I thought I was already in love, so what is this I am feeling now? You tell me, Liam, you tell me!"

As she started to weep, his arms were around her and there was no more yawning chasm, just the strength of his body against her and the hardness of his mouth, no longer gentle as it had been when he had first kissed her, but searching, demanding something she didn't understand and yet would have given him unhesitatingly in that moment if he had asked for it. When he led her over to the divan, it was she who attempted to prolong the embrace. As she did so, Liam took her hands in his, kissed them, and pulled himself away from her.

"Listen, Beth, it would be the easiest thing in the

world for me to make love to you at this moment."
He kissed her hands again and held them against his
waist, his head on one side, the tone of his voice as
ironic and stagey as the Irish brogue in which he now
spoke. "Y'see, darlin' Bethie, I'm one of the feckless
Irish, making love at the drop of a hat, the turn of
a head, the twinklin' of an eye." The phony brogue
disappeared, leaving only desperation in his voice.
"But I'm not going to do that, Beth! What would
happen to you if anything came of it?"

"Maybe they would let — it — happen."

Beth felt the laugh shake his body. "I'd be labelled
a fortune hunter and you'd be packed off to the country
until it was over. Your life would be ruined. Finished."

"What shall I do?"

"Speak to your mother, speak to your father, speak
to anyone who'll listen. Get the goddamned marriage
put off. Tell them you're too young, tell them you're
ill, tell them the strain'll give you a nervous collapse
— anything to postpone matters. God knows where
that will lead to, but at least we can buy some time,
and time is our only ally."

But Beth knew that the moment had gone in which
she would have made a commitment to him from
which there was no turning back. If the feckless
Irishman had made love to her, that would have
lessened the confusion in her mind and her emotions.
Maybe it would have helped her forget that she was
supposed to be in love with another man and on the
verge of being happy with him for ever after.

As Liam helped her put her hat back on, smoothed
the veil over her face, she put up one gloved finger

and touched the cleft in his chin, the dimple where he smiled. "For luck," she said. "Maybe dimples hold good luck."

"The luck of the Irish," said Liam O'Connor, smiling at her. The dimple deepened with his smile, and Beth thought of the Irish of New York scattered across its face, more trouble than the others put together, he had said, more bereft, more deprived in this *goldene medina,* this el dorado, than any of the others. As she did so, she felt a superstitious terror clutch at the heart she had lost so unreservedly, so precipitately to Liam O'Connor.

Was it as simple as that? Beth had reason to fear that what had happened to her was even more complicated than losing her heart to a man, and an unsuitable one at that.

She had lost her heart to a city; she had lost her heart to life. Back in the brownstone, sitting alone in her bedroom, she realized it was impossible to separate the man from his setting.

"My God," she said out loud, "there's a world out there!" Put into words it sounded trite, but the impact of her discovery escaped definition in words. It could only be understood in the heart. When she thought of the nature of her existence up to her meeting with Liam O'Connor, she saw herself moving like the clockwork trains her brothers used to play with around the figure-of-eight track, so different from her father's railroads, which spread like complex veins and arteries across this land of which she knew nothing.

Her awakening had been as sudden as the smack on
a baby's backside that gives him his first breath, and
she felt like gasping and screaming with the marvel
of it all.

And yet — if this were all that had happened, could
she not still marry the count? She would be a rich,
titled, privileged woman, and the world would be her
oyster. Could not Count Maximilian von Schönstein
be part of it? Could he not still be her husband?

Her husband. How could she ever have agreed to
marry a man about whom she knew nothing? He had
barely had a conversation with her, never kissed her
lips, and she had willingly been signed, sealed, and
delivered into his impeccably gloved hands.

Beth shivered. For a moment, the lightly accented
voice she recalled seemed menacing rather than hypnotic. And yet, even as he entered her thoughts, the
confusion began. She remembered the liquid dark eyes
moving over her, caressing her as his hands and lips
had never done, and the shiver changed to a thrill
of sensual pleasure.

Time. Liam was right. She needed time to discover
the unknown man she had consented to marry, and
time to discover the unknown Elizabeth LaPierre
Holman she had just uncovered in the company and
the arms of another man.

Chapter Eight

New York

Ada Holman returned from Philadephia in a much happier frame of mind. Her brother-in-law had returned to the fold, and she had managed to calm Medora down enough to take her repentant husband back.

Her mood was further lifted by the news that her husband had worked out a financial settlement with the count and that enquiries into his background were very satisfactory indeed. Count Maximilian von Schönstein came from one of the most elite of the Austrian noble families, with a magnificent palatial townhouse on the Schwarzenbergplatz near the Ringstrasse and vast estates in Bavaria and Ischl, where the emperor himself spent the summer.

The information about his fortune was somewhat vaguer. Like most Europeans of his class, it didn't seem to be so much in hard cash as it was in landed possessions. There were some magnificent family emeralds that would be Beth's on her marriage. For the honeymoon he planned an extended trip to the Middle East on the Royal Mail steamship *City of Rio de Janeiro*, a magnificently appointed liner.

Ada was thrilled for Beth and for herself. So many things in her life seemed to be falling into place. William, Jr., was doing what his father expected of him. What did it matter to her if there were rumours that William spent time in the Waldorf's Peacock Alley, Hester Street, and other places of equally dubious reputation? She had never heard of most of them, nor did she care to, so long as William took an interest in his father's affairs. Let him sow his wild oats, and then perhaps he would settle down to a good marriage. And Jonty had a wonderful idea for Henry. Since he liked studying, why should they not do something *à la mode* about it? Broaden his experience? It was therefore decided that Henry should attend the University of Tübingen in Württemburg, Germany, for a couple of years.

Ada Holman sat in her Japanese boudoir ecstatically going over plans with her daughter. "Oh, Beth, my dear, think of what the count has planned for you! Rowing in a caïque up the Golden Horn, the palaces of all those sultans in Syria and Mesopotamia! It sounds so gorgeous when he talks about it! I'm so thrilled for you!"

"Mama —" Mrs. Holman looked at her daughter and saw there were tears in her eyes. "Beth, what is it? Are you ill?"

"I think I must be, Mama. Maybe it's because I'm still so young, but I don't want to leave home just yet. Could you let me wait another year, until I'm a little older? Vienna is so far away, and how often would I see you and Papa? Oh, Mama, please say we can postpone the wedding for a year, *please*!"

Mrs. Holman stared at her daughter, dumbfounded. What in heaven had happened to the child who had tried to persuade her to allow the marriage to take place this spring?

"But, Beth, why this sudden change? A few weeks ago you couldn't get married fast enough! If you'd said anything *then*, something could have been done, but too much has been arranged now. All the agreements have been signed, all the dates fixed. It would look very odd to postpone the wedding now."

Tears were streaming down her daughter's face, and she had collapsed against the chair, her body racked with sobs. "Please, no, I can't — You must put it off, you must, you must!"

Truly dismayed, Ada cradled Beth in her arms. "This is terrible, Beth. You must indeed be ill. I'll send for Dr. Daniels — he'll give you something to relax you, make you sleep. It's quite normal for a young girl to feel like this before her wedding day, sweetheart. You'll feel better soon when you see the count again."

Ada nearly lost her balance when the full weight of her daughter's body sagged against her in a dead faint. Panic-stricken, she screamed out for William, Jr., who was in the next room. Between them they got Beth to her bed and summoned the doctor.

Alarmed by Beth's collapse, William, Jr., remembered something he had been told by a friend. Beth had been seen on the Lower West Side, on foot, in the company of a man. At the time he had been incredulous, thought it a case of mistaken identity and dismissed it out of hand. Now he realized it was about the time his mother was away — and here was Beth fainting, and apparently refusing to get married. Could it be that —? Horrified, he decided he had better tell his mother what he had heard.

When he finished, Ada Holman looked as if she had been turned into a pillar of stone. For a moment she stood immobile, not even appearing to draw breath. Then she said quite quietly, "Thank you, William. Say nothing of this, not even to your father. Leave it to me."

Ada spent some of the worst hours of her life waiting for the sedative the doctor had given Beth to wear off. Even with her iron control she was unable to stop her imagination from running riot. The worst possibility was, of course, that the fainting meant that Beth was — expecting. If that was the case, then the game was over. Failing that, much could be done — and would be done.

As the first shafts of light penetrated the thick velvet curtains of her bedroom, Beth opened her eyes to see her mother standing by her bed.

"Mama."

Her mother's voice was clear as fresh ice, and just as cold. "On the afternoon of June the sixth, you were on the Lower West Side, with a man. Walking. Who was he and what were you doing?"

The possibility of subterfuge was over. All Beth could do now was to tell the truth, throw herself on her mother's mercy, appeal to her feminine instincts, her maternal love. Slowly she sat up in bed, clasping her hands around her knees to steady herself.

"I had accepted an invitation to see something of New York, Mama, from a gentleman called Mr. O'Connor. I know he would not be considered suitable by your standards, but you might feel differently if you had spoken to him as I have. Oh, Mama, there is so much out there I know nothing about! I know nothing about anything, not even the man I am marrying, and until I went to — well, all the places we went to — I didn't realize it."

Her mother didn't appear to have heard a word Beth had said. The thin, cold voice came through lips that barely seemed to move.

"Has he taken advantage of you? Apart from the fact that he should be horsewhipped for even speaking to you — has he taken advantage of you?"

"No, Mama. He is an honourable man."

"An honourable man, is he? O'Connor — oh, my God, would that be the Irish peasant who didn't even have the brains to turn up here on the right day?"

"He's not a peasant, and it was his handwriting — oh please, Mama, let me just wait, I'll not see him again, anything. Please!"

The rage finally burst out of Ada Holman in a parrotlike screech in as uncontrolled a display of emotion as Beth had ever seen from her mother. "Don't you plead with me, you hussy! My God, every girl in New York would give her eyeteeth to be in your shoes, and you throw it all away on some verminous mick from the slums! You must be mad, my girl! Well, let me tell you what's going to happen — you'll be watched night and day until the day of your wedding, so don't think you can run away with this sleazy romeo who thinks he can catch himself a quick fortune! I can only thank God your upbringing saved you from giving in to him!"

"It didn't!" There was a terrible triumphant sound in her daughter's voice. "*He* was the one whose upbringing stopped him! I would have done it, Mama. I would have done it!"

Ada Holman literally foamed at the mouth as she responded, the spittle hitting Beth's face like sleet. "You slut! Where you got it from I cannot think, but not from me, that's certain. I tell you right here and now, Elizabeth, that you are going to be saved for the count, whether you like it or not. You'll walk down that aisle on your father's arm as planned, and your likes and dislikes have nothing to do with anything that happens on that day. You'll be guarded round the clock, madam!"

Staring over her mother's shoulder at the window that looked onto Fifth Avenue, Beth felt the walls closing in on a prison more confined, more threatening than the one she had known before.

Every night there was a bodyguard at her door. He wore livery and was called a footman, but he made little attempt to hide the gun he always carried. By day, Beth was never on her own. Newport was considered safer than New York, but she was still constantly accompanied so there would be no possibility of a letter dispatched or a note received. Else was "let go." Not that anything had been proved against her, but she was known to be sympathetic to Beth, and there was the risk of her being suborned.

Although the guarding of Beth was remarked upon, it was not considered extraordinary. It had happened before in New York society, for there was always the danger of elopement, an illicit marriage, a loss of virginity. Dr. Daniels had assured Ada Holman that, as far as he could tell, Beth was "*virgo intacta*," as he delicately put it, and certainly was not pregnant.

Ada breathed a sigh of relief, for she could cope with anything else. "In love" she could deal with. "In love" was as thin and insubstantial as air, as easily dissipated as a fortune could be if one's children fell into the wrong hands.

There remained, however, one major problem, that of Max von Schönstein himself. How could they risk giving him access to Beth? In a few words Beth could tell him a great deal, and all their precautions would come to nothing. Beth was certainly clever enough to realize that she could stop the marriage by telling the count what her family didn't want him to know.

The solution arrived at by her mother ensured that Beth would be given in marriage to a total stranger. It was explained to the count that it was customary in New York society for the engaged couple to see each other in as public a manner as possible, to avoid any gossip and rumour that might tarnish the young woman's reputation. At first he seemed surprised, but he accepted the conditions put upon him with his usual good nature and good manners.

The young lovers saw each other at public balls,

picnics, and theatrical performances chosen by Mrs. Holman. They never exchanged a word in private. If his fiancée's lack of vivacity or the absence of any signs of her former adoration surprised the count, he showed no sign of it. After all, it made no difference to the agreement he had struck with her parents.

William Holman, Sr., had never been enamoured of foreign titles. He had, however, signed the papers and he rarely reneged on a deal — certainly not for such inadequate reasons as a downcast expression or a broken heart. He who had the gift of the masterstroke had himself been won over by an orchid on a bed of moss, all the way from Colombia.

Chapter Nine

Vienna

Tetragrammaton — Emmanuel — Agla — Adonay.
They sounded magical, the mystic names in raised
gold letters about the ivory frame on which the crystal
stood. What they had to do with the images that
surfaced from time to time in her mind was beyond
Gisela's understanding, but her mother said that it
was appearances that mattered.

"People are more impressed with the truth, darling,
if you are making passes over the crystal or dealing
the tarot, because they can *see* that. And it will be
much prettier if you don't go into real trances — all
that shuddering and shivering is so unattractive! I
really don't think you should be a medium...No, I
see you more as a *clairvoyant*."

Concerned about the effect of Gisela's powers on her sanity, Leo Fischer cautioned Franzi, "Leave Gisela's mind alone. We are learning more and more the importance of dreams and what goes on deep in the human mind. A colleague of mine is devoting much of his research time to the study of dreams."

Franzi sniffed. "I'm delighted to hear that a man is at last paying some attention to what we women knew all along. If you don't want me interfering with her gift, Leo — and you don't deny she has a gift, do you? — then find me a teacher for her, if one exists."

Leo Fischer looked sombrely at the pretty blonde woman sitting opposite him. They were taking dinner together al fresco at the Casino Zögernitz in Döbling. The evening was beautiful, calm and clear; a light breeze tickled the strands of Franzi's hair against her cheek, blowing the ruffles of her dress against her face. The light was softening into dusk and the candlelight was tender to Franzi's skin, on which the first faint lines were beginning to show.

Was it that which saddened him, he wondered, or was it too much of the *vin-de-paille* from the cloister cellar of the nearby monastery that made him want to weep instead of laugh, reminding him of retribution and mortality? What lay ahead of them both, and that funny little fawn they had inadvertently produced between them? It might indeed be better for Gisela to have a chance at something other than the theatre and the profession that went along with being an actress. One way or the other, not much of her childhood was left if her mother's plans were anything to go by.

"A teacher does exist." There was a chill in the wind, and a few leaves fluttered from the beech trees around the terrace. One fell onto the table, and Leo picked it up and stroked the drying skin stitched between the veins. "He is a man of great skill and much learning, but he is a man of my race, and you have been anxious to distance Gisela from that part of her inheritance."

"Only for her sake, Leo! I am no *Judenfresser*, and you should know that. If he is the best, then that's what I want for Gisela."

"Oh, he's the best. He came from Moravia, I believe, but before that he was in Russia — somewhere, sometime. His patrons are powerful men, and he will only take on Gisela if he wants to. He cannot be bought with money or your charms, *Liebchen*. He will have to be persuaded by Gisela herself."

Franzi's eyes glittered. It was not like the sparkle of the stars that had begun to appear in the night sky above them, but a phosphorescent glitter over murky depths. It reminded Leo Fischer of the oily gleam on the surface of a stagnant pool, signifying decay and death.

"I will speak to her, Leo, never fear. She will know what is expected of her."

The sadness gnawed at him and he answered her irritatedly. "Neither of us knows what is expected of her; he alone will have the answer."

"What is his name?"

"Islenyev. But he is more commonly known as Arcanus the Magician."

The trill of Franzi's laughter bubbled into the air

between them, a self-consciously pretty sound. "Oh Leo, is he one of those performers one sees in the Prater? I might just as well ask the services of Kasperl, the clown from the Punch and Judy show!"

Why did she have to remind him of Kasperl, with his melancholy nature showing beneath the humour? There was an uncustomary roughness in his voice when Leo replied. "No, you might not. This is no circus clown from a meadow by the Prater Haupt-Allee. You joke about things you don't understand."

Franzi leaned across the table toward her lover, her breasts swelling above the frills of her bodice, concern on her face. She had read his mood incorrectly and she must quickly put matters right. "*Liebling*, Leo, forgive me. I'm just a silly woman and you are right. I understand nothing about such matters and am so fortunate to have you to help little Gisela and me."

Her breath seemed to him as hot as the *Föhn*, the debilitating summer wind that brought madness and despair; her perfume was like the fragrance of pot-pourri, lying like ashes in an urn, a reminder of the lost, dead roses of summers past.

Chapter Ten

Vienna

A group of cavalry officers rode past the carriage, the sound of their spurs blending with the sound of their laughter. Through the carriage window Gisela saw their fur coats, the shine of the silver cords that held them together, and the polished gleam of their high boots. By her side, her mother sighed and clicked her tongue against her teeth.

"Lovely men. Ah, such lovely men." She toyed with the pearls around her neck, touching them to her lips, laughing softly as if at some private reminiscence. Gisela glanced up at her mother and thought about what she had been told over the past few days. She was going to meet a friend of her father who would understand the visions she saw and who would help her. In return, he would expect something from Gisela, although her mother had been evasive about the nature of the bargain that would be struck.

No matter. The point had been clearly made that she was to do whatever it was this man required, for only she could seal the agreement. Passively, Gisela watched the snowflakes fall on the iron railings around the magnificent palaces and on the people who strolled or hurried by on the street. She noticed they were mostly in twos — a man and a woman or two women together. Sometimes they passed a group of army officers, and just occasionally she saw a woman standing alone as if waiting for someone.

"Who are those women, *Mutti*? Mostly they wear shawls and not coats, and it's so cold outside."

Her mother followed the direction of Gisela's pointing finger, and her mouth twisted in a smile of disdain.

"Line girls." The scorn sputtered through her words. "They walk the line on the pavement along which the authorities allow them to walk. They, darling, are the lowest of the low. That's why it is important to listen to your mother and obey her. Remember them when you are alone with this Islenyev — Arcanus, as he calls himself."

"Won't you be there. Or Leo?"

"No. He has asked to see you alone. Undisturbed."

There was a momentary faltering in Franzi's voice, and she turned quickly to look again at the line girls beyond the windows of the carriage. The sight of them seemed to rally her, and she flung her arms around Gisela, squeezing her tightly. "And tomorrow, little precious, we shall go for a sleighing party in the Höllen Valley. Won't that be lovely?"

"Lovely, *Mutti*."

The carriage drew up outside one of the most impressive *Palais* on the Schwartzenbergplatz, which Gisela recognized as the home of one of her father's wealthy banker friends.

"This is where the gentleman is staying," said her mother.

The staircase up which they were conducted was lavishly decorated by the celebrated artist Mackart. The ceiling was covered with paintings, the oils glowing richly in the dim light, for only a few of the chandeliers had been illuminated. Gisela watched the legs of the aged footman ahead of her, knotty calves bulging beneath his white hose, heard the sound of his laboured breathing echoing in the cavernous space around them.

Suddenly she was frightened. She heard the sound of her own breathing, was aware of a strange rasping noise coming from her mother's throat.

At the top of the stairs the footman stopped and turned to her mother. "You must leave her now, *gnädige Frau*. The child must continue alone. I will give her the light." He held out the heavy silver candlestick he had in his hand, and the thick white candle guttered and flared at the movement. The weight of it was such that Gisela staggered for a moment. She put out her other hand to grasp it.

"Come with me, *Mutti* — at least come to the door!" She didn't recognize the sound of her own voice. It was like the sighing of the wind down the winter streets.

"No, I cannot. You must go alone."

Her mother's voice was also different, harsh, all its soft crooning quality gone. Before her daughter could plead with her again, she had turned and started down the staircase, her skirts rustling around her like dead leaves.

"There." The elderly footman pointed to a set of double doors trimmed with gold in the shadows at the end of the corridor. "Do not knock. He expects you." Gisela listened to the creak of his buckled shoes as he moved away into the darkness.

The doors were heavy, and she had to put the candle down and push with all her strength. As the gilded handle turned, she felt them move smoothly and silently away from her, swinging under their own weight.

"Gisela Valeska."

The voice came from the far end of the room like thunder between the mountains, along the limestone cliffs of the Wienerwald. At first, all she could see was a multibranched candelabrum on a vast expanse of table, which was covered with a black silk cloth. Straining her eyes to see into the shadows beyond the pool of light, she got only an impression of a massive chair in which someone was seated. In spite of her fear, she felt herself drawn on toward the light. A moment later she saw him for the first time.

Even seated, he was the tallest man she had ever seen. His arms stretched well beyond the carved arm-rests of the giant chair, his long, gnarled hands extended before him. He was wearing loose, flowing robes of black, but Gisela got the impression he was thin, for his cheekbones stood out like a bas-relief in a face framed in long bronze-coloured hair streaked at the sides with gray.

His eyes were a curious light shade of a colour Gisela

couldn't make out from where she stood. It was not the colour that was important, however, but the way his eyes penetrated, twin rapiers into her own eyes, mind, soul. She couldn't look away as they held her, pinned, motionless in time and space.

"Come, child."

The thunder of the voice had now become like the purring of a leopard in the shadows. Drawn on by the eyes that held her, she moved toward him, her feet silent on the thickly carpeted floor.

"Put your candle on the table. Stand close to it, so I can see you."

She did as she was told and his eyes moved slowly over her. When they came back again to her face she thought they were ice blue, but then, quite suddenly, they seemed to become pale gold in the candlelight. Gisela now saw there was a crystal on the table, about the same size as her own, but in a stand of ebony.

"You like the speculum?"

Bewildered, Gisela followed his glance. "The crystal?" They were the first words she had said in the room, and she was surprised to hear that her voice sounded normal once again. The discovery strengthened her. "I don't know. I don't see the purpose."

Thunder rolled again between the mountains, and she realized he was laughing deep in his throat. He clasped his hands loosely in front of him and she thought to herself, "His hands are as long as a pair of hands and feet put together."

"Do you know who I am?"

"They call you Arcanus the Magician. Also Islenyev."

"So they do, but do *you* know who I am?"

She looked again into the pale eyes and, for some reason, somewhere in the shadows, she heard a child laugh, a few words in a language she didn't understand, a flicker of happiness.

"You are Alexei."

Of a sudden the gaunt hands unclasped and the long frame leaned forward from the chair toward her.

"That I am, Gisela Valeska, that I am. And you are who they say you are, and what they tell me you might be. I am Alexei to you, and to no one else. It is between us."

Gisela nodded. Suddenly her fear was gone and there were questions she wanted answered. "Why did you laugh about the crystal?"

"I did not laugh about the crystal, but because your reply was the one I hoped for. The crystal is only an instrument, a means of channelling what you have inside you."

He indicated a chair behind the table, close to the crystal and the candelabrum. "Sit down, Gisela, and tell me what you see and feel in this thing of no purpose."

The chair was too large and low for her, so she knelt upon it, her elbows on the table. "It looks just like mine, except that mine is set in ivory."

"There is more. Your beryl is from Moravia, and mine from Siberia."

"Does that make a difference?"

"*You* make the difference. You see nothing?"

Gisela shook her head. She suddenly felt desperately anxious to please the giant across the table, but she couldn't see what wasn't there.

"Put your fingers on it."

"Do you want me to make passes over it?"

The rumble in his throat was there again. He shook his head, the long bronze hair swinging on his shoulders.

"No, that will come. Just touch it with your fingers. At your age, it is enough."

The surface of the beryl was cool, smooth to the touch, like walking in bare feet on a marble floor. Suddenly, in the pads of her fingertips, Gisela felt a warmth, a tingling. The only feeling to which she could compare it was the sensation when she hit her elbow sometimes. She looked up to tell him, but she could see that he knew already.

"Just move your fingers lightly over the surface."

As she did so, the beryl seemed to become hazy, as if it needed cleaning or as if something had dulled the surface. Her eyes were drawn down into the depths of the speculum which seemed to have become black. There were small pinpoints of light, like stars, in the darkness. Now it was not as if she had bumped her elbow but like the time she had once bumped her head, very hard. White clouds appeared as the blackness started to dissolve before her eyes. She gave a little cry.

"Tell me, child."

"A young man, on horseback, like the cavalry officers I saw coming here — only his uniform is different, some sort of cape. He's riding like a wild man, not in lines like a soldier, but I'm sure he is a soldier. Tears are streaming down his face and his sword is drawn. There's a woman somewhere, and she's taken something from him. He wants it back.

and yet he doesn't want it back, for it means he loses
her. And so he must kill the man, for if he loses her
he doesn't want the man to have her. Ah, how he
suffers — the pain, how he aches — it is you!"

As she swung away from the crystal, a cry tore from
her, echoing through the room, his own cry answering
it, then fading again into the black corners of the past.

The giant called Alexei was staring at her, dry eyes
filled with a grief beyond tears, but the voice still
thundered as it had when he had first spoken to her.

"The past. There is no doubt about the past, for
it is done and seen to be done, and the gift cannot
be counterfeited. There, my child, is the purpose of
the crystal. It only holds what you can give it. You,
Gisela, need no chants, no prayers, no incantations
such as these."

Alexei Islenyev pointed to the letters at the base of
his crystal, and then to the candelabrum. Around the
base of the latter Gisela saw the words "Elohin, Elohe."

"Then why do you have them, if you are like me?"

"For the world, Gisela, for the world."

So *Mutti* was right. Even this man said so, and she
believed him without question. Gisela looked again
at the crystal. It was clear once more, with perhaps
a suggestion of darkness moving to the side, but it
could have been the shadow cast by the candle flame.

"Did you lose your gift?"

"For a while, and then it returned to me."

"I am glad."

Alexei moved suddenly back against the great chair,
and Gisela saw his hands clench over the armrests,
the tendons standing out like tree roots.

"Glad? Sometimes the gladness is when the gift goes,

and when it comes again it means a terrible joy is past. You, child, will know that one day. For the moment, your gift is pure, clear as spring water, as the ice crystals for which the Greeks named the beryl. But I cannot wish for you to be spared that pain, for it is perhaps one of the greatest of all the world's pleasures."

There was something so terrible and so sad in his eyes that she didn't want to understand. He leaned toward her and she was relieved to see he was smiling at her. Although he had laughed before, this was the first time he had smiled, and Gisela saw for a moment the little boy she glimpsed briefly in her first vision.

"You will come again." It was not a question, but a command.

"Yes. You will teach me the tarot?"

"You already know it, but we will do what we did with the speculum. You must come alone."

"I know. I won't be afraid this time."

"Were you afraid?"

"Yes. My mother said I must do whatever you wanted, and I didn't understand why that upset her so much. She'll take me skating tomorrow."

The blackness on the giant's face was like the blackness at the heart of the last vision she had seen. "So, the lies have reached this place! And yet you were sent. Would they sell anything, everything?" He stopped and looked at Gisela. "Say nothing of what happens in this room. Nothing. Promise me your silence."

She nodded and he continued. "You may go now. Come back in a week's time. My host will let you know."

Gisela crossed the room without looking back, and it was only when she was outside the door that she realized she had left the candle on the table. It wasn't important anymore, for it suddenly seemed quite light out in the hall amid the soft glow of the paintings, the glitter from the chandeliers. She went to the top of the stairs and looked down.

At the foot of the stairs she saw her mother. Franzi looked as if she had been turned to stone, as if she had been standing there a very long time.

"Gisela?"

"Yes, *Mutti*. I forgot the candle."

"Darling!" Her mother was flying up the stairs toward her, hugging and kissing her and sobbing all at the same time. "Are you — oh my little one! — let me look at you — tell me — tell me it wasn't too terrible!"

"It wasn't terrible, but I cannot tell you anything. I have promised."

Gravely, perplexedly, Gisela stared at her mother. She seemed to have been even more frightened than she, Gisela, had been.

"Ah, dear God! My little heroine, my angel! Perhaps that is best — yes, yes, it is for the best."

Torn by remorse and guilty relief at her daughter's composure, Franzi Valeska tried to kiss away whatever it had been that had elicited the cry she had heard from the child, obliterate from her mind the answering cry of the man to whom she had given her greatest treasure. Perhaps kissing would stop the dreams that would come in the night after each visit to the palace on the Schwartzenbergplatz as she guided Gisela's first steps on the path to a great and glittering future.

Chapter Eleven

Vienna

Sometimes Gisela saw Alexei every week; sometimes it was not for a month or so. It was not difficult to keep silent about the nature of her visits, because she took pleasure in the secrecy of the bond she had with him. Although it had been Leo Fischer who had first suggested Arcanus the Magician to her mother, her continued visits to him had caused a rift between her parents. Gisela did not understand why and had not asked the reason. She was sorry she no longer saw her father as often but was not too disturbed by his absence. His role had always been a peripheral one in her life, and what right had he to criticize her mother? He had not married her but drifted in and out of their lives as it pleased him.

Leo Fischer left Vienna for a prolonged absence to study with a renowned clinician in Berlin, and Franzi quickly found herself other admirers. They came and went, filling the elegant apartment on the Asperngasse with laughter, compliments, song, and a variety of predominantly military uniforms: lancers' tunics with waterfalls of golden braid down their backs; cavalry officers' furs in winter, mantles of blue with decorated shoulder-straps in summer; the tight-fitting trousers of the infantry; the gray ensembles of the Royal Hunters; guard officers' toques cascading with green and white feathers. Occasionally there would be a government official looking positively drab in his black suit, bowler hat, and gray tie fastened with a pearl stickpin.

Gisela's presence was an added attraction for Franzi's establishment. Seated in a small gilt-painted chair behind an oval table, with her crystal and her tarot cards, she performed for her mother's friends. The apartment on the Asperngasse soon acquired a reputation for being one of Vienna's most original and fashionable salons.

Receiving vibrations and intuitive messages from the tarot was one thing; learning all the ways of using the cards was quite another. With the twenty-eight cards of the Major Arcana and the fifty-six cards of the four suits that made up the Minor Arcana, there was much to remember. The spread of the cards on the table was an art in itself: the Horseshoe, the Card Royal, the Gypsy spread — the variations seemed endless.

Most fascinating of all were the figures of the Major Arcana and what Alexei had to say about them. There was magic and mystery in the names alone: the Chariot, the Lovers, the Hanged Man, the Wheel of Fortune. Gisela discovered that Alexei had been named for the Magician in the Major Arcana.

"He is the man of inner knowledge, the interpreter of what lies before him on the table and what he sees before him in life. His is the card of Will, for it is not enough to be given the gift. One must also understand how to use it."

Under Alexei's tutelage strange things began to happen when Gisela saw the figure of Juno placed near the Fool, or the Lightning-struck Tower near the Star. She began to see how hope affected ruin and how idealism modified the death card in a spread. Pictures formed in her mind, the images moving between her and the cards instead of forming in the crystal. Very often there was no image at all, but the words flowed from her. She was not in a trance and was quite conscious of what she was saying, but where the words came from she didn't know.

"What card am I, Alexei?"

"You are not one of the cards, Gisela, any more than I am merely because I am named for one. However, it seems possible that the High Priestess will be important to you. Arcanus the Magician, and Gisela the High Priestess."

Alexei Islenyev laughed, his pale eyes surveying the young girl across the table from him.

"Good. I like Juno with her golden peacock. You said she was wise, enlightened, the perfect woman."

"Yes, and she is also ignorant and shortsighted, shallow and selfish."

"Are there always two sides? Is the Magician also something bad?"

"Of course. He is the card of indecision and failure, one who uses his skill for evil or destructive ends."

She didn't have to ask if that applied to him, because she could see from his eyes that it must be so.

In the real world, the one that lay beyond the great doors of the room in the mansion of Alexei's patron, such things as death and destruction, illness and disgrace had to be carefully predicted, or preferably not predicted at all. Gisela learned to take refuge in the dual nature of the cards, always seeing the best rather than the worst after one particular occasion when she had told a *Rittmeister* in the dragoons that she saw defeat or disgrace for him in some small and remote place "in Bohemia, where my crystal comes from."

There had arisen a sudden murmur of agitation and shock in the room, and the dragoon captain himself appeared visibly shaken. This was hardly surprising, since his next posting was to the small garrison town of Bilin, in Bohemia, and he was due to leave within the week. At the end of the evening, Franzi Valeska had an urgent talk with her daughter about diplomacy and discretion.

"Gisela, my love, is there really any need for you always to be the voice of doom for so many of our friends? Surely there must be all kinds of nice things you can tell them about money and love and so forth? People don't want to come out for an evening's entertainment and then hear that they are going to contract a serious illness or be ruined financially!"

"What can I do, *Mutti*, if that's what I see? You know what the gypsies say, that the cards never lie."

"I know, darling, and I'm not asking the cards to lie. I'm only asking *you* to lie, just a little, for my sake. Or do you see social ruination for me in those cards of yours?"

Gisela had not tried to see anything for her mother, and both the cards and the crystal had spared her any unwanted visions. She did not want to see again the man in the shadows with the knife to her mother's throat.

"I will ask Arcanus what I should do."

"He will understand. He is a man with powerful connections, and I cannot believe he made them by foreseeing plagues and pestilence for the great ones of this world."

When Gisela asked Alexei on her next visit to him, she thought at first he had not heard what she had said. He clasped his hands around the great silver candlestick she had carried in and stared deep into the flame. When he finally answered, it was as if he spoke to himself.

"Where does the secret doctrine come from? Did the gypsies learn it from the crusaders when they returned from the Holy Land? Could we use it to find the Holy Grail once more? Could we use it to find the secret tunnel underneath the Great Pyramid and thus unlock the secrets of astrology, the riddle of the sphinx? Whatever the answer is, it is clear to me that this wisdom is not one of Eastern fatalism, which believes our fate to be immutable, unalterable. I believe we have a say in our destiny."

Alexei looked up at Gisela, and it seemed to her that she could see the candle flame in his eyes, a flickering gold.

"Remember, High Priestess, that we all come to bends in the road where the signpost points in different directions, and we must choose. Perhaps it is better to tell the man who goes to Bilin that there is a possibility of disaster, that Bohemia holds for him special dangers and he should be aware of them. If you tell him there is little hope, then he may make of it a self-fulfilling prophecy and bring about his own end. There are always choices, even though you may see there are only difficult ones for the *Rittmeister*. I always remind myself that the Magician in the Arcana is also called the Juggler. So, Gisela Valeska, throw your predictions in the air and let the world catch them as they may."

"Does that mean sometimes telling a lie?"

"It means sometimes not telling the whole truth."

Even as he said this, however, Alexei Islenyev appeared to become angry. He rose from the chair in which he always sat and came around the table, moving over to the windows across which the curtains were always drawn. It was the first time in their meetings that he had moved from his seat, and Gisela was as awed by his great strides as if he had taken flight before her eyes. His voice thundered toward her.

"And yet I play with words, and you and I both know it. As Arcanus the Magician, I practise mendacity and evasion again and again."

The movement of his heavy robes had released a scent like incense in the room, hanging like smoke in the dim light. Gisela felt the hairs on her arms stand up, prickling against the sleeves of her dress. "You see something for me, don't you?" she asked. "You always have, but now you see more and it makes you frightened."

His back was to her when he replied, and he seemed to be staring out of the windows as if the curtains were not drawn across them. "Somewhat frightened, but I am often afraid of what I see. That's why I have learned to juggle."

The silence lay heavy between them as he turned to face her. "Are you going to ask me what I see?"

At first she shook her head, but then she could bear it no longer and the words burst from her. "Now I know how the *Rittmeister* felt! All I want to know is that there are choices for me — but I know you will say yes to that. I'll ask what my mother's friends always ask — do you see a man?"

"Yes, but I also see a woman, and I always see the same woman when you touch the Empress in the tarot."

"I the High Priestess, she the Empress. What of the man? Who is he?"

"He is either Hercules with the lion at his feet or he is the Fool. I suspect he is both."

Alexei came across to where she sat and knelt down beside her. He put his hand on hers and she felt as she did when she touched the crystal. It was the first time he had approached or touched her. "Gisela, it is almost time for what I see to happen, and when it does the gift will disappear. Because of this you will be unable to warn someone close to you of terrible events that cannot be changed. Then the gift will return."

The smell of incense was very strong, and it made Gisela think of tombs and catafalques, change and decay.

"You said there were always choices."

He stood up, towering over her, his great beak of a nose accentuated by the shadows, cast by the candle. "The choices that will lead to these events have already been made, and some will not be made by you."

"Then I must must sit and wait for these things to happen?"

"No. You can go out and meet them head on, headlong. I shall not see you again for a while because I have taught you all I can for the time being."

The dismissal was so sudden she felt that it was a rejection. "Why can I not go on seeing you?"

"Because we would be wasting each other's time."

"For a while, you said. When will that time be over?"

"We will both know when that happens."

Alexei Islenyev watched her walk away from him across the room, the silver candlestick in her hand. She was a foot taller than when she had first come to him, the dark hair no longer loose on her shoulders but coiled in rich swathes around the strong face. When she leaned forward to grasp the candlestick, the swell of her breasts was clearly visible under her lace blouse, the scent of her femininity as marked to him as that of the peach and apricot blossoms that flowered between the vines in early spring.

She was still far too young for what would happen, but her childhood was over now. That early-blooming womanhood would cost her, for a time, the gift that had brought her to him, and there was nothing he could do about it.

"*Adieu, ma petite sorcière.*" The words, in the language he had once used for love, echoed across the empty room and against the door which had now closed behind her.

Book Two

Enemies Concealed

Chapter Twelve

Karlsbad

When summer came, Franzi and Gisela moved out of Vienna to escape the heat, staying at first near Baden bei Wien under the foothills of the Julian Alps, on the edge of the Vienna Woods.

It was, at the beginning, a time of great felicity. Wearing light dresses of white lawn, muslin, and lace, they ate fresh crescent rolls for breakfast as they looked down from their little villa on dew-fresh fields and limpid streams. In the evening, they read or entertained each other on the piano, singing songs together.

As the weeks passed, however, Franzi grew restless. "We are so out of circulation here, so out of touch! I need to know what's going on, to exchange gossip with friends, to show off my new summer frills! There's no one here to see how charming we look together, darling — well, no one who counts, that is."

Just as she so often saw reality reflected in the crystal, Gisela realized that her mother could only really see herself if she were reflected in other people's eyes. She needed compliments, the sweet fragrance of flattery, to know that she existed.

"Where shall we go then, *Mutti*?"

"To Karlsbad, precious. I hear it's lively there this year."

So Bohemia and Karlsbad it was, where the liveliness Franzi sought was ensured by the town's closeness to the German frontier, with easy access to both Berlin and Vienna. Instead of renting a villa, they stayed at the Hotel Schloss so that they could be surrounded by people who counted, those reflective surfaces Franzi needed so much.

Gisela was quite happy, for she was still her mother's most constant companion. Together they walked along the Alte Wiese, took the waters at the Schloss Brunner, relaxed in the charming coffeehouses under the lime trees. And, for the first time, Gisela was allowed to accompany her mother to the casino in the evening.

"It's nice to be without a permanent escort for a change," thought Franzi as she regarded her daughter across the damask napery, cut glass, and silver of their table in the casino's dining room. An orchestra played softly among the palms, the tone of the violins as sweet and melting as the sorbet in silver bowls before them. Franzi toyed with hers, taking sips of her *Pommery sec*, watching Gisela spoon the melting ice into her mouth and licking her lips in delight.

Amazing how well her father's looks were turning

out on the child, now that she was beginning to grow into early womanhood. Of course, the dark hair and pale skin, the shadowed eyelids curved over the secretive eyes, the long, strong mouth went quite against the current trend of desirability. Only the straight, strongly marked eyebrows were *à la mode*, strictly speaking, unlike her own blonde, bubbling self. But Gisela would do very nicely. That sinuous, slender body and fluid walk already attracted attention. It was so — so unchildlike. But then, she was no longer a child, this daughter of hers, not since — Franzi's mind shied away from the thought she would have to face with the completion of the phrase.

Why did this Islenyev not ask to see her again? There was no trouble between them, she knew that, and he had taught Gisela marvellously well. Their salon was the talk of Vienna. Perhaps it had been the newness that mattered, her extreme youth, as it was for some men. No jewels or gifts had come from the relationship, but she and Gisela had both benefited indirectly, and the child had some form of security for her future.

They would have this summer together before she started to think about another arrangement for Gisela. Amazing also how the child seemed completely unmoved by — again, Franzi's mind swerved away from contemplation of something she had not thought would be so difficult. What else was there, after all, for women such as herself and her daughter?

"Gnädige Frau."

The voice came from behind her, smooth, strong, and sensual as *Kaffee mit Schlag*, deep roasted Viennese coffee with thick cream and the sweet bite of cinnamon.

Franzi saw Gisela lick up a last spoonful of sorbet and stare up at whoever was standing behind them. There was a movement as the man came around the table, and Franzi saw him for the first time.

She recognized him, of course. One saw him at the opera, at Sacher's, at the *Burgtheater*, but he had always seemed inaccessible, too rich for her blood. The smooth dark hair around the perfectly shaped head of one of the noble ones, *die Adeligen*, the elegantly cut moustache framing the perfectly proportioned mouth, the aquiline nose, the lazy eyes of the sensualist and man-about-town, connoisseur of rare wines, fine paintings, beautiful women. He moved with the grace of the superb cavalry officer he was, the strength of a man who has learned to spend hours in the saddle in the service of the empire or on long, arduous days in the mountains hunting chamois and bear. The eyes that moved over her, the strength of the hands that grasped the spare chair at the table, suggested a combination of wildness, sensuality, and the cultured exclusivity of the highest Austrian nobility, the *Erste Gesellschaft*.

"I see two beautiful women alone, and I wonder how such a thing can be. Are you not, madame, with the *Burgtheater*?" Before Franzi could reply, the gentleman gave a deep bow. "But allow me to introduce myself. I am Count Maximilian von Schönstein."

With the practice of more years than she cared to think about, Franzi turned toward the count and bowed slightly, showing an inch or two more of her breasts. Her little hand flickered over the frills of her bodice and then touched a strand of blonde hair. "Why yes, Your Excellency, how clever of you! I am Franzi Valeska."

"I thought so, but you are so versatile in your roles that I couldn't be entirely certain. I have seen you in —"

The count listed virtually every role Franzi had played in the last few years. She was delighted, allowing her laughter to trickle forth in silvery cadences as he spoke, watching the sensual eyes move over her body. Suddenly, he turned toward Gisela. "And this is —?"

"Forgive me, Your Excellency. This is my daughter, Gisela."

"Your daughter? Impossible!"

It was a line Franzi had heard many times before, but never had it been expressed with such fiery disbelief, such delighted amazement. Gisela's social education had been complete enough for her to realize how important this meeting could be to her mother. She stood up and made a little curtsy to the count. "Count von Schönstein."

"Charming, charming! Have I not heard of your daughter's name in connection with an exceptional skill as a clairvoyant?"

"Why yes, Your Excellency. Gisela is acquiring quite a reputation for her readings of the crystal and the tarot at my salon in the Asperngasse."

"Then you must certainly invite me when the season begins again and we are all back in Vienna. Meanwhile, would you both allow me the honour of being your escort this evening?"

"Oh, Count von Schönstein, the honour would be ours!"

He remained with them all evening, leading them, one on each arm, through the casino. He insisted that they gamble for him, choosing all the cards and numbers. "Come on, little crystal-gazer, I have had no luck at all. Let's see if you can change that for me!"

Although it had nothing to do with Gisela's skills, they were very successful. Franzi didn't think she had ever felt so triumphantly happy in her life. Even if he only wanted her for a week or so, at least people would observe the nature of her conquest. Her stock would rise in the eyes of those who counted.

She had no doubt that the evening was a prelude, but what the course of events would be she wasn't sure. Would he ply her with notes, trinkets, little favours, or advance matters more swiftly? She wondered. He was, of course, in control and he would make those decisions. She didn't mind, for part of the thrill of the game was the suspense.

At the end of the evening, the count escorted them to their carriage, helping Gisela in first and seeing her settled before he came to Franzi, who waited on the steps of the casino. Before she could make the pretty farewell speech she had planned, he had spoken.

"You are staying at the Schloss?"

"Yes, thank you, my —"

"Your room number?"

Taken aback at the abruptness of the enquiry, the businesslike note in the mellifluous voice, she gave it to him.

"I will be there in an hour. Send away any servants and leave your door unlocked. Your daughter, I trust, will not be disturbed?"

"Why no, there is a dressing room between —"

"Good." A kiss of the hand, a bow, and he was gone, leaving Franzi standing on the steps of the casino.

On the trip back to the hotel, Franzi sat silently with her thoughts. Gisela dozed on the seat opposite her. The evening's finale would have been almost — well, humiliating, if he had not been of the highest nobility. She was not used to being treated in such a manner, for most men had to cajole her for her favours. Oh, she and they knew she would surrender, but there was a form to these things. Still, it was impossible to accuse a nobleman of not being a gentleman; it was a contradiction in terms.

Franzi reminded herself of his consideration for Gisela. And such haste certainly seemed to suggest extreme desire, perhaps even infatuation. Franzi felt her heart thump wildly within the whalebone-and-steel corseting which she knew she would remove without hesitation for such a catch, whatever misgivings she might temporarily have.

A little more than an hour later he was with her, entering her bedroom door and locking it behind him. When he spoke, the creamy sound had returned again to his voice.

"Extinguish the light, Franzi."

"Certainly, Count, if you wish it, but would you not prefer —?"

"No." She listened with a thrill to the laughter in his voice. Franzi heard the clink as he removed a weapon of some kind, and then the rustle of his clothing. So considerate after all, she thought, giving him a generous glimpse of her skin glowing in the dimming light.

As darkness fell over the room the count was upon her. It was as sudden as that, with no preliminaries and none of the tender consideration Franzi had read into the instruction about the light. It was as close to rape an anything she had ever experienced because of the violence in his actions, his commands, the very movement of his body. He stayed with her for about an hour. There was none of the pillow talk at which she was such an expert, the tantalising love play for which she was noted. He turned her on the bed as if she were a mount he was trying out for the first time, talking to her only when it was necessary to explain what he wanted. Finally he left her as abruptly as he had fallen upon her and started to get dressed once more.

Franzi put out her arms to him and began to tell him the things she felt he would want to hear her say. When he spoke, it was with the same tone of voice she had heard on the casino steps.

"No. I am the only one who speaks when we meet. Next time you will not cry out your pleasure for my benefit. It has no interest for me. You understand, Franzi, actress of the *Burgtheater*?"

She understood. For this man, her pleasure only interfered with his. It was her subjugation in which he was interested and from which he derived satisfaction.

She could not wait for him to return to her bed.

At first Gisela was sorry that her mother had found another lover at Karlsbad. Something about the count disturbed her, but she had no visions or intuitions about him. After a while, she began to enjoy his company. He himself insisted she accompany them on rides in the country, dinner in the evening, gambling at the casino.

Franzi had never looked more radiant. There was a bloom on her skin, a lustre in her eyes, a sinuous softness to her usually bouncy step. The summer moved pleasurably toward their return to Vienna, which was to be in the count's private railway car.

Watching the landscape flash by as she drank a glass of sparkling white wine, Franzi reflected on the extraordinary turn of events in her life. She couldn't wait for the new season to begin and for the chance to show off her new conquest. For that is what he is, she told herself, turning the glass around in her hands and watching the bubbles explode — whatever he does to me in the darkness. At the thought, Franzi felt her thighs tremble, aching for the sensual fury, the hard hands, the barked commands of the nights to come.

At that moment he returned from the observation carriage, where he had left Gisela, escorted by one of his servants. He sat down opposite her and poured himself a glass of wine. As he put the bottle back in the silver ice bucket, he said to her, with the abruptness that was often in his voice when Gisela was not present, "My visits to the Asperngasse will only be to attend your salon, and for no other reason."

She was taken aback, fearing he meant to finish their affair. "Are you concerned about your reputation — with your family, or with the emperor?"

Franzi could see her question had angered him. He leaned toward her. "I am *concerned* about nothing, I am afraid of nothing. How could a relationship with a *Burgtheater* actress affect me in any way? Even one who allows me to do the things I do to her — hmm?"

Finally he had stung her into anger. She leaned toward him, slamming her wineglass on the table. "That is no judgement of me, Count, nor of my character — but of yours!"

She had scarcely finished speaking when he left his seat and came across to her, putting his hands around her throat. She could feel his fingers against her neck, cutting off speech and air, and she put her hands up to his, started to struggle. Even as she did so, he brought his mouth down against hers, hard, as he always did, bruising her, as he always did. And, as always, she felt sexual excitement stir in her at the violence.

When he released her, he was laughing. "Were you afraid?"

"Yes. I thought you were going to kill me."

He was stroking her neck now, pressing his thumbs into her collarbone and then pushing his fingers down the front of her dress. "But that's what you like, Franzi, isn't it? So, you will come to me when I send the word."

Relief flooded her. "Where?"

"At Sacher's. Anna Sacher will assign you a room. You know of that part of the establishment, even if you haven't been there."

Of course she knew it; all Vienna knew it. He was treating her like a whore. She also knew she would fly to him as if her feet had wings.

"Yes, I know it. I will be there."

"Of course you will be there!" Abruptly he released

her, returned to his seat, and poured himself another glass of wine. When Gisela returned, he was his charming and courteous self again, the perfect gentleman. After enquiring after what she had seen in the observation car, he excused himself to prepare for their arrival in Vienna.

Gisela looked at her mother. Franzi's colour was high, her eyes sparkling. "Will the count help you in getting good roles at the *Burgtheater, Mutti*?"

"I think so, darling, because he knows the director personally."

"Will we be holding the salon again?"

"Of course, but the count wants to be discreet in our — our relationship, in using his influence. There is so much jealousy in society, as you know."

Franzi sighed and looked out of the carriage window at the spire of St. Stephen's Cathedral outlined against the cloudless blue sky. It was time to think about Gisela once again, and what was to be done about her. It seemed that this Islenyev wanted no more of her for the time being, so she was free for other admirers.

Maybe — the thought suddenly struck her — maybe the count could arrange something far more prestigious than they could have hoped for only a few weeks ago. He seemed quite charmed by Gisela, and surely there was some member of the nobility he needed to oblige, impress, or repay. Even men in his position had such demands put upon them, and it might strengthen her own bond with the count if she had such a card to play.

A warm burst of love rushed through her and she

flung her arms around her daughter. "Oh my darling child, what a winter this will be — the happiest we have ever known!"

Their laughter floated up into the blue sky above St. Stephen's Gothic spire. It seemed the very best of times to be living in this, the most beautiful city in the world.

Chapter Thirteen

Vienna

Franzi found the season quite as wonderful as she had anticipated. She purchased a wardrobe of dresses from Spitzer and a collection of new hats from Paris which she fastened to her blonde head with long rhinestone pins in the latest fashion. Her life was a whirl of gaiety, of after-theatre parties and dinners amid the Oriental splendour of the finance barons' palaces, to which she was often conveyed in the count's equipage with its gold-striped wheels and the family coat of arms on the door.

She landed a plum part in a new historical drama and had the additional thrill of knowing that her lover watched her perform from the front rows, which were reserved for the nobility. She visited Sacher's regularly. As she explained to Gisela, "It's so much more convenient for the count. He spends much of his free time at the Jockey Club, darling, and I join him afterward."

Gisela was not taken to Sacher's, but she was taken to tea — *Jause* — at Demel's by the count and then, surprise of surprises! — to the Riviera, just like one of the "idle rich," a true "lady of leisure."

These were expressions her mother had used when the count had returned from a late autumn hunting trip in Bohemia and announced he would be taking them both for a *Katzensprung*, a flying visit to Cap Martin. When he had left the apartment, Gisela broke into a wild dance around the room. "*Mutti*, the count is going to take me as well! Oh *Mutti*, he is so kind, kinder even than Leo was to us!"

"Yes," said her mother. She watched the slender figure whirling about and felt a little stab of fear.

Gisela's happiness did not prevent her from hearing the tension in her mother's voice. She stopped her wild waltzing and went over to Franzi's side. "Is something wrong, *Mutti*?" Franzi gave a light laugh as though the matter were a mere nothing.

"I'm a bit concerned, darling, that you will be spoiled by his kindness — no, *Liebe*, before you protest, let me explain what I mean. We must never forget, you and I, that we are working women, not the idle rich, and that we are closer to the *Zweite Gesellschaft*, the Second Society, than we can ever hope to come to the count's class. He is so protected by his rank that he doesn't have to worry about who the next mayor of Vienna will be or whether the people are rioting in the streets. He doesn't even have as much anxiety as the emperor shut up in the Schönbrunn, getting up at five o'clock every morning and worrying about the Magyars or the Serbs or the poor Empress Elizabeth."

Gisela had never before heard such a long political speech from her mother, and it startled her quite as much as hearing that she was becoming spoiled. "You don't usually worry about those things any more than the count does, *Mutti*. Have you seen Leo lately? He used to talk about such things, and you used to get annoyed with him."

"Yes, darling, I know, and I find it all such a bore. And yes, I saw a friend of your father yesterday, and how I wish I hadn't! I only start fretting over things I can do nothing about, and it will give me wrinkles!" Here, Franzi gave one of her silvery laughs and patted her hair as she gazed at her reflection in the gilded mirror behind Gisela, as if to reassure herself.

"I don't understand, *Mutti*. What has all this to do with the count taking me with you to the Riviera?"

"It has this to do with it, darling. While you are having a good time you must remember we are only borrowing the count's privileges. They are not ours by right, and we shall have to make plans for you in the spring. Remember, Gisela, that we are not ladies of leisure; we are working women."

"I know, *Mutti*, and I shall work hard at my acting and dancing classes, I promise you, as well as at the tarot and the crystal, just to please you."

Bemused, Franzi looked at her daughter's earnest

face. Sometimes Gisela's ingenuousness baffled and exasperated her, but any gentle probing about her visits to Arcanus the Magician were answered with silence.

They travelled to Cap Martin in the same private carriage that had brought them back to Vienna, stopping first at Nice. Holding back the chenille-trimmed velour drapes, Gisela stared in unabashed wonder as she received glimpses of a Europe she had never seen before.

"You like travelling by train, Gisela?"

The count was standing by her seat, smiling down at her, his face tinted with a rosy glow from the coloured glass at the top of the carriage window.

"I love it, Count von Schönstein, it's so exciting!"

"Then one day I shall take you with me on the Orient Express across Europe, and to Sofia and Constantinople and on to the Orient itself."

"That would be beyond my wildest dreams!"

She heard the silky sound of the count's laugh as he repeated, "Beyond your wildest dreams, Gisela? Well then, we must try to do it."

"I would love to see the Orient."

Count von Schönstein sat on the seat beside her and crossed one impeccably Savile-Row-tailored leg over the other, flicking off an invisible speck of dust.

"Ah, the Orient! Did you know that the Turks were turned back at Vienna, and that they say the Orient begins on the other side of the city's first tollgate?"

"No, I didn't know that, but I meant the Orient like Constantinople."

The count laughed again. "One day, I promise you we shall go through the Bosphorus and see the seraglios of the great sultan caliphs. Constantinople is the real gateway to the east — and we could sail back across the Caspian Sea.''

His melodic voice washed over her, and the exotic names sounded like the magic words on the speculum, musical and spellbinding.

"Oh how *Mutti* would love that!''

"Yes.'' Count von Schönstein stood up and bowed to Gisela. As he did so, his face again glowed in the light of the stained glass, rich and powerful. "Then that's what we shall do, Gisela, one of these days.''

When they reached the coast, they went by carriage to Cap Martin, which was on a quiet wooded promontory between Mentone and Monte Carlo and was so exclusive it was patronized by the emperor himself. The days were a busy round of carriage rides and visiting, and the nights were filled with parties and soirées, eating at the smartest restaurants such as Noel et Patard's.

For Franzi, the joy of Cap Martin was being with the best people and doing the right things at the right time and place. For Gisela, it was seeing the sea for the first time, running along the edge of the shore in bare feet, holding up her skirts and shrieking with delight as the waves soaked her to the skin and splashed her lips with salt. It was also the joy of seeing her mother so happy.

From the terrace of their villa Count Maximilian von Schönstein watched Gisela, dark hair flying in the breeze, her unrestrained laughter echoing over the sands toward him. When she saw him standing there she waved, and the count raised one hand in an elegant salute.

Suddenly she turned in his direction and ran up

the sloping shore. When she reached him, she flung her arms around his waist, forgetting manners, rank, her mother's constant reminders of her place in society.

"Thank you, thank you for everything, for making us so happy!"

"Gisela! You are soaking! Look what you have done to the count!"

Franzi stood at the glass doors of the salon, her usually studied voice shrill with anger. She was looking at Gisela as she had never looked at her before, and it brought the young girl abruptly to her senses. She saw the wet mark she had left with her embrace across the front of the count's waistcoat and stammered in dismay, "I'm so sorry, Your Excellency — I didn't think —"

"You must think — you must think at all times, do you hear me?" Franzi's voice sounded more normal now, but there was still an underlying note in it of something other than anger.

Count Maximilian von Schönstein stood quite still where the edge of the terrace met the sand and looked at Gisela. "It's nothing, nothing at all, Gisela. On the contrary, it is always pleasant to be — appreciated."

He touched the wet, dark hair with one hand, while the other slowly moved across the dampness on his waistcoat in a slow, caressing movement.

When they returned to Vienna Franzi started her salon once again, and Gisela sat in her gilt chair with the crystal and the tarot cards before her. But the crystal remained strangely clouded, as if something had muddied its frozen water. She saw nothing in its prisms.

Occasionally it went black and Gisela saw the starry pinpoints of light that presaged a vision, but nothing came.

She told the tarot without insight, from the positions of the various cards and the interpretations taught her by Alexei, but no flashes of inspiration came to her when she saw the Chariot alongside the Hierophant or the Star close to the Fool. She paid particular attention to the Empress, Hercules, and the High Priestess, but they too lay mute on the silk-covered tabletop and would not speak to her. No one knew of this but her, so the bureaucrats, the court officials, and the officers still came to have their fortunes told and went away happy. She was better at prevaricating and pretending than she had been the winter before.

Mutti had got over her anger and coldness, but her mood had lasted well into their return to Vienna. Gisela understood. She knew how much her mother would hate to lose the count, and it would be terrible if it were because of anything she, Gisela, had done. When the count took them to hear the music of Mahler or Brahms or the two Strausses, or when she was invited to accompany them to one of the winter balls, she was as circumspect and discreet in her behaviour as she could possibly be. Her mother would tease Gisela when she saw her looking at the young men, particularly those in the reserved seats at the opera or the theatre — "Ah, that's young Fürstenburg, isn't he handsome, darling? *Now* who are you looking at? Oh, you have your mother's good taste! That is Count Lichtenstein."

Carefully, Franzi collated her information and plotted her course. There were two or three possibilities

she had in mind, all from the Austrian nobility, and
all without a permanent mistress. From discreet
enquiries she had ascertained the ones who preferred
very young dark-haired girls, and from her own obser-
vations she noted the ones who eyed her daughter.

It was surprising that no one had approached her
about Gisela, but it could be that it was generally
believed she was still associated with Islenyev. He had
powerful friends and there were many who feared him.
Franzi decided she would have to make the first move
herself, especially since Gisela was so disappointingly
unflirtatious. The days of carnival were fast approaching — *Fasching* time, when Vienna's giddy whirl spun
even faster. A strange madness came over the city at
this time of year, a snapping of the fingers in the
face of reality, a whistling against the powers of
darkness and disillusion.

Franzi had her eye on the son of one of the most
prestigious families in the land. She was aiming very
high, and she knew there was little chance of the sort
of arrangement she wanted for Gisela without the
count's help. He would have to be the go-between,
and she must choose the moment well for her request.
She would not ask him at Sacher's — no, never there.
She did not seem to exist for him there. He was as
violent, as impersonal as ever, keeping her waiting
sometimes for over an hour and then staying with
her for five minutes, using her, and leaving. Other
times he would keep her there for hours until she
thought she would die of exhaustion.

Outside the room at Sacher's he was courteous to
her. Inside it he was never anything but offhand,

contemptuous, even brutal. The effect on Franzi Valeska was just as it had been the first night at the Schloss
hotel in Karlsbad. She found the role of victim irresistible. Disgusted with herself after their encounters,
she tried to justify her willing submissiveness.
"It's the title, his position in society, the chance of
advancement for myself and my darling Gisela," she
told herself. But she knew, without a shadow of a
doubt, that those facts played only a part in her
enthrallment.

She decided to speak to him after he had attended
one of Gisela's performances at the Asperngasse. At
such times the count was at his most lighthearted and
conversational, and liked to sit and drink coffee with
them, sharing the cakes he brought from Demel's, the
confectioner on the Kohlmarkt, where he sometimes
took Franzi and Gisela to tea. He would usually linger
a few moments after Gisela had gone to bed and discuss
the next round of parties and balls with her.

Yes, she thought, he plans to spend an evening here
just after the *Industriellen* ball. I must see Gisela looks
her most charming for him. As she formed her plan,
Franzi felt the stab of fear that had come to her a
few times lately and pushed it impatiently away. How
stupid she had been in Cap Martin! Both before and
since that occasion the count had shown nothing but
polite concern and affectionate interest in Gisela's
welfare. He did not make the slightest flirtatious
remark, had not made even the subtlest of advances
toward Gisela in all the time they had known him.
It was just her own insecurity about the tiny lines
of time she saw reflected in her mirror that was making

her jealous. For her own sanity, the sooner she found a protector for Gisela, the better.

There was a large group of visitors expected for their first salon after the *Industriellen* ball. The evening would begin as usual with music, song, and refreshments, but it would all be very informal, very relaxed — one of the delights of an evening at the Asperngasse. Men and women sat in groups exchanging gossip or gathered around the piano, listening to the music or singing along with it. About halfway through the evening, Franzi gave the signal for the guests to seat themselves in a circle around the small gilt chair and the table on which the crystal and cards were read.

Franzi found it worked better if Gisela joined them later in the evening. It added to the sense of drama when she appeared through the long velvet curtains behind her chair, carrying the crystal and cards in her hands, whereas, to Franzi's surprise, her presence early in the evening tended to put a restraint on the gathering. It had to be something to do with Gisela's powers, for in the year 1897, and in this society, a fifteen-year-old was considered an adult.

Gisela was an adult. Many of those present knew about Arcanus, and many of them used establishments where there were girls younger than Gisela. Franzi had been shown private art and literary collections that made the *Decameron* pale by comparison. Could it be that her guests' reaction to Gisela was because she seemed so naïve, so unworldly?

How she could have produced such a child Franzi could not think, what with all the men who had passed through the apartment and through Franzi's experienced hands. She had known what Leo and others had been hinting at when she took Gisela to Islenyev, and if the child had run away from him screaming she would never have taken her back, never. Well, she didn't *think* she would have taken her back, but since there had been no financial rewards there had been no need for such a decision. Gisela was usually quiet and withdrawn for a day or two after one of her visits, but that had been all.

It had been a relief to see how well adjusted Gisela was to the life she would have to lead. Or was it perhaps that she was merely unfeeling? It didn't matter either way, Franzi supposed, but if the girl displayed a little liveliness and colour it would go down far better. After she had talked to the count she would have to have another talk with Gisela. With a man like the Russian, being with a child was enough, but for a young nobleman such as Franzi had in mind, something different was required.

Franzi sighed at her reflection in the mirror and returned to her toilette. There were times when she regretted her moment of madness with Leo Fischer, the instant attraction that had driven them to making heated love in their host's bedroom within an hour of meeting. But no — no regrets, she thought. How can I regret one of the few moments in my life when my gasps were genuine and my response real? Gisela is indeed a love child, and I love her more dearly than anything else in this life of mine.

"*Mutti?*"

Gisela was at the bedroom door, tall and slender in her yellow silk dress, the ruffles high about her slim neck.

"Darling!" Her love suddenly overwhelmed Franzi, filling her with an emotion that felt disturbingly like grief. catching in her throat like tears. She threw her arms around Gisela, hugging her and kissing her extravagantly until she had regained control. "You look so beautiful — how fortunate you are to be able to wear that colour! It's so fashionable at the moment and it's not at all a good colour for me."

With unsightly tears now under control, Franzi went over the evening's arrangements with her daughter as she always did: who was coming and why; what she had learned about this government official, that army officer; what it would be nice for this loving couple to hear. There was nothing to be gained in discussing her other plans for the evening, for she had yet to assure herself of the count's cooperation.

The guests for that evening were the usual mix. There would be two composers, a brilliant young doctor who was also an up-and-coming playwright, bankers, an architect, an artist, two or three members of the First Society, and, of course, Count Maximilian von Schönstein. His Majesty's army would also be well represented. Only the playwright was new to the salon, so the evening should more or less run itself.

It was one of the best gatherings at the Asperngasse that season. The music was wonderful, the conversation brilliant and witty. When the count arrived, slightly later than everyone else and more gorgeous than anyone else in magnificent dress cavalry uniform, Franzi felt her cup of happiness brimming over. She caught sight of herself in one of the many wall mirrors, cheeks attractively flushed, lips parted in laughter, and thought she had never looked better. Lightly clapping her hands together, she called out to the guests in her pretty voice.

"Dear friends! You are having such a splendid time

that I wonder whether I should bring more serious matters to your attention! But some of us need to know whether we should plan a journey or stay at home, whether we should find a new lover or find something new and amusing to do with the old one!"

Franzi's silver trill of laughter rose above the amused response of her guests as they seated themselves around the small table.

"Gisela!"

Franzi held the velvet curtains to one side as Gisela entered the room carrying the crystal and the tarot cards. Smiling, quietly self-assured, the yellow silk dress rustling around her, she seated herself at the table and closed her eyes for a moment. A hush fell over the assembled company as they waited for her to speak. The long-lidded eyes opened slowly and surveyed the men and women in their jewels and decorations, the ones who waited with undisguised eagerness, those who assumed a cool detachment. Count Maximilian von Schönstein stood behind the chairs, his eyes never leaving her. When her glance reached him their eyes held each other's for a second before the count turned from her gaze with a smile. At the front of the circle, Franzi watched them both and felt the little tickle of pain touch her heart once more.

"Arthur? The crystal speaks to you. Is there an Arthur in the room? You practise my father's profession, but you speak to the world through your words, as the crystal speaks to me through pictures. Ah —"

There was the rustle of the yellow silk dress as Gisela turned toward the playwright, whose look of mild amusement changed to one of surprise.

For the writer she saw an important breakthrough, enormous success in the next few years; for the high court official she predicted a complex matter of protocol which would give him great problems before he brought it to a successful conclusion. Only Gisela knew that the crystal merely sputtered tiny points of light at her, that the tarot only did for her what it could do for anyone else. It did not stop her from seeing a great coup for one of the bankers in the next year and warning him about his holdings with the Rothschild railway. Neither did she hesitate to give advice to one of the composers about the need to return to his more serious composition. She did not forget to add the little light touches that kept her audience amused, as recommended by her mother: hints about clandestine meetings at the Thalhof Hotel in Reichenau, revelations about private terms of affection used by one of the couples in the room. Gisela herself often didn't understand what she was implying at this point in her performance, but she trusted to her mother's judgement. From the reaction of her audience tonight, *Mutti's* information was right on target.

"Come on, Franzi, let's hear what your daughter has to say about *your* future! Perhaps she will see a wonderful role for you by our new genius Schnitzler here, eh?"

The two women laughed across the room at each other, the blonde mother and the raven-haired daughter looking at each other, loving each other.

"Well, darling, what do you see?"

"Happiness, *Mutti*, always happiness, just as you told me."

Only Gisela knew that the beryl lay black before her, the tarot mute. Even the stars in the crystal had gone.

"The clouds are moving across the crystal now. The vision is passing from me." The husky voice grew silent, and the young girl's head dropped forward slightly, like a flower too heavy for its slender stem. A little sigh escaped her lips.

"Gisela seems genuinely tired tonight," thought Franzi. Perhaps it was just as well, because she could be persuaded to go straight to bed when the company had left.

Gradually the guests departed, their voices drifting up from the street below, mixed with the sound of carriage wheels and horses' hooves against the cobbles. The male smell of cigars mingled in the salon air with the scent of jasmine and tuberose, the rich fragrance of cognac.

"Bring Gisela in, Franzi, and we'll have our coffee together."

The count leaned back against the rose damask sofa, a gold-tipped Sobranie between his fingers, his eyes moving over his mistress's body. Franzi's flushed cheeks felt even hotter, her breathing ragged. How she wanted him! Perhaps she could persuade him to stay tonight, to make love to her here for once. It was difficult to know what sensual means of persuasion she could use, since the initiative always came from him. He was uninterested in pretty shows of reluctance, flirtatious suggestions, the slow and seductive removal of petticoats, the unlacing of bodices.

"Gisela was very tired tonight, Count, and I have

sent her to bed. But I did indeed want to talk to you about Gisela, without her being present."

"Oh?" The count sat up slowly on the sofa and extinguished his cigarette. "Is there something wrong?"

"Well, yes and no. As you know, Gisela is now fifteen, and although she has her extraordinary gift, she has little else."

"Little else? Gisela is a beautiful young girl."

"Exactly!" cried Franzi with relief, seeing her opening. "And it's going to waste in this apartment! She shows no interest in anyone, encourages none of the few advances made to her, does not seem to have a flirtatious bone in her body. But —" Here, Franzi lowered her voice for dramatic effect. "I *know* there is the possibility of a relationship with the son of Baron Bartholdi, for he has expressed a strong interest to mutual friends, and I think Gisela would like him. However, it is difficult for someone in my position to arrange such matters — with the family, that is, for one should at least have their tacit agreement — and an introduction from you would be so advantageous for Gisela. I do not want her to be *used* by this young man and then cast off without some arrangement — you understand?"

Franzi had been uncertain what reaction she would get to her request. Lack of interest or a reluctance to get involved would not have surprised her, but she had not expected the rage that exploded from the normally aloof and insouciant Count Maximilian von Schönstein.

"Dear God, madam! Are you asking me to procure

a lover for your fifteen-year-old daughter? Are *you* a procuress for your own child? Never, I tell you, never!"

Sometimes he frightened her in the room at Sacher's, but he didn't frighten her now as he sat there accusing her of prostituting her own daughter. How dare he try to make her feel guilty? It was because of him and his kind that women like herself and her daughter existed, after all!

"Why not, pray, Your Excellency? Is the baron's son too good for my daughter? I don't think so and I think he will jump at the chance of having her! I ask you as a courtesy; he is of your class, and I thought you would prefer it that way. But I have no need of your help — Gisela's looks have already done all that is necessary. I know that from what my friend told me, and she is very experienced in such things. I shall use her as our matchmaker instead!"

"I forbid you! I absolutely forbid you to set Gisela up with that — that degenerate!"

"Degenerate? Not according to *my* enquiries — he is young but experienced, his first amours having been arranged by his father through his own mistress. He is not diseased, has no unnatural appetites. It will be heaven for Gisela!"

They were both speaking in whispers, aware that the cause of their battle lay not far from them, and the words hissed and spat between them like bullets.

"Heaven? What do you know of heaven?"

"Little enough, God knows, Count von Schönstein, and that is why I try to snare a piece of it for my daughter! I will *not* turn back from this undertaking!"

The anger and violence hung between them, heavy

and palpable in the pretty little salon in the Asperngasse. The candlelight which Franzi preferred was dim now, as the candles sputtered to an end in the candelabra on the tables.

"Then we are finished, you and I. There are plenty of other depraved little *cocottes* in this city, and I am tiring of your flesh, Franzi. There are other bitches in this city who do not sell their daughters."

Pain filled her, worse than anything she had ever known before. But she had acted all her life and she would need to give one of her best performances now. She was laughing at him, mocking him, the trill of her laughter running like quicksilver through her speech.

"Rest assured, Your Excellency, that I shall redouble my efforts for my daughter! Threaten away, insult me if you must — but by this time next week Gisela will be in one of the grandest mansions on the Ringstrasse being made passionate love to by a dream of a man whose title is as noble as your own — a Titan in bed — as inventive and skilful as any woman could wish for!"

The crescent-shaped dueling scar on the count's cheek was scarlet against the skin drained of colour; the tendons in his neck stood out like whipcord. His breathing sounded as it did on the nights when he drove himself in a fury of lust, hour after hour, in the room at Sacher's.

Franzi could not have foreseen such consequences. How could she? She was an actress, not a clairvoyant, and the crystal had been dark that night, the cards silent beneath her daughter's fingers.

Chapter Fourteen

Vienna

The sound echoed through Gisela's sleep, and in her dream it was the sound of the owls calling in the trees outside the villa at Baden bei Wien as she and *Mutti* played *Taroque* on the terrace together.

"Ai — ee — ai — ee — oooh!"

She was pulled from sleep into the half-darkness of her bedroom, with the early-morning light filtering through the curtained windows.

No, not owls, she thought confusedly, but a woman's voice. Not *Mutti's*, but the voice of Maria, the maid, who should be moving about her first task of the day by now. The screaming started again, degenerating into the raw, coughing gasps of someone in an hysterical or epileptic fit. Gisela got out of bed and ran toward the salon from which the screaming came.

At first all she could see was Maria's plump back, heaving as if she were vomiting, bent over something on the floor near a satin-covered sofa. Then Gisela saw a foot, and a silver high-heeled shoe lying close to it.

"Mutti!"

At the sound of the cry, Maria turned with her arms outstretched. "No, Miss Gisela, don't! Don't come closer! I'll fetch Otto — God help me, I shouldn't have screamed like that and brought you here, but it was the shock — no, there's nothing you can do now, please, Miss Gisela!"

Maria pushed at Gisela in an effort to hold her back, but she was around her in a second, crouching by the body on the floor.

Franzi lay on one side, curled up, one arm stretched out, the other across her body. Her hair had fallen forward across her cheek and shoulders, mercifully hiding the stab wounds from view. But the blood from them was everywhere, congealed on the lace ruffles, the carpet, the blonde curls of the dishevelled hair.

"Mutti, Mutti." This time it was not uttered as a cry, but gently, as though Gisela sought to soothe the woman who lay lifeless before her. She put out her hand and touched her mother's arm, even though she knew it was a gesture without purpose. Why had the crystal remained clouded last night? Why had it not been given to her to save her mother when she had been able to warn complete strangers of danger in any corners of the empire of Franz Joseph?

"Why?" she heard herself say aloud. "Why?"

As she heard the sound of her own voice, the sound of Maria's breath rasping beside her, panic and grief filled her. She flung herself upon her mother's body, trying to gather her up into her arms, stroking the hair back from Franzi's dead face.

"No! No!" In this frenzy of denial of what she knew to be true, the tears finally burst from her. It was as if the dagger that had taken her mother's life was at her own throat, and she prayed she might die in that moment, not be forced to live without her mother.

"I'll get Otto, I'll get Otto," Maria repeated. Gisela heard her running heavily across the room, then the sound of the salon door being closed behind her.

Dazedly, Gisela drew away from her mother's body and looked down at her nightgown, which was spattered with smears of blood. When she looked up she saw that there were signs of a struggle in the room around her. A small table lay on its side by the sofa, the lamp and ashtray of faience which had been upon it were in pieces on the floor. It was difficult to tell what else had happened, because the room was littered with glasses, cigar and cigarette ends, plates of half-finished food. As she was about to turn back to her mother, Maria returned with Otto, the doorman. She saw the shock on his face change to compassion as he looked at her.

"Come, Miss Gisela, come downstairs and wait with us until the officers come. I have already sent Klaus for them. They will take care of everything."

Gisela shook her head. "No, I'll stay with her until they come."

"Is there anyone you would like us to send for? A relative, perhaps?"

Gisela felt as she sometimes did in dreams, when she tried to talk and her mouth would not obey her; her tongue felt as thick as flannel. "Leo — my father — is still in Berlin — I can't think of — yes, if you would send for Count von Schönstein. He — you had better tell him."

She felt the strength draining from her so powerfully she wondered she could not see it pour from her, as tangible and bright as her mother's blood. She wondered if she would ever be able to use her legs again, walk away into emptiness from her last contact with the only person in the world she had to love.

Crouching there over her mother's body, she realized suddenly that this was the first of her visions she had seen fulfilled. From somewhere in the past came the scent of lilacs, the sound of her mother's laugh sparkling like white wine in a crystal glass.

The authorities summoned by Klaus were efficient, courteous, and even more considerate upon the arrival of the count. As he swept into the room they stood swiftly to attention.

"No! No!"

Gisela heard him say what she had said, watched as he crouched over her mother, touched her hair as she had touched it. She saw him shake, put his hands over his face, and then, as if suddenly becoming aware of Gisela's presence, rise to his feet and turn to her.

"Gisela — you shouldn't be here."

"She wouldn't leave until you came, Your Excellency. We tried to get her to go with Maria, but she wouldn't move."

"Come, Gisela."

Numb, obedient, she followed him through into the small boudoir that led off the main salon. The count led her gently to a chair, helped her into it, then knelt down before her and took her hands in his. His face was level with hers, and she could look straight into the beautiful brown eyes. He smelled faintly of sandalwood and cigar smoke.

"Gisela, listen to me. I will not leave you alone to cope with this, I promise you. They tell me your father has been sent for, but I realize there are difficulties there."

"Yes, he's getting married."

"I know. Now, the police will want to question me, as they will everyone who was here last night — but particularly me, for I was the last person to see your mother — apart from, that is —" His voice trailed away and Gisela felt the hands holding hers tremble. "I can only thank God I went on to the home of friends who can vouch for my presence. And I thank God, Gisela, not just because of the officers who will question me, but because I can assure you that I — that I —"

"No!" Gisela shook her head, the tears streaming down her cheeks. "I would never think that of you — I couldn't, because you were the best thing that ever happened to *Mutti*. I'm so glad for her that she had you!"

Count von Schönstein put his arm around her and held her against him. Gisela felt the grief shaking his body, his tears against her neck, trickling down into the neck of the robe that Maria had helped her into before the police arrived. "Don't cry, Count von Schönstein, don't cry."

She slowly put her arms around his shoulders and his head sank closer against her. Tentatively, lovingly, she placed her hand on the smooth, soft hair and soothed him as if he were now the child. She thought of Cap Martin and the affection that had overwhelmed her, of watching his hand move over the damp traces left by her wet hair. The salt she now tasted on her lips was from his tears and hers, and the love she felt was born of grief, not gratitude.

"Don't cry," she repeated. "You were so kind to *Mutti* — don't grieve."

The count raised his head from her shoulder, his eyes luminous with tears, bright with passion. "Dear Gisela, I have said I will take care of everything, and here you are taking care of me! No more 'Count von Schönstein' or 'Your Excellency,' you promise me? Grief and suffering makes equals of us all. I call you Gisela and you must call me Max — yes?"

"Max."

His smile was brilliant, as sparkling as his tears. He put his hands on each side of her face, and Gisela felt his fingers touch the lobes of her ears, his thumbs caressing her chin. "There, already it comforts me."

Dizzy with grief and shock as she was, it nevertheless struck Gisela that she had never heard her mother address the count by anything but his title. "Max," she repeated. The realization made the honour paid her all the more precious, the single syllable glowing bright in her mind in this moment of deprivation.

"Gisela." The count took his hands from her face and patted her gently on the shoulder. "I will take care of everything."

She wanted to take his hands in hers and kiss them in her gratitude, but she remembered her mother's words. "You must think at all times," she had said.

The careless time was over forever. The first gesture had come from him, and so must the second. She must never forget the lessons her mother had taught her.

Chapter Fifteen

Vienna

The Emperor Franz Josef led the Corpus Christi procession in June 1898, as was the custom. The pomp and panoply of the double empire was at its most magnificent in this show of shows paraded through the streets of Vienna. Franz Josef travelled in his gold state coach drawn by eight white horses, stopping at the altars of three of the city's churches. At each stop he knelt in prayer, a candle in his right hand, his left hand on the pommel of his sabre. The mayor of Vienna followed in a coach pulled by six horses, and the cardinal blessed the population.

At the count's invitation, Gisela attended the parade, watching from the vantage point he had obtained specially for her. For her, carnival time and the months following it had been a grieving time, but the count had insisted she should go. "I have to attend in my official capacity, but I will come afterward and we shall go out somewhere. It is time we should do so, Gisela."

Why, she didn't know, but in the moment when the cardinal blessed the people, Gisela felt some of the blackness leave her soul. She looked up at the blue sky above her, felt the warm June air on her face and her spirits lifting in response to the music, the majesty of the occasion, the promise of summer in the fresh air. When the count came afterward to call on her, he saw immediately that something had changed.

"You feel better, Gisela."

He was smiling at her, and she felt laughter bubbling up inside her from a source she thought had dried up forever. "Yes, I do, I feel better," she said in surprise.

"Well then — shall we have a little spree? *Ein Hetz*, Gisela! Say yes!"

The count was laughing; it was the first time she had seen him laugh in months, and it suddenly struck Gisela that he was really quite young behind the uniform and moustache, almost certainly younger than her mother had been. Just a young man laughing at her in the June sunshine.

"*Ein Hetz* — yes, yes, yes!"

"Let's go to the Prater then! But first I must change from my ceremonial uniform. I shan't take long and you can wait for me in the carriage."

It was no hardship to wait in the count's beautifully appointed equipage outside his *Palais*, with the sleek carriage horses standing patiently in their harness, attended by liveried grooms. Gisela's feeling of unreality deepened when the count reappeared, running lightly down the steps in a dove-gray suit, soft hat pulled rakishly forward, a silk foulard in the neck of his shirt. Was it really for her company that he laughed, that his eyes danced, that his voice sang with happiness?

"You waited! You didn't run away! Here we go!"

And she was laughing with him, the lace ruffles of her white dress blowing against her face in the breeze, the ribbons on her hat fluttering behind her, and her heart beating like all the drums in the Corpus Christi parade.

Afterward, it was all a blur of sensations: their laughter together, and her heart beating — and how handsome he was; how all the women stared at him. He went with her on some of the rides, and he won her favours: a doll, coloured ribbons, a tortoiseshell comb for her hair. She knew she would keep them forever.

"Do you want to see the Punch and Judy show next?"

In her mind's eye Gisela saw Punch beating Judy with his stick, thought of the screams, the violence, the sadness.

"No, I don't think I want to see it this time."

"Are you hungry, then?"

"Very!"

They ate *Tafelspitz* — tender boiled beef with applesauce and horseradish — and followed it with some of the famous yeast cake of Vienna, *Gugelhupf.* The count ordered champagne.

"Champagne? with *Tafelspitz*?"

"Why not? Ah Gisela, why not!"

He laughed at her over the rim of his glass as she wrinkled up her nose at the explosion of bubbles on the surface of the wine.

On the way home in the soft twilight they sang the words to the Strauss melodies they had heard in the restaurant. At one point the count stopped the carriage and jumped out. When he returned, he was carrying a bunch of roses, yellow and pink, which he had bought from a street vendor.

"For you, *süsse Mädel* — sweet girl."

Sweet girl, he had called her. Gisela experienced for the first time the ineffable pleasure of being admired by a handsome young man.

"Thank you, Max. You give me compliments — lilies of the valley — and you give me roses."

"And you have given me some moments of happiness again. Gisela, I have to go away for a short while, but when I come back, would you let me take you away for a holiday?"

Would she go on holiday with him? She would go anywhere with him — even if it were only to the Prater again, just for the fun of being with him. He saw the answer on her face, and he leaned forward and grasped her hands and the roses she held between his own.

"*Süsse Mädel*, the world is your oyster. Where would you like to go?"

She shook her head, overwhelmed. "You choose, Max."

"Very well — let's go to Bad Gastein. It's a fairy tale of a place, fit for sweet princesses."

So, she was called a princess now, and by one of the chosen ones. It seemed infinitely better than being a high priestess, and if the gift had departed, so much the better. If bad things were still to come, let them come as they did for other people: unheralded, unforeseen. Let the present remain unclouded by visions seen in the speculum, or in a hand of cards laid out on a table.

Max was away for a few weeks in the early summer, as he had said he would be. When he returned, he took Gisela to Bad Gastein, just as he had promised her.

And, just as he had said, Bad Gastein was a fairy tale, a romance of coloured lights and illuminated crags and waterfalls. Gisela floated through the days on the cloud of euphoria that had surrounded her since Corpus Christi. If they had gone back to Baden bei Wien or Karlsbad the memories of her mother might have been far more than the bittersweet nostalgic ache they were for Gisela during this month. When she thought of her mother laughing at the casino in Karlsbad or in the villa at Cap Martin, it was like eating *Sachertorte* on a sensitive tooth: exquisitely painful but swift in passing. The moment of horror in the salon at the Asperngasse had become as insubstantial, as unreal as the first forewarning she had had as a child. Self-absorbed, she gave herself up to the dreamlike quality of the present.

However, the count was no dream. He was the reality of which Gisela dreamt in the night, when the nightingales and orioles sang outside her bedroom window, open to the honey-scented air of the villa garden.

Franzi Valeska's daughter was both an innocent and as knowledgeable as only a courtesan's daughter could be. From an early age she had known what happened between a man and a woman, the art which had been an important part of her actress-mother's life. When Franzi Valeska had said, "We are working women,"

Gisela had known what she meant — that love-making was a coinage, just as much as any golden *Kreuzer*, and that it was the stuff of which the lives of such women as Franzi were made.

At the time Gisela had given no thought as to why she had chosen to appear ignorant to her mother. Now, night after night, lying in bed in a villa in Bad Gastein, she wondered about it. It seemed to have had little to do with her own fears and a great deal to do with how she felt about her mother. That maternal warmth, those arms that encircled her, those lips that kissed her, played another role in another world. By cloaking herself in ignorance she had held on to the image she treasured and denied the value placed upon Franzi's warmth by others.

Mutti was dead now. The police had carried out a lengthy investigation, Maria had told her, and even the count and all his friends had been questioned more than once. The judgement of the court of enquiry had been that Franzi had been killed by one of her lovers, and Gisela had been given to understand that there had been many, both during the relationship with her father and with the count. Part of her grief had involved finally coming to terms with the true picture of her mother — and part of the healing had been brought about by the count himself.

Count von Schönstein was the only man Gisela could recall who had never flirted with her mother while she was present, caressed her publicly, or spoken outrageously or suggestively to her. He had treated Franzi with a strangely distant courtesy, and limited their physical familiarity to kissing her hand. There was now some confusion in Gisela's mind as to whether he had ever been her mother's lover. Protector, she thought, just a protector. Perhaps there really were men who only wanted a pretty actress to escort, a cheerful apartment to visit from time to time. Max had always been tolerant of Gisela's presence, and that had not always been true of other men, including her own father.

It had always been men who separated her from her mother. Deep down she had resented it, and this resentment had made her want to remain ignorant of the way of life that brought about that separation. Max had scarcely kept her mother away from her at all, and she had for once been able to accept her mother's two roles — that of actress and that of mistress.

As she tossed and turned amid the rumpled sheets, Gisela saw quite clearly what she wanted from Max von Schönstein. She did not want only to laugh with him, be escorted by him, be visited from time to time. She wanted him to make love to her. "Make love to me, Max," she whispered, wondering if lightning would strike, if disgust and rejection would follow. What she felt was not guilt or horror, but a sensation like a flickering tongue of fire that licked over the surface of her skin as if she were running a high fever.

He had taken her dancing that night, and she had worn vivid colours for the first time ever: a dress of emerald-green and garnet instead of the pinks and ivories of her childhood summers, and it was made of taffeta and shot silk. Everyone had stared at the count and the striking fifteen-year-old girl with the long dark eyes and the cloud of hair. The world probably imagined they were already lovers. Would that we were, she thought, would that we were!

Lying over the back of a chair across the room, her

glorious dress shone in the moonlight. On an impulse Gisela got out of bed, pulling off her nightgown as she went, picked up the dress from the chair and pulled it over her naked body. The silk and taffeta were cool against her skin, and yet she experienced the same sensation she had when she thought of making love. "Max," she said out loud. "Max." Holding the dress up around her, she started to dance across the room, waltzing to the music of the night-birds beyond the window in the deserted garden. As she whirled round toward the bedroom door, the handle moved and the door started to open.

Gisela wasn't afraid. She knew who it was and why he had come. Whether it was coincidence, wish fulfillment, or visionary power she didn't know, but she felt she had made it happen. She had brought him to her. His first words confirmed her intuition.

"Sorceress, Gisela Valeska, I saw you in my mind dancing in the moonlight, and I had to come." The count's voice was hoarse, ragged with emotion.

"How did you see me?" She heard her own voice, a whisper, yet as clear as a trumpet echoing across the room.

"I don't know. You are the sorceress and I am the slave. You brought me here."

She did not doubt that what he said was true. She had danced in her magic dress until he came to her. A sense of her own power filled her, and she felt as if she could float above the ground, fly through the night sky, touch the stars.

"Yes, I called you and you came to me."

"I am yours to command, sorceress."

"High Priestess. Arcanus called me the High Priestess."

Chapter Sixteen

The Orient Express

Once, when she had been a child and thought of herself as a child, he had promised her the Orient. Now, he gave it to her. From Vienna on the Orient Express, through the Porta Orientalis into Rumania and the Balkans, to Constantinople across the Black Sea from Varna.

Gisela saw it all though eyes dazzled with Max, blurred with his beauty. Their laughter and sighs rang in her ears as she saw her own passion reflected in the velvet eyes across the snow-white damask of the dining car, the baccarat crystal on its surface reflecting the light from the huge gas chandeliers above.

Max von Schönstein gazed at the face opposite him. Gisela was framed by the teak-and-rosewood panelling behind her, its gilt flowers lustrous in the soft light. For a while he had wondered if she had attracted him merely because of her virginal freshness, and if the effect on him would be as evanescent as was customary for him in such matters.

He had been wrong, and he was delighted. When the young girl's sensuality had been released by their first love-making, her charming originality had bloomed into a gorgeous lushness that had taken him by surprise. He was not in the least bothered by the world seeing him with a very young mistress, but Gisela's looks had flowered into a mature beauty as exotic as anything to be found in any seraglio from Constantinople to Baghdad. The wardrobe of purples, scarlet, and emerald he had chosen with her prior to their departure emphasized this new hothouse charm. He had insisted too, on some ivory silks and satins, against which her skin and hair glowed in savage splendour.

Gisela was wearing ivory now, with diamonds and pearls, and she quite eclipsed the delicate aquarelles by Delacroix and Seymour in their gold frames between the windows of the dining car. The smoothness of the skirt, cut on the bias to emphasize the unfashionable slenderness of her hips, showed off the subtle lines the count now found more erotic than the rich curves he used to prefer.

She has dazzled me more than I thought possible, he thought to himself. The seduction was mine, her skills are all mine, and yet it is the woman herself who attracts by what she is, not by what I have given her.

"You are magnificent, Gisela."

She smiled, her strong white teeth dazzling, her eyes elongated further by the smile. "I know."

There she had surprised him again. She threw back her head, the low rich laughter coming from her throat, and he saw the firm square line of her jaw. "And how do *you* know it? Do you see it in the crystal?" He pointed to the glass of Napoleon brandy in front of him.

"I see it in your eyes. I no longer see visions in the crystal."

"Ah." There was a strange awkwardness about his laugh, as if something had made him feel ill at ease.

"And you know why?" she continued. "It's because we make love, did you know that? The virtue that was the gift passed into the love."

"I must satisfy you, then?"

Her kid-gloved hand touched the wrist of the hand holding the brandy glass, and he felt the electricity run through him. "Satisfy me? You fill me, Max, and there's no room left for anything else. It's just as Arcanus said it would be."

"You should not forget the skills he taught you, Gisela. When we return to Vienna, I shall set you up in a salon so brilliant that it will be the talk of not only Vienna, but Paris and Berlin and — yes, even New York!"

"New York? That's so far away! Would people there really be interested in me?"

"Of course! Clairvoyance and spiritualism are all

the rage — and there's so much wealth there. It has to be seen to be believed!"

"You have been there?"

"Oh yes, more than once. I was there earlier this year."

"Could there be any more wealth there than here?" Gisela's gesture took in the gold-rimmed porcelain dinner service, the gold-lettered menu with its ten courses, the heavy silver cutlery.

"As much if not more than here. At the opera I saw the wife of one of the richest men in New York wearing a rope of pearls around her waist — and from it hung a giant uncut ruby which she kicked before her as she walked!"

"*Really*?" For a moment, the gorgeous woman opposite him became a little girl again, her eyes wide with wonder.

"Really. And they dine off plates of gold in houses as grand as any of our palaces, grander than many I know."

"Could we go there sometime?"

"Perhaps we will. Your gift and your looks could make your fortune. Rich men like to know what the fates hold for them. That kind of fortune is something they cannot control."

"It's the one thing none of us can control."

A shiver, a flicker of light, stars in the crystal before her, and then it was gone, leaving only the familiar sadness around her heart.

"What is it, Gisela?" There was disquiet in his face again.

"Nothing, just a shadow. Take me back to our compartment, Max. Make love to me."

They walked through the ladies' salon with the Louis XV chairs and the tapestry hangings imitating Watteau's *fêtes galantes* to their private suite. By the time the count had loosened the flowered damask drapes from the cords that bound them, Gisela was waiting for him on the silk sheets, her arms held out for him.

He had thought the obsession would pass once he had taken her. He had thought that was all that would be necessary, though the strength of his obsession had disturbed him. The mere idea of anyone else having her had filled him with a black rage he had never felt before over a woman. Such anger he had experienced, yes, in a duel, but a duel was an affair of honour. This was different, and yet he had been driven to seek satisfaction with the same intensity he had experienced during the duels that had given him the scars on his body, which had brought death to others.

At the thought of the young nobleman to whom she had nearly been given, rage filled him again. He looked at her lying on the bed and it seemed to him that she metamorphosed before him, the long slender legs tapering away into a creamy, shining blur in the pale light as though she were a mermaid.

"Sorceress!" he cried out. "What have you done to me?"

He watched her mouth curve into a smile, and she reached out to him, her hands moving over his body, around his waist, drawing him down to her, the smile changing to a gasp as he thrust himself into her.

"No one else, Gisela — no one, or I kill him!"

She did not answer him but wound around him the legs he had seen change but a moment earlier.

Now, as he brought his mouth down hard against hers, it seemed to him that her limbs had become serpents twined around him as he struggled to establish his feeling of supremacy over her.

"*Compagnie Internationale des Wagons-lits et des Grands Express Européens.*" Gisela looked back at the great train as they left the railway platform in Vienna and read out the message printed in raised bronze letters above the windows.

"You have a good ear, Gisela, a talent for languages. Next you must learn English — we can see to that in the next few weeks."

Gisela was relieved she was not going back to the apartment on the Asperngasse. No amount of redecorating could wipe away from her memory the blood-stained body of her mother on the floor of the salon. On one of the fashionable streets just off the Ringstrasse, Max had obtained for her another apartment which was being furnished and decorated to her instructions while they were away.

Gisela's unerring instinct for the right ambiance, the perfect setting for her original looks, had amused and intrigued her lover. She had forsaken the rococo Orientalism of her mother's apartment for the new flowing lines of the decorators and painters who were beginning to make their presence felt in Vienna and Paris. She chose soft, curving lines, floral motifs — irises, waterlilies — in pastel shades, offset by the gleam of butterfly wings, the brilliance of a peacock's tail.

As Gisela walked in the door of the new apartment

it seemed to fold around her in perfect harmony, and the slim figure of the young woman became its centre.

"Perfect, Max!" she cried out in delight, whirling around to face him. The shot silk of her skirt became part of the kaleidoscope of colour. "Everything is perfect!" At one side of the room she saw her crystal and the tarot cards in their case on the small table she had retained from the Asperngasse. Suddenly she knew she must look at them.

"What are you doing, Gisela?"

"I must look at the cards. They are telling me to read them."

"Still not the crystal?" His voice was flippant, lighthearted.

"No, not the crystal. It will still be dark for me, I know."

Her great amethyst-coloured cloak swirling around her, she sat down. Her long, slender hands shook as if the rings she wore on nearly every finger were suddenly too heavy for them.

"Just the ten-card spread — it will be enough," he heard her mutter. Breath suspended, feeling as though time itself were suspended, he waited to hear what the tarot would reveal to her.

Gisela took the twenty-two Major Arcana cards from the pack, separated the Fool and the Magician from them and placed them together on top of the pack. A smile crossed her face as she picked up the Magician, and he heard her say, "Arcanus." She then shuffled the pack and placed ten cards on the table in front of her. Leaving four cards facedown to one side, she proceeded to go over the remaining six.

It was impossible to tell from her expression what, if anything, she was seeing. The young woman leaned forward over the table, frozen in concentration, hands flat on the black silk cloth. She did not look up until she had turned over the remaining cards and looked briefly at them. Her eyes seemed to him like the deep, black lakes he sometimes came across when hunting in the mountains.

"The Empress is with me again," she said, "and the two lovers, as I hoped. But they are reversed — how can that be? And if you are Hercules, then why is the Empress with you, and not the High Priestess?"

"Gisela!" The count strode across the room and put his arms around her. "What are you talking about? What is wrong with the cards being reversed, and what do you mean when you say the Empress is with you again?"

Gisela was still looking at the cards, searching for a clearer meaning to the disturbing panorama they had shown her. "Yes, yes, the moon is reversed and that is a good sign — and the star can be read both ways. But the Empress — who is she? She is important to me, and now she seems to be important to you. I haven't seen that before in the cards. Do you know the Empress Elizabeth, Max? I hadn't thought of the real empress being the tarot Empress, but — did you — have you been her lover?"

"Gisela!" Max von Schönstein's laughter filled the room. "That's almost a blasphemous suggestion, my sweet girl! The Empress Elizabeth is exquisitely beautiful, completely inaccessible — and ineffably cold. To my knowledge, no one is her lover, including Franz

Josef! Perhaps what you are seeing is a more exalted clientele than even I myself have dreamed of for you. Only time will tell."

"Only time will tell," Gisela repeated, looking at the cards once more. "And there is the Fool as well, somewhere in time, somewhere in the future."

"But that's me, Gisela! I am a fool — a fool for you, always and ever. There's no mystery there — it is Count Maximilian von Schönstein who is the Fool!"

He almost convinced her with his laughter and his cajoling tone and the strong hands that caressed her, his mouth hard against her breast. Desperately she turned to the present, putting behind her the tarot's confused signals, its hidden message.

"Max, if I am to be such a star, then I must have information."

"Information?" Puzzled by both what she said and the sudden change in her mood, he looked up at her.

"Yes, information. It surprises me what I can tell even when the crystal is dark, but I need more. *Mutti* knew all the gossip about the people who came to the Asperngasse — and not just about their love affairs. Politics may have bored her, but she was no fool, my mother. Even the most correct of the military and government officials could be flattered and cajoled into confiding in her. She was my eyes and ears. Can you do the same?"

"The same? My dear Gisela, I can do even better!" The count jumped to his feet and started to pace the room excitedly. "I may not have your mother's shell-like ear into which to pour sweet nothings — and everythings — but I have something even more valuable. Rank. My God!'' He whirled around and came back to her, grasping her shoulders. ''What possibilities this gift of yours has! It never occurred to me before, but you could be more than a star performer, Gisela. You could be a power to be reckoned with — with my help, of course. Have you ever given private readings before?''

''No,'' replied Gisela, startled at the strength of his reaction. ''It was always in front of a group in the salon, picking out individuals — but you know that.''

''Darling girl, suppose you gave private readings as well! Do you not see the possibilities? You could draw out information that would be useful to the country — or, by God, you could *give* information, facts the government would like others to hear and believe!''

''Others? Information?'' If she understood correctly what he was saying, then her performances suddenly became more than a party game or an evening's entertainment. ''What exactly are you asking me to do, Max?''

The count's eyes glittered as though he had a fever, but his voice was calmer when he answered. ''You don't have to worry about that, Gisela, not yet. You will see. It will be such fun — a real spree!''

Gleefully he pulled her up from the chair and waltzed her around the room until she was out of breath and laughing with him, all the confused messages of the tarot forgotten.

''Come, you must change into your most incredible dress, sweet girl, and I shall take you to the opera and then to Sacher's. We must attract a starry clientele to these doors, and we might as well start right away!''

The starry clientele were not slow in coming. In a matter of weeks, visiting the salon of Gisela Valeska became one of the chic things to do in Vienna. Even when the count was away on business in New York during the winter of 1898 the nobility, the bankers, the military men, and the politicians flocked to her doors.

For the times when he would not be there to give her information or instructions, Max decided to introduce her directly to his government contact. Gisela was worried about this development.

"Darling Max, I don't want to be seen in Beethoven Street visiting the police, even such a distinguished member as your friend."

"Sweet girl, what makes you think I would expect something so vulgar of you? And you underestimate the status of my acquaintance — had you really thought I was working with mere policemen? No, Gisela, you have been receiving information from a staff captain with the Royal Dragoons. Our contact is Baron Eihrentahl.''

Stunned, Gisela began to realize the significance of what she was doing. It had seemed such a game to her. When guests arrived from St. Petersburg, or from Zagreb, Prague, or Bratislava, she made them especially welcome and took particular note of what they confided, passing on anything she had been asked to convey. Sometimes the messages made sense to her; sometimes they did not.

Besides, she learned a great deal because of her own skills. Men were surprisingly willing to tell the most incredible things to a clairvoyant and were as willing to talk about their friends and enemies as themselves. Gisela heard secrets she was sure they would not have told their mistresses during the most intimate pillow talk. Gradually she was building up a wealth of knowledge about the rich and powerful in Vienna and beyond. When amorous suggestions were made to her, she had only to remind her client gently of the count's membership in more than one duelling fraternity, including the prestigious German national duelling corps, Silesia, and the importunings soon ceased.

With the planned visit to Baron Eihrentahl she could no longer pretend she was playing a game. "How will I meet him, Max? Should he be even thinking of coming here?"

"He won't be, and it's all arranged. A closed carriage will take you tomorrow to the Eighth District. Don't worry — it's quite respectable, full of young doctors and lawyers. You will meet him at rooms he has taken on Floriani Street in one of the big houses there."

"Will you come with me?"

"No, the baron feels it is better I stay away."

"Tell me something about him, Max. Is he old, dry as dust, frighteningly correct like the emperor?"

The count laughed. "He's very correct, and he's approaching middle age, but there is more to him than that. He's an army man as I could never be an army man — it's his life. He has written histories of nearly every place where he has served and mapped

"Come!" barked a voice from inside. Her escort opened the door, bowed to Gisela, and left her.

Baron Eihrentahl sat behind the largest desk Gisela had ever seen; she couldn't help wondering how they had got it through the door.

"*Gnädige Fräulein*, please come in. I am pleased to meet you."

The baron came around the desk and extended his hand to her. He walked with the straight spine of the professional soldier, and the angle at which he held his head marked him out as a member of the First Society. Gisela saw it again and again in Max and his friends: a tilt of arrogance, insouciance, of the chosen ones who felt they owned the world.

There, however, any resemblance to Max ended. There was no idle humour, no insouciance in the eyes that were looking so closely at her. The expression in them was sharp, calculating; they focused on her briefly and then moved beyond her, as if they were more accustomed to ranging over wide landscapes, distant vistas. His fine-drawn features betrayed no hint of softness, and he didn't have the oval-shaped head of the Austrian aristocracy. His was square, emphasized by the light graying hair which was cut *en brosse*.

Nor was there anything in those sharp blue eyes to suggest that this man responded in any way to her beauty — and Gisela knew how striking she looked in black silk and sable, with diamonds glittering in her ears. Piqued, and then suddenly amused by her own reaction, she smiled dazzlingly at him, her awe of the occasion dissipating with the need to charm. She was rewarded by a flicker of something other than calculation before his gaze distanced itself once more.

"*Herr Baron.*"

"Please, *Fräulein*, sit down." The baron indicated a chair on her side of his desk. "It will not be necessary to curtsy to me again. We do business together, so rank can be forgotten."

"Rank is never forgotten."

The response was out before she had thought about it. The baron had returned behind his fortress of a desk, but she could see that the fine-chiselled mouth beneath the gray moustache was smiling.

"You are right, of course. So, curtsy in future if you wish — but I think you will not."

She did not reply this time, but waited for him to continue. The smile had disappeared as quickly as it had come.

"*Fräulein* Valeska, we have been interested in you since the days on the Asperngasse."

Gisela was surprised. "I thought Max — Count von Schönstein — had brought me to your attention."

"Partly, but we have been aware of you since the matter of the *Rittmeister* who went to Bilin."

Now he had truly surprised her. "Why? Who told you about that? I remember him, but chiefly because my mother was annoyed that I had upset him so much."

"Yes, you upset him a great deal. The gentleman in question had served in other garrisons in which we knew information was being given to the Russians. In his previous posting he had been close to the Russian border in Kolomea, in eastern Galicia. In Bilin we — caught up with him."

"My God, no wonder he was so nervous!"

"Precisely. For a while we thought your revelation might affect our plans, and we had to check on whether you — well, let's just say we investigated you."

In its own way, this interview was turning out to be as revelatory as her first meeting with Alexei. "My God!" she repeated. "I was just a child!"

"Even children can be used, sometimes without their knowledge. But we satisfied ourselves that you were not being manipulated — at least, not in any way that made you our concern."

"And now *you* wish to manipulate me, *Herr Baron*?"

The blue eyes focused on her, sharp and clear. "We both wish it, *Fräulein*. Am I not right?"

"Yes, I would be happy to help the emperor in any way I can."

"Good, because that is why we are both here. So, to business." He picked up some papers from his desk, put them down again as if he had changed his mind and asked her abruptly, "What do you know of the different peoples who make up this double empire of ours, *Fräulein* Valeska?"

"Not very much. My mother told me what I needed to know, but she wasn't interested in politics. My father was interested, but he passed out of my life a while ago. He is Jewish."

"I know." Gisela remembered what Max had said about the baron's Jewish blood, but she didn't notice any reaction on his part. "I won't bore you with detail, but perhaps I can describe the magnitude of our task." The baron leaned across the vast expanse of mahogany between them, his hands stretched out on its surface, his gaze now fixed far beyond her.

172

"So many peoples make up this empire of ours! Let us begin with the Magyars — all that stubborn mysticism — how well I know it — my mother was Hungarian. Then there are the Slav races. And there is constant tension between the Germans and the Moravians, and the Poles to the north of them. Not to mention the Italians south of the Brenner — and the Serbo-Croats, Ruthenes, Slovaks. Beyond our borders lie those who work at creating agitation from within to weaken us. Oh, it's easily done, because each man thinks his group should have greater power and privilege." Here, the baron paused for a moment and looked at her as if to assure himself she was still listening, then continued.

"The monarchy, in the person of the emperor himself, is all that unites us. And, as you and I both said, that is why we are here. You, *Fräulein* Valeska, will play your part in keeping us a move ahead in this great game of chess we play with human lives. At the moment, the court and the Balhausplatz are virtually the centre of Europe. We work to keep it that way."

Gisela was as much impressed by the fact that the baron had bothered to tell her these things as by his knowledge, which was almost certainly very basic for a man in his position. It made her feel warmer toward the distant, erect figure behind the desk.

"What can I do?" she asked simply, and was answered first by the smile that deepened the fine lines around his eyes.

"More of the sort of thing you did with your recent visitor, Hodlizcka, the Magyar high court official. Even the lady in his life had uncovered next to nothing for us — yet he told you things that were of great value to the *Kaiserliche Königliche* consular service."

"I am glad it was useful. How do I get the information to you and receive my instructions while the count is away?"

"From me, directly, by private delivery, and this will continue even when the count returns. The messenger will come to you every week. If there is nothing for him, just tell him so. It would be better not to come here again, unless absolutely necessary. If, however, an emergency arises, you must feel free to return."

"What sort of emergency, *Herr Baron?*"

The clipped voice softened, but the new gentleness only added a feeling of menace to what he said. "There are constant threats against the royal family, for instance. You never know what you might hear, *Fräulein* Valeska."

His reply brought home to Gisela the seriousness of what she was doing, what had started almost as a game, to please Max. She gave a little shiver, and the baron added, "Don't worry. It's unlikely you would be entrusted with that kind of information. You are — " Here, he hesitated a moment. "You are very beautiful and very successful, but I understand you do not sleep with your clients, and men usually confide that sort of secret in bed."

Gisela was jolted by his remark, as if the clipped voice had physically assaulted her by speaking of such intimacies in the same tone as he had given her her potted history lesson. Forgetful of his rank, she was stung into angry response. "I find it insulting, Baron

Eihrentahl, that you should speak to me so casually of such personal things. Have you forgotten your own observation? As you yourself said, men tell me things they do not tell their mistresses. I am very beautiful, indeed; I am very successful — indeed. I don't sleep with my clients — indeed. And I am told more out of bed than many are told in it. Add that to your dossier, Baron!"

Gisela stood up, drew her sables around her, and looked down at Baron Eihrentahl behind his mahogany fortress. "May I leave now?"

It gave her some pleasure to see that she had startled him. He got up and came around the desk to her. "Forgive me — I was trying to reassure you, and, instead, I have offended you. It was not what I intended. I think —" The baron hesitated, then added, as if surprised at the discovery, "I think I intended it as a compliment."

"I am not here for compliments." And yet, was that not one of the things that disconcerted her, that he had paid her none? Was she becoming like *Mutti*, looking for lilies of the valley from every man?

"You are right. Of course you may leave — I'll call for the guard. The empire is grateful to you, *Fräulein* Valeska."

"Thank you."

Baron Eihrentahl picked up an envelope from the desk and handed it to her. "Here is the code message with which the messenger will greet you, and the seal which will be on all the letters. Destroy it when you know it — it's very simple. Use what paper you wish for your own communications, but it might be better if your correspondence looked like a — a —" Baron Eihrenthahl looked uncharacteristically at a loss for words.

"A *billet-doux*, Baron?" Gisela completed the sentence for him.

"Precisely."

She could not resist adding, "It shall be the colour of lavender, Baron Eihrentahl, and scented like *Mai-glockchen* — lilies of the valley."

She could see he was laughing. Even the luxuriant moustache couldn't hide it. "Why not lavender to match the paper, *Fräulein*?"

"If you prefer."

Baron Eihrentahl shrugged the square shoulders that up to then had seemed so stiff. "I have no preference."

"Then I shall surprise you." This time she could hear his laugh, a sound as clipped as his voice, as if it were a skill that had become rusty.

As Gisela followed him to the door she looked around the room, something she had not done when she came in. It was sparsely but luxuriously appointed, and she noticed that there were many maps on the walls. On an impulse she went across to examine one of them and saw that it was delicately tinted with an exquisitely painted vignette in one of the corners.

"This is lovely. Is it one of yours?"

"Yes." She could hear the surprise in his voice. "I do some mapping."

"I know." Her turn to say that now. "Turkey — Constantinople — I have been there."

"I know." Eyebrows raised, she turned back to look

at the *Herr Baron* with his short military haircut, his rigid stance, his piercing blue eyes. If it had been any other man, she would have thought the exchange mildly flirtatious. With this man — impossible.

"Do you know everything about me?"

"No." The lightness she had imagined in his voice was gone, and he was as he had seemed when she had come into the room: cool, formal, polite. "It is clear your dossier is incomplete." He put his hand out to the door and suddenly asked, "How old are you, *Fräulein?*"

"Seventeen."

He shook his head. "Impossible."

His response suddenly made her feel sad. "Life can make you old, Baron Eihrentahl. My gift makes me old."

"Gift?"

She saw that if he had thought at all about her clairvoyance, he probably thought of it as parlour tricks. Well, maybe he was not so far from the truth, after all. "The reason I am useful to you."

"Ah, yes, that." The baron bowed sharply from the waist and held the door for her. "Good-bye, *Fräulein* Valeska."

It was only in the carriage that Gisela realized she had no idea how old he was and hadn't even thought about it, although he had asked her age. Perhaps it was because she hadn't thought of him as a person at all. Just a military cipher, she thought, moving his chess pieces around in his emotionless, detached way. Why Max had described this man as a romantic she couldn't in the least imagine.

Chapter Seventeen

Vienna

Max returned from New York in January in time for most of the public balls and for carnival time.

He was not prepared for the progress Gisela had made, and it took him by surprise. She was now fluent in Hungarian, and in addition to working on her French she had begun to acquire some English. She usually had information of some kind for the messenger who came every week to the apartment, and Max found it amusing that she would neither tell him how the exchange of messages took place nor allow him to be present when it occurred.

"The baron said it would be better not to compromise you in any way from now on. We deal directly with each other."

"Ah, that old stick-in-the-mud! Don't worry, sweet girl, I'll not spoil his little game with you — if that's the only game he plays?"

"Oh, Max! He didn't even look at me as though I were a woman!"

"Then he must be even colder than I thought, for you are more beautiful than ever, Gisela."

It was hard to believe she was still so young, for there was an ageless quality to her beauty. The strong planes of her face contrasted with the slenderness of her frame, and there was a maturity in the directness of her gaze, the sure dexterity of the jewelled fingers that dealt the tarot cards. The new sophistication of her dress — the vivid colours, gold lamé turbans, bold jewelry — gave the impression of a woman of the world rather than of the young girl she still was. There was now something evasive, elusive, in his mistress that the count had not sensed before he had left her and it both disturbed and excited him. On an impulse he caught her to him and said, "Come, Gisela — tell the baron's henchman you will be away for a while. Let's go to Paris, sweet girl — hmm?"

"Paris? Oh, Max. Wonderful, marvellous — let's!"

In a matter of days he had swept her up and carried her away from the new intrigue which he himself had started and which now seemed to threaten the absoluteness of his role in the creation of one of Vienna's new sensations.

Paris seemed much like Vienna to Gisela. She was kept within a very narrow circle by Max, and she saw nothing of the new movements in the arts that would change the Western world as the century turned. However, her French improved and her wardrobe grew, and the count's fascination with his creation was intensified when he saw the effect Gisela had on Parisian society.

Max had never frightened her before, but here in

Paris she saw something she had only glimpsed previously. Frenchmen were not as impressed by the count's battle scars as his countrymen, and one young Frenchman went beyond love letters and flowers and attempted to force his way into their hotel suite. There was a brief, ugly struggle which culminated with Max's calling the Frenchman out.

It was not the violence in Max's nature Gisela feared — he was not violent toward her — but the euphoria she sensed the violence gave him. From the moment the white-faced young man had been escorted by his friends from the room, Max had been in a state of ecstasy she had thought could only be released by their love-making. It stayed with him through the intervening hours until the cold gray dawn when he left with his seconds for the Bois de Boulogne. During those hours he had not slept with her and she had felt quite alone in her terror. The possibility of death didn't seem to have occurred to him, and the usually sensuous softness of his dark eyes had become a harsh glitter, as if he were held in the throes of some feverish delirium. Cold with fear, Gisela lay in the darkened bedroom and waited.

The light had hardly begun to filter through the curtains when the bedroom door opened and he was standing there, still in his cloak, his boots, his gloves. She opened her mouth to speak, but he put a finger to his lips.

"Hush! Say nothing. It is over."

As if he were performing an extension of the ritual already brought to some terrible conclusion in a clearing in the Bois, he approached the bed and started to turn back the coverlet, the blanket, the sheet, one by one, with solemn, almost military precision. Only then did he remove his gloves and place them on the table by the bed. Slowly, tenderly, he pulled the silk nightgown from her. When he had done so, he stood and looked at her for a while before he spoke, as if assessing the value of an *objet d'art*

"Yes, yes, you are worth it." His voice was formal, measured. "If he dies, he will not have thrown his life away for nothing. It was an honourable meeting between gentlemen."

Max bent forward and kissed her on the lips, and then she felt his hand moving over her body lightly, quickly, until she could have cried out with wanting him. She didn't speak or move, however, feeling fear as well as desire stirring inside her. There was a demoniac intensity about his movements that terrified her. And yet she wanted him. The attraction was even stronger because she knew he had committed the deed out of passion for her.

Suddenly, out of nowhere, his mood changed, and the tension in the room lifted. He threw himself on the bed, kissing her, laughing, folding his cloak around her body.

"What a joke life is, Gisela, what a spree, what a laugh! Were you frightened, sweet girl? Were you frightened?"

As he rolled them both in his cloak across the bed, she felt the buttons of his jacket cold upon her skin and the strength of his thighs around her legs. The tension inside her dissolved. She, too, felt the laughter of relief welling up and spilling out of her.

"Of course I was frightened! You're mad, you're crazy, and you're wrong! I am *not* worth it — you could have been killed, Max! Then all this loving would have been over!"

"Never, never. I'll never die, *süsse Mädel*, not I! Tell me again — you were afraid for me!"

"I was afraid for you, I was afraid for you. There, is that good enough for you? I was afraid!"

With a roar, he rolled them both off the bed and on to the plushly carpeted floor. There, for the first time since he had called out the young Frenchman, they made love — still wrapped in his cloak and with Max still in his clothes.

Afterward Gisela could see the marks of the metal buttons on her skin, like medals of combat, gifts from the victor. Did that make her, she wondered, the spoils of war? By evening the little circles had faded, and she was sad. Only a small scratch on the back of Maximilian von Schönstein's hand bore witness to the events of the early dawn and to the fact that he had fought another man for love of her.

When Max went to America again that summer, Gisela's original beauty was captured by one of the great painters in that brilliant period of Viennese art. He surrounded her with waterlilies and snakes, the lines melting and sinuous, her face vivid and strong in the midst of those swirling lines. She could see that the count was delighted with it on his return, but he was also disturbed by it in some way, as one is by the memory of some dreams.

"He understood you, sweet girl. You are a sorceress and you can turn before my eyes into a serpent, a sea creature, a waterlily."

"Really, Max? Has this happened?"

"Yes. It is part of the hold you have over me."

The serious tone in which he made his reply worried Gisela and reminded her in some strange way of the Paris duel. To change his mood she started to tell him about her new admirer, who was a member of the Austro-Hungarian Bank and a fervid Czech nationalist with powerful Russian connections and a complicated love life. She soon had Max laughing at the man's pecadillos and erotic peculiarities without betraying any of the confidences and information that went every week on rose-scented stationery to Baron Eihrentahl. At the big house in the Eighth District, it would be the timetable and the itinerary of the banker's travels to his ladyloves that would be of interest, rather than what he did once he got into the bedrooms of Prague or Ragusa.

Gisela wondered if the baron had had a surprise when the messenger brought him a pink envelope smelling of roses instead of lavender or lilies of the valley. She doubted it very much — such a trivial part of their conversation would not be remembered by such a serious man. It was of no importance to her, either. However, what had begun as something she had done to please Max had now turned into something more than that. There was a pleasure in these powerful games, a heady euphoria at her own skills of manipulation. Her gift of clairvoyance was something that happened in spite of her and over which she had little or no control. The only sensation to which she could compare the feeling the game of intrigue gave her was the way she felt when she and Max were making love. She began to understand how Max felt about duelling.

Gisela's happiness and reputation grew through the year of 1899 as they all moved toward the new century. She looked forward eagerly to the challenges it would bring to her, for she had never felt stronger and more sure of herself. The crystal was still dark for her, but Max was her world and she was his High Priestess, his sorceress. It was a confident, radiant Gisela who awaited his return after the count's usual visit to America in the summer of 1900.

Chapter Eighteen

Vienna

It was nearly autumn when the count returned, and the wind that blew through the black pines along the limestone cliffs of the Wienerwald already carried the chilly promise of winter on its breath. Gisela had not been surprised by Max's long stay overseas, for the ways of the First Society were still mysterious to her, and she would no more have wondered at his absences than she would have questioned his extravagances. She had at times been lonely, for her relationship with Max did not allow for friendships, even with other women. The salon, however, had prospered, and the messages had continued to go to the Eighth District throughout the summer.

   She had carefully planned their first reunion. When the maid announced him, she was lying on a couch in the salon, dressed in ivory satin, an outsized cravat of soft white tulle high around her slender neck. On the wall alongside the couch hung the portrait by Klimt, a study in shimmering jewel colours. Her husky voice reached him clearly across the room.

"The British resident from Baghdad tells me that the desert around Tehran is ringed with beautiful mountains, and that there are gorges of crystal water running down from the snows of the Alburz, if you go to Shimram."

"Gisela. You are more beautiful than I remembered."

"Of course." She rolled over onto her back on the sofa, sighing and stroking her thighs through the slim-fitting skirt. Her voice now sounded as it did when they made love — velvety, breathless. "Yet another admirer tells me that Bologna is the most romantic city, with arcaded streets, courtyards of pink and yellow stucco. Where shall we go, Max? Where shall we go, you and I?"

"Wherever you wish, *süsse Mädel*. The choice is yours."

She laughed, and Max von Schönstein felt his body respond to the sensuality in the sound, the allure of this girl who never ceased to amaze him.

"Come here, Count."

It amused him to be ordered so imperiously, as no one else would dare to command him. He stood penitently by her side, looking down into the luminous eyes.

"You are not in uniform, I see."

"No. Don't you like my beautiful new *tailleur* from Savile Row?"

"I prefer uniforms. Take it off."

He did as he was told, allowing his clothing to lie

at his feet where it fell. All the time her eyes moved over his body, but she did not try to touch him. Instead, she started to pull the long satin sheath of her skirt up over her hips, her body writhing as she did so, her eyes finally meeting his as she freed the gleaming folds from her hips. Beneath the skirt she was naked.

A smile of triumph crossed her face as his body responded instantly at the revelation. "So, the choice is mine, Count? Then straddle me."

She flung her arms above her head as he mounted her, and she cried sharply as he thrust himself inside her and moved against her body, supporting himself with his hands on each side of her slender waist.

"Better than Tehran? Better than the Alburz?"

"Better, better! More, Max — longer, harder — it's been too long, too long!"

The sweat was pouring from him, and he thrust his hands beneath her and held her up against him as the climax hit him, watching the eyes in the painting rather than the eyes of the woman beneath him. In that moment it seemed to him that the water serpents wound themselves around his body and the moisture between them was created by the waterlilies folding around his limbs.

"Mermaid — sea serpent! What more have you dreamed up while I was away?"

She was laughing at him again, triumphant, sitting up now and removing the ivory dress so that it fell on the floor with his clothes. He saw again the perfect circles of her breasts, tipped with carmine, like the secret lips of her body.

"No — this time it is for you to surprise me."

He knelt on the floor before her, between her legs, and pulled her hard against him, tasting her, and himself upon her, hearing her cry his name over and over again.

Outside the bedroom window dusk had fallen. Against the neutral light Gisela could see the perfect spiral of smoke from Max's cigarette, the gleam of his large gold signet ring, the faint outline of the scar on his cheek. He moved, and the embossed patterns of his smoking jacket caught the light. Gisela sighed with happiness. They had moved to the bedroom where they had made love again and then slept together. She felt replete — with champagne, with life, with love. She listened with pleasure to the sound of his voice.

"Persia would be wonderful, and it's been a while since I was there. We would have time for that, I think."

"Time? When must you go away again?"

"Oh, not until after Christmas. My commanding officer would like to see something of me, and I have business in Vienna. I will be having visitors from America, papers to sign."

"Really?" Gisela sat up in the bed, excited. "Will you bring your visitors here?"

Max laughed and, with an elegant flick of the wrist, tipped the ash off his cigarette into the crystal ashtray on the side table near him. Then he inhaled deeply once more.

"I think not, Gisela. It would hardly be fitting in this case."

"Fitting?" Max had never before shown any need for concealment about their relationship. "Why?"

"Because I am arranging my marriage."

Six words. He had said six words. She heard them separately, each word apart, not linked to the next.

It wasn't a sentence, because sentences had meaning, and this one didn't. It lay there between them, a miscellany of sounds. Meaningless, without content.

In the silence between them Gisela heard the beating of great wings, just as she had when she had seen the raven and the beautiful girl on the bed, the blood, the agony. When the whirring in the air around her had ceased, she opened her mouth to speak, but no sound came out. Max von Schönstein got up from the bed in one graceful movement and crossed over to the chair by the window. When he turned back to look at her she could see the sweetness of his smile.

"But there should be some time for a holiday, because the wedding is not planned until next year. How the Persians will love you, Gisela! It will be entertaining to watch the gleam in those insatiable eyes of theirs — hmm?"

As if suddenly noticing that something was wrong, the count leaned forward and looked at her quizzically. "What is it, sweet girl?"

This time the words came out, but she could only repeat what he had said to her. "Because I am getting married?"

Max von Schönstein crossed his legs and flicked away some cigarette ash. "Yes, *Liebchen*. It should not make too much difference to us. In fact, I shall have to spend less time in America now that the groundwork is all laid, and she will, of course, be living here. When she goes back to visit her family we shall make our little excursions and so on, just as we did before. Everything will be much the same."

There was still a sense of disbelief, as if he were suddenly speaking a new language and she was misinterpreting what he was saying. It had to be, for he was so unmoved, so unconcerned, so much the same Max he always had been.

"I don't understand, Max. I don't understand what is happening. I thought we were lovers — I thought we were in love."

Max seemed surprised, taken aback at her reaction. Carefully extinguishing his cigarette, he got up and came over to the bed. Tenderly, he looked down at her.

"And so we are, Gisela! You don't think I would let you go? How can you think such a thing of me? We are lovers and shall continue to be lovers." He caressed her hands, her arms, her shoulders. Only when he tried to kiss her did she pull away from him.

"I thought there was only me. All this time, and you were arranging this? All this time — while we made love?"

If anything, he seemed even more surprised. "God in heaven, sweet girl, you know I cannot marry you, don't you? Did you expect me to remain single? I haven't been sleeping with her, you know — that would have been disastrous! If it makes you any happier, one could describe it as a business arrangement with a very rich partner."

"But you will make love to this business partner, in the end?"

"It is expected of me, and it would hardly be fair to her to do otherwise."

"What is she like, this business partner?" Gisela thought of poor, plain, wealthy Anna Gould whom she had seen in Paris and who was married to that quintessential playboy Boni de Castellane.

Max looked as if he were about to answer her, and then hesitated. His eyes were fixed upon Gisela, and for one wild moment she wondered if either her beauty or her distress could make him change his mind. However, when he finally spoke, his reply gave her no hope.

"Charming, as well as very rich. Rather gauche, of course, with a formidable mother, but all that may change. She has a certain style of her own."

"Does she know about me?"

"Of course not!"

"So, we have something in common. Besides you, that is."

Again, Max's eyes moved to her face as if he sought there the answer to an unspoken riddle. "Yes — yes," he murmured, as if to himself rather than to her, "you have something in common. And yet you are different, worlds apart." He smiled and appeared to pull himself back into the present from wherever his thoughts had taken him. "But I have made you happy, haven't I? And I shall make her happy. I'm good at making women happy — it's the thing at which I excel in this world. Swordplay." Max laughed lightly at his little joke and threw himself back on the sheets.

Still filled with disbelief, Gisela looked at his handsome, smiling face. "What do I like, Max? What makes me happy?" Not stopping to wonder if her questions were sarcastic, angry, or filled with grief, he answered her.

"You? Ah, you like tenderness, sweetness, inventiveness, because you are young and I am your first. You like to play at ordering me around — it is exciting, obeying your orders. You, sweet girl, are insatiable, demanding."

"How did you know this, at the beginning?"

He shrugged his shoulders and frowned. "I don't

know, but it's a skill I have. You read the tarot; I read women. Some, of course, are easier than others, like your mother."

He had broken the spell, the shock that held her almost in a trance. The pain that should have hit her when he had spoken of his marriage struck her full force with her anger, and she turned on him, her nails scratching his hands, his face.

"Bastard! Don't you speak of my mother like that!"

She had caught him by surprise for a moment, but at the feel of her sharp nails on his skin, he grasped her wrists and pinned her on the bed beneath him.

"Why not, little one, why not? You knew about her, and yet you became my mistress. What is so different now?"

"You respected her! You were a gentleman to her! That mattered to me!"

The count brought his face down close to hers, and she could feel the hiss of his breath on her mouth. "Never, never, never in bed! Your mother wanted nothing to do with respect in bed! She didn't know it until I showed her, but she was tired of respect, of sweet nothings, pretty sayings. I could see that, and I treated her roughly, harshly, with as much contempt as possible! Why do you think I made her come to Sacher's?" Max von Schönstein's mouth was virtually upon hers as he disclosed the secret she had never guessed, not even when her mother had appeared angry with her. His words bruised her lips, her teeth, her very soul.

"To humiliate her, yes, that was part of it — but it was you I wanted, little girl, all along. You, you, you! Snake-woman, sorceress, crystal-gazer!"

He had slandered her mother, had used her to reach

the daughter, had arranged a marriage throughout their love affair. And now he was saying that she was guilty too, that she had seduced him by some power or other. And yet, even if she had been physically strong enough to stop him, she knew that she would have allowed him to continue as he pulled off his robe and started to make love to her.

As he took her, Gisela felt for the first time what it was to be like the girls she saw on the streets of Vienna, walking a line dictated to them by someone else, living on someone else's terms. Even as the familiar rush of sweetness engulfed her, that thought finally gave her the strength for what she knew she was going to do.

Max didn't speak to her afterward, but fell into a deep sleep. When he awoke, Gisela was sitting in a chair close to the bed. She was fully dressed, her hands folded in her lap. Her expression seemed remote but composed.

"Sweet girl, come back to bed."

She shook her head and smiled at him. "No, Max, and you must leave my bed now."

He shrugged his shoulders in his charmingly self-deprecating way and smiled ruefully at her, his sensual dark eyes glinting in the subdued light. "You are still angry with me, after such a love-making?"

She answered his question with one of her own. "Tell me, Max — if my mother had not died, had you still planned to have me?"

Max looked surprised. "Of course. It was virtually over between us, and Franzi would have passed on quite happily to someone else. She wanted a nobleman for you, so she would have been pleased in the end. Her death was unfortunate."

"Unfortunate," Gisela repeated incredulously. "And you think I would have gone to you?"

"I know you would have come to me."

He was right, and she knew it. If her mother's death had not stopped her, why would her presence?

"Go now, Max."

"Very well. I will see you this evening."

"No. We will not see each other for a while, I think."

She could see she had made him angry for the first time. He clenched his fists, and his voice shook when he replied. "Don't give me orders, Gisela. I do what I like."

"I have been thinking about that, and I don't think that's true anymore — with me, I mean. I have only to tell Baron Eihrentahl that I want you to leave me alone, and I think he will see to it. I am an important source of information for him now. I know he can make things difficult for you with your regiment as far as postings are concerned, and with all the leaves you like to be able to take."

"Sorceress!" he spat at her through clenched teeth.

"Yes. That's one of the reasons you will leave me alone."

"You'll never be rid of me, Gisela. You'll come crawling back to me on your hands and knees, begging to have me back in your bed."

Gisela paused a moment and then replied, "That is possible and I know it. But I want you to go now, and to stay away until — until —" Here, her voice faltered.

"Gisela." Max's voice was gentle, his eyes tender. "How can you?" He started to approach her, but she immediately stood up and walked to the bedroom door.

"I am leaving the apartment now and I shall stay

away all day. I shall return for my evening *conversazione* and you will be gone. The baron would prefer it done that way, without drama, I am sure."

Disbelieving, defeated, he stared at her. She had outmanoeuvred him. Nineteen years old, female, a kept woman, and she had beaten him. Her new contacts were far too powerful to offend, even for a member of the First Society. Besides, with all his debts now paid, his properties secure and a million or two dollars to spare, why should he jeopardize all that for a *cocotte*?

"I shall never forget this, Gisela."

"Neither shall I."

He had spoken out of vengeful anger, but she had spoken with suffering and love. It was still in her voice when she said, "Good-bye, Max."

In a moment she was gone from the room, and he felt the rage inside him, choking him. Twenty-four hours earlier he had had a beautiful young mistress who was the talk of Vienna, a hand in the power games of the state, and a marriage arrangement that had taken care of all his financial problems. Now he was left with only the marriage.

The image of his bride-to-be floated across his mind. Elizabeth LaPierre Holman. The eyes — the mouth — the hair. Such a strange, such an uncanny thing, the likeness between the two women. Max von Schönstein smiled and stretched himself out again on the bed. He had not, as yet, given much thought to what it would take to please that particular girl, and he should set his mind to it. He knew his fiancée was fascinated by him, and by his title, but for all her restricted upbringing he sensed a spirit of adventure in Elizabeth Holman, a longing for something new and different.

So be it, he thought. I will allow Gisela long enough to regret my absence, and during that time I shall devote myself to my wife. By this time next year I shall have Gisela in my arms again.

At the thought of her, the rage rose in his throat once more and the feeling of humiliation he could no longer deny. "Power?" he said out loud to the empty room. "She has power? An illusion, a farce for the gullible — that's all it is, just party tricks! If not, by now she would have —"

The count's half-finished sentence echoed through the empty room. He imagined for a second that he saw it, hanging like ectoplasm in the scented air, and was momentarily afraid if might reach the High Priestess whose party tricks he had just derided. At that moment he could not help thinking of a party trick still talked about by Viennese society: the extraordinary significance of a raven seen in a crystal bowl in a Ringstrasse mansion.

Chapter Nineteen

New York

Brides often cry on their wedding day, and it is not unusual for their mothers to weep as well. The tears of Ada Holman and the new Countess von Schönstein were, therefore, commented on but not considered remarkable. Most of the guests were too wrapped up in the trappings of the occasion to be concerned with the inner feelings of the principal players. Envy and awe were their chief emotions, and they would have been skeptical if anyone had told them they should feel anything different. The bridegroom was too handsome, and the von Schönstein emeralds too magnificent to allow for anything else.

"*Lucky* Beth!" sighed her contemporaries as they glimpsed the bride's misty eyes behind her veil. They shivered deliciously when they saw the count's dancing dark eyes and the duelling scar on his cheek. The bridegroom's gentle attentiveness to his silent bride was remarked upon by all those present, and the demeanour of the bride herself seemed entirely suitable for the occasion.

The only truly uncontrolled moment occurred at the quayside, when Beth said good-bye to her younger brother, who had returned from Europe for his sister's wedding. Henry had been distracted and tense throughout the day, and when it was his turn to kiss his sister, they both broke down. Beth clung to him, sobbing, and the rest of the family could see the young man's shoulders shaking convulsively. Distressed, exasperated, exhausted, Ada Holman tried to part them, grasping ineffectually at her son's jacket.

"Henry, please, you are upsetting Beth, and she must be so tired by now. Come along now, do."

Jonty Shotover moved quietly away from the family group and went over to Henry's side. "Henry, please let her go." He put his hands gently on Henry's shoulders, and said, "Come, Henry." At his touch, Henry released his sister and walked back toward the rest of his family.

Count von Schönstein took Beth's hand. "This is hard, I know, but it will only get harder the longer we stay. Let me help you up the gangplank, Beth. We can wave from the deck as long as you wish."

Beth turned from her husband and started up the gangplank, stumbling over her long skirts, her heel catching on the uneven surface.

"Take my hand, please."

Hand in hand, the count and countess then walked up the narrow planking to the ship.

"We can stand here, Beth."

"I would rather go to the stateroom."

"If that is what you wish."

The onlookers on the quayside were surprised to glimpse only a brief wave of the hand from the count before he followed after Beth.

"Well! I do think he might have let her stay," said Ada, cheated of her last moment of drama.

Henry looked at his mother. "That will have been Beth's decision," he said. Then he turned and walked away.

"Don't worry, Mrs. Holman. I'll look after him," said Jonty and hastened after Henry's departing figure.

"He's such a comfort," thought Ada to herself as she took her husband's arm and turned toward the waiting carriages. Behind them, the ship's whistle echoed across the dockside.

The evening meal in the ship's ornate dining room had been superb. The orchestra played light classical airs, Viennese waltzes. Beth ate virtually nothing, and she did not want to dance.

"I have eaten enough and danced enough today." She looked across the table at this stranger who was her husband, and although she had thought she had no more tears left, the tenderness in his eyes made her want to cry.

"So have I. Come, Beth. I think we have some talking to do, you and I."

"Talking?" The unexpected response had caught her by surprise.

"Yes, talking." He was looking at her now with both tenderness and amusement. "Come, we are both tired after today. I have known easier days on official duty at the Hofburg with the emperor."

Their stateroom would not have looked out of place in the brownstone on Fifth Avenue. It was actually a suite of rooms fitted out with every luxury, glittering with gilt and glass, the floor-coverings like velvet underfoot. A tray with decanters and glasses stood on a low table in the sitting room. Through the open door into the bedroom Beth could see the sheets on the bed, the covers already turned neatly down. The count followed the direction of her glance.

"Ah, but it's not as simple as that, is it?"

"Simple?" Maybe it was because she was so tired, but Max von Schönstein didn't seem to be making any sense at all. She waited for him to continue.

"Beth, I'm going to sit down here and pour myself a drink. If you want to sit down with me, I would be delighted to pour one for you too, for I would like to tell you what I know about you."

The strength seemed to have gone from her legs, and she sat down abruptly, opposite him. The count continued to talk as he poured out two brandies and handed one to her.

"Between the beginning and the end of last year things changed between us. We saw less, rather than more, of each other, which is unusual between two people who intend to get married — whatever your mother may have pretended to the contrary. I was afraid of losing you."

"Afraid of losing me?"

"Yes. Does that surprise you? This is, I think, a time for honesty between us. I went into this, I confess it, because you are an heiress — but you must know that. I found, to my surprise, a woman I could love.

That made it hard when your brother William told me about the newspaperman."

She could not believe it. He had known about Liam, and yet he had married her. "Why? If you knew, how could you go through with all this? Why didn't you spare us both?"

"Because I didn't want to give you up, and because I understand, a little, what happened."

"How could you?" she cried. "How could you know? Supposing — supposing he had seduced me?"

"I was prepared to take that chance, but I don't think he did. Let me explain, Beth, what I think happened, and you can tell me if I am wrong. I think he seduced your mind, this newspaperman — and more than that, much more. You saw your own city for the first time, and New York seduced you quite as much as the Irishman's blue eyes. My dear Beth, you are not made for such narrow circles as your Millionaires' Row, Newport, Bar Harbor. Elizabeth LaPierre von Schönstein, you were made to be a woman of the world!"

Max was leaning forward now, his dark eyes shining, his expression as animated as she had ever seen it. "Beth, you will adore Europe, the East — oh, give it a chance, give *me* a chance!"

His intuitiveness and insight had stunned her into silence. She had not expected it any more than she had expected he would plead with her. Yet a last vestige of suspicion remained. "I have to give you a chance. I am your wife now, and I have no choice. Why should it matter to you?"

"Because I want it all!" He was standing up now, glass in hand, pacing the room. "I am selfish, I am greedy, and I want the extra luxury your money will

bring. I want the New York connections your family
will bring. But I also want your approval, your liking,
maybe your love. Is that too much to ask, Beth? Only
you can tell me that — not your mother or father,
or anyone else."

"I don't know," was all she could think of to say.
"I don't know if it is too much, not now, not at this
moment."

"Then I can wait until you do."

"Do you — do you really see me as a woman of
the world?"

"Very much so. In Europe you will grow, you'll
see."

Already he understood her better than her mother,
or anyone else close to her. She found that consoling,
warming to the heart.

"And now I shall say good night. We are both tired
and will sleep better without each other. There is a
perfectly good divan in the small salon there."

Before Beth could express any opinion, her husband
had bowed gracefully and departed through the door
to the small salon-dressing room. He closed it firmly
behind him.

Beth slept better on her wedding night than she
had for weeks, with the great liner rocking gently
beneath her. When she woke the next morning, she
discovered that Max was already up, sitting in the main
salon and drinking coffee. He smiled delightedly at
her when she joined him.

"You slept well, and you don't have to tell me. I
can see it from the colour in your cheeks. How do
you like your coffee, Countess von Schönstein?"

She could not resist the shiver of pleasure her new
name gave her. "Black, please."

"Come, sit down, and let us plan the day."

They walked the deck arm in arm, admiring the seascape and commenting on the other passengers. By midday she was laughing at his jokes. That evening, she danced with him to the Viennese waltzes she had heard with such anguish the night before, admiring the grace and strength with which he guided her round the floor and aware they were being admired. When they returned to their suite and he closed the door of the little salon behind him, Beth had an empty feeling inside her as she walked slowly into the bedroom.

The next night, Max took her gambling in the ship's casino, scolding her laughingly for her aggressiveness and daring. "Such rapacity! You are terrifying to watch, *süsse Mädel!*"

"*Süsse Mädel?*"

"Sweet girl." He said it with such tenderness, a hint of shyness in his voice, that she felt suddenly protective, almost maternal toward this patient husband of hers.

Back in her stateroom Beth stood at the little table and watched him pour a nighttime brandy for them both.

"I don't now how to say this — I — you —"

The count put down the decanter and looked at her with the tender glance that had taken her so much by surprise. "You don't have to, Beth. I'll be with you in a short while. It will be all right, you'll see."

It was more than "all right," much more; it was not wrong at all, no anguish, no regret, no feeling of violation or humiliation, as she had feared. It had not been the act of love itself she had been frightened of, but whether she should be doing it with this stranger to whom she had given nothing but her millions.

She could not speak for her heart, but she could

for the pleasure he gave her body, and she was already feeling the liking and approval for which he had asked. And her laughter. She heard it ringing out over their heads as they woke together in the morning and he teased her gently about her tousled hair, her sleepy eyes — "But you have been in bed hours, Countess, so what have you been up to for such a look, hmm?" Even as she laughed, he made love to her again. Beth felt passion replacing the shyness and apprehension of their first love-making, and she made her first discovery of the climax of love.

"You seduced me, Max."

"You are a woman who can only be first seduced through the mind."

There was a triumphant sound in his voice, and she knew he was thinking of the one he had called "the newspaperman." That too was all right, for he was entitled to such a feeling. He had forgiven her, wooed her, and won her. And she was glad, glad, glad that he had done so.

Together they saw the desert around Tehran, ringed with snow-capped mountains, and visited the tower from which the Zoroastrians flung their dead for the vultures. They picnicked in the moonlight in the fairy-tale gardens tangled and scented with roses, filled with the song of the nightingales.

It would have been an amazing experience for anyone. Wrenched from the narrow confines of her previous existence, Beth found it beyond any dream she could have imagined. In her thoughts, Liam O'Connor and his life seemed more unreal and improbable than the Arabian nights that surrounded her.

They made their way slowly back to the Western world that awaited them, moving through Marseilles, Avignon, Arles, Nîmes, across the face of the map Beth looked at each night on their travels, until they reached Vienna.

She was thrilled with her first glimpse of the city. The lush countryside around it, the towering cliffs of the Wienerwald, the vineyards, and then the magnificence of the Ringstrasse, seemed perfection to her.

Her grasp of German was good now. As Max said to her, "Of course it is good, sweet girl, because you learned most of it in bed, and there is no better place to learn a language."

"What languages have *you* learned in bed, then?"

"Ah —" Max looked contritely at her from under his lashes and said, "— my wicked past! You promised not to reproach me with my wicked past. But — if you must know — French, Persian, American —" He begged for mercy as she pummelled him with her fists.

Bavaria, however, was vastly different from Vienna. The only representatives of Max's family Beth had met had been his best man — a distant cousin who was in the diplomatic service and spoke good English — and an uncle who had come instead of Max's mother to the wedding. A day after she and Max arrived in Vienna, Max took her out to the gloomy and formidable structure in the remote Bavarian countryside where his mother lived with her widowed daughter.

The two women were as gloomy as the ornate and ramshackle edifice in which they seemed content to spend the rest of their days. Dressed in styles of a bygone era, peering at Beth from behind their identical lorgnettes, they were more removed from her experience than any of the exotic people she had seen on her honeymoon. She realized that they reminded her of the Zoroastrians — it was all too easy to imagine these two throwing the remains of Max's deceased father from one of the crumbling, crenellated towers of the château for the ravens who swooped around the estate. Horrified at these morbid thoughts, she yearned to depart from this landscape of threatening dreams.

Max didn't find anything strange in the atmosphere; he behaved much as he had on their travels. But here Beth could not respond to his gaiety and laughter; she sat silently watching him talk and joke with his unresponsive mother and sister. One evening she caught sight of herself in one of the badly mottled mirrors in the main salon, sitting in a row with the other von Schönstein women. Terror filled her; she imagined she saw the dust and cobwebs of this magnificent Bavarian ruin creeping over and around her, tying her to the rickety chair beneath her.

"Take me away, Max," she begged him when they were alone that night in the cavernous bedroom.

"Of course, sweet girl. You said nothing, so I supposed all was well. We'll leave tomorrow."

Contrasted to Bavaria, Vienna seemed even sweeter. When Beth tried to visualize Max's mother and sister, it was as if the lorgnettes had been masks, for all she could remember was untidy gray hair and eyes like black slits that stared unblinkingly at her, or at Max.

The ornate, opulent style of the Ringstrasse did not intimidate her in the least. Beth might not have had a title before her marriage, but she was accustomed to living like a princess, to attending elaborate, formal evenings at the opera or the theatre, to going to balls, to giving orders. She understood the importance of protocol and pecking order, for she was from one of the most rigid social hierarchies in the Western world, where new money had an even greater need for such reassurance than old wealth.

Travel had broadened her mind, conversation had sharpened her natural wit, and physical passion had fulfilled the promise Ada Holman had seen in her daughter. When they passed through Paris on their return to Vienna, Beth had chosen a new wardrobe. Her flair for what suited her had delighted and surprised the count. Instead of the frumpy, gauche colonial his friends were expecting, he arrived with a more than merely presentable woman on his arm.

Vienna in 1901 seemed to Beth a dream of a city, full of charm, style, and dash. Vienna had flair. Vienna was enticing, as enticing and seductive as Max von Schonstein himself. She found it easy to slip into its quicksilver stream of laughter and music, to allow herself to be beguiled by her husband's amusing, laughing friends. Compliments here were called lilies of the valley — *Maiglöckchen* — and the fragrant flattery was everywhere.

There were wonderful parties at the great *Palais*, like the one hosted by the Macedonian millionaire Nicholas Dumba, who had amassed a fortune trading in the Balkans. There were visits to the Prater, the great fairgrounds of Vienna, to enjoy herself like a child who had never before been so indulged. She had not been allowed to go to Barnum and Bailey's circus at Madison Square Garden, but she went for the first time in Vienna. It arrived in four trains of sixty-six Pullman cars, and set up in a meadow by the Prater Haupt-Allee. When Max took her, she felt deliciously guilty, as if she were disobeying her mother.

Beth, however, did not dwell much in the past. She was revelling in her freedom, in being the wife of Count Maximilian von Schönstein, in seeing the look of surprise and admiration on the faces of his friends when they met Max's American heiress. She wanted nothing more than to be in this city on the Danube, that great river stretching across the plain to Hungary and to some far-off delta on the coast of the Black Sea.

Max told her that the court of the Austro-Hungarian Empire was the centre of Europe. She felt as if she were at the pivotal point of the waltzing, spinning universe as she and Max attended balls, soirées, gala openings. Autumn arrived, and with it came the annual ritual of hunting in Bavaria.

"You can come if you wish, Beth, but I will not be away long and we always spend whole days in the mountains. You would have to be on your own with my family."

"Oh dear, Max, I really don't know what we would find to say to each other! I shall stay here, for there are things to be done. And I have friends here now."

There was indeed work to be done on their town house, and a lot of correspondence to catch up on. Beth was particularly anxious to write to Henry in Tübingen and assure him that all was well with her and that she was happy.

On a fine autumn day, when a soft wind was blowing the scent of falling leaves into the city and a ripe, golden sunshine illuminated the mansions of the Ringstrasse, Beth parted from Max for the first time since their wedding day almost a year before. With an eye to making purchases for the *Palais*, she had arranged to attend an art exhibition that afternoon with the wife of one of her husband's friends, Baroness Tenka von Mayerdorf.

The morning, however, was her own. She made her way to her own boudoir and rang the bell for her maid.

"Eva, can you find me any of the count's writing paper with his crest? I would like to write some letters to my family and friends."

"The *Herr Graf* keeps it in his study, ma'am. I will instruct one of the footmen to fetch some for you."

"No, don't bother. I will use the count's study — it would give me pleasure."

"Very well, ma'am. I will see that there are fresh pens and ink ready for you."

Beth had been in Max's study only once before, when he had shown her the *Palais*. He had rarely used it since their return to Vienna, and it was usually kept locked, as such rooms were if they contained personal papers and were not in constant use.

The room seemed redolent with Max's presence. Beth could smell his cigar smoke around her, imagine she caught a whiff of sandalwood in the air. Smiling to herself, she sat down at the desk and ran her hands over the surface. Max's laughter suddenly seemed so real in her imagination that she looked about her, startled.

Süsse Mädel. I am his sweet girl, she thought, I am so lucky, after all — lucky, lucky Beth, just as my friends said when I didn't believe them. Sighing with contentment, she started on her first letter.

When she had finished writing to her mother, she thought how thrilled Ada Holman would be if the letter arrived with the count's official seal. Beth knew he had one; it wasn't on the top of the desk or in any of the pigeon holes, so, hesitating a moment, she started to open the desk drawers one by one. None were locked. They contained various pieces of correspondence and what looked like account books and ledgers. There was still no sign of the seal, and she wondered if he had, perhaps, taken it with him. She opened the last drawer and was about to close it again when she saw the small pile of letters tied together with some scarlet tape. The top envelope had a New York address on it.

Beth had never before thought of handwriting as being either masculine or feminine, but there seemed to her to be something unmistakably female about the curves and scrolls of the letters in this script and their flow across the page.

"My wicked past." Max had spoken amusingly, contritely about his past amours, and they were only to be expected, she knew that.

But why should he keep these letters tied together in such a manner? She had been given to understand that he had rid himself of his past. Piqued rather than distressed, Beth took the letters from the drawer, intending merely to look at the signature, or so she told herself.

Gisela. The "G" was round and strong, the "l" rising high above the vowels. The final "a" had a flourish of a tail. Beth was now more than piqued, for the name gave the unknown female some dimension. She flipped the letters in her hands, angry at Max, and at herself because she was spying on him. Suddenly, two words leapt off one of the pages at her.

"*Süsse Mädel.*"

Jealousy tore at her, instant, agonizing, and she cried

out, "No one but me — he says that to me! I am his sweet girl — I! Not you, not you!"

She threw the package onto the desk and one of the letters fell from the tape. When Beth picked it up she saw the date at the top of the sheet and the hot anger turned to something bleaker, colder, lonelier. The letter was dated only the week before. Unable to stop herself now, she started to read it. It was quite short.

Max.

I'll not change my mind. Not yet. I hear she is charming and seems to love you, poor fool! Stay away from my bed. Americans are not like line girls, or even Franzi Valeska. I don't think this one would find an arrangement like ours at all cozy or gemütlich, as we Viennese women are supposed to. Pay a few debts before you bring an angry papa down around your head from New York.

Baron Eihrentahl sends his regards — or would, I am sure, if he knew I was writing to you.

Gisela

The letter revealed far more than her husband's wicked past. It had been incontrovertibly written in the present, and he had obviously been pleading with some woman, some former mistress. *He* was begging, and she was resisting! Not yet, she said.

This, then, was his love for her, a thing of convenience, a matter of money. Was he really in Bavaria now, or was he with this Gisela? And who was Franzi Valeska?

Who, for that matter, was Beth von Schönstein? She had thought herself free, she had thought herself loved. She had thought herself a woman. Max had said she was meant to be a woman of the world. He had been so wrong. She was a child, an innocent who shook with tears, alone in a desert called Vienna, emptier than the sands around Tehran. A poor fool for loving him, as this woman had said.

Rage filled her, so violent that she cried aloud, "What shall I do? Dear God, what shall I do?" Through the tears that burned her eyes she looked at the address on the letter, and the jealousy tore at her, twisting and cutting, and doubling her over with pain.

"Gisela." She heard the name echo around her husband's study, sighing and whispering around the walls. She looked again at the address.

Chapter Twenty

Vienna

As Gisela's carriage passed the Houses of Parliament on the Ringstrasse she saw the new fountain they were building with its statue of Pallas Athena. Alexei had told her that the goddess had sprung forth from the head of her father, fully grown and wearing armour. Oh fortunate Athena! It seemed the only way to come into the world if one was a woman. Alexei had also told her the goddess had chosen the olive tree as her special gift for Athens, and the city had become hers.

"I hold out no olive branch to anyone," thought Gisela, "and Vienna has never seemed less my city than it does at this moment." She had seen it first through her mother's eyes, then through the count's. Now she felt blinkered, cut off from her surroundings.

And yet she had not left the heat of the city that summer but had shut herself away in her apartment.

She felt more like the Hermit in the tarot than the
High Priestess. In her previous life she had never had
to think about the Hermit's qualities of caution,
circumspection, and self-denial. Now they seemed
worthy of as much consideration as the card's reverse
implications: imprudence, immaturity, foolish acts.
Musing on the aged man with the lantern of occult
science in one hand and the staff of magic in the other,
she felt a closer kinship with him than with anyone
else.

If only the crystal would speak to her again, there
might be some comfort there. It was not so much that
she desired reassuring visions, but that she sought
confirmation of the gift that made her unique. She
was tired of pretence and subterfuge, of saying she
saw triumphs where there was only darkness, lovers
where there were none.

She had thought of trying to see Alexei Islenyev,
but he had said she could not until the gift was hers
once more. These must be the sufferings he had hinted
at, and she consoled herself with the thought that after
a period of time her clairvoyance would return. Alexei
had so reassured her when she was still a child and
unaware of what the world was like.

Did she know that now? Yes, of course she did. It
was about survival. She hadn't thought of killing
herself, and she couldn't have explained why. Oh yes,
she hoped Max would be hers again, and now she
knew he wanted her in his life. And yet she had turned
him away even though, as he had predicted, she longed
for him.

As the carriage turned off the main Ringstrasse onto
the quiet, elegant street where she lived, leaves from
the lime and plane trees fluttered into the open
window. She watched them settle on the floor in front

of her. It's autumn, she realized with a vague feeling of surprise, and I thought the summer would never end. What shall I do with the winter ahead of me?

As Gisela put out her hand to the carriage door and prepared to descend, blackness surrounded her. There were pinpoints of light on the edges of her vision and she thought, for a moment, she would faint. At the same time, there was a sudden prickling sensation at the top of her spine, a tingling in her fingers.

She was being watched. By whom, or why, she couldn't tell, but there was hostility surrounding her in the quiet street, menace in the shadows of the autumn afternoon. Her heart pounded in her chest; the sound seemed to echo between the facades of the elegant buildings.

There was no one in sight as she got out of the carriage and entered the building, but the sensation was still powerfully present as she climbed the stairs and entered her apartment. Outside the window she heard the sound of her carriage clattering away across the cobbles. Gisela went to the window and looked down to the street.

A woman stood there, looking up at the window. Pale face, dark hair — that was all she could see. Yet even as she turned away, Gisela knew that this woman was responsible for the feelings she had experienced a few minutes earlier.

Stars now disturbed her vision more strongly than they had before; when they cleared she saw the crystal across the room glowing as brightly as the lamp lit by the servants for her arrival. Gisela watched the light coalesce into a single star, the crystal glowing violet around it.

Her legs shook beneath her. Stumbling over her skirts, she crossed to the speculum. The star remained, surrounded by colour, but no vision presented itself to her. Hands shaking, she picked up the tarot pack and pulled out one card.

She knew already what it would be. Not Hercules, the High Priestess, or the Magician. It was the Star card, with the young girl pouring the water of life from the urn she held. Storms weathered, faith, hope. A strong card for women, symbolizing the person who comes into one's life to change it forever.

"But to change it for good!" Gisela cried out. "Why then does she threaten me, this woman outside my window?"

There was only one way to find out. Gisela ran across the room, pushed open the door, and drove herself along the corridor and down the stairs before she could lose her nerve and turn back. Flinging open the door into the street, she almost stumbled over the woman she was seeking.

She was crouched at her feet, head down, but Gisela could see the knife in her hand. And, even as she saw it, she knew that it was no longer she herself who was in danger, but this visitant who had brought back to her the visions in the speculum.

"No!" Bending down, she grasped the hand that held the knife, heard the rattle as the metal hit the cobblestone. The woman looked up. Pale skin, dark eyes and hair, straight brows, firm, mobile mouth, a strong jawline. As soon as she saw her, Gisela knew her.

"Dear God," she whispered, and yet her words seemed to resound around her in the empty street. "I am looking at myself — you are my double, my *Doppelgänger*. More than that — much more than that. God in heaven, you are the Empress."

Chapter Twenty-One

Vienna

There was a comforting warmth in the room from the *Kachelofen* — the white porcelain stove with its shining brass door — and the scent of roses in porcelain bowls and lilies in tall vases. The stunning, dark-haired woman drew the dusty-pink silk drapes together over the windows and pulled the bell tassel by the stove. Neither woman had spoken since coming into the house. Beth watched as Gisela sat down on a sofa close to an extraordinary painting that echoed the style of the salon. Beth spoke first.

"Klimt. I was to see some of his paintings this afternoon."

"You came here instead. Why?"

"Because of the letters. You *are* Gisela?"

"Gisela Valeska, yes. And you are —" Beth saw a

flicker of pain in the other woman's eyes. "You must be the Countess von Schönstein."

"You called me something else outside, or maybe I misheard it. The Empress."

"Yes." Their conversation was interrupted by the arrival of the maid. Gisela ordered brandy and coffee and waited for the girl to leave before she leaned forward and picked up the knife that lay on the table between them.

"You got this in the East."

"In Isfahan, yes."

"You came to kill me and then decided to kill yourself instead. Why did you change your mind?"

"I don't really know. I just knew I couldn't go through with it once I had seen you, and I knew I couldn't kill Max. That left only me."

The maid arrived with the drinks on a tray, and Gisela stood up and took them from her. "You needn't stay, Kathi, I will pour them myself." She prepared two cups of black coffee with generous amounts of cognac. When she handed one to Beth she said, "Drink it. You really must, you know. We have many years to cross in the next little while."

With the warmth of the brandy and coffee, Beth felt the shaking in her body start to subside. She looked across at the other woman.

"Who is Franzi Valeska?" she asked.

"My mother — she was my mother. But how do you know about her? Did he tell you?"

"He told me nothing. I found letters. He knew your mother too?"

The other woman's smile twisted. "Yes. I'm sorry you found the letters. I also was told nothing, and I also thought of killing you."

Beth asked the question she herself had been asked. "Why did you change your mind?"

"What had you done? If anyone was to be killed, it should have been him, and I couldn't have done that. You were an innocent."

"An innocent." The brandy-laced coffee seemed to have numbed Beth's nerve endings, and some of the pain had now dissipated. "I am no longer so innocent as not to realize, from what I have seen in Vienna, that you and he could have continued your relationship. Why didn't you?"

Gisela looked intently at the American girl. There was a vivid colour in her cheeks and her eyes glowed feverishly. Yes, they were very much alike, but she could now see the difference a country and a culture had made between the two of them. It was not anything as simple as an accent or a way of dressing, but something far more subtle. Perhaps it was the way they held their heads, or their expression, the way they used their hands. She couldn't exactly say how, but they were as alike and yet as dissimilar as the Old World was to the New. Beth was about to repeat her question when Gisela finally answered.

"Because I cannot share him."

Beth understood only too well what this extraordinary woman meant. Extraordinary, yes, she thought. She too saw the likeness, but there was a jagged edge to Gisela Valeska, an exotic dissonance that was not part of her own personality. Beth suddenly felt lost, afraid. "What do we do now?" she asked.

Gisela Valeska looked surprised. She leaned back and wound her arms about her body, rubbing her shoulders with her hands as though she were cold. Beth suddenly saw in her mind the serpent-woman on the wall of Baroness von Mayerdorf's dining room.

"Nothing. We go on. Or, rather, I go on. You have Max, and you hold all the cards." At this, Gisela put her head back against the hard gilt edge of the sofa and laughed. "Cards!" Her voice had become harsh and brittle.

"But he doesn't love me. He wants you back, so he can't love me."

"Listen." Gisela Valeska now sounded angry, but Beth knew that the anger was not directed at her. "Your husband, Countess von Schönstein, loves no one. Except, perhaps, himself — and that is why it's possible to go on. It is Max's own skill with women that interests him, not the woman to whom he makes love. Your marriage will work precisely because Max will never love anyone. I am not saying he won't take a mistress or be unfaithful to you, but that will be of no importance to him. If you want him, he will always be yours, on his terms."

"What if I, too, cannot share him?"

"You would be well advised to try, Countess. The alternative is failure and grief."

"Or divorce."

"You say that so easily. Is it accepted so readily in your country?"

Beth thought of Aunt Medora and her mother's horrified rush to Philadelphia. "No."

"Then it is not an alternative."

There was no way out of her dilemma, it seemed. She looked into the eyes of the woman she had come to kill and thought of the moment she had seen the face so close to her own. "Why did you call me 'Empress'?"

"Ah." The anger went out of Gisela's voice, and

it now sounded almost tender. "When must you return, Countess?"

Beth thought of the empty *Palais* on the Ringstrasse and of the Baroness von Mayerdorf, who had expected her two hours previously. "I have all the time in the world."

"None of us has that, Countess, but I will take some of yours, if I may. Come."

Beth followed Gisela to a table in one corner of the room. It was covered with black silk, and on the silk stood two brass candlesticks, a pack of cards, and a crystal ball in an ivory frame. Startled, Beth looked at Gisela, and it was as if the dissonance in her, the strangeness she couldn't explain, suddenly fell into place.

"You saw me. You are a medium."

"I saw you, but I am not a medium. You have always appeared to me as the Empress, but always in the tarot and never in the crystal. Yet today you appeared as a star shining in the speculum."

"You are a clairvoyant."

"Yes, although for more than two years I had lost my powers. Sit down." Gisela indicated the chair on the far side of the table and sat down herself, without waiting for her guest. She picked up the tarot pack, riffled through it and extracted one card. "There you are as you have appeared to me through the years." Beth sat down and took the card held out of her.

The tarot Empress sat upon a throne, a crown on her head and a sceptre in her hand, two strands of pearls around her neck. Her eyes stared straight ahead of her.

"Tell me about her."

The clairvoyant spoke softly, quickly, the words running clearly but continuously, flowing as though she were in a trance, although there were no physical signs of such a state. "She is the card of action, achievement, material wealth, fertility. She is resolute, strong, representing the best in women."

"Does she have no faults?"

"Of course, but I would not call them faults. There is good and evil in everything, and this is also the card of dissipation, indecision, anxiety, and fear. It depends on the hand I cast for you. Would you like me to do so?"

Beth nodded, and Gisela held out the pack to her. "Shuffle them for me from the bottom of the pack, then make three piles on the table in front of you with your left hand."

Beth did as she was told and watched as Gisela spread the cards in front of her in a fan shape until the entire surface of the table was covered and there were only a few left in her hand. The clairvoyant stared at the spread for a while before she spoke. "So, Countess — you become the Empress once more. When I see your future, some of my own is revealed to me."

The single lamp near the table cast a soft pool of light over the two women. Darkness had now fallen outside, but there was no need to call the servants for any more light. The cards on the silk-covered table; the Diviner and the Enquirer were all that mattered, the lamplight embracing the two women, the darkness held beyond them. Again, the words flowed from Gisela, and Beth found it difficult always to grasp their meaning, for the clairvoyant sometimes seemed to be speaking in riddles.

"We are linked, you and I, and not only by this

Hercules, this man we cannot share. It is a personal bond, but I see larger things at stake: war, nations overturned — these things will also affect our lives. I see that from the reversed Emperor and the Lightning-struck tower. I see Hercules, of course, and the Magician is here once more — but here is the Fool again. I have seen him before, but I don't know yet who he is. A man, yes, an idealist, an individualist who cannot conform to society's patterns, a fool in material matters. His presence is even stronger now than it was in the past — he is close to you — not here, I mean, but in the spread."

Liam O'Connor, thought Beth. She has seen Liam. It has to be him. Excitement filled her, and then anguish, and she asked, "Do you mean this is someone in my future, someone I have yet to meet?"

Gisela looked up, caught by the anguish in Beth's voice. "The link is already there, I think, but there is too much — he is too important not to reappear once more. Besides, the three of us share some future space — somewhere, somehow."

She looked back again at the cards and Beth watched her body tense, her hand touch the card of the Empress. When she looked up again her eyes burned as they had when their glance first met on the street outside.

"Why did I not see it before? No matter, it comes clear to me now. Empress, you carry a child."

Beth's sense of shock deepened, and she shifted abruptly in the chair as if to free herself from the spell cast by the lamplight, the cards on the black silk, the mesmeric gaze of the clairvoyant.

"Not that I am aware of — you must be mistaken."

Gisela gave a little laugh. "The cards never lie, Empress. I do, sometimes, but the cards — never."

"Then I am trapped."

"You always were. That, too, is in the cards, but so are the Chariot and the Star. They represent victory, peace gained, although the cost will be great."

Beth turned and looked at the beryl, its pale green facets translucent in the lamplight. "Do you still see the star in the crystal?" she asked.

Gisela pushed the cards together and returned the beryl to the table. Her hands echoed its shape in space, as if she caressed it without touching it. Suddenly she gave a little cry.

"The clouds are clearing away — it's so long since they moved! I see a river between steep banks, a house high above, surrounded by great trees, like the beech-woods below the Wienerwald, the willow copses along the Danube — but no, no, this is not Vienna, although the house reminds me of the Ringstrasse *Palais*. There's a room now — no, a hallway, green-and-white marble, circular, a great door — with glass, like a fan, at the top of it. I see light through the glass — gold, red, lemon-coloured light. You were happy here — but this is not then, this is not now, this will come. Now I see a bird, like a raven, but I don't think it's a raven — ah — now I see the other, the —" Suddenly Gisela pushed the crystal from her, turning her head away from it. "No!" Her shuddering cry filled the room and she stood up, swayed, and fell to the floor.

Beth ran to Gisela's side, bending over her, taking Gisela's hands in hers. They were as cold as marble. Suddenly they held on to hers so hard that she winced. The clairvoyant's eyes opened, staring up at her.

"My God, what am I doing? What did I see?"

"I don't know, but it made you faint. Slowly now, here, let me help you."

Side by side on the sofa, the two young women stared

at each other. At that moment, the resemblance between them was striking, one the mirror image of the other.

"What did I see?"

"You don't remember?"

"Not all of it — some of it, but much of what I saw has been wiped from my mind, I know that much. What did I say? Try to remember, Countess — what did I say?"

"You seemed to be talking about my being happy at first, and then something happened. You talked about a bird, like a raven, and then you said, 'Now I see the other,' and then you cried out, 'No!' and — you fainted."

"A bird again — the other —" Desperately, Gisela tried to recall the lost images. "— the setting, the place — did I tell you that?"

"Yes," said Beth, and she could hear the incredulity in her own voice. "I know the place. You couldn't possibly know of it and yet you saw it. It was my parents' house in the Hudson Valley near New York. But nothing else was clear."

"One thing is clear, even if the vision never returns," said Gisela. She leaned impulsively toward Beth, clasping her hands. "You must always be careful, Countess, when you go to this house on the Hudson — or never go there again if you can help it."

"I don't know — at this moment I wonder if I will ever see it again." Beth suddenly felt exhausted. "I think I had better leave now. I don't want the servants or the Mayerdorfs sending out search parties for me."

"I will order a carriage for you."

"Thank you, *Fräulein* Valeska."

"Gisela, Countess."

"Beth — or Empress, if you prefer."

Gisela smiled. "And I am the High Priestess — but that is so pompous, don't you think, between friends, or enemies?"

"Perhaps. Shall we meet again — Gisela?"

"That much is certain. I have yet to meet the Fool in your life. I won't ask you any more about him now, although I think you have identified him, no?"

Beth did not answer. There was no need, although her thoughts were not only of Liam O'Connor. They were also of the child she carried, and of the father of that child. Max. As the single syllable sounded through her mind, she saw the sensual glance of those languorous brown eyes, heard the teasing laughter in his voice, and knew that hating her husband was not going to be as easy as she might have imagined. She was a woman who had been seduced through the mind, and her thoughts were now betraying her, just as her body had betrayed her on the third night of her honeymoon when she herself had invited Max von Schönstein into her bed.

Gisela Valeska seemed to have read her thoughts. "We have solved nothing, have we? If anything, it has all become more difficult — and yet, there is something I can do, something that will give us both a breathing space."

Hopelessly, Beth looked at Gisela. "What is there you could possibly do?"

Beside her on the sofa, the clairvoyant smiled suddenly, almost mischievously. "I can send a letter to my love," she said.

Chapter Twenty-Two

Vienna

It was a long time since she had climbed the stairs behind the aged footman with his laboured breathing and his knotted calf muscles. Yet it seemed to Gisela as if time had stood still and she was a little girl again. Maybe if she turned around very fast she would catch a glimpse of *Mutti* in the shadows below. Fear gripped her and she hastened after the servant. How could she want to see her mother's expression of sorrow and desolation as she had all those years ago?

"Thank you, I know the way now. You can leave me." She took the candlestick from the servant and walked toward the great doors.

"Gisela Valeska, High Priestess."

"Alexei. Juggler."

She heard a soft rumble of laughter, the echo of a small boy's laugh within the sound. There was no longer a table at the other end of the room. The furnishings had been rearranged, and Arcanus was sitting in the same massive chair, but by the windows, over which the curtains were drawn. As Gisela walked toward him she saw the tremendous hands, the bronze hair sprinkled with gray, but, above all, the hypnotic eyes.

"You have not changed."

"You have, High Priestess."

Gisela's laugh was bitter. "It was as you said, Magician, and now the the vision has returned. But you know that."

"There is much I don't know. Tell me." Arcanus indicated the chair opposite him in the window. Gisela placed the candle on the small table between them and sat down. Alexei Islenyev looked at the strong jaw, the sensuous, mobile mouth, the dark eyes whose bold glance held his. His eyes passed over the rich curve and colour of her costume in its vivid, stained-glass tints.

"Suffering has made you beautiful."

"What a price to pay for beauty!"

There was humour in his voice when he replied. "A very good bargain, it would seem to me. Suffering makes most people ugly. But tell me, where is Count von Schönstein?"

"On his way to serve in Cracow, at the fortress there.

It was suddenly discovered he was needed by his regiment."

"And the Empress?"

"On her way back to her country with her unborn child."

"And you?"

"I? Ah, I shall continue to do what I can for the empire — I think you know about that. Maybe — who knows? — I shall take a lover!"

Gisela laughed, but Arcanus did not appear amused.

"Cracow is not the end of the earth, Gisela Valeska. It was a good solution, but there is such a thing as leave, even for someone coerced into being a career soldier."

"Am I never to be free?" She moved restlessly in her chair. Arcanus did not answer her question. Instead he leaned forward and touched her hand. It was only the second time he had touched her, and she felt the contact in her head and her heart, like the vibration of a great cathedral organ.

"You dance on the edge of the abyss, Gisela. Follow the Empress and go to America."

"Is that what you see in the stars for me?"

"I do not always look to the stars for answers, any more than you do. It was good sense that led you to ask the baron to remove the count from Vienna for the time being."

"You know everything, don't you?"

Again he did not answer her question, but continued, "You will find the baron not averse to your departure for America, at least for a while. There are many expatriates in New York who would flock to you and whose undertakings would be of great interest to him. There are as many anarchic pan-Serbs, pan-Slavs. and Czech nationals in that city as there are in Prague itself."

"I will think about it."

"Do that." As if he had suddenly become aware he was touching her, Alexei Islenyev withdrew his hand swiftly and looked away from her toward the curtained windows. In that moment Gisela knew she must ask him the question that had haunted her for so long.

"Alexei, when my mother first brought me here, she was greatly distressed, as if something terrible was going to happen. I know my mother too well to think it was fear of the unknown or some superstitious terror of the occult. That was not the fear I saw in her eyes." Gisela hesitated and then forced herself to continue. "Did she think she was buying your gifts and your powerful connections with — with me?"

"Yes."

She had dreaded his answer, but she had at least hoped he would dress it up in pretty words, prevaricate, pretend he didn't know what she meant. She felt defiled, sick with rage.

"My mother — my own mother."

"Yes," he repeated. Gisela felt her anger turn toward him, and it was easier to deal with the feelings released by that second "yes."

"Then why didn't you take me? Was I not your type of little girl?" The words spat from her, ugly and obscene.

The rage in Gisela's voice was as nothing to the

thunderous anger of his response. "Because I do not *take* little girls! It is a canard that has followed me here, that was put about by my enemies in Russia when I got too near to truths that others did not wish noised abroad. It is the kind of accusation difficult for someone considered a Holy Man to live with, particularly if he is close to the Imperial family. It was, and is, false."

"Then why didn't you deny it to her? Why didn't you tell her? Wicked, wicked woman that she was!"

Once more he touched her, holding both her hands in his, and the anger was gone from his voice. "Because as long as she thought you were in a relationship with me, she would not give you to anyone else."

"Sell me, not give me! I was for sale, Alexei, wasn't I? You don't give away an eight-year-old virgin for free — I was for sale!"

"Yes." Again that cold "yes" tore at her, ripping away more of the illusions to which she had clung, but this time he continued on with words of consolation for her, words of understanding for her mother. "But your mother knew that there was not much that could bring security to the Franzis and the Giselas of this world. I am not, God help me, justifying what she did — but you, her daughter, should despise the society that made such a thing seem desirable to a mother who loved her child very much. This was not a wicked woman but a woman of pitiably few resources who died because of the life she lived. It will be hard for you to live with these things, but you must find peace with them for your own sake, and your mother's."

Revulsion filled her. She would do as Alexei had suggested. She would take herself far away from the lilac and the lemon blossom, the line girls of Vienna. She would forget *Mutti* and Max in another, newer world.

Book Three

The Fool

Chapter Twenty-Three

New York

The main dining room of the Waldorf-Astoria was decorated like King Ludwig's palace in Munich, from the frescoes to the pale-green marble pillars. Beth was glad she had chosen to stay in the more restrained elegance of the St. Regis, but she had wanted to meet Jonty Shotover on neutral ground and this was what he had suggested. She looked at Jonty's bland, pale good looks across the table and was struck all over again by the unreality of her life.

"How are my mother and father?"

"Very well, since they are under the impression you are blissfully married and on your way to New York for a short visit. The fact that you are not blissfully married and are already here would change their state of health very fast, I can assure you."

"What did Henry tell you?"

"What you told him. That, for reasons you chose not to specify, you will be away from the count for a considerable period of time and intend to have your child here. A child about whom, I gather, your husband knows nothing. Do you intend to keep silent forever?"

"No, but I didn't want him to know before I left. They might have let him come back from Cracow and I might have had difficulty leaving. When I wrote to Henry, he suggested I leave on a visit and get in touch with you first when I got here. He said you would know best how to introduce my parents to the idea that I intend to spend as much of my life here as possible."

"Dear Henry — he has such faith in me!"

"Of course, because you are so good at handling Mama," said Beth. She looked up and caught an expression on Jonty's face so unlike anything she had previously seen there that the question which followed came almost involuntarily from her. "You really care for Henry, don't you? Are you — and he —?"

She couldn't finish the sentence. She had spent a season in Europe where such things had been visible, if not considered completely acceptable, but she could not bring herself to complete the thought.

"Yes, we are. Now we each have secrets to keep, haven't we?"

"Oh my God."

Jonty's pale skin looked more waxen than ever, and the hand he put out for his wineglass was shaking.

"Hard as it may be for you to believe, it is mutual, and I really care for Henry. It was hell to suggest he should go to Tübingen, but it was best for both of us. It has made no difference to how I feel — I don't yet know if Henry's feelings remain the same. But your mother is my employer, as it were, and it was an explosive situation."

"Oh my God," said Beth again.

"How too boringly you repeat yourself, Countess! Let's change the subject. Where are you going to live? With your parents? When am I to inform them you are here?"

With difficulty Beth returned to her own problems. "No, I don't want to live with my parents, not ever again if I can help it. Henry said you have connections and would find me a place that would be suitable. The count thinks I have merely left on holiday, and he is unaware there is a problem between us. I see nothing wrong with my parents also being told that I am on an extended visit while my husband is with his regiment in Cracow."

"But tell them about the baby. They'll be so thrilled at the idea of a little noble person in the family that your mother won't look for the holes in your story. No need to mention forever when you talk about staying in New York — just let it creep up on them. And when I say them, we both know we really mean your mother. None of this matters to your father. It is woman's stuff," Jonty said, a note of self-satirization in his voice.

"I agree. Have you any idea where I should live? I guess it had better be in an area of New York I'm familiar with, but I'd like to avoid being too close to my parents."

"There are new apartments being completed on Central Park West you could look at — brick and stone construction, with every luxury. Even with your money, Beth, it's a big investment, especially since your plans are still what one might call fluid, and you're not used to apartment living."

"Oh no, that sounds perfect. There were very nice apartments in — " Beth stopped. She didn't want to think of Gisela Valeska, although her anger and jealousy had gone. But thinking of Max was painful, just as it had been painfully easy to make love again when he had returned from Bavaria, laughing and joking and enfolding her in his cloak, the feel of the cold air still on his skin. Oh yes, he had sensed something was wrong, but she had felt he couldn't be bothered to pursue the matter. It had not been important enough, now that he could pursue Gisela Valeska again.

"Very well. When shall we say you arrived?" Jonty gave her a disarming smile and she thought of what he had told her about himself and Henry. The initial shock was over, but it added to her feeling of confusion.

"In about a week's time I shall send them a wire saying I had to make a quick decision in order to book a passage, that the arrangements for the apartment were made through a friend in Europe — and that I am expecting a baby. Can we at least get my signature on some agreement for an apartment by then?"

"I am sure we can. Do you mind my asking where you are staying?"

"At the St. Regis."

"Delightful. You'll be fine there. I guess we shouldn't repeat this assignation, my dear Countess. You are not likely to see your parents here, but you could run into mutual friends or your brother William. And people could jump to amusingly wrong conclusions, couldn't they? I suggest you lie low for the next week or so. Will you trust me to find you an apartment?"

"Of course."

The look Jonty Shotover now gave Beth made him seem a million miles removed from her image of him as a social butterfly. "Beth," he said, "I'd like to feel that what I told you didn't turn you against Henry. He values your good opinion and needs your support, more than he needs that of William or your parents."

"I'll always care about Henry, Jonty, because he has always cared about my feelings."

He smiled. "It's getting busier, Countess, and I think you should go back into hiding."

"You know where to find me."

That night, she lay in her hotel bed and thought about Jonty Shotover and her brother Henry, and her older brother William, who in his early twenties was already showing the physical signs of his alcoholism and dissipated life.

"And here I lie," she said out loud into the darkness, "pregnant, with a broken marriage that my husband doesn't even know is broken. In fact, the only people who know are me, my brother and his lover, and a clairvoyant who is my husband's mistress!"

Meanwhile, somewhere out there to the south of her was a blue-eyed Irishman with whom she had once fancied herself in love. At this moment she couldn't have said if she still loved him, or Max, or both of them, or anyone at all. Against the darkness she saw the Fool on the tarot card laughing at the edge of the abyss, dancing even as the world crumbles away at his feet.

She spoke into the darkness again. "Liam, I am the the biggest fool of all."

Watching the skaters on the lake in Central Park as she passed, Beth envied the young women's graceful movements, but only for a moment. She remembered how rigidly structured her life had been when she had been one of them, and she marvelled at her newfound freedom.

For free she was and the irony did not escape her. The confines of her former New York prison had been so narrow that her present dilemma seemed like liberty itself. The day before, she had taken a cablecar down Broadway, past City Hall to Battery Park and seen the bay shining in the distance. It had been a freezing-cold day, but no one had paid her much attention and there was no one to demand that she return.

On her way home the warm smell of bread and rolls reached across the road to her from a bakery and she went in. She was surrounded by people who spoke German and she even heard the distinctive Viennese dialect at a table she passed. But oh, the bliss — the *Gemütlichkeit* — of the fact she went unnoticed!

Eyebrows would have been raised in her area of town at the sight of a woman eating alone. Here, nobody bothered her.

Even though she had known little of the city, Beth was aware of how much New York had changed in the short time she had been away. The comparatively new *Palais* and government buildings of Vienna seemed to be part of the past, but one could not mistake the extraordinary Flatiron building — or even her own apartment — for the constructs of an earlier age. Standing at the window of her empty apartment, her signature barely dry on the papers that made it hers, she waited for her mother to arrive.

Dear Papa, she thought, when you settled some of your millions upon me and bought me a husband, you set me free. Beyond the doors into the hallway she heard voices and Jonty's distinctive laugh. Bracing herself, she turned to face her mother for the first time since her departure for Europe.

"Beth, sweetheart!"

Beth had forgotten how large her mother was. Enfolded in that steel-and-velvet-clad embodiment of power and prosperity, Beth looked over her mother's shoulder at Jonty Shotover. He gave her a wink and a thumbs-up signal.

"You look so — so *European!* But you look so thin! And for the life of me I cannot think why we are standing in this terrible empty little box when you could be at home! And Jonty keeps dropping hints to me — but you're too thin — oh Beth!"

Words tumbled pell-mell from Ada Holman as she alternately clasped and unclasped Beth, holding her first away from her and then close, as though they moved in some ritual dance together.

"Mother, I'm fine, I really am, and this isn't a box, you know. It's a beautiful apartment — very exclusive. And yes, I have some news for you. I'm expecting a baby in May."

This time the words her mother poured forth were accompanied by tears. Beth wondered if she were correct in sensing both guilt and relief in the outpouring, and prayed she was right. A guilty and relieved Ada Holman would be easier to cope with than an aggressive, narrow-minded Ada Holman with her overpowering drive to dominate.

"But you can't stay here — it's not furnished! When will the count be joining you? Oh what nonsense all this army business is! It never got in his way before, did it?"

"No, and that's part of the reason why he must spend some time with his regiment now. There's a possibility of trouble in Macedonia, and the Bosnian Serbs —"

"Goodness, Beth, that's all double-dutch to me. Such a messy thing, politics, and the poor count having to get caught up in it! Never mind, you're safe here, and surely they'll allow him to come over for the birth of his own child?"

Before Beth could frame an answer, her mother had rushed onward. "But you've no furniture yet. Where are you sleeping? Where are you eating?"

"I'm staying in a hotel, Mother."

"Oh my God, Beth!"

Appalled, Ada Holman stepped back and stared at her daughter.

"It's perfect for my needs, and I shall stay there until I move in here."

Meeting Beth's eyes, her mother was taken aback by the expression of steely determination she saw there. She could hardly fail to recognize it, for it was a reflection of her own will. "Doctors," she protested feebly, "what about doctors?"

"I saw one in Vienna, and I shall need to make appointments here. Perhaps we could make them together."

Pacified, Ada Holman turned her thoughts away from Beth's aberrant behaviour and threw herself into organizing that part of her daughter's life into which she had been invited.

Standing at the uncurtained window looking down on the passers-by far below, Jonty listened to the voices of the two women rising and falling as a background to his own thoughts. Presently he said, "We should be leaving, Mrs. Holman. Don't forget your bridge party."

"Oh my goodness, yes — it had quite slipped my mind. I declare, Beth, life is so busy at the moment it would be far easier to see one another if you were at home — but never mind, we shall fit everything in."

"Of course we will, Mother."

Across the empty room, her mother's court jester smiled sweetly at her and Beth could almost see the cap and bells of his trade. Perhaps it was Jonty Shotover that Gisela Valeska had seen in the tarot, the only Fool to enter her life. It seemed highly unlikely that Liam O'Connor would want anything to do with

242

a pregnant woman whose marital status was complicated and whose family considered him a dirty Irish peasant.

Chapter Twenty-Four

New York

There were now drapes of fine white book-muslin across the windows overlooking Central Park, and beneath them a velvet-covered window seat with pillows of deep rose and ivory. There was an antique Chinese rug on the floor with a rose background and blue and gold flowers. The sofas and chairs were covered with a rose-blooming chintz, and cane-backed chairs sat at the dining table. Plants filled the windows and porcelain bowls were scattered around the room. It was as far removed from palace or *Palais* as Beth could make it.

She had heard from Max. He had spoken lyrically

of the baby, said he was coming over but had not yet appeared. With relief Beth read what he had to say about continued trouble among the Serbs and of a possible transfer to the garrison in Zalesczyki. He also wrote about court balls and plans for a vacation on the Dalmatian coast.

Gradually Beth began to realize that what she had heard described in her mother's set as a "marriage of convenience" was also in Max's interest. A divorce without a divorce. This did not make her as happy as she had presumed it should have done. For the moment, however, she found herself preoccupied with preparations for the birth of her child.

Without willing it to happen, Beth found herself caught up in choosing layettes and buying a baby carriage of polished white wood trimmed with gold, like one she had seen in Madison Square. All her power and energy were channelled into nest-building for a baby who would, it seemed, be fatherless to all intents and purposes.

It was only when her labour pains started that Beth realized how isolated she was. There were her doctors and her nurses to call, and she called them, but apart from these there remained only her mother.

When Ada Holman reminisced about the birth of her first grandchild, she invariably said, "And I left dear Mrs. Astor right in the middle of a hand of bridge and went *straight* to Beth's side."

Beth's baby was a girl. Her first reaction was one of relief, for she was sure Max would have been more interested in a boy to inherit his title.

"Beth," said her mother, "she's perfectly beautiful

and she looks just like you. You never really discussed names with me for a girl. What will you call her?"

"Liane."

"Oh that's lovely! So European and yet so easy for everyone to pronounce. How did you think of it?"

"I — I just like it," was Beth's reply.

The apartment was soon filled with flowers and gifts for the baby. Friends of her mother and a few of her own contemporaries brought chocolates and champagne and magazines for her to read.

In one Beth came across an article about the district attorney for New York, William Jerome — "the terror of the Tammany and the Tenderloin," as the writer called him, "a crusader with a conscience." The writer was Liam O'Connor. Heart thumping, Beth read it through, and then again and again until she knew it by heart, by that thumping, jumping heart of hers that could hear the Irish lilt through every word on the paper in front of her.

Before she could consider, reconsider, or do the sensible thing, she had taken paper and pen and had written to him. She wrote without planning what she wanted to say, without thinking of cause or effect or how to go about it, or whether she should be going about it at all.

Dear Liam,

I loved your article in Puck, *I really did. I am so glad that a crusader with a conscience like William Jerome has a crusader with a pen like Liam O'Connor. A clairvoyant in Vienna*

*told me I should see you again. Do you believe
in such things? My phone number and address
are at the top of this letter. I would be glad
if you would contact me. I never had the chance
to return your hospitality.*

Sincerely, Beth

It seemed silly when she read it through. Gushing
and forward, yet stiff and cold at the same time. She
sent the maid out to post it before she could change
her mind or alter a single word.

She was astonished, shaken with delight, when a
week later his reply arrived.

Dear Beth,

*Thank you for loving the article. Call me
if you are serious about returning my hospitality. You also owe me a pair of gloves.*

Liam

She phoned at once, her hand trembling so that
she had difficulty holding the receiver. At the sound
of his voice she could see his face vividly, as if he
were already in the room with her, and she felt the
physical response in her body.

"I don't believe it. You sound just the same."

"Yes, well, the Irish brogue is a difficult one to get
rid of, I'm afraid."

"Sorry, that was such a stupid thing to say."

"Well, this is a kind of stupid thing we're doing,
Countess, isn't it? Am I not likely to be slung out

on my ear at best, or run through with a sabre at worst?"

"No chance. I have my own apartment."

"Wow, you rich girls. Oh — and congratulations, by the way."

"You mean about Liane?"

There was silence for a moment at the other end of the line, but when he replied he sounded as laconic as ever. "Sure, couldn't miss it. Your mama had it all over the papers."

"She's sweet. Not Mama, the baby, I mean. Will you come and see her?"

"I'll come and see you."

"Oh."

"Change your mind? That's all right." Suddenly his voice was clipped, distant.

"No, no — it's just that it's all so — so easy. I'm not used to such ease."

"A bit repetitious in style, Countess, but I know what you mean. When shall I come?"

"Tomorrow?"

"No, but I can come the day after."

"The day after is better. Tomorrow never comes."

She heard him laugh. "Not bad. I take it back about your style. Okay, see you the day after. In the afternoon, about two?"

"Wonderful."

And it was wonderful, although she wasn't sure she really knew what it was she was doing. As Liam had said, it was stupid. Thank God she was just that: stupid, with a lack of conscience that was positively frightening. For the first time since her arrival in New

York, Beth went to examine herself in the mirror, concerned about what an observer might see.

Even to her own eyes she appeared very different from the girl who had left New York nearly two years ago. She looked older, and it was a look that had nothing to do with exhaustion after her daughter's birth, since she had hired a nurse in addition to the other servants she already employed. No; this change had more to do with greater sophistication in her way of dressing, the way she did her hair, and above all the way her eyes looked at the world.

It also undoubtedly had something to do with sexual experience and everything to do with suffering. One could not wait in the streets of a strange city outside the apartment of one's husband's mistress, knife in hand, and not keep some reflection of that moment on the face in the mirror.

One reflection, however, was not there, one that she had hoped she might see. The reflection of Liane. Another woman, far more experienced than she, looked after her baby's physical needs and instructed her in the practical aspects of motherhood. Yet Beth needed no one to tell her that motherhood was something that happened inside, and that it had not happened to her. When she looked at Liane in her cradle, at the head that was shaped like her father's and the mouth that was already somewhat like her own, all she felt was a kind of surprise that a child existed. It was not that she felt hostility or even that she didn't feel protective. It was rather that she didn't feel involved. And she felt deeply guilty that she couldn't love Liane instantly and without reservation.

Beth had not been the least concerned about her

appearance for the past few months, but now she cared desperately. Whatever else she was unconcerned about, she knew that she wanted to sweep Liam O'Connor off his feet as she had done two years ago. She was embarking on a campaign, a campaign to win him over to her cause, and selecting the right dress suddenly felt as vital to her as finding the right thing to say when Liam walked through the door.

He was right on the hour. The cool and collected greeting she had planned dissolved into a smile that trembled, a stammered welcome that might have been given by the seventeen-year-old she had been when she had first met him. She had forgotten — how could she have forgotten? — the impact of that face, the eyes, that smile. How could she have forgotten she had been willing to give herself to him within hours of their first meeting? Was he as shaken as she was? Did he, too, remember? "I love you," he had said. "I am in love with you."

Liam O'Connor stood in the rose-and-ivory sitting room and looked at the figure from what he referred to as his "brownstone blackout period." After the initial madness and anger had subsided he had laughingly discussed it with his friends, and everyone had agreed it had been simply a logical extension of O'Connor's desire to screw the rich. With time he had completely accepted this theory.

Her voice over the telephone had given him the first jolt, and he had not told anyone about her invitation. He would have found it difficult to make ribald jokes, to have laughed about ersatz countesses or poor little rich girls. He had accepted her invitation in the hope of laying a ghost.

Some ghost. The same girl and yet not quite the same, in her tight-fitting, emerald-green dress with the collar of ivory braid high up around her neck. The same eyes, and yet not quite the same; the same mouth and yet — no, he'd not think of the mouth or the memory of that kiss. The unaccustomed feeling of vulnerability made him suddenly belligerent.

"Why am I here, Countess? For old times' sake?" She stiffened, and instantly he saw her as he had seen her two years ago when he had challenged her in her mother's sitting room.

"No. I have a proposition to put to you."

Liam raised his eyebrows and Beth flushed. "I expressed that badly —" Suddenly, she was angry. "Yes, it *is* for old times' sake and I *do* have a proposition to put to you, and that was a cheap shot, O'Connor!"

"I didn't say anything, Countess," he protested.

"Your eyebrows did."

"I'm not responsible for my eyebrows."

Laughter burst from both of them in unison, nervous and relieved laughter, not far removed from hysteria.

"That's the Irish in you, O'Connor."

"Liam, remember?"

"Beth."

"Hello, Beth. It's been a while."

He saw her body relax as she sighed deeply. "Oof, I'm glad that's over. Sit down, Liam, and let's have a drink. What will you have?"

"A touch of old Charleston 'n Savannah, if you have it."

Her smile was wide, delighted, delicious, and Liam felt its impact on his mind, his memory, his skin, as if she had touched him.

"Darling Gran — I really loved her."

"I thought all nice girls loved their grandmothers."

"I'm not a nice girl, not anymore."

He took the drink she had poured, carefully avoiding touching her hand. "Can't believe that, but do you want to tell me why?"

"Not since I waited on a street in Vienna outside an apartment to kill my husband's mistress."

"Ah, Beth!" He made no attempt to conceal the pain her reply had given him.

She shook her head and broke in on whatever he might have been about to say. "No — I want to tell you first. It all has to do with my proposition, you see."

It was easier to tell than she had imagined, because it was as if it had all happened to someone else. Vienna and its Ringstrasse and Max all seemed to be on a different planet from New York and Central Park West.

"And so you see," she finished, "I am free for the first time in my life."

There was silence in the room for a moment, and Beth couldn't tell from Liam's face what his reaction was to her words. Then he asked, "What about your daughter, who is, after all, his child? Doesn't she curtail your freedom?"

"No." She wanted to be honest, whatever it made him think of her. "I'm only afraid she is going to make little difference in my life. I'm having difficulty grasping that she's part of it, and I really don't know if that's because of Max or because of me."

If her coldness had shaken him, he didn't show it. "What, then, is your proposition?"

"That you provide the cause and I provide the money for it."

Liam O'Connor was looking confused. With a gesture she remembered only too vividly from their first meeting, he ran his fingers through his dark, curly hair. "What cause, Beth? Let me get this straight — you are saying you'll bankroll me to any good deed I want?"

"More or less, yes."

"What's in it for you?"

The cold businesslike tone of his enquiry jolted her into action, and she jumped up from her chair and crossed to the window. "A purpose in life — what difference does it make to you why I am making this offer?"

"It only matters if I am part of the deal."

"Since you can choose the cause, I am hardly trying to buy your principles. As to your —" She hesitated and then continued, "I don't imagine you waited around for me."

"Nope."

He made no effort to expand on that one laconic syllable and she was glad. It hurt quite enough, however irrational that hurt might be. "So let me help with the one thing I have to offer. Money."

Liam suddenly slumped down in his chair, long legs sticking out in front of him, and started to laugh. "Countess, there's one thing you still do to me that you did two years ago. You still catch me unawares and take my breath away. Let me see now, which cause do you fancy? This town's full of 'em. Shall I pick me an anarchist from Tompkins Square? Or would you prefer a Social Populist, a Zionist, maybe an Internationalist? What shall it be, Beth?"

She was afraid she would cry if she lost control, so, struggling to hold on to her composure, she kept her voice low. "I thought you might like to start a magazine."

Liam wasn't laughing anymore, she noticed. He leaned forward and looked straight up into her eyes. "You're serious, aren't you?"

"Perfectly. You're the only one being facetious here."

Again the gesture she remembered, as he ran his fingers through his hair. "I apologize, Beth, but I felt such a damned fool for coming here."

"And I was beginning to think I was a damned fool for asking you. Does this sudden sobering-up mean you would indeed like to start a magazine of some kind?"

"Yes. A group of my friends — well, we've been kicking a couple of ideas around for a few months now. We think we've a viable one, but we've just not been quite able to get it off the ground."

"I am offering you wings."

The new tenderness of his expression and the warmth of his smile made Beth's confusion worse. "You are, Beth, you certainly are. I have a suggestion to make before we discuss sordid details, such as how much. Would you like to meet my friends and hear what we have in mind?"

"That seems like a good idea. Why not bring them here next week sometime?"

The blue eyes glittered with delight. "I should warn

you that some of them are kind of uncouth, Beth, a little crazy. Not what you're used to. Are you sure that —?"

His voice tailed off as he heard her laugh. Her laugh was low and musical, like her voice, and it filled the room and his senses. He felt the madness start to return.

"How do you know what I am used to, Liam O'Connor? I'm married to a man with a crazy family in a run-down castle in Bavaria and a mistress who's clairvoyant, who sees visions in a crystal ball and reads the tarot. And whom I quite liked. She calls me the Empress and herself the High Priestess, and you know what? She reminds me of me — of me! So let me meet your crazy bunch and see how they compare with mine!"

Liam O'Connor watched the slender body that seemed untouched by childbirth sway as she walked to and fro, hugging herself with amusement. She turned to look at him over her shoulder and her smile dazzled him as it had two years previously. Goddamnit, it looked as if he were hooked again. Why goddamnit? he thought to himself, since this time you get some of daddy's money and no strings attached. There was an answer to that, but he didn't want to pursue it for the moment. He didn't have affairs with married ladies. That thought threw a cold dash of reality onto the flame that had begun to burn in him once more. Beth had finally sat down opposite him, and he leaned toward her.

"I don't want to ask you this, Beth, but I must. Where does Count von Schönstein fit into your plans?"

Beth looked at him defiantly. "He doesn't. Max is a million miles away in Cracow."

"You don't really think he'll stay there, do you? My God, he has a daughter he hasn't seen and a wife—"

Beth interrupted him. "— and a wife who means nothing to him except for her money — and that he has in abundance. Under the terms of my marriage agreement, there is a settlement that is for him, and him alone. I have my own money, and he has no claim on it in any way."

He wanted to hold her, comfort her, kiss away the ache in her voice. Instead he said, "I don't think it's going to be that simple, Beth. I'm not asking you to change your decision — I'm too selfish for that — but you mustn't forget that the count is a complex man who lives by a set of rules that should have disappeared in the Dark Ages."

Beth leaned back in her chair and surveyed him challengingly. "Are you afraid of him?"

"Yes, and I think you should be as well."

"Don't worry. Even if he leaves Cracow, or any other garrison they send him to, he'll not move far from Gisela Valeska or Vienna. It is a matter of pride to Max to get her back; more than that, he's infatuated with her. You would understand if you saw her."

"I must have misunderstood. I thought she had ended the affair because of you, and because of her own hurt when he married you."

How to explain Max to Liam O'Connor? How to explain what he could do to logic and common sense and reason? Even when one knew what he was like. "If you knew Max as I do — it's not that simple, as you yourself just said to me. He is — he is —" There was a movement from the chair opposite her, but she was not sure if it was impatience at her weakness or disbelief. "Enough of that. Let's just say that I feel safe while there is a clairvoyant in Vienna called Gisela Valeska. She will draw him to her."

Before he could express an opinion one way or the other, she had deliberately changed the mood of the conversation. When she next spoke her tone was light, playful. "Remember I said that she saw you, Liam? Well, she did, and she said she, too, would meet you at some time in the future."

"Oh really? Was I doing an Irish jig in her crystal ball, or what?"

"She saw you in the tarot. You know which card you are? You are the Fool, O'Connor, dancing on the edge of the abyss, your own man, full of idealism but hopeless in practical matters. I hope one of your friends has a good financial head on his shoulders."

"Her. One of my friends has a good financial head on *her* shoulders." He could see she was waiting for more, so he changed the subject. "So, I'm the Fool, am I, Empress? Well, that's true enough and I'll not argue with it."

He got up to leave, and Beth remembered something she hadn't understood in his letter. "Gloves — you said something about gloves."

"Ah yes. I left my only pair on a hall table on Fifth Avenue two years ago."

"I owe you a pair of gloves, then."

It wasn't all she owed him. She owed him everything and she owed him nothing; it hadn't been only a pair of gloves he had left on Fifth Avenue. "Consider the debt repaid by the offer of a magazine," he replied with a flippancy he was far from feeling. "'Bye, Beth, I'll be in touch."

In touch. The phrase stayed with Beth all day and into the night. Her dreams were a confused sequence of images, one after the other: of Max, laughing, teasing, making love to her and arousing her to passion. Even as she reached a climax in her dreams, it was Liam's face she saw, Liam's voice she heard, and the larger heavier body that encompassed hers and brought her to ecstacy. She awoke suddenly, perspiring, panting, horrified at the indiscriminate nature of her fantasies

Would either man do for her, then? Was there nothing particularly special about either of them for her in this matter of falling in love, loving, lovemaking? Why was it all so very different from what she had read in Else's "True Love Stories"? How could she even wonder such a thing when she already knew the answer. How could she first have fallen in love with Max, then fallen in love with Liam, and then with Max all over again, and now —

Only it didn't matter now. He had said "nope" and "she." He was no longer hers for the taking.

When the dreams returned, Liam was gone from them, and there was only Max. He was angry now, angry with her, pointing to the duelling scars on his face, white against the tanned skin, suddenly whiter than reality, as white as his teeth had been when he had laughed and cajoled her into passion in spite of herself.

Chapter Twenty-Five

New York

Because so many of Liam O'Connor's group led irregular lives or had jobs with odd hours, it took more than a week to get them together. In Beth's class one generally knew where most people were at any given time. In this other society, it was not the difference in the structure that was remarkable; it was the lack of it. Eventually a date was set, although the numbers who would attend remained uncertain. Beth was not in the least concerned, as long as one member of the group was the financial advisor known only as "she."

"She" and Liam were the first to arrive. "Hello,

Beth, let me introduce Anna Grabēz, the one with the head on her shoulders," said Liam. His eyes were fixed on Beth's face.

"God, man! You make me sound as exciting as wet flounder. Hey, Beth — some place you've got here."

Anna Grabēz was anything but dull, and it was indeed some head she had on her shoulders. Set atop a tiny face and tiny body, it was covered with a mass of flaming red hair. Although she appeared to be barely five feet tall, she bounced into the room, voice booming, and the impression she gave was of someone very large in stature. The effect of her clothes, which were brilliantly coloured and in violently clashing patterns, seemed calculated rather than accidental.

Liam's financial expert shot past Beth, removing her shawl from her shoulders as she went and draping it over one of the ivory chairs. Beth looked back at Liam and saw that he was grinning at her.

"Crazy enough for you?"

"No, that is not what I was thinking." She could hear the acid in her voice and feel her lips tightening as if she chewed on a lemon. Liam O'Connor continued to grin like an idiot.

"Just for a moment there, you looked and sounded like your mother."

Before she could think of a retort the rest of the group had started to arrive.

There were five in all for this first meeting of the magazine consortium: two women, three men, and Beth herself. The other woman was called Gloria Baker; she was the daughter of Lithuanian Jews, herself born in New York, and somewhere in her mid-

thirties. Her husband, Lester Baker, was a gentle,
bearded man of German extraction whose intelligence
shone in his eyes. Both had extensive newspaper and
magazine experience, and their writings ranged from
academic treatises to exposés. They had close links
with many of the city's ethnic groups, and Lester,
surprisingly, spoke Mandarin and some other Chinese
dialect. When Beth asked him why, he replied,
"Because I wanted to," in a tone that suggested he
was surprised she found a reason necessary.

The other man was about Liam's age, and Beth felt
the same discomfort with him as she did with Anna
Grabēz. He was untidily dressed, unkempt and loud
of voice, his conversation peppered with oaths. His
greasy hair was fair but his skin seemed tanned and
his eyebrows were dark. When introduced to Beth, he
ran his eyes over her with an unabashed frankness
that made her wish she could close the door in his
face.

"Tug Bailey at your service — any service at all
for you, little lady." Beth smelled whiskey on his breath
as he passed. "Hey — Anna!" Beth watched him kiss
Anna Grabēz extravagantly, his hand patting her
backside. Beth noticed that Liam seemed completely
unmoved by the sight, and decided that perhaps Anna
was, indeed, merely his financial advisor.

But even as Beth thought this, Anna came back to
Liam, wrapped her arms around him and said,
"C'mon, Liam, let's hear what Beth can do for us."
Giving Beth a genuinely friendly smile she then
pushed Liam down with her onto the sofa.

Beth's misgivings subsided once the talk started. It

swiftly became evident how bright, organized, and
motivated these people were. Their basic idea was for
a magazine covering the multicultural diversity of the
city. They wanted to deal with both the good and
the bad: the hardships experienced by new arrivals,
the corruption of Tammany and Tenderloin, and also
the richness of the cultural heritage brought by the
immigrants to New York from all over Europe. Above
all, they wanted to cover the new cultural explosion
in the city: the Yiddish theatres on the Bowery, the
nickelodeons, the black music slowly moving out of
the Tenderloin brothels and into more respectable
nightclubs.

Gradually, Beth found herself caught up in the
intoxication of their talk, their enthusiam, their exper-
tise. It seemed to her that the very texture of New
York lay at the fingertips of these people: rich, complex, beautiful. She could see it, smell it, feel it in
her rose-and-ivory sitting room, and she felt dizzy with
excitement.

She was also made aware of Anna's role in this pool
of talent. Feet firmly on the ground, she guided them
through what was necessary and practical, as well as
what was "wonderful" or "marvellous" or "fun to
try." For all her eccentric appearance and outlandish
language, she was the pragmatist in this gathering
of dreamers and intellectuals.

Decisions were made; solutions were found; agreements were reached. When the meeting broke up for
refreshments, the euphoria in the air was based on
solid possibility rather than mere wishful thinking.

Beth's role was simple. They told her how much

it would cost and she had given them carte blanche. "But," she had added, "I would like to be part of it — in touch with it."

"Of course," said Gloria Baker. When the formal part of the evening was over she had come to sit by Beth and talk to her. She smiled, and her broad, plain face was transformed by the beauty of that smile. "None of us here could possibly approach your perspective, Beth. Lester's and Liam's parents are from the professional classes, but your position — "

"Would my position be of any interest?"

"Sure! Who wouldn't want to read what the daughter of a robber baron has to say? Dear God, Beth — your set are the stuff that dreams are made of! Forgive me, I don't mean to offend you."

"It isn't the first time I've heard the expression. Does your family live in the Jewish area of New York? Liam took me there, once."

"Did he?" Gloria's shrewd eyes examined Beth carefully. "Yes, they do, but my father wants as little to do with me as possible. I am his *Amerikanerin* of a daughter who married a Gentile and became a daughter of Babylon. There are many like me in the ghetto who rebel against Orthodox parents. In many families it's a fight lost in one generation."

"It's so difficult to be a dutiful daughter." How stupid that sounded, thought Beth as soon as she said it, but Gloria simply nodded in agreement. "I know what you mean," was her reply.

Over Gloria's shoulder Beth could see Liam and Lester Baker talking earnestly together over some newspaper article one of them had brought with him.

To the right of them she saw Anna Grabez standing close to Tug Bailey, laughing up into his face. Their bodies were almost touching. As she watched, Liam's glance flickered over the pair and returned again to the newspaper on his lap.

Lester and Gloria were the first to leave. Anna casually announced, "Liam, I'll leave you to your own devices. Tug'll see me home — eh, Tug?"

Tug grinned widely and shrugged his shoulders. "Sure thing, anything to oblige." Anna picked up her shawl from the chair and wrapped herself in its purple-and-green paisley swirls. "See you later." The two left together, their laughter echoing down the hallway. Speechless, Beth turned and looked at Liam.

"Am I 'your own devices'? Is that what she meant?"

"She meant I am free, just as she is free."

"To do what, pray?"

"Whatever. No one owns Anna, nor ever will. She believes that marriage makes women chattels, possessions, that it is a thing of the past."

"Oh, I see what you mean. Free means free to sleep with whomever you want."

Liam was silent for a moment and then said, "I know this is difficult for you to grasp, Beth, but it's quite usual in our circle. There shouldn't be one set of rules for men and one for women."

"I never thought there should be. I feel just as negative about promiscuous men as I do about promiscuous women."

"I am expressing this badly."

"You certainly are, but then I can't think of a good way to express it. Let me try to sort one thing out — is she basically your girl?"

"She is basically my girl."

"And you feel all right about that?" Beth gestured in the direction of the hallway.

"I feel all right about that."

Beth leaned against the closed door and stared at him. It seemed to Liam O'Connor that her eyes were fathomless pools in which he was drowning beneath the weight of his lies, his subterfuge, his longing.

"Then I think," she said quietly, "that you and Anna Grabēz are as primitive in your own way and as much in the Dark Ages as Max, whose set of rules seems no worse to me than your lack of them. He buys, and she gives for free. He puts a price on love and devalues it; she makes it worthless by offering her favours to every Tug, Dick and Liam in New York."

She had struck closer to home than he cared to admit and it made him belligerent. "You still believe in fairy tales and love stories, do you, Beth — in spite of everything?"

She looked startled, and he felt that it was by something he had shaken loose from the shadows of her mind. "Yes — I suppose I must."

"Beth!"

Beth looked up at him, at the bluest of eyes, the cleft in his chin, the dark, curly hair. And when he put his arms around her his body against hers felt as it had when she had dreamed about him. She wondered if she too was as indiscriminate as Anna Grabēz, and if it didn't really matter to her which man was holding her.

At the thought she saw in her mind Tug Bailey and Anna undressing each other with their eyes, their bodies touching.

"No!" She pushed him away, suppressing her tears with her anger. "I am not going to be your consolation prize for the evening, O'Connor, something you snatch from a grabbag of girls when the fancy takes you or when Anna is with someone else. Go and stop someone on the street if you want to make love — it makes no difference to you who it is!"

For the first time in his life Liam O'Connor felt violently angry toward a woman. It confused him. How could he both want her and hate her at the same time? He would have liked to shake her, force her back into her genteel salon, throw her down on the rose-covered sofa and tear her expensive dress from her, pull her dark hair loose over those alabaster-pale shoulders. The strength of these emotions terrified him into action. Without a word, he turned away and let himself out of the apartment.

Beth stood where he had left her and said what she had not been able to say when he was present.

"I want you too much, Liam O'Connor, to take turns with you. I want you for me alone and I cannot share you. Not with anyone."

I cannot share. The words reminded her of Gisela Valeska, and of Max von Schönstein, whom she had thought was hers and hers alone. She had not been prepared to share him either. Was it she who was unnatural, she wondered, or was it the attitudes of the men with whom she elected to fall in love?

Chapter Twenty-Six

New York

The magazine was christened *Facets* and the title designed so that the letter T curved decoratively over and around the other, simply drawn, letters, so that the word "Faces" became part of the title's significance. There were more meetings at Beth's apartment, more staff was hired, and premises were found near the Puck Building on Lafayette in a structure designed in the Romanesque style of the 1890s.

The weekly get-togethers at the apartment grew larger and soon included other members of the New York intelligentsia, none of whom had any connections with Beth's brownstone world. Her mother

would have considered them beyond the pale by virtue
of both their abundance of intellect and lack of means.
Some were actually quite comfortably off, but their
passion for things cerebral would have made them
immediately suspect.

With the arrival of the first prolonged heat wave,
Beth's small daughter made her presence felt by object-
ing strongly to the airless nights and humid days. Ada
Holman had left for Newport, protesting at her daughter's refusal to accompany her but leaving Beth an
open invitation to use the house on the Hudson.

"Heaven knows it can be hot enough out there —
Newport is so much cooler — but it's fresher than
the city. Give the caretaker a few days' notice and he
can open it for you. You can take your own staff."

Beth was loath to take favours from her mother,
but when she looked at her daughter's face, scarlet
with rage and discomfort, and felt the now-familiar
prick of guilt at her own sense of detachment, she
decided to go.

Besides, she had had enough of the state of affairs
between herself and Liam O'Connor. They had not
spoken to each other alone since the first meeting of
the founders of *Facets* and it was a ridiculously
uncomfortable situation. When she saw his blue eyes
dancing as he spoke to other women, and particularly
Anna Grabēz, she felt the hot knife of jealousy stab
through her assumed air of indifference and prayed
that no one noticed.

When she announced at the weekly rendezvous that
she was going away for a while, she saw Liam's direct
blue gaze fasten on her. He avoided her as usual for

the duration of the evening, but as everyone left she saw him hanging back and was caught by surprise at the surge of elation inside her.

"Where are you going? Out of the country?" The enquiry sounded idly polite, casual.

"No, just to the Hudson. Liane is feeling the heat. It seems only fair to take her out of the city." Beth heard her own voice, as detached and coolly courteous as his.

"Certainly. Will your husband be joining you there?"

She looked at him, startled. "No. I thought I told you — it's not likely he will ever join me. There is trouble in Macedonia and Gisela Valeska in Vienna."

"And you think you are that unimportant to him?"

"I know I am that unimportant to him. He has what he wants from me. Even his daughter hasn't brought him here, has she?"

Unable to hide the bitterness in her voice, Beth dreaded hearing the pity she anticipated in his reply. For, pretend as she might, the depth of Max's indifference had taken her by surprise. He had, by now, almost given up the farce of exchanging letters. Liam's response, however, was not what she had expected.

"You once told me how much you liked the Hudson Valley. It will be good for you, too. Besides, you should get to know your daughter. It's hard on a child to be an orphan when both parents are alive."

Her answer blazed with anger, for he had pricked the guilt that surfaced all too easily in her.

"Don't you *dare* to criticize me!"

Liam O'Connor flung his hat on the hall table and

moved toward Beth. His hands grasped her by the shoulders and she felt his fingers burning her through the thin fabric of her dress.

"I *will* dare to criticize you, Beth von Schönstein, because it seems I'm the only one who will. No mama, no papa, no husband to do it — and everyone here thinks you're wonderful and gorgeous and oh, so modern with your absent count and your endless money to fling at causes. You need me, Beth; if for nothing else, you need me as a thorn in your side!"

She did need him, but not to show her the error of her ways. On this hot summer night when her blood raced at the thought of his flesh against her skin, she needed his body against hers. She looked up at him and this time she knew that his eyes were saying all the things she was thinking of and longing for. She waited, but the words she saw in his eyes didn't come, so she met his anger with hers.

"Do I? But you don't need me, Liam, do you? You're so wonderful and gorgeous yourself, and oh, so modern with your free love and your oh-so-available girl friend! I don't care a damn about your criticism! It amuses you to say I'm sometimes like my mother — and maybe I am, God help me — but when *you* start tut-tutting at me you sound more like her than I do!"

She heard their breathing, harsh and rough, felt his hands slide down her arms to her elbows, curve around them and pull her against him. Perspiration trickled between her breasts and she could see it glistening in the hollow of Liam's throat, the cleft in his chin. Then, suddenly, he was smiling and rubbing her elbows with his hands, as though he were comforting her after a fall.

"Ah, Beth, it's hopeless. Who am I kidding? I look at you across your elegant sitting room filled with my friends who are now your friends, and I watch them laughing and flirting with you, and you so bright and brittle in your new role — and I want you to be the young girl I kissed in a cab, not this complicated woman who threatens to screw up the love-'em-and-leave-'em arrangements of my sex life."

The joy that filled her seemed as painful as anger or jealousy, because he still had not committed himself to her, or to anything. She put her hands on his chest, holding them there as though she resisted him.

"The young girl was complicated as well. You have forgotten, Liam. It has always been complicated between us. It will never be easy."

His head close to her, the incredible blue eyes looked into hers, without mockery or anger anymore. Just tenderness as he said, "But you don't want me. You said so, remember?"

"I meant I didn't want to be one of your love-'em-and-leave-'em ladies."

"Do you want to be my complicated one?"

Difficult to refuse, when his lips grazed her cheek as he asked the question, her hands still resting on him as he moved his arm around her and held her close to him.

"Don't make me say it, Liam. I can't."

"I have to. The lady of the manor always has to give permission to the peasant to make love to her."

"There you go again!" Beth tried to break away from him, but he stopped her and she heard him laugh.

"I'm sorry, Beth. I'm always flippant when I'm the most serious. Listen — it's too damn hot standing here. Go to the Hudson, Bethie, take your baby and your entourage, and I'll come visit you. I'm not big on talk at such moments as these, but you and I have some sorting out to do. Agreed?"

Beth nodded, unable to trust herself to speak.

"Now, go to bed and get some sleep. I'm going to do the same thing, only I'll be lying there thinking about what a fool I am when I could be in your bed making love to you. Your fool, Bethie, just as you said I was."

He kissed her gently on the cheek, picked up his hat and let himself out, closing the door behind him.

Beth stood there, feeling the dampness of the fabric against her back where his hands had held her. She put up her hand and touched her cheek where he had kissed her. "Complicated," she said out loud, and the word seemed like an endearment to her. Life was only simple when one was directed by someone else in a narrow line that led from Fifth Avenue to the Hudson, on to Newport and back again. Complicated was the price she was prepared to pay for freedom, especially if Liam O'Connor was part of the bargain.

Beth had forgotten how much gold leaf there was inside the house on the Hudson. After the clean, spare lines of her own apartment, she felt oppressed by her mother's decor.

There was more to it than the decor, though she didn't want to think about the other reasons. As she had first walked into the green-and-white marble reception hall, Gisela Valeska's vision had come back to her. Beth looked up at the fanlight that was part of her earliest memories and some of the clairvoyant's words came flooding back.

"I see light through glass — gold, red, lemon-coloured light. You were happy here — but this is not then, this is not now, this will come."

It now seemed to her she had been happy here only in contrast to the rest of her life, to the brownstone prison on Fifth Avenue. Now, after one night in the *beaux arts* monument to money her father had built for her mother, she moved Liane and herself to the simpler Greek porticos and interior decor of the guesthouse which lay close to the main mansion. It contained more chintz and wickerwork and she felt comfortable there. Besides, her "staff," as her mother had put it, were a mere skeleton crew compared to the battalions it took to run the main house for the few weeks each year it was used by the family.

The Hudson Valley cast its spell once more as Beth walked along great alleys bordered by sumach and fir, pushing Liane's carriage and feeling the breeze on her face. She stood on the steep green cliffs above the Hudson River, looking down on the yachts and boats and across at the wooded slopes of the opposite bank with the Shawangunk Range in the distance. She felt the beauty of it fill her with the contentment it had given her as a child.

Not complete contentment, however, for she was waiting for Liam O'Connor to come and make love to her. There could be no pretending it was a decision made in the heat of the moment, some present moment that had overwhelmed and swept them away. It was something they had mutually agreed to, not in cold blood — no, never that — for she had time to think about it, to change her mind and withdraw. She suspected Liam had wanted it like that, to give her a time and space for reflection. "I'll come and visit you — we have some sorting out to do," was all he had said, and she herself had refused to put any sort of acceptance into words. "I can't say it," she had told him.

There was no saying to be done now, she knew that. It would happen; there was no longer room for self-deception. This was what she had wanted all those months ago when she had read the article in *Puck* and phoned its author. This was what she wanted here in the house on the Hudson, and there were no barriers anymore, only the waiting to be got through.

He did not keep her waiting long. One warm afternoon, Beth walked around the house from the lawn overlooking the river and he was there, standing by the porticoed front door, a valise at his feet, hat in hand, his shirt open at the neck. He smiled to see her coming toward him in her white dress, ruffles blowing in the breeze by the river, and his heartbeat quickened at her answering smile, the flush in her cheeks as she glanced at his valise.

"How did you get here? I had forgotten you'd have to make arrangements." So seductive, she thought, those Irish eyes that first startled me so across my mother's sitting room, and all I do is ask some pointless question in a voice that sounds prim and cold, even to me!

If there had indeed been a chill in her voice, Liam had not noticed it. He put out a hand and touched a strand of her hair, smoothing it away from her face, and his voice was gentle. "Oh you rich girls who don't have to think of such things! I flew through the air — no, I came by the Hudson River Day Line. Then a guy with a trap gave me a ride here." The hand that smoothed her hair caressed her shoulders, and they moved close to each other, their bodies touching, effortlessly, all tension gone. "Know what he said?"

Beth could feel the laughter and joy filling her, mingling with something far more powerful as his thighs touched hers and his hands stroked her back, the curve of her spine. "No. What did he say?" His voice came to her, muffled, as he kissed her neck, her hair.

"He said, 'You'll like it, working up there. He's a queer old dude, but he's fair.' "

He kissed her mouth even as she laughed. "I hope I can live up to my father's reputation."

"As a queer old dude?"

"Stop making me laugh, O'Connor. We have to talk."

"Darling Beth, I did say we had some sorting out to do, but I didn't come here to talk — I came here to make love to you, and we both of us know that. Let's stop fooling ourselves. Let's make love, Beth — what other way can we make sense of this crazy situation? Not by words, that's for sure — ah, God, Beth, say yes!"

In answer she took him by the hand and led him along the neatly raked gravel path that led to the great doorway of the main house. Beneath their feet, the fine loose stones crunched, the only sound in the warm summer air besides their breathing and the high-pitched whine of a cicada in a sumach over their heads. No words, he had said. He was right. Words would make no sense of anything. Better to act on impulse, rashly, foolishly, in the manner she had been taught to despise. Here, in the heady heat of a July afternoon, it was the only thing that made any sense to her.

It was dark inside the great house, cool and empty. Their footsteps echoed across the mosaic floor, quietening as they reached the rugs from Isfahan in the upper hallway that led to Beth's childhood bedroom.

Liam O'Connor looked around him at the panelled walls, the French paintings, the silk drapes around the bed, at the all-embracing luxury that had enveloped Elizabeth LaPierre Holman from the day she was born. How was it possible that he, Liam O'Connor, whose grandparents had clawed their way out of the hellhole of Bandit's Roost and Battle Alley, could be so crazy for this rich man's daughter — and the titled wife of a European degenerate, God help him! — that he could be standing here of his own free will surrounded by the proceeds of crooked stock deals, land fraud, tenement rents. Free will? He had none left. She had bought him with her millions, compromised his principles when she had offered him *Facets* on a golden platter. In the dim light filtering through the heavy tasselled drapes, he saw she was loosening her long dark hair with a slow sinuous movement of her arms, her sleeves falling away from the pale, creamy skin. Desire struck the breath from him as she unfastened the bodice of her dress.

"Beth, I love you." As his breath returned to him it was all he was able to say. Not the money, not her millions — it had happened in spite of the millions he hated so much. Just the girl, hesitating now as he stood there staring at her, the soft bodice of her dress held against the half-concealed curves of her breasts. He moved toward her and placed his hands over hers, taking them away, pulling the dress from her body. "Beth, I love you," he said as he undressed her, kissing her smooth skin as it was uncovered, desperately pulling off his own light summer clothes, repeating the same sentence over and over again. Naked now, kneeling beside the bed, he placed one hand over her breasts and cradled her chin with the other. Her dark eyes stared back at him, their expression beyond interpretation, fathomless.

"Won't you say it too? Is it only this foolish, crazy Irishman who'll say it?"

He could read those beautiful eyes now, and what he saw was anguish, and something more which he thought was fear. She looked away for a moment before answering. "I don't know! I still don't know! Look at the mistakes I've made in the name of love, Liam." He made a sudden movement and, as if she took it as rejection, she grasped his hands in hers, thrusting them between her thighs. It was a gesture so unadorned, so unlike anything he had imagined of her, when he had imagined such things, that he was sure she could read his amazement as he had seen her fear.

"Let's make sense by making love, Liam — no words. Show me, make love to me."

He made love to her as she asked, without words or laughter or dalliance. He was stronger, heavier than she had imagined when she, too, had imagined such things, and he was heavily muscled, his torso and thighs enveloping her, swallowing her up beneath him. This urgency unleashed upon her had nothing to do with flippancy and laughter, or love me and leave me, or anyone will do. His body came against her hard and fast and long, and she heard him cry out like a bull as he took her. Then it was her own voice that she heard, crying out his name.

"Oh my love."

"Close, Bethie, close. Careful, or you'll be saying it soon." He kissed her gently as he spoke, and the tenderness of the tone took away any sting there might have been in the words.

At least she now knew something she had not known before they had made love. She had to have him. It didn't matter that she couldn't say the words. Words did not make sense. Only what had passed between them made any sort of sense at all. She said his name; it was all she could find to say. "Liam. My Liam."

"That I am, and there's no getting away from it. You bowl me over, lady." His hands traced the lines of her body, the geography of this new erotic landscape. He felt her hands move almost tentatively over his back and thighs, the touch as light as a butterfly, and he was struck by the memory of the moment when she had taken his hands and thrust them against her.

"You are so muscled. Is it all that street-fighting you told me about?"

Liam laughed and placed her hand on his upper arm. She felt the muscle tighten and then relax beneath the skin. "More than street-fighting. I work out."

"Work out?" Beth moved her hand across his chest and he flexed the muscle there as her hand touched it.

"Yes — with boxers, professional fighters, for fun.

I like it. Biff, biff." Lightly, he brushed her chin with his closed fist, imitating the sound of the punches.

Beth took his fist and kissed it. "Why?"

"I was an incorrigible fighter, so my father decided that boxing would channel my aggression. He'd worked his way to law-abiding lawyer, and his father before him had worked his way up from the gutter, and he knew how quickly you could lose it all — particularly if you're Irish, and particularly in this tough town."

"That tough town."

"Right. I'd forgotten where we were." Liam sat up on the bed and looked around him, then back at Beth. Her long black hair covered the satin pillow and her skin gleamed white against the ivory sheets. She smiled at him and he covered his eyes. "Fifth Avenue princess, you dazzle me."

"I'm glad. It won't be easy for you to love me and leave me if I dazzle you."

She too had her uncertainties. In thinking of his own, he had forgotten that. He turned back to her, held her close against him. "Beth, I promise you — I, listen, I know why you said that and I'll tell you something. I'd have forced myself on you weeks ago, but I was scared too. I knew two years ago when I fell in love with you that it was trouble. There'd be no quick roll in the hay with you, and then off to fresh fields and pastures new." He pulled her up against him and looked around the room once more.

"Look at this, Beth — you don't even notice it, do you? I said don't let's talk, but — my God, have we got some talking to do! By rights, I should have been paralysed by all this — *stuff*, but all I could think of was you. This place scares me out of my wits!"

"You? Why you?" Beth looked at him, lost, won-

280

dering for a moment if he too understood her own
fear. "It scares me, and that's why Liane and I are
living in the guesthouse." He felt her shiver against
him, and the warm surface of her skin suddenly seemed
chill.

"Tell me."

When she had finished, she waited for him to laugh,
perhaps to kiss away her fears, to be amused at her
gullibility. Instead he said quietly, "You take this
woman quite seriously, don't you. She made an impression on you."

"Yes. I can understand why Max — why he —"
Beth stopped and Liam said nothing for a moment.
When he spoke again, she heard the roughness of anger
in the tone.

"I can't, but I won't pretend to be sorry. Whatever
you felt for me two years ago, we probably wouldn't
be here now if your husband had been to you what
he should have been."

Beth couldn't reply because she didn't know the
answer. Now that they had made love, it seemed
impossible to her that she would have denied him.
She ran her fingers through the dark, curly hair as
she had seen him do two years previously on Fifth
Avenue, losing herself in the gesture, in the feel of
his hands on her body, mouth on mouth, passion
increasing once more, the fears and doubts vanishing
with the return of desire. She heard herself cry out
on an inhalation of breath as if she would draw him
inside her, body and soul, in one intense spiralling
vortex.

Chapter Twenty-Seven

The House on the Hudson

Liam moved into the guesthouse, and into Beth's bedroom. He spent hours playing with Liane with an unselfconscious delight that Beth envied, talking baby talk to her and peeping at her through his fingers until the baby crowed with pleasure. The domestic staff were as amazed by this behaviour as they were by his obvious role in their mistress's life. As the nurse said to Cook, "If it wasn't for the fact that Madam was expecting when she came back from Europe, I'd think he was the father. And more's the pity he's not, for all the good that other foreign one is to Madam or Baby."

When moonlight silvered the river, they walked for miles, for darkness was their friend. They had agreed to keep a low profile in the area so as not to draw attention to themselves. Obviously they could not stop the usual gossip from the domestic or grounds staff, but they could avoid direct confrontation with her parents' set in such places as Saratoga Springs and certain resorts in the Adirondacks.

It was then they did the talking they had said they must do. Beth had so much to learn about Liam. When he told her about his grandfather working his way out of the Hell's Kitchen of Rat Trap and Ragpickers' Row, killing himself with work so that his son might become a lawyer and live in the discreet prosperity of London Terrace, Beth began to understand a little more about this complex man with whom she had fallen in love.

"You have told me more about your grandfather than you have about your father. Why is that?"

"Perceptive woman, aren't you? I have a problem talking about my father."

"Could it be that success gave him some of the qualities you despise?"

"Sharp Beth, my clever one! Yes. Worst of all, he became ashamed of his own father." Beth watched him clench and unclench his fists and swallow hard, as if he were close to tears. "God, Beth, the man was dying — dying of a life of fighting and working his guts out for his family, and my father would find any excuse not to go. I was the one who was with my grandfather when he died."

"No wonder you believe that riches corrupt. The wonder is that you had anything to do with me at all."

"Wonder indeed that I'm crazy about you, can't take

my eyes off you, can't take my hands off you. Talk to me, Beth. Explain to me why I love you. Tell me about yourself.''

But she couldn't, and besides, there was so little to tell. Her life was a straight, narrow line compared to Liam's, a life without shade or subtlety. Until he had come along, a life without dimension. "There is nothing to tell. I am what you see.''

"You *are* Circassian walnut, gold leaf, Italian marble?''

"I'm afraid so.''

"Then you are even more dangerous and mysterious. How could you have lured me into your arms?''

"Let's not try to understand — let's just remain enigmas to each other.''

In the stifling heat of the afternoons, the cooler hours of dusk and evening, they would return to the mansion to make love. All fear and inhibition gone, they would run together through the house, the sound of their laughter echoing through the oval reception hall, beneath the ancient Italian ceiling of the massive dining room. Liam would watch Beth dancing ahead of him along the upper corridor, shedding her light muslin dress as she went, laughing back at him. Her skin would become suddenly golden in the rays of the setting sun which filtered through the oval windows at the top of the staircase and dappled bronze lights in her dark hair, and it seemed to him she was indeed Circassian walnut and gold leaf, all the things he feared, everything he wanted and desired.

He told her his illusion, and watched the laughter leave her eyes. "Is this marble, Liam O'Connor? Is it?'' she demanded and pulled him down onto the priceless rugs and wound her arms around him, warm and gold from the sun, those arms that lured him and from which he had no desire ever to escape, nor did he have the will to do so.

Eventually, however, he knew he had to return to New York. He had difficulty persuading Beth to stay on awhile longer. "Do it for Liane, Beth. I've got work to catch up with by now, and if you come back with me, I'll get nothing done." He hesitated a moment, and then forced himself to bring up the matter he had not wanted to think about during the last few weeks.

"I can't live with you in New York, Beth — you know that?"

She hadn't been thinking ahead at all, and although she asked him, "Why not?" she knew the answer.

"I know you'll quote Moravian troubles and Viennese clairvoyants at me, but we can't forget the real possibility that the count could come back into your life."

"Please, Liam, don't."

"I don't want to, believe me, but I can't live with you, and we've got to be realistic about it. Besides, we cannot entirely forget your parents."

She knew he was right. She hated the thought of parting from Liam, but compared to the pain of the past, this hurt seemed only a moment of inconvenience in the flow of her present happiness.

After Liam had gone, Beth occupied herself by writing about New York and Newport society as her mother had known it, as Gloria Baker had once suggested. She spent more time talking to Liane than

she had done before Liam's arrival. She found baby
talk difficult, so she settled for talking as if to another
adult friend. It seemed to work for both of them. The
baby smiled at her mother with as much pleasure as
if she had recited a nursery rhyme, or played peekaboo
as Liam had done.

When she finally decided to go back to the city,
Beth wrote ahead so that Liam would know she was
arriving. Within an hour of her return he was at the
door of her apartment. She knew as soon as she saw
the expression on his face that something was wrong.
Before she could speak, he held her tightly in his arms
and started to explain.

"I think your clairvoyant is in town, Beth. And
whatever the Serbs or the Slovenes may be up to, you
know what you said to me. That you were safe as
long as she was in Vienna."

"Where did you see her?"

"I didn't — I heard about her at Martinka's. It's
the magicians' holy of holies, a supply house on the
west side of Sixth Avenue, between Twenty-ninth and
Thirtieth."

"Can we find out more?"

"Even better. We'll go and see her."

Chapter Twenty-Eight

New York

It was still warm in the city, but the humidity was less oppressive than it had been before Beth's departure for the Hudson Highlands. They took a streetcar to Martinka's and Beth found out more about the place.

"What were you doing at a supply house for magicians?"

Liam shifted uneasily and squeezed Beth's hand. "Checking on Anna. Let me finish before you jump all over me. Anna is a Bosnian Serb by origin, and she's got herself mixed up in some sort of organization supporting revolution in the homeland. As far as I can make out, they want to get Macedonia from Turkey and Bosnia-Herzegovina from Austria."

"Macedonia again, Austria again."

"Small world, isn't it?"

"But why here in New York? What can a Serb back in the homeland want from someone so far away?"

"Money, money, money to flow back to the freedom-fighters, that's what."

"What's Martinka's got to do with all of this?"

"Two brothers, Antonio and Francis, run the place. They've been here a few years now — used to be on Broadway near Duane, moved to Sixth Avenue about five years ago. They were born in Prague and then moved to Vienna, to some big theatre of magic there before they emigrated. A lot of immigrants from that part of Europe drop in and out of the place every day, and it's become a kind of informal exchange centre for information. As far as I can tell, Francis and Antonio have nothing to do with secret societies or subversive organizations, but they do know of Gisela Valeska. They happened to be talking about her to a customer when I was there."

"Will we see her there?"

"No. Francis' wife, Pauline, is trying to arrange for us to attend her first séance — or whatever it is a clairvoyant does. I said I was a newspaper reporter and wanted to cover it."

It would have been difficult to miss Martinka's. Above the entrance were the words Palace of Magic in gold letters, and the window was filled with the bizarre and curious objects of a magician's trade. The interior was dark, gaslit, lined with shelves stacked with more of what the window had contained. A skull, gleaming with a macabre whiteness, stood on a table near the entrance to another room in the back. In contrast with her exotic surroundings, the woman standing behind the counter looked reassuringly ordinary. She was hemming what looked like a triangular flag, and she looked up from her work and smiled at them.

"Mr. O'Connor, isn't it? We got the reply yesterday, and Francis has written you a letter of introduction. Here you are." She reached under the counter and handed Liam an envelope. "The lady is staying at the Waldorf, but her performance is in a private room at Rector's." She gave a little laugh. "Francis says I shouldn't call it a performance. She's no player of tricks, according to my husband. She's real."

Beth looked at Liam and he could see the reflection of an intense emotion on her face. "Why does he think so?" he asked.

"Because a friend he respects from the Kraky-Baschik theatre of magic in Vienna investigated her for — well, for someone. He could see no tricks. There were things he couldn't explain."

Outside on the street Liam put his arm around Beth. "You're shivering. Are you afraid your husband will be there?"

"No, and I'm not really afraid. That's not what I'm feeling. You haven't seen her yet, so it's difficult to explain. Rector's — isn't that one of the lobster palaces on Broadway?"

"That's right. Just the place to meet an actress or to take a dancer for a late-night supper. It'll be interesting to see who's in the audience. Husbands and wives, or husbands and mistresses."

"Or wives and lovers."

"Don't, Beth." Liam's voice was rough. "I'm not crazy about being reminded of my role in your life as kept man."

Shocked, Beth stopped walking and turned to him.

How can you say that, Liam? You support yourself; you are your own man."

Liam put his arm around her shoulders and held her close to him. "I can say it, Countess, because to all intents and purposes I am employed by you. And as to being my own man —" His hand caressed her back, oblivious of the passers-by. "That I am not, my love. I am yours, your man. For better, for worse, I am yours."

Beth was reminded of what she didn't want to remember: that she was married, that she had taken a lover, and that this man in her life cared far more than she did about both of these things.

Beth gave a great deal of thought to what she would wear to Rector's. Finally she chose a dress in a heavily embossed white brocade, with the revers of the bodice cut low over her breasts and the shoulders veiled in ivory lace that rose to the point of her chin. The skirt was cut on the bias, smooth over the hips and flaring out at the hem. For her jewelry she had chosen diamonds and black pearls. Her maid dressed her hair high on her head in elaborate coils, and a small headdress of tiny black feathers, with one long white feather curling around one side of her face.

Liam stared at her, transfixed. "You look magnificent. You look about ten years older. You terrify me."

"Wonderful." She spun out the first syllable of the word in her deep voice. Suddenly she seemed a stranger to him, not the girl whose body he knew inch by marvellous inch, whose hands upon him filled him with a sense of his own manhood he had never experienced before.

Beth smiled and turned to pick up her wrap from the chair beside her, and to his relief Liam saw again the girl in her blue dress in his Greenwich Village rooms, the young woman unfastening the bodice of another white dress in the house on the Hudson.

Rector's reminded Beth of Vienna. The decor was richly embellished, elaborately rococo, a mixture of glossy dark woods, scarlet velvet, and damask, gilt everywhere and on everything. There was a note of abandon in the laughter of the women, an extroverted ebullience in the men's voices that seemed more reminiscent of Europe to Beth than the New York she had known. The members of her new circle of friends had changed that view, but this was her first close-up look at the city's painted and perfumed women, at nattily dressed men with heavy gold chains across embroidered vests, diamonds big as pigeon eggs on their fingers. Somewhere in the background she could hear gypsy violins.

An attendant escorted them to one of the private rooms upstairs, examined their invitation, and ushered them through the door. The room was already quite full, and all eyes focused on them as they were shown to their seats.

"Do people know you, or is it because you're such a stunner?"

"Both." Her smile dazzled him, and her eyes glittered as though she had been drinking champagne. "I recognize a few of my parents' friends — some influential people."

"The psychic world is very chìc at the moment with your set — your ex-set."

On a raised dais before them two men were setting up a small table covered in a black cloth. From behind the heavy velvet curtains emerged a portly middle-aged gentleman. His flowered waistcoat emphasized the well-fed rotundity of this figure, and the rich voice booming from beneath his whiskers suggested fine amontillado, the crisp skin of a juicy canvasback duck.

"Ladies and gentlemen! Please give your warmest welcome to a lady whose beauty is matched only by the brilliance of her great gift. Welcome to the fair city of New York! Welcome, Gisela Valeska!"

There was a moment's pause, a murmur of expectation, and Gisela Valeska entered through the curtains, the crystal and the tarot in her hands.

She was more remarkable to look at than Beth remembered. The sweep of her long, dark eyes, the sensuousness of the full red mouth above the strong, square jawline were dazzling. Her dark hair was fastened up, but a few long tendrils escaped around the hairline, black as ebony against the creamy skin. Her earrings reached to her shoulders, and the diamonds in them blazed in the lights.

What was most startling to Beth was the gown Gisela had chosen to wear. She remembered her as a tall, slim figure sheathed in purple in a room of brilliant colours, standing before a painting in vivid shades. Tonight, however, she was wearing a dress of white satin. Beth heard Liam's intake of breath beside her, felt the movement of his body as he turned toward her. She turned to him, heard the shock in his voice.

"She's your goddamned double!"

There was nothing to say. Was that why she had chosen to wear white? Because she had wanted to say with her appearance, "I am not like this woman. There is no link between us. I deny whatever there is that binds us together."

Gisela sat down behind the low table and placed the crystal and the cards on it. Up to this point she had been sombre, almost expressionless, her eyes fixed somewhere beyond her audience. Suddenly she looked at them and smiled and there were murmurs of appreciation. A couple of the men whistled softly, and Gisela turned in their direction and laughed, a provocative throaty sound. When she spoke her voice was as Beth remembered it: husky, lightly accented, her English fluent.

"Ladies and gentlemen, you are here to see signs and wonders, and that is what I shall give you. But there will be no puffs of smoke, no apparitions, no strange voices emanating from my mouth." Her long fingers lightly touched her lips and her gaze languidly swept around the room. "No. The signs and wonders I shall reveal will be judged by you in the coming weeks, months, and years. Yet there will be some you can judge now, for they will come from inside some of the people in this room — from the mind and the heart." Here, Gisela allowed her fingers to move over the gleaming satin of her dress. "So, if you do not want the truth, if you fear what I may reveal — and I will see many things in the next hour — perhaps it would be best to leave now."

The glittering dark eyes surveyed the room. No one moved.

"So." Gisela's gaze returned to the crystal. Her hands moved over it, describing its shape without touching it, and her breath was audible in the silence that had fallen over the crowded room. When she next spoke it was to say only one word.

"Gold." There was a long pause before she spoke again, and her eyes never left the crystal. "There is much gold in this room — honestly and dishonestly is it here. But that is the natural state of things in this world, and so it is here in this country, the *goldene medina* of my father's people. These are good years that shine like gold itself, but some in this room will suffer — four, five years from now. I see gold again, but this time I see a city — not this one — on a beautiful bay that shines in the sun — that is the gold maybe? — no, no, it is not — I see an entrance, a name — golden again — Golden Gate?"

Someone muttered, "San Francisco," and another voice asked, "Is there going to be another strike?" Gisela seemed unaware of the interruption and continued speaking. "There is terror in the streets — a riot perhaps? — no, not caused by man but by the earth itself tearing apart, bringing suffering to many in that city of gold." She paused here for a moment and then said, "I see a six — and now I see a seven, and there is gold again, but in this city now, and there is fear again for many, close to the time of which I have just spoken — I see copper and bronze, they are significant — and gold disappearing — vaults, panic — removal. Some who are rich in this room will know poverty once again."

There was a murmur of alarm in the room and this time Gisela sensed it. She looked up from the crystal and smiled at her audience. "But it is better to be forewarned, no? We get the bad away first so that I can tell of the good — and there is so much good, so much that is fascinating about some of you that I know! How do I know? Ah, you judge me, tell me if I am right. You —" She turned to a man sitting in the front row and addressed him by name. He looked startled and wary, then gradually relaxed and started to laugh with the rest of the audience as Gisela told him what he did for a living, hinted delicately but suggestively at some of his personal likes and dislikes that had to do with the lady who sat by his side. The audience began to roar with amusement and appreciation. Swiftly, expertly, she passed from one to another, sometimes addressing the man or woman, sometimes looking into the speculum. Once or twice she asked a member of the audience to come up and lay out the tarot cards for her. By now the room was completely under her spell. Under cover of the audience reaction Liam spoke to Beth.

"She's very good at what she does — this part is her act and she's done her homework well. But that first stuff — I don't know, but I got the feeling she didn't plan any of that. Notice how quickly she switched what she was doing when she realized the effect it was having? She's not convinced me yet — maybe she's not entirely a performer, but when she is one, she's the best."

Liam had barely finished speaking when there was a sudden movement from the stage. Gisela Valeska was standing up, her hands pressed against the table, her eyes staring into the distance once more. When she spoke there was a new urgency in her voice, a sense of it being driven by some force beyond the woman herself.

"There is a wind coming from the north and a great cloud — brightness and fire — I see four living creatures, but they are not human, for they have four faces and four wings, and they shine, they shine like copper, like bronze, like gold. Something burns in the midst of them like torches, or burning coals. Beneath them is a great wheel shining like crystal, and the sky above them is like the crystal also — and their wings beat like thunder, like the sound of fighting and tumult, a war to tear the nations asunder, somewhere beyond the golden city and the empty vaults of gold. But you will be drawn into it, and my country — ah, my country — gone, gone forever — changed and crushed beneath those crystal wheels, those shining creatures — always, forever —"

This time there was not a sound from the audience. This was something beyond agitation about dwindling bank reserves or devastating acts of nature. For a moment all were held in a silence as inexplicable as the cosmic events the clairvoyant had described.

It was Gisela herself who first broke the silence. With a sudden movement she turned, eyes staring blindly, in Beth's direction. Unfocused, empty, they stared through and beyond Beth.

"The Empress," she said. "The Empress is here."

Slowly, as if something were pulling her upright, Beth got to her feet. The two women in white stood and looked at each other across the room, across the heads of the men and women who were invisible to them both at that moment. Beth spoke first.

"You are right. I am here, High Priestess."

"Empress."

Gisela smiled and Beth felt the tears well up in her eyes, but whether they were of sadness or anger or fear, she couldn't tell. Then Gisela extended her hand and indicated Liam sitting beside her.

"I see you have brought the Fool to meet me, Countess," she said.

Disconcerted, Liam looked from one woman to the other as the room exploded into laughter around them.

Chapter Twenty-Nine

New York

The white muslin curtains fluttered gently on a breath of air that had blown across Central Park from the East River. Liam looked at Beth. She was sitting on the velvet cushions, staring out of the window, her face concealed from him.

"I understand," said Liam.

Beth turned toward him slowly, as if waking up out of a trance. "But you still don't quite believe her, do you?"

"Depends what you mean by believe. She's very impressive, however —" Liam hesitated.

"Tell me. I'd like to be convinced she is less than she seems, I truly would."

"I said I understand, because she casts a spell when you're there with her and I got carried away by it, believe me." Liam went to sit by Beth on the window seat and started to tick off on his fingers the main points of Gisela's performance.

"First and foremost, she'd made sure who was coming. It was by invitation only and someone had given her the dirt on a selection of people from the audience. Easily done. Agreed? Having said that, I have to admit that's the easiest part to explain, and it could even cover how she knew about you being there, and about me."

"She knew about you in Vienna."

"So you say, but she could just have been guessing there'd be a man in your life by now. And, hell, she knew tonight there was a man in your life, because I was sitting right there beside you. Anyway, let's go on to the more difficult stuff — all that rigmarole about gold. You don't have to be a clairvoyant to guess we'll have another financial crisis in the next few years. They come and go, Beth. We had a beaut in 1893, with dwindling gold reserves, the Pullman strike, and a drought affecting the corn crop. Your parents' friends went so far as to cancel various social events, which'll show you how serious it was."

"How about San Francisco?"

"Beth, honey, San Francisco is built on a fault! You could get an earthquake anytime. It's already been shaken several times, and that sure as hell would lead to panic in the streets."

He demolished Gisela's predictions so easily. Even Beth herself was beginning to wonder how she could have been so overwhelmed. "The men with wings — how about all that? Where did that come from?"

Liam put his hands on either side of Beth's face, blue eyes twinkling at her. "When you were a little girl, were you a good little girl, and didn't you always go to church like a good little girl?"

"Of course I did, but I don't see what that has to do with this."

"Plenty. Did you read your Bible?"

"Only the bits Mama told me to read."

"There's the problem! You were too good. I'm an Irish Catholic — well, was — and I recognized those men with wings. Come straight from Ezekiel, they do."

"Ezekiel?"

"Yup. An Old Testament prophet with as great a sense of the dramatic as Gisela Valeska. Can't remember much of it, but enough to recognize it. 'As I looked, behold, a stormy wind came out of the north and a great cloud with brightness round about it — and from the midst of it came four living creatures — and over the heads of the living creatures was a firmament shining like crystal' — something like that."

"Was he talking about war?"

"As far as I can recall he was describing the Godhead, but it's still great stuff for describing war."

He made it all sound so unremarkable. Beth put her arms around him. "I admit what you say convinces my head, but it makes no impression on my heart or my soul or *something* in me. I can't explain why, but that's how it is."

"There's something else this Gisela Valeska has

going for her, Beth. She's beautiful. Many of the mediums and clairvoyants in New York at the moment are homely, to put it charitably, and — don't get angry with me, my darling — beauty makes a hell of a difference, whether you like it or not. This woman is stunning."

"You are my *Doppelgänger*," Gisela had said to her. "She's your goddamned double," Liam had said that evening when he had seen Gisela. Why that should make her feel bound to her husband's mistress she didn't know, but it did. Beth took Liam's large boxer's hands in her own, spreading her slender fingers against his and pulling them into her lap.

"You've answered all my questions except one, and only she can answer that for me."

"I know. I know that's why you'll see her again. A word of advice: Don't go see her at the Waldorf. See her here, on your territory, Beth. Invite her to come here, to you."

Alike and yet unalike, similar and yet different. This time Gisela Valeska was wearing the vivid colours in which Beth had first seen her, a walking dress of scarlet with diamond-shaped inserts of white lace, lace lining the scarlet collar pulled up around her face. As she looked around Beth's living room, Beth remembered how she had looked around Gisela's apartment off the Ringstrasse.

"Your Fool has changed you."

"You seem unchanged to me."

Gisela laughed. "I have no Fool in my life." She removed her long white gloves and sat down. "You wish to know about the count."

"Is he in Vienna?"

"Yes. He is part of my reason for being here in New York."

"Selfish as this sounds, you were some kind of safeguard for me when you were in Vienna."

"You are right." There was no vanity or pleasure in the tone of Gisela's voice. "As for myself, I intend to spend only a short time in New York — long enough for some obligations I have to fulfill — and then I go on tour. And I have acquired a protector." Her smile was seductive, slightly amused, as if she had surprised herself. "I couldn't in Vienna."

"Max would have hurt you, or him."

"Oh no, that is not the reason." The amusement was gone now from her smile. "When he was near me, I could think of no one but Max." Gisela put up her hand and stroked the high collar. "An ocean between us has made a difference. In Vienna he burned me, consumed me; I could see or think of no one else."

To an outsider, Gisela's words would have seemed overly dramatic. To Beth, who knew only too well what she meant, they were only a statement of fact.

At that moment the sound of Liane's laugh reached them from a room nearby. Gisela smiled at Beth. "Your child?"

"Yes, you were right in Vienna. I have a daughter."

"May I see her?"

Beth carried Liane into the room and Gisela swept her up into her arms, kissing her, talking in English and Viennese. "But she's so wonderful! How lucky you are!"

"You think so?"

"Of course. Don't you?"

Beth didn't reply. She watched Gisela settle back on the sofa with Liane in her arms, watched the unselfconscious ease with which she responded to the baby's gurgles. Then she said, "I listened to what you had to say about Max and I felt nothing, nothing at all. I cannot imagine how I could ever have wanted to kill you for such a man."

"For such a man." Over the head of the daughter Max had never seen, Gisela looked at Beth. "Such a man, Countess, is easy to kill for. You forget, so let me remind you. If he wishes to charm you, he is difficult to resist. Do not be lulled into a false sense of security. When we spoke before, I wasn't sure that you wanted to give him up. Is it the man you were with the other night who has changed your mind?"

"Yes."

"All the more reason to be careful. Max makes a fetish of jealousy and honour. With him, these things are at the root of his existence."

"But he doesn't want me!"

"Ah, Beth, appearances are everything in a life like his. Have you ever thought about why he is still in the army? It gives him cachet in the empire, and it also provides the occasional danger that adds spice to his life. The facade is everything, Countess, and the heart means little to such a man and the society he represents."

"And yet you love him."

"Do I, Beth? What *is* love?"

Of all the questions in the world, this was the one she was least qualified to answer. Beth shook her head, speechless.

It was at this moment that Liam arrived, letting

himself in and walking through to the sitting room. The two women and the child were close together, and as the two dark heads lifted at his entrance, he had a sense of some secret between them, a fusion that went beyond the extraordinary resemblance of these two beautiful women. Gisela Valeska spoke first.

"I saw you in Vienna."

"So Beth tells me."

"And you're not sure you believe. Well, I cannot blame you. Such a mixture of trickery and reality, my act — is it not?"

She saw he was disconcerted and smiled at him the dazzling smile he had seen at Rector's. Then she turned to Beth and said, "Ah, *liebe* Beth, that dimple, those eyes, that body — he is so gorgeous, no?"

The laughter of the two women rose in the twilight that had begun to move into the room, and the baby smiled with them as though she were part of the female conspiracy that bound them together, leaving him beyond their magic circle. Beth held out her hand to him, drawing him to her. "Liam."

"Liam — Liane." Gisela looked from the child on her lap to the man. "Beth, he is not the only Fool walking on the edge of the precipice. You have many things to hide."

Liam blinked, as though he were coming out of a trance. "I've been talking to a good friend of yours, Miss Valeska," he said abruptly. "Colonel Edward Delaney."

"Ah, Eddie!" Gisela turned delightedly to Beth. "This is the person I spoke of — he arranged the tour for me."

"What do you know of him?" Liam asked her.

"All that matters, sir. He has plenty of money and he is crazy for me — that's what he says to me: 'I am so crazy for you, baby,' he says. How I love the way you speak here! So — so picturesque!" Gisela laughed and then looked at Liam with some anxiety. "He has plenty of money, hasn't he?"

"Plenty, but not much of it honestly come by."

Gisela shrugged her shoulders. "Then we should suit each other very well, no? I also come by my money by uncommon means, wouldn't you agree, Mr. O'Connor? He is having a railway car fitted out for me, and we shall travel all over — Boston, Philadelphia, Chicago."

Liam looked now at Beth. "What about your husband?"

Beth replied with a calmness she was far from feeling. "Yes, he may well come here, and that's why Gisela is leaving New York as soon as possible. My guess is that he will go first to my parents — bridges to mend and so on. Max is good at that. Jonty says they don't know about you; they just think I'm mixed up in some artsy Greenwich Village set."

"Jonty? Oh, right, one of the little brothers of the rich." Beth saw Liam's mouth twist in contempt.

"They have their uses. Personally, I think Max will go after Gisela, but if he knew about you, then you might be in more danger than me."

Gisela agreed. "I don't think he would kill a woman for love." She had spoken almost casually, but no sooner had she finished her sentence than her eyes widened and her body went rigid. The child in her arms started to cry. Beth took Liane from Gisela. "She's probably tired. I'll take her to her nurse."

When she returned, Liam was giving Gisela a glass of brandy. She looked up at Beth and smiled apologetically. "Forgive me — a momentary discomfort and the child sensed it. I really must go." She seemed suddenly remote, strained. "Perhaps you would come and see my travelling circus, Beth."

Deliberately, Beth tried to lighten the mood. "I'd love to, if only to see this Eddie who's so crazy for you."

Gisela laughed, but the tension was still plainly there.

After she had left, Beth questioned Liam about Colonel Edward Delaney. "Is he really disreputable, Liam?"

"Oh yes, a real shyster — charming, clever, and completely unscrupulous. He was born somewhere in the South. I don't know too much about his background, but he was up on oil-stock fraud charges and got off on a technicality, something to do with the charges being laid in one state when the offences occurred in another. At the moment he's involved in the building of rail cars, and he's also connected with the publishing of *City Highlights*, which makes *Town Topics* read like a church periodical — and I don't have to tell you about that little number."

"Not for babes, prudes, idiots, or dudes — I know. It would explain where Gisela got her information for the evening at Rector's."

"Right, and probably he helped her with the guest list as well. It struck me at the time they were an unusual cross section of New York society, but Eddie Delaney's friendships cut right across class lines."

"Is he really a colonel?"

"I think so. I've heard there was a little matter of diverting treasury funds in Alabama at one point in his career, so he got out of the army." Liam looked sombrely at Beth. "I hope Gisela Valeska is as clever as she seems. You need a long spoon to sup with the devil, and this guy's for sure one of the devil's disciples, if not the devil himself."

"It's not the devil's disciple she has to fear," was Beth's reply. She looked at the sofa where Gisela had sat; she remembered the slender, scarlet-clad body rigid with fear, and the expression in her eyes. She remembered now when she had seen it before. It had been in Vienna, when Gisela had visualized the house on the Hudson and had fainted at what she had seen there.

Chapter Thirty

New York

The walls of the rail car were of inlaid wood, the lamps of brass. The floor was covered with Persian rugs and the luxuriant pelts of various exotic and unfortunate wild beasts. There was coloured glass in the windows, and both doors and windows were hung with crimson velvet draperies. A vast brass bed dominated the adjoining sleeping quarters furnished with heavy mahogany furniture and foliage and flowers.

"Its a palace on wheels — fit for a king," said Beth in admiration.

"Or the queen of clairvoyants, ma'am." Colonel Edward Delaney was six feet tall and fifty years old;

his personality seemed overpowering in the furniture-filled carriage. The colour of his clothing was subdued, but the stock in the neck of his shirt was a vivid green, pinned with a diamond, and there was a doorknob of a diamond on one finger.

But this was no rough diamond of a man, however unrestrained his sartorial splendour. His voice had the same honeyed lilt as Beth's Grandmother LaPierre, and his smooth-as-cream manners did not appear to be a recent acquisition, a thinly veneered part of a poseur's stock in trade. Beth had felt the power of his charm from the moment she met him, and she had to admit he was very different from what she had expected — a Diamond Jim Brady, perhaps, whom she had once seen at the Hotel Lafayette with his actress-mistress, the golden Lillian Russell. Apart from the spectacular gems worn by both men, they had little in common, including the size of their cigars. As he spoke, the colonel was extracting a small, slender cigar from a box labelled Between the Acts, and he asked Beth's permission before lighting it.

"I wish we could persuade you, Countess, to travel with us. The showman in me hates to see such a resemblance go to waste! Two beautiful women, one the mirror image of the other — it'd cause a sensation, ma'am. Won't you think about it?"

"I'm afraid, Colonel Delaney, that I have commitments here in New York. There's not only my daughter, but the birth of the new publication I'm involved with."

Liam had refused to come with her, reminding her that where Gisela was, so might the count be as well.

"Only dudes like Eddie Delaney fight duels anymore in this country. I can only use my fists, and I know what that bastard of yours would do. He'd refuse to fight back and call me out. It wouldn't be the first time Eddie Delaney's been in such a situation."

"He's not my bastard, Liam."

"Yes, he is, Beth my love, and you're only postponing the moment when you have to make a decision about him. I think you should divorce him."

Divorce. He said it with such ease! Beth thought about her mother and father, and of her Aunt Medora. In spite of everything, she couldn't help thinking of the devastation such a decision would cause her mother, which would be compounded by her remarriage to a penniless Irishman.

But more than that, beyond that, was the thought of Max. Possessive, proud, unpredictable as he was, it was far safer not to draw his attention to her life in any way. Here, in the presence of Gisela Valeska, she was even more aware of the need for avoiding his renewed interest. She looked across the over-embellished rail car at Gisela.

"May I ask you about something you said the other night at Rector's?"

"Of course, but I cannot promise to remember. Some of it, yes, because it came from Eddie, but much of it is lost to me."

"I was wondering if you know the writings of the prophet Ezekiel?"

"Ezekiel? — No. Should I?"

"Something you said was very like his words. He is an Old Testament prophet, from the Bible."

Gisela threw back her head, her laughter cascading. "I have no knowledge of the Bible, Countess! Many in my mother's profession went faithfully, or dutifully, to church, but not my mother. She told me she had no time or need for such pretence, and the opera school had no religious instruction. If I spoke such words, it is possible I heard them somewhere, but I have no recollection of it."

"I see." There was nothing further Beth wanted to ask. She believed and Liam did not, and repeating Gisela's answer to him would make not the slightest difference. She changed the subject. "Where do you go on your tour?"

"Boston, New Haven, Hartford, Philadelphia, Chicago, then on to the South and to New Orleans," replied the colonel, smiling at Gisela. Ruefully, Beth realized that Gisela would soon have seen more of her country than she had

As the thought crossed her mind, so did the face of her husband; Max, laughing, teasing, waltzing around the foyer of their Ringstrasse *Palais*, his great cloak swirling to some unheard music in the air.

Her eyes caught Gisela's and she knew that the clairvoyant was aware of her thoughts, as if in that moment her forehead was transparent and their minds were as one. Colonel Delaney spoke.

"I'll leave you two ladies alone for a while. An honour to have met you, Countess." He bowed to Beth and said to Gisela, "I'll not be far away." Their eyes met in an exchange of undisguised erotic intimacy before he left the carriage.

Gisela Valeska surveyed Countess Elizabeth von

Schönstein. The big, curly haired Irishman had indeed changed Max's wife from the lost, deranged creature she had met in Vienna. It was difficult to imagine this self-possessed woman crouching in a street with a knife in her hand, hell-bent on either killing her or self-destruction. "Well," she said, "do you like him?"

"I don't know, but I can certainly see why you do."

Gisela laughed. "He is so charming, no? Such a gentleman!" Suddenly she was serious. "I don't know what you may imagine of me or my life, or even why I should want you to know this, but he is only my second man."

Beth was so taken aback that she couldn't think of an adequate response. Gisela continued. "I met him at the Waldorf-Astoria, in the Palm Garden. We were introduced by my contact in New York, who had been talking to him in the men's café — Stockbrokers, is it not called? — and he paid court to me from the moment we met. Flowers, gifts, pretty words, and soon we were together." The laughter was back in Gisela's voice as she added, "Don't worry, I'll not bore you with intimate details. Such gossip doesn't interest me as much as it did my mother — ach, how she loved her *Tratsch*! — I like only useful gossip."

"Useful for what?" Beth asked. Gisela didn't answer, and her next remark made it clear she was thinking now of other concerns. "Remember what I saw in the speculum in Vienna, Empress. Whatever it was, and it was not clear, don't let your love for this man blind you to that vision."

The two women looked at each other, silent. There

was little further to say. What passed between them took place on another level and had already been communicated.

Beth had left by the time Colonel Eddie Delaney returned. He found Gisela sitting before the mirror in her sleeping compartment dressed in a tea gown of garnet silk and brushing out her long black hair. He slid his hands over her shoulders to caress her breasts beneath the loose wrap. Gisela leaned back against him, allowing sensation to wash over her, filling her with nothing but desire, aware of nothing but the erotic response of her body and his.

"Ah, Eddie, that feels good — harder, closer." She put her hands over his, massaging them even more firmly against her, feeling his own arousal behind her.

Eddie Delaney had disarmed her with his pretty accent, the vocabulary that sounded so exotic to her, the array of offerings that had arrived at her hotel door. Once in her bed he had charmed her with his complete absorption in her, his fascination with every inch of her body. He set about love-making with a single-minded determination — as if he had a plan of campaign — that Gisela found quite entrancing.

Besides, it couldn't have worked out better than that the man who knew so much of the intrigue and secret life of this amazing city should have proven so attractive to her. It had not been planned that they should sleep together — at least, she didn't think it had been intended. He had seemed so foreign, so American, and that had been exotic in itself. Now, with his talk of honour, and protecting a lady, and the duels he had fought in cities with names so unusual she could barely pronounce them, he seemed more Viennese than the Viennese. That too could have its uses. Heaven forbid it should be necessary, but it gave her an extra feeling of security all the same.

"Anyone ever told you that that little girl looks just like you?"

"Yes. I called her my *Doppelgänger* once." Pinpricks of light sparkled before her eyes and she closed them, concentrating on the feel of Eddie Delaney's hands. Kneeling on the floor behind her, he pulled open her gown, stroking her belly, her thighs, his lips against her neck and bare shoulders.

"What's that mean?"

"My double — it's from an old German folk tale. Not a good thing, Eddie, to meet your double."

"Why's that?" Eddie Delaney came around between Gisela and the mirror, his arms around her waist. She held his head against her and felt his mouth on her flesh start to erase the fear created by the aura of light she saw in the mirror. Still the words came to her, tumbling out unbidden.

"Because one of the two has to die, Eddie. One has to die."

She saw in the glass Max's face, rosy in the light from the window of another railway carriage, when she had been a little girl and he had promised her the world.

Chapter Thirty-One

New York

Beth got back to her apartment to find Henry and Jonty Shotover waiting for her. Overjoyed, she flung her arms around her brother. "I'm so glad to see you! It's been so long. Where were you all summer, after you finished at Tübingen?"

"Travelling, mostly in Italy — Beth, Jonty and I have to talk to you."

She knew immediately what was wrong. "Max is in New York."

"Yes. He's at the Fifth Avenue house at the moment. Mama is away, but he's doubtless regaling Father with tales of battles against wild Slavs and the need for his apparent desertion of his wife and daughter. He'll be here shortly."

"Do you want us to stay?" Jonty asked.

"No, I'll see him on my own. I want to talk about the possibility of — of divorce." Beth could hear the tremor in her own voice as she spoke the word. "Or raise the subject, or something. I'm not sure until I see him."

"I wouldn't do that, Beth." It was Jonty who spoke.

"You're just thinking about Mama."

"No, I'm not. Believe it or not, I'm thinking about you. We've heard rumours that the count is spending wildly — there was one party in Paris that cost literally thousands of dollars — quite put Boni de Castellane to shame, we gather. A divorce would mean losing his monthly allowance and having to live on the original settlement. I wouldn't be surprised if a fair amount of that wasn't already gone. If you bring the matter up, you could find yourself in a lot of trouble."

Beth looked at them both despairingly. "What shall I do?"

"Go along with the way things are for now. If you really want a divorce eventually, make absolutely sure you have grounds. Maybe desertion is a possibility — I don't know, but with the hunting season coming up in Bavaria he's not likely to stay here," said Henry. "For God's sake, be careful what you tell him. I'd guess this is just a play-it-safe visit, and he'll be gone in a few weeks."

Beth shook her head. "Do you know about Gisela Valeska?"

Henry and Jonty looked surprised. "Sure," said her brother. "She's the talk of the town — what's that got to do with this?"

Beth felt drained at the thought of trying to explain everything. "She's — she was Max's mistress, and he's come here because of her, not because of me."

Jonty looked impatient. "Come on, Beth. Women

like that are a dime a dozen to men like the count. No, it's to assure the continuation of his income, that's what he's here for. Reassure him and he'll go away happy. He'll not find it in his interests to listen to any story he may hear about — er —"

"About Liam?"

"Right, and that's the other reason I don't suggest talking about desertion. The least he'd do is threaten to countersue, Beth."

"I thought I was free," she said. "I'm as trapped as I ever was."

Jonty's smile was sunny, belying the words that followed. "Heck, Beth, we're all trapped. Didn't you know that?"

Even as he spoke, the bell of the apartment rang and they heard Max's voice in the hall. Beth had forgotten its smoky quality, the lilt of his Viennese accent. She had forgotten how seductive it could be.

"Beth, *Liebchen*! My God, but you are so beautiful!"

Before she could speak she was swept into his arms. The smooth skin that always seemed slightly cold was against hers, the dark eyes that always seemed slightly feverish looked into hers. What does he see? she wondered. Please, let him see nothing, nothing at all Almost instantly he released her. "Mr. Shotover — and Henry — what a pleasure! How was Tübingen? And Italy, wonderful Italy! You know it well too, don't you, Mr. Shotover? Or so I am told."

The message was quite clear. At some point this summer Henry and Jonty had been together, and Max was making sure they knew he was aware of it.

"Such a pleasure, Count von Schönstein. Beth, we'll be on our way."

Now she desperately wanted them to stay. When she said good-bye to them at the door, it took all her courage not to ask them to remain. When she walked back into her sitting room, Max was sitting in one of the chintz-covered chairs with a relaxed and sinuous elegance, as if their situation was the most normal one in the world.

"This is so quaint, Beth, so American, so — homey, is that not the word? Dear Beth, isn't life amusing? Who would have thought we should not see each other for so long? Wars and rumours of wars, and long cold nights in Cracow and God knows where else — who would have thought it? As my English friend would say, life is sometimes such a *scream!*"

The final word hissed from him like a shower of sparks on cold metal, and her cheek still felt cold from where his skin had touched hers. She steeled herself to speak.

"What do you want, Max?"

"What a strange question for a wife to ask! Are you really feeling so indifferent toward me, *süsse Mädel?*"

"Never call me that — never, never call me that!" The hot anger Beth felt gave her back her energy and her willpower.

"No." Max looked thoughtful. "You are no longer just a sweet girl, Beth. There was frankness between us at the beginning, when we both had our cards on the table — cards!" He laughed abruptly. "And it was good, was it not? We had fun together, fun making love, you and I, and you were such a good little girl learning all her lessons, hmm?"

"I'll never sleep with you again, Max."

To her surprise, he sounded calm when he replied. "Not if you don't want to, *Liebling.* I only made love to you when I did because you asked me into your bed, remember?"

She nearly struck him. Her hand went up, and then she saw the heat in his eyes, as dangerous and unpredictable as the eyes of some wild creature. "Pity," he said, "such a pity we cannot continue with the way things were. You in your life and I in mine."

"But we can. Isn't that why you are here?" To her relief his reply was the one she had hoped to hear.

"I think it's the best solution, don't you? Except that it seems such a waste for you to remain celibate." He was looking straight at her as he spoke, and Beth forced herself to go on looking at him with eyes she hoped were expressionless.

"That way is not for me, as you know, *Liebe*. No, no," he repeated, and Beth heard the change in his voice as he asked, "You know that Gisela Valeska is here?"

She was all he wanted, just as Beth had told Henry and Jonty, just as she had always known. In Vienna, Gisela had said Max could love no one and that it was not the woman to whom he made love that mattered. If that had been true once, it was not true now, and she feared for Gisela. "I don't know what you are talking about, Max," she replied.

"Oh yes you do. You knew in Vienna and that is why you are here in this *gemütliche* little hideaway. *Das ist mir ganz wurst*, Beth — I couldn't care less. I only want to find her. Then I'll go away and leave you to your little life."

There was a terrible hunger in his voice, a sound unlike anything she had ever heard from him before. But then, how long had she known him? How much time had she spent with this man? Just enough to make a child he hadn't even asked about, but not long enough for much else.

She said nothing, and for a moment they stood looking at each other across the room.

Suddenly, with the spring of a leopard he leapt up

and moved across the floor to her side, pinning her against the mantelpiece. Beth could feel the hard marble edge against her spine and the pain in her wrists where he held her. Feeling genuine terror, she started to struggle. "Max, let me go — my God, you're mad!"

It was as if her words had suddenly snapped him out of a trance. She saw him blink, felt his body suddenly relax against her, the pressure on her wrists slacken. A moment later he was laughing, the violence gone from his eyes.

"Oh Beth, such a calumny! All I was going to say was that I would take you by force — I can't say 'rape,' can I, because you are my wife. I'm entitled to you and no one else can say that, can they? Wouldn't it be amusing? Wouldn't you like to go to bed with me after all this time, *Liebling*?"

As he bent toward her, Beth shoved him away and he stumbled backward, laughing as he did so, filling the room with that carefree sound, lilting like dance music. "I'm just teasing! There is only one I want and I shall have her, you know. I'll find her, Beth — my silly sweet girl, my wonderful, beautiful girl, I shall find her! And you know what, Beth? When I do, she will run to me and she'll never resist me, not my Gisela."

Laughing still, Max turned on his heel and left her. As he left, Beth could almost visualize his great cloak swirling around him and hear the music she associated with the time of their happiness together.

Shaking now, she crossed to the telephone and dialled Liam's number. The sound of his voice was what she wanted to hear, not the half-mad, melancholy gaiety of her husband's Vienna.

Half an hour later Liam was with her, his arms around her. Beth allowed the physical contact to erase the memory of another body against her, another pair of hands. As she touched Liam, felt her own response to his rock-hard boxer's body, the reassuring sanity of those direct blue eyes, she realized how afraid she had been of her own reaction to Max. She had not really needed Gisela's reminder of Max's power to charm; she knew it only too well. She felt relief, and joy as she realized that, for her, Max's allure was part of the past, part of Vienna, gone forever.

"He's gone, Liam."

"I know, my darling, I know."

She had meant more than that, but explanations were not necessary. Only Gisela could understand what she meant — Gisela, for whom Max had come looking. Would her southern colonel set her free from Max von Schönstein?

"Do you want to tell me about it?"

Gone. She felt the relief and joy exploding into laughter, and she leaned back in his arms, listening to the sound of her happiness echoing round the room, watching the concern in Liam's eyes change to amusement.

"Are you hysterical, Beth? What is this? Why are you laughing?"

"Because I'm happy — because I'm in New York with you — because I'm in love."

"In love? What is 'in love,' Beth von Schönstein?"

"You show me."

Liam picked her up in his arms and carried her to the bedroom. "Show me," she repeated, again and again, an incantation against the powers of evil, the destructive force of the one who had left her to find another, setting her free. "The one I want — the only one I want —" Unconsciously, she echoed her husband's words, erasing him from her mind with her mouth against her lover's mouth, her hands pressing muscle and sinew and sex, leaving the imprint of him against her palms, the scent of him deep in her flesh. Driven by her need, Liam took her with urgency and passion, sensing only her longing for reassurance, not realizing that, for the first time, Beth von Schönstein was his and his alone. Afterward, he watched as she slept in his arms, regretting that there were things he must ask her and things he must tell her that would break this circle of security they had created for each other.

When she opened her eyes, he was smiling at her. "You look beautiful and I love you, and —" He paused.

"And I shall have to tell you what happened. I don't want to think about it, but —"

"Then let me tell you something first. Whether it makes any difference to what happened here, I don't know." Liam gently brushed her hair away from her face. "Beth, Gisela Valeska is not just a clairvoyant. I thought there was more to her than table-tapping, but I couldn't swear to it. Honey, she's a spy."

Her mood of contentment broken, Beth sat up. "What are you talking about? What's she spying on, or whom? Colonel Delaney, the army — what? Liam, you're not making sense!"

Liam laid a hand gently on her arm. "Listen, Bethie. It's no coincidence she was in Martinka's, no coincidence she linked up with Delaney. I'm not sure about his role in all this; maybe he doesn't know he's being used. Honey, she's been digging into various pan-Serb, pan-Slav organizations. One of the more active and extremist members of one group has just been found dead in mysterious circumstances."

Beth drew away from the reassuring pressure of his hand, shock and disbelief on her face. "You're not trying to tell me she's an assassin, are you? That's utterly improbable, Liam!"

"I'm not saying she did it with her own hand, but I think she put together enough evidence for someone else to do it. Don't have any more to do with her, Beth. Forget all about this Gisela Valeska. She's playing a much more dangerous game than the tarot, and I don't want you to find yourself involved."

Beth pulled the sheets around her, as if she suddenly felt the need to emphasize the distance he had put between them. "Anna — Anna Grabĕz," she said.

How acute she was, he thought angrily. "I don't follow you," he said, and he immediately cursed himself for such an idiotic response.

"Of course you do, Liam. Anna has fed you all this stuff. What did you tell her, for God's sake? She hates our relationship and makes no bones about it. I can never decide if it's pure jealousy — which I could understand — or because I have made you betray the purity of your principles. It's as if I had taken your political virginity — for Anna, I think I have."

Liam felt his own anger growing at her reaction. Beth had guessed right; most of the information had come from Anna. She was also right when she said that Anna had taken the exclusive nature of their relationship very badly, and her motives might indeed be suspect — how he regretted divulging the nature of his interest in Gisela Valeska to her — but Liam believed her. Anna had close links to many of the subversive organizations in New York, for emotional as well as journalistic reasons, and it had been the cause of constant friction between them in the past. He sat up, swung his legs over the side of the bed, and started to look for his clothes.

"Come on, Beth — it's Gisela Valeska who's the problem, not Anna. Don't let's get sidetracked. You haven't yet told me what happened here, but I'd guess she came up in the discussion, didn't she?"

"Yes. He's come here to find her, and even if I knew exactly where she was, I wouldn't tell him."

Liam's anger started to melt at the steely note in her voice, that note he had heard two years ago in her Fifth Avenue mansion. He turned and reached out for her hand. "Beth, darling Beth — you should have sent him after her, let them fight it out between them, destroy each other if that is what's to happen."

"It's not that simple. If Max destroys her, he destroys me."

She had spoken before she had consciously thought of what she was saying. As she heard the words it seemed to Beth at that moment as if she too saw beyond the veil of the present and into the future.

"You're wrong, Beth, you're so wrong! Throw them both to the wolves, or to each other — it's the same thing. Forget about Gisela Valeska."

Beth didn't answer. She could hear the urgency and the love in Liam's voice, but it was as if a mist had descended between them, obscuring their view of each other. How could she make Liam understand what she felt in her heart: that her fate was still bound in some way to that of Gisela Valeska.

Chapter Thirty-Two

Chicago

Colonel Edward Delaney was a sensualist, but first and foremost he was a businessman. When he saw an opportunity to make money — particularly if someone else did most of the work and took most of the risk — he seized it. He was a financial opportunist and as deserving of the title robber baron as any Holman or Vanderbilt.

When an acquaintance in the newspaper world, Ludo Pasić, had introduced him to Gisela Valeska, he had been dazzled and delighted. Rarely did commercial ventures come in such splendid shape as that of the Viennese clairvoyant, and her act was already the talk of New York. If he could not persuade her to some joint financial venture, at least he might coax her into bed with him. Either way, he couldn't lose — and there were not too many undertakings of which that could be said.

To his surprise, his amatory conquest had been reasonably swift. A week of flowers, jewels, champagne, candies, and a magnificent full-length sable cloak, and he was invited to the lady's bed. Once there, he was so intoxicated by her that he had the unaccustomed feeling that it was she who had made the conquest, not Eddie Delaney.

Nevertheless, she happily fell in with his plans, both in bed and out of it. Rarely had he encountered a combination in a woman of both class and lack of inhibition. He found it a heady experience.

The tour met immediately with unqualified success, and by the time they reached Chicago word of the amazing and beautiful clairvoyant had gone ahead of them. They were sold out and people were still clamouring for tickets. Gisela was happy when they extended their stay; the city's air of raw energy and excitement delighted her. Looking out at the forest of telegraph wires, the shrieking and smoking locomotives, the grimy towers of industry, and the vast financial institutions, she found it not in the least ugly. "So American, Eddie," she said, "so alive."

Sometimes they held performances in one of the rail cars and sometimes in the local hotel, if it was suitable. In Chicago the colonel booked the best assembly room in the Palmer Hotel and it was filled every night. Some nights they returned to the train and others they stayed in the hotel's honeymoon suite, which had been done up Egyptian-style, the sofa shaped like Cleopatra's barge, the lamps perched atop bronze sphinxes and the clock set in black marble pyramids. "So American, Eddie!" Gisela said with delight, which somewhat puzzled the colonel.

Most of all, Eddie Delaney looked forward to showing Gisela the southern United States. He had promised they would take a vacation together in his part of the world, and the names flowed from him in exotic profusion: Charleston, Savannah, Chattanooga, Mobile, Memphis.

Confined as her quarters were, and exclusive as her relationship was, Gisela felt less claustrophobic than she had in Vienna. Beyond her rail car stretched the prairies, plains, and mountains of a land that appeared to have no boundaries. So unlike Europe, where borders were crossed with the frequency of sunrise and sunset. The euphoria in Americans that seemed to spring from confidence in their future and enjoyment in the present bore no resemblance to the surface madness disguising the deep melancholy of her own decaying Viennese society.

Gisela was not much given to philosophical thought: Things simply happened, and there you were. Nevertheless, an upbringing by a mother whose dictum had been, "If you are sad, you must hide it; men don't like it," had left its mark. As a young girl Gisela had learned about the melancholy and malaise existing in most human beings.

Here, change did not mean decay. Change was for the better. This was the land of dreams come true;

no one had to tell her that, it was in the air around her.

Still, Gisela was relieved to be away from New York. She had done there what Baron Eihrentahl had asked her to, and done it successfully. What was more, it had introduced her to Eddie Delaney. He was enough to stop the true flashes of clairvoyance, the clouds from he crystal. After one particularly spectacular night when she had held her audience spellbound, Eddie had said, "When you put on a show, lady, you put on a show!" That was all it had been: a performance, and she wanted it to stay that way.

Better, perhaps, that she should have been prescient. And yet, what difference would it have made if she had known that Max von Schönstein was in Chicago? Could she have foreseen the moment when he burst into the bedroom of the rail car and found her asleep with Eddie Delaney in the big brass bed? Would it have made a difference?

When Gisela woke up and saw him standing there, she thought at first he was one of her visions. So foreign, so alien, so beautiful, Max smiling at her, as if the man lying beside her wasn't there at all.

"Max!"

Colonel Delaney woke up at her cry, saw the figure standing there and went for his revolver, which he always kept on the table beside him.

"No." There was a gun in Max's hand. "I'll give you satisfaction, if that's what you want, *mein Herr*, or I can kill you right now."

"Why would you do that, sir? You are not known to me."

"I am known to the lady. More than that, she is mine."

"Our present positions in this room would seem to make that statement a lie, sir."

"Our present positions in this room give me the advantage, sir. As a military man yourself, you cannot deny that."

"No, sir. If it's satisfaction you want, then you'll get it. I should warn you, sir, I have fought duels before."

Max's laugh was soundless, a movement of the mouth. "So have I, *mein Herr*, so have I."

At last Gisela found her voice. "No, Max, no! This is not Vienna; you cannot do this. I'll come with you — anything — just so long as there's no violence, please!"

It was the colonel who turned to her, and his expression was angry. "Stay out of this, Gisela. It has nothing to do with you. It is a settling of accounts between gentlemen — do you understand?"

Dully she listened as Eddie said, "If you withdraw, sir, you have my word as a gentleman that I will join you outside. Or do you want seconds? That will take me a little time."

"No need for witnesses, I think. Do you agree?"

The colonel nodded. Gisela heard Max say, "*Servus*," in his elegant Viennese, as he bowed and left the room, pulling the door on its wrecked hinges closed behind him.

When it was over, and Eddie lay dead on the rough grass and cinders of the railway siding, Gisela went into the city and sent a wire to her contact in New

York, Ludo Pasić. Then she went back to the rail car in the siding, where Max waited for her, as relaxed and comfortable as if he were in his *Palais* on the Ringstrasse.

"I can't get you out of this, Max. You have gone too far this time."

"Sweet girl, I always go too far, you know that. You needn't concern yourself about me. I, too, have a friend in high places."

"Your wife's father?"

"Heavens, no! Better than that — his wife's pet courtier, his younger son's *amour*. I shall see you in Vienna, Gisela — *Liebe, süsse Mädel*, sorceress!"

Chapter Thirty-Three

New York

Ada Holman's little parlour of Japanese bamboo, jewelled crickets and butterflies had stayed that way longer than any of the other reception rooms had remained Italianate, Gothic, or mediaeval. For some reason it had continued to give her pleasure, and it was to the parlour she returned after she had read the letter. She sat by the window overlooking Fifth Avenue with the missive still in her hand, as if held there by some magical force, unable to put it down or to tear her eyes away from the horror of its contents.

"I am ruined," she said aloud. "I am ruined." For the first time she felt old, painfully aware of the arthritis threatening in her hip and of the extra girth around her waist even the whalebone armour couldn't conceal which made it more difficult to breathe while dancing, climbing stairs, or reading such news as the letter in her hand contained.

The sound of her own voice saying such a terrible thing gave her the strength to put the letter down and ring for the butler.

"I want to see Mr. Shotover, Jenkins. I don't know where he is, but find him."

The butler allowed himself to look mildly surprised at the coincidence. "This was just hand-delivered, ma'am, and I believe it is from Mr. Shotover. I was about to bring it up when you rang."

Jonty's note was brief: *I will be at Murray Hill very soon after you receive this. I beg you to use your discretion and to take no action until I have spoken to you.*

Discretion. It was the first word Ada Holman said when Jonty arrived and was shown into the parlour where she still sat, the letter from Max von Schönstein on the desk in front of her. "Discretion? You beg me for discretion, Jonty? How can discretion save me from the disgrace this letter brings? My son-in-law is a murderer, and my youngest son is — my son is — and with you, Jonty! With you, of all people! The one person I thought I could trust implicitly! Or are you trying to tell me this is all a pack of lies?"

Ada Holman had never before seen Jonty Shotover when he wasn't smiling. As always, he was well turned-out, but his face was uncharacteristically white and haggard.

"I can't tell you that, Mrs. Holman. All I can tell

you is that with discretion your position in society may be saved. But many things will have to change — in all our lives."

"I am being blackmailed — the count is threatening to tell my husband — and everyone — about you. Pray tell me what changes can put an end to that!"

"Only facing the consequences will put an end to it, Mrs. Holman."

"We can't even think about it! What do you mean?"

"This is what I've been able to do so far. The count is a killer, but he's the only one of us who will get away scot-free. I have helped him out of the country, and I advise discretion. If he is arrested, we are all ruined. Only with him gone may something be salvaged."

"Can we trust him at all?"

"No, but he can do little damage where he is. The woman in the affair has also left, using her own contacts, and I am given to believe he will stay in Vienna as long as she is there. Since she is a material witness to the killing, she is unlikely to return. The count assured me of his silence on — on various matters — if I helped him, and yet he has written to you. I got a note after he had left telling me he had done so. That's why I am here."

"Jonty, how could you, how could you!" Betrayed, devastated, Ada Holman finally broke down, the tears coursing down her cheeks.

Jonty Shotover stared at her, exhausted. When the first paroxysms were over, he said gently, "Forgive me, but I must sit down. I've had no sleep for forty-eight hours and I shall collapse if I don't." Without waiting for her permission Jonty sat down opposite her, rubbed his face briefly with his hands, and then continued.

"Whatever you might like to say about Henry and myself, please forgo it for now. We have more urgent matters to deal with. What you probably don't know is that Beth is involved with the newspaperman she met two years ago. There's a real possibility she may defy the count's threats and try to marry this man."

"Oh my God!"

"Precisely. Beth is capable of it — you know that, don't you?" Ada Holman said nothing, but her horrified expression said it all. "If that happens, then everything will collapse for you socially. As for the other matter, if Henry and I absent ourselves for a while, nothing much will happen. There are too many skeletons of that nature in other closets I personally can threaten to rattle, I assure you. But Beth, now that's a different matter. You'd never live it down. We must find something to do about Beth."

Ada Holman firmly grasped the straw she knew could save the situation — the straw she could refuse to turn into gold, the gold Beth professed to scorn so much.

Mother and daughter faced each other across the rose-and-ivory sitting room. Ada Holman took Count von Schönstein's letter out of her purse, held it out to Beth, and watched her while she read it.

"You already knew?" asked her mother.

"Yes, and I've talked to Jonty."

Beth looked at her mother's face. "You know about Liam." Jonty, she supposed. He had more or less said there would be other things on her mother's mind. "Perhaps it's as well, because you will have to know sometime that I intend to start divorce proceedings and eventually marry Liam, if he will have me."

Ada Holman sat down on one of the sofas and put the letter back in her purse, snapping the clasp shut. Her expression, when she looked up at Beth, seemed somehow both sly and triumphant. "I am quite sure there'll be no problem in making Mr. O'Connor take you. Well, not as things stand at the moment. You're his ticket to fame and fortune, are you not, Beth?"

"I'm more than that, Mother — far more than that!" Beth's passionate voice filled the room.

"Really? That is indeed fortunate, because I am here to remind you of the terms of your marriage settlement. If you become involved in an action for divorce, it is in your father's power to have the agreement declared null and void. The clause was put in to protect you against possible action by the count, but it will serve equally well against you. I shall have no difficulty convincing your father as soon as he hears about Mr. O'Connor, and I don't need to tell you that, do I? If you start divorce proceedings against the count, you will find yourself cut off from the comfortable income that enables you to live in the manner to which you have become accustomed — and the manner to which Mr. O'Connor has become accustomed, I understand."

"Liam wouldn't care a jot whether I were rich or penniless! In fact, he would prefer the latter!"

"Really?" said Mrs. Holman. "Then he must be

stupider than I thought. A numbskull as well as an adventurer! Lord, Beth, you'll be in the gutter sooner than even I'd imagined!"

Ada Holman almost looked as though she were enjoying herself. Her eyes glittered and her fingers were clasped tightly over her purse as she leaned toward her daughter. "What would happen to your little literary enterprise if all the money suddenly disappeared? Am I not right in thinking everything would collapse and that the incomes of many more people than you and Mr. O'Connor would disappear? And Beth, unless you go along with what I require of you, there is no more money. None."

Beth did not try to argue, call her mother's bluff. This was no bluff; this was what would happen.

"None, even for Liane?"

"I shall apply for custody of Liane, and that's the only way she would see any of the family money. There's not a court in New York that wouldn't back us, and you know it."

"You wouldn't!"

But she would, and Beth knew it. Desperately, she stared at her mother.

"Then what do you want of me, Mother? Surely you don't expect me to go back to Max after what he has done!"

"After what *you* have done, I think you mean, Beth — no, I couldn't expect that."

"Mother, he killed someone! How can you compare anything I have done to murder?"

"If you hadn't left him and come running back here, possibly none of this would have happened. And don't try telling me stories about how he was off to — oh, wherever it was he was off to — and that there was another woman. You just used those as excuses to get back to this no-good Irishman, didn't you?"

Surely it hadn't been like that. Surely she had loved Max once — the handsome, laughing man who had first made love to her and shown her the world?

"So Max goes, and I stay, is that what you're saying? I don't divorce Max and I don't marry Liam, is that it?"

"Not exactly. If things are to remain financially the same, you are not merely moving in with this man, or he with you. I imagine you have already been questioned by the police, and it won't be the last time, whatever influence your father and I can bring to bear. No — you'll have to get out of the country until it all blows over. You don't have to go to Vienna, but at least it will appear you are supporting your husband and that your marriage still exists."

"Appearances. That's all that matters, isn't it?"

Ada Holman did not bother to reply. The answer was self-evident and Beth's question a statement of fact to her, the credo by which she lived. She stood up, and as she did so she swayed and held on to the arm of the sofa.

"I don't know which is worse, you and this man or Jonty and Henry. How could it have happened, when you were given so much! I can only thank God Jonty didn't corrupt William, because *someone* has to help your father, and Henry will also have to leave the country for a while. Thank God for William!"

Since William had spent the last month in a sanitarium on Long Island drying out, it was an extraordinary observation. But it seemed alcoholism was more acceptable than either homosexuality or adultery. Beth looked at her mother. Despite the barrier between them, she saw the suffering on her mother's face, the trembling of her hands, the slight limp as she walked to the door.

"May I at least see Liam and talk to him? Surely you'll not cut off the livelihoods of so many people if I only do that?"

"I have not said I'll cut *them* off, Beth. I have said I'll cut *you* off. Very well. Let him know that his income is not in jeopardy. Don't be too surprised if he isn't as crushed as you might expect, Beth. Never trust a man!"

Stunned, Beth stared at her mother. What hidden drama from her mother's past had prompted that particular aphorism, which burst hot and bitter from some fire banked beneath that steely surface?

"Mama —" But even as she put out a hand and touched her mother's arm, she was pushed violently away.

"I wanted everything for you, Beth, everything, and you had it at your fingertips, and then, right in your hand. And you threw it away. It was nothing I did — you did it all yourself. Not me, you! That fortune hunter could never have touched you unless you had let him!"

Beth was thankful to feel anger replacing the pity she had started to feel. "What about the 'other woman,' Mama? What about her?"

"Other women?" Her mother's voice was incredulous now. "Other women are nothing, less than nothing. Other women are a fact of life. There will always be other women. The thing to avoid is being the other woman oneself. A marriage in which the wife keeps up appearances can never be threatened. That's all that matters, Beth — the marriage and not the nonsense that goes with it. That's for the other women, and they're welcome to it!"

Passionately declaring her denial of passion, Ada Holman pulled on her gloves and added, "Break it off, Beth. Now, today. Finish it."

They had never made love in Liam's apartment. The walls were thin, the tenants of the building mixed, and although most went about their own business, there were always those ready to sell interesting titbits to *Town Topics* or *City Highlights*. When Beth saw the place again, she thought about the daffodils that had been on the table, heard the slap of his hand echoing across the intervening years that separated Beth the dreamer from Beth the realist.

"I told you Gisela Valeska was trouble."

"I never denied it, but the trouble was not of her making. She told me in Vienna that Max loved no one, but I think she was wrong. I think he loves her."

"You call that sickness love? He pursues and kills, and you call it love?" Liam's voice was incredulous.

"I don't know what I call love, Liam. I don't know."

"Thank you — I think you just told me why you're here. We're finished, aren't we?"

Beth couldn't trust herself to speak. She turned away

so he wouldn't see the tears in her eyes and shook her head.

"Then why are you here? Slumming, perhaps? Are you hoping a change of pace will rekindle the flame? Are you looking for a guilty thrill by letting a penniless mick have you on his threadbare coverlet?"

"How can you say that, after all we —" the tears choked her and she struggled to stop them falling.

"All we what, Beth? A few tumbles in the hay — no different from Anna and me, eh? And after all you said about her!" Pain drove him to hurt her as much as she was hurting him.

Somehow she found a gap in the wall of tears and managed to reply. "You can hurt me, and you are, terribly, but that's not true and you know it. You'll never convince me you really feel like that!"

"Why not? Would you rather believe you hurt me too? This is less painful and spares my guts, Beth. Would you deny me that?"

"No, and if you prefer it, then believe it. I'll believe what I want to believe."

"We still haven't come to why you're here, then. The count has killed the colonel; Miss Valeska has got herself smuggled out of the country by her dubious contacts; the count has got himself smuggled out by your mama's dubious contacts. And yet we're not talking divorce or marriage, are we?"

"If it were that simple, I would be where I want to be — with you."

"Three cheers for me. So how come it's not happening?"

"Money, Liam, money. My mother has been cleverer than we gave her credit for."

The message carried by Ada Holman seemed even more pertinent in the less-than-luxurious surroundings of Liam's rooms. Liam was silent for a while and then he said, "A ruthless woman."

"Absolutely without mercy."

Desperate, not really believing his own words, he said, "We've made a good start, circulation is building up well — we could do it."

"We can't risk it, Liam. Gloria and Les have given up everything to make this work, you know they have. *Facets* is their life now, and we've taken on other employees. Do you really want to risk throwing all those people on the streets? I know I can't."

He couldn't plead anymore; it was against his nature. All he knew how to do was fight when someone hurt him. Gruffly, he asked, "What are you going to do?"

"I shall set up a financial arrangement with our lawyers for the continuing support of *Facets*. Then I'm going to take Liane and leave the country for a while. Jonty and Henry want me to join them in Italy, and I think I shall do that."

The look of distaste on Liam's face was unmistakable. "How can you stomach it, Beth? Doesn't it anger you to think about what that little leech has done to your brother?"

"I've had some time to get used to the idea, because I've known since I came back to New York. I was shocked, yes, and I had difficulty accepting it, but I was never angry. As I told you, I don't know what love is anymore. If I ever did, that is."

"You did once." Desperation made him struggle once again against the instinct of years. He started to move toward her. Beth let the tears fall now, because she had said what had to be said and she could not be betrayed by her own weakness, or his. But when she saw him moving toward her, she said, "No, don't touch me, Liam, because if you win, then we both have lost."

She saw rejection on his face, hostility for her, for her mother, for everything she stood for. The past, she thought, remind him of the past.

"We're buying time, Liam. Remember how we said that to each other when things seemed far more hopeless than they do now? Time is on our side."

She had been seventeen then. She was still not twenty. Beth suddenly remembered the egg timer near the chafing dish in her parents' dining room in its silver frame, the sand running soundlessly from one crystal into the other, inexorable, waiting for no one and for nothing. Nothing at all.

Book Four

Metamorphosis

Chapter Thirty-Four

Italy

You cruise through the Ageans Islands from Piraeus, and the time passes. Walking in the gardens of Roman villas, thence by landau to Siena, up through Viterbo, Orvieto, Montefiascone, driving through the hills to Florence — and the time passes. In Florence, you take rooms above the Piazza Goldoni, overlooking the Arno and the Ponte di Carraia. And the time passes. You cannot make up your mind whether to winter in a *palazzo* on the Grand Canal in Venice, or in one of those villas dotting the hills around Siena, with their terraces and topiary and fountains in the open countryside. You laugh with Henry and Jonty and toss for it, and the villa outside Siena is chosen.

There is much laughter, surprisingly enough. Beth feels guilty about it at first, and then not even that anymore. They are such fun, these two lighthearted young men, so devoted to each other, and to you and Liane. And they know so much! When the winter is over, all five go travelling again, through the icy Splugenpass from Switzerland back into Italy and to Lake Como. Then on through the Bergamesque Alps to the gentler slopes of the Aprice Pass into the Val Cominica, the countryside changing before their eyes: waterfalls, villages shrouded in foliage, small glades surrounded by trees. Love isn't a fairy tale. Italy is.

Encouraged by Jonty and Henry, Beth sends back articles to *Facets* — on Tuscan cities, on the world of American emigrés, on the monasteries in the hills southwest of Florence, southeast of Siena. On anything and everything that catches her fancy, and her fancy is never short of inspiration.

The sand continues to run through the glass, soundless, unnoticed. Almost.

Liane starts to walk, and to talk, and to become a person in her own right, and much more interesting to her mother. She has hair lighter than either of her parents, and her grandfather's eyes: penetrating, clear, like topazes. Beth is cajoled into happiness by the discovery of her daughter, and the love she begins to feel is uncompromising.

Another winter passes and they buy an automobile, a large Panhard-Levassor, to motor across France to Pau, along the border of Spain, up through Périgueux, Limoges, Bourges, and Blois to Paris. An article on the pleasures of motoring is sent back to *Facets*. Gloria

Baker writes and tells Beth she has gained quite a following and to keep the articles coming. Liam never writes, and Gloria doesn't mention him. Only certain shades of blue disturb Beth sometimes, when the light shines on them in a particular way, reminding her of those Irish blue eyes of his.

Her mother writes frequently, as though nothing untoward had happened. Isn't it too dreadful about those Serbs, or whoever it was, murdering poor King Alexander and his queen? Such a primitive crowd! What a shame Beth was away when Prince Henry of Prussia visited the Vanderbilts! Motorcars terrify her, and a dance called the cakewalk disgusts her. She fears both signal the death of civilization as she knows it. Beth should just *see* the new Hotel Astor going up opposite the Olympic! And so on, and so on.

It becomes easier and easier not to go back, not to think of going back. In 1905, Henry, Jonty, Beth, and Liane explore the Abruzzi, take the cure in Salsomaggiore for Jonty's hayfever, start to talk about a permanent base and some sort of schooling for Liane. They postpone decisions for another year. There are too many friends to visit: sculptors, painters, writers, other Americans like themselves. Life is rich and unfettered. Beth can see no traps now, and that's all that matters, keeping them beyond the mind's eye.

There is no man in her life. Only Jonty and Henry, and that, too, is a love that is easily recognizable and free from pain.

1906, and Strauss writes "Waltzentraum," keeping the sweet Viennese dream alive amidst the rise of socialism, as Sigmund Freud turns fifty. A year earlier, two hundred thousand had marched to the Ringstrasse during the November strike. The sands continue to filter through the glass, and the signs are there for all to see. If they want to see.

In San Francisco, the earth trembles, violently, and remembrance is thrust upon Beth. Frenetically she gathers up her loved ones and drives, drives, drives, up to Paris, down the length of the Italian peninsula, and on to Sicily, to Trapani, on the coast southwest of Palermo, back to Naples.

The earth trembles in New York, in October 1907. There is a financial panic, a run on the Mercantile International Bank, and Ada Holman's cable finally reaches Beth in Rome. Her father has had a heart attack and is very ill. He is dying.

Beth's bubble bursts as Gisela Valeska's prophecies touch her life once more. Four years and then *pop!* Just like that.

Jonty will not return, but she and Henry leave taking Liane with them.

Chapter Thirty-Five

New York

It was 1907, yet nothing seemed to have changed on the quayside since she had left four years earlier. The city, however, *had* changed. It was brighter, busier, taller than ever. The Park Plaza had joined the Hotel Astor, and there was now the Hotel Algonquin just off Fifth Avenue on Forty-fourth, where American friends in Europe had suggested Beth stay. The Ziegfeld Follies had arrived, and the Jardin de Paris. During a performance of *Mamzelle Champagne*, Harry Thaw had shot the man whose architecture had started to change the face of New York. It was not over a building, but over a girl. "Cultivate the externals" had on this occasion been taken to an extreme, or, perhaps, to a logical conclusion.

Inside the Murray Hill brownstone, it was as if time

had stood still since her childhood. Beth watched her daughter looking at her surroundings, wide-eyed with apprehension. Some of Ada Holman's rapacious decorating instinct had abated over the years, and much of the interior remained as Beth remembered it.

Beth was not anxious to subject Liane to a long death-bed scene, but she wanted her father to feel a moment of immortality when he saw his own eyes looking back at him from his granddaughter's face. She watched William Holman's pale face gather into the supreme effort of a smile when he saw Liane. Then he closed his eyes once more. Beth took her daughter to her mother's parlour and left her with one of the young housemaids.

Watched by Ada, William, Jr., Beth, and Henry, William Holman sank slowly through the night and died in his sleep shortly before dawn. Beth looked at the inert form of the father she had never really known, and felt a pang of grief so sharp that it took her unawares.

Although the financial panic of October had undoubtedly hastened William Holman's death, the estate had been left in good order. Nothing had been left to chance by that most careful of men, and although the collapse of the Mercantile Bank had lessened his fortune by a few millions, he had left his heirs well provided for. To the grief Beth was feeling for her father was added a feeling of incredulity that a loss within such a context of affluence could have brought about the end of his life. What passion he must have felt for his millions that the disappearance of some of them should have cost him his life!

Beth had known they were a wealthy family, but she had never known how wealthy. The sums discussed by the lawyers made her dizzy with zeroes, as they danced in her mind and across the pages and pages of the will read to the family members assembled in the dining room. Behind her brother William's head she could see the egg timer in its silver stand, still sitting on the massive, carved sideboard, the sand held in the lower sphere. Time passed, time consumed.

How would William manage? Her mother told Beth he had been relatively stable for the past eighteen months, but what would this new responsibility do to him? He seemed quieter, less brittle than she remembered, but since she had not seen him for so many years it was impossible for her to know if this was because of their father's death or a permanent change.

The will made clear that they were all heirs to the Holman fortune and that nothing about their lifestyles would alter. Beth's Uncle Cecil, the once-wayward husband of Medora, had been appointed a joint administrator of their father's business affairs with William, Jr.

William had spent time in Philadelphia with Cecil and Medora when it became necessary to remove him from New York. "Cecil seems able to reach William in way your father and I were unable to do," Beth's mother told her. Beth wondered if it could be that it took one sinner to understand another. Certainly, the standards of William and Ada Holman had been impossible for any of their children to live up to.

Sitting there in the family dining room, Beth had difficulty controlling the involuntary smile that started to cross her face. If there was one thing her mother had managed to inculcate into her daughter, it was a strong sense of her own imperfection. She could not

speak for her brothers, even for Henry. In Siena or
Florence or Rome, they had not discussed such things.
Happiness was often dependent on forgetting, not
remembering.

Happiness and forgetfulness. Liam. In her black
dress, behind the mahogany dining table, Beth felt
the first surge of sexual longing, an agonizing feeling
of impatience at her self-imposed celibacy. That was
the trouble with coming back. New York meant Liam.

And yet — what was there to stop her now from
marrying him? There were no clauses in the will that
would alter her financial position if she did so. She
was finally free to make the decision. All that remained
was the problem of Liam O'Connor himself.

He might be married. She could hardly expect a
young, virile, handsome man to remain celibate for
four years, whatever quixotic decisions his former
mistress might have made.

She would not think about that. Nothing mattered
but finding him. When Beth looked across the table
at her mother, who now seemed smaller, more fragile,
she felt the familiar guilt. This time, however, the
guilt was not because of the treachery of her thoughts,
but over the realization that she would do anything,
everything possible to marry the man her mother had
once called a "verminous mick from the slums."

Liam had moved. It disturbed Beth that she could no
longer picture him in the familiar setting but must
place him in limbo. The man in the rooms above
Liam's said he had been gone for more than a year,
but he thought he was still somewhere in the area.

"Try Hyppolyte Havel's. Last I heard he'd taken up with that crowd."

"What crowd?"

"Anarchists."

It didn't sound much like Liam, but it did sound like — no, she wouldn't even think of that possibility. Shutting out the unwelcome thought, Beth hurried on through the Village.

Greenwich Village remained much as it had been when she left New York. As gaudily painted as ever in shades of green, carmine, blue, and black, cafés such as The Vermilion Hound, The Dragonfly, Little Russia, and The Samovar were still there. She could still have had her fortune read in tea leaves, if she so desired, to the music of a gypsy violin. Was that so very different from the crystal or the tarot of Gisela Valeska? Yes, she thought to herself. Yes. Don't ask me why, Liam, but yes.

At that moment she saw a familiar figure coming out of Polly Holliday's. Swathed in shawls and scarves, red hair flying loose in the autumn breeze, it was unmistakably Anna Grabēz. She looked down the street and as she saw Beth, her expression registered shock.

"My God, where'd you spring from? Oh, right, I read your papa died. D'you get to own all the slum properties now, Beth?"

"There *are* no slum properties now. They were sold long ago." Dear God, why did she feel the need to defend herself or her class at such a moment?

"Oh excuse me, you just get the cash. Good for you."

"And for you. It's paid your wages for the last few years."

Anna gave a short bark of a laugh. "Not mine, honey. I haven't worked for *Facets* in a while."

"Then can you tell me if —"

She was interrupted by Anna. "No, I can't. I've no intention of helping you get in touch with Liam O'Connor. You may find him sooner or later, but not through me, babe." Suddenly, Anna's air of sardonic hauteur broke down, and she leaned toward Beth, grasping the iron railing beside her as though to restrain herself from physically lashing out at her.

"Listen to me, Countess von Schönstein — stop playing games and get out of our lives. So the little rich girl's decided to dip back into the bargain basement and see if she can pick up where she left off, eh? Get out, Beth. Get out and leave Liam alone! You're no damned good for him and he's far too good for you — only you'd never understand that, would you? To you, he's just convenient when you fancy being laid by a peasant and getting a cheap thrill out of the whole episode! Then what do you intend to do? Go back and snicker with your fop of a husband and your pansy friends about your night in the sack with an Irish bum, eh? Isn't that it? Leave Liam O'Connor alone!"

Beth couldn't speak. She started to back away, her legs trembling and nausea rising in her throat. Anna was wrong, so wrong, but obviously Anna cared, and Beth hadn't thought she'd felt so strongly about Liam. Anna had already started to walk swiftly away, her shawls blowing in the wind. Beth turned to leave.

"A moment of your time, ma'am."

A man who had been standing in the doorway of Polly Holliday's was gesticulating at her. He was short and fat, with very long hair and sideburns, and Beth had never seen him before. "I couldn't help overhearing, ma'am. Are you looking for Liam O'Connor, journalist and pugilist?''

"Pugilist?''

"In a manner of speaking, and that's where he's most likely to be at this moment — where he practises the pugilistic art. I could tell you where if — that is — if you could see your way to — I have many expenses — if you could help defray the cost of survival in this cruel world?''

Beth opened her purse and pulled out a handful of silver.

"Ah, so kind, thank you. Liam O'Connor, ma'am, is almost certainly at O'Rourke's gym, which you will find in the erstwhile familiar haunts of the Irish of this great city of ours.''

The loquacious panhandler gave Beth an address she recognized as being close to Columbus Park. She remembered what Liam had told her about that area of the Upper East Side: of Bandit's Roost, Battle Alley, Rat Trap, and Ragpickers' Row, all of which had been razed in the 1890s for Columbus Park itself. It was the area from which his father's father had managed to elevate himself and his family, and although not nearly as dangerous as it once had been, it was unknown to her. She hailed a cab and gave the driver the address.

The air in O'Rourke's gym was a blue and gray haze, redolent of the smell of alcohol, fried onions, and liniment. The voices around Beth seemed to have been made husky with the atmosphere, hoarse and rasping with the smoke that hung in the gaslit air. But there was also vitality, as shown by the laughter, the shouted epithets, the bursts of excited discussion, the remarks hurled in her direction.

"Here, lady, let me buy you a drink! Here, lady,

356

I'll let *you* buy *me* a drink — ah, don't be like that!
Give us a smile — that's more like it!"

She couldn't resist turning and smiling at the men
who shouted good-naturedly from the bar, its bottles
and glasses gleaming like jewels in a darkened cave.
She heard their appreciative whistles and laughter at
her response, and she felt an unexpected elation at
their noisy appreciation.

That, then, was how Liam saw her again, after life
had put four years between them and he had given
up hoping. The smoke curled around the tall, slender
figure in black moiré, the light shining on the expensive sheen of the fabric as she moved, throwing into
relief the high plane of her cheekbones, the strong
mouth, the long, dark eyes. She was wearing no hat
or veil, and the wind had blown the cloud of her hair
loose around her face so that her skin seemed more
like ivory than he remembered. But as a flame of
recognition danced in her mesmerizing eyes, he saw
the colour rise in her cheeks.

"Liam." Soundlessly, her lips shaped his name.
They stood still in the midst of uproar, a gulf of four
years and lost dreams between them. How could he
cross that divide and hold her, kiss her, yell at her,
convey to her the hell she had put him through, the
hell it was to realize she still shook him to the core
and he didn't want to feel that way. Anymore.

Her eyes were moving over him, and Liam O'Connor
became painfully aware of his seminaked state, his
torso bare, the sweat dripping from his face, running
down his back. As if he had made love, as if they
had made love — in an apartment, in a house on
the Hudson. He ran his fingers through his hair, felt
the sawdust on his fingers from his sparring partner's
gloves and the floor of the ring.

"Hi, Countess." Start if off, somehow, anyhow.

"Can we talk?"

Her voice shook him. He had forgotten it could do that: husky, a strange little vibration somewhere behind the words. In the moment it took for him to find his own voice again someone at the bar shouted, "Hey, O'Connor, if you don't want to talk to her, I will! How about it, Countess?"

"Barney." Liam turned to a black man standing behind him near the ring he had just vacated. "Pass me my clothes, eh? Tell Col I'll be back to see him tomorrow."

"Sure thing, Liam." A bundle of clothes was handed over to Liam from behind the ring attendant.

"Excuse me a moment while I put these on. Don't want to be arrested in the street, do we?"

The pain in his eyes was still there, but he had smiled at her and joy shone in Beth's own answering smile.

"Ah, Beth," he said, and disappeared behind a canvas screen in one corner of the gym. Around her Beth could hear the whistles and catcalls, the grunts of the men in the ring, the squeak of their boots on the sawdust floor, the sharp instructions barked at them by their trainers watching at the ropes.

In a cab again with him, space on the seat between them, a polite exchange of conversation.

"I'm sorry about your father."

"Thank you. I felt — feel — grief. I didn't think I would feel anything."

The driver spoke. Where you wanna go?"

"Oh, right." Liam gave an address still in Greenwich Village, close to Bleecker Street.

"You didn't move far."

"No. It's still quite close to MacDougall. How did you find me?"

"I crossed a gentleman's palm with silver."

"Thirty pieces, by any chance? Was it anyone I know?"

"Not that I'm aware of. Do you feel — betrayed? Still?"

"Yes."

He felt her start to tremble, longed to put out a hand, heard his voice rough and abrupt as she seemed about to do the same thing herself. "Don't. Don't lay a finger on me, or I'll kiss you to death. That's how angry I am, how betrayed I feel."

"Don't tempt me, Liam, don't."

"Why not? You tempt me, goddamnit, when I should hate your guts. Where've you been for four years? And don't give me a travel itinerary like that stuff you've been sending back to *Facets*!"

"Stuff? It's good and you know it, even if it's not like yours."

"What do you know about mine?"

"Everything. I read it all."

"Yippee. Did you keep it under your pillow?"

"On my bedside table."

"Ah God, Beth."

"I mean it."

"I know you do. That's the hell of it."

Fingers moving across the cracked leather of the cab seat, touching, intertwining, his fingers on her wrist, her pulse pounding as if it would burst through the blue-veined skin. "Yes, she said, "that was the hell of it."

But it hadn't been. It had been good in Italy and she had been happy. How could she explain that now, or justify it to herself? How could she understand it now that he had touched her again, and she knew he still wanted her? She could no more explain it than she had once been able to understand how she had fantasized that two men were both making love to her.

The new apartment was grander than the old one, with more space and slightly better furnishings. Beth looked around for signs of a permanent female presence, but suddenly his arms were around her, his mouth on hers. There was passion in his kiss, but his voice was light when he spoke.

"Are you going to let me make love to you before you leave again for the Continent?"

"Let? I thought I'd have to persuade you because you'd hate me so much."

"I do hate you so much, but that has nothing to do with this."

Not hate nor anger nor betrayal, nothing but mouth against mouth, skin against skin, her hunger for his touch, his hands on her breasts, hers on his thighs, and the scent of his body still warm from fighting. The power of him, the rhythm of him moving against her, and the moisture of him, the sweetness of her release. So long, so long, and yet the time had passed — minutes passing from one sphere to another, sand in a silver stand.

"Why did I do that?" His hand was stroking her hair, but she heard the groan he gave as he spoke.

"Because you wanted to." The hair on his chest was curly and springy beneath her fingers, wet with fighting and love-making.

"More than that. Want is easy. You want, you take, so long, babe, and that's it. You — ah, you tie me up in knots." Liam took a handful of her hair in his fingers and tugged at it gently.

"I haven't wanted and I haven't taken. I don't know what that proves, but that's the way it's been."

"Are you trying to tell me there's been no one for four years?"

"Yes."

"Ouch. What am I supposed to feel, Beth?"

"That's up to you. I want to talk."

"You mean you're not going to just take me and leave me again?"

"Oh, Liam!" Suddenly she was crying four years of tears, for herself and Liam O'Connor, and — it was undeniable — for her father, who had been a stranger to her. There was also grief for the frightened, vulnerable face of her mother showing for the first time beneath the iron control and self-satisfied expression of a woman with the world at her feet.

Liam held her in his arms until the worst was over, and then they talked. They talked of legal agreements, and wills, and a future free of anger and separation. Suddenly the complicated world between them seemed simple.

Chapter Thirty-Six

New York

"Where have you been, Mamita? I don't like this house!
I want you and me and Henry to go back to Jonty
— please, please!"

Beth held Liane close to her, the love she had once
thought she would never feel flooding over her, and
stroked the hair that was so much lighter than her
own — *"crème caramel,"* Jonty called it. "As soon
as we can, darling. Your grandmother is so unhappy
because of Grandfather's death and we must comfort
her for a little while longer."

"Then can we go?"

How could she tell this child that she was planning
to marry and to settle in this city that was foreign

territory to her? Postpone it, prevaricate a little. Tell her another day when things are better. What things? When would it be better?

"Soon — but you'll like it here, Liane. I've had no time to show you how wonderful it can be. You'll see."

"*Then* can we go back to Jonty?"

"Soon, but now I must see how Grandmama is. Henry is going to take you to the park, and tomorrow we'll go riding."

Liane raced off to find Henry, her fears temporarily forgotten. That was a comfort, thought Beth. She must remember that, at Liane's age, children are quickly soothed by offers of immediate pleasures or distractions.

She found her mother amid the butterflies and crickets of her parlour. It looked as if she had been trying to write letters, but when Beth came in she sat staring in the direction of the shuttered windows.

"Mama, let me put on some more lights. Have you been trying to write in this gloom?"

As her mother turned toward her, Beth was shocked by the look on her face. She seemed to have deteriorated further in the last twenty-four hours, her face more drawn, the eyes deep in their sockets.

"I know what you are thinking of doing, Beth. I guess that's where you have been, isn't it?"

"What are you talking about, Mother?" Beth stammered, angry at her own reaction. She had not intended to prevaricate with her mother, and yet here she was, behaving like a child caught in a misdemeanour.

"I am talking about Mr. O'Connor. Your father's

will puts no barriers in your way — he refused to do that — and there's nothing I can do to stop you now."

Beth took a deep breath. "I'll not pretend with you any longer, Mother. I intend to get a divorce and marry Liam O'Connor. I will do it as discreetly as possible and cause you as little discomfort as I can."

"Discomfort." Her mother gave a little laugh and looked up at Beth, the hollows beneath her eyes deepening and darkening in the artificial light.

"Beth, I am dying."

The words sounded like the measured striking of a clock between them, signalling the end of her hopes. Even before she had heard any of the details, Beth knew she was hearing the truth.

"I have cancer, Beth. I have known for quite a while — even before October when your father was taken ill. I thank God I never told him, or anyone. It seemed pointless to worry your father over something he could do nothing about — it is inoperable, you see. All the doctors can do is to keep me as comfortable as possible." Here, Ada Holman gave another little laugh and continued. "All I have left is what your father built with his money and I with my social skills. I know this is the twentieth century, but in my circles nothing has changed. There is no such thing as a discreet divorce, and I personally doubt there ever will be. I am begging you, Beth, to leave me the one thing I have left. My reputation. Beth, I beg you — please."

With her mother's desperate eyes upon her, grieving for both her parents, Beth felt an ineffectual and impotent rage for herself and Liam. She had to admire the iron will that had stopped her mother from seeking support from anyone when facing her own suffering. And now this woman who had never begged for anything in her life was asking Beth to keep up the appearance that had always been of first importance to her. Shaken, Beth knelt down and took her mother's hands in hers. "I'll stay with you. I'll be there. I shan't leave you, I promise."

"And you'll not do this — this thing, Beth?"

She couldn't say the words. She shook her head and held her mother in her arms, noticing how suddenly her mother's solid frame had dwindled into this weakness which, trembling against her, was as powerful in its frailty as it had been in its strength and now dictated her daughter's course of action.

Later on that day, Beth told Henry. He put his face into his hands and said, "Oh God — what about Jonty."

Beth grimaced. "You're just like me. All I can think about is Liam."

"But you'll do what Mother asks?"

"You know I will. Henry, I'm going to ask you to stay as well for Liane's sake. I shall be spending a great deal of my time with Mama, and I don't know how long it will be. Liane's already missing Italy and this is no atmosphere for a little girl. Ask Jonty to spare you for now — although I think he should stay away. I'm sure he'll understand."

Henry looked at his sister. "Do you think Liam O'Connor will understand?"

"I don't know."

"Surely he will if you are asking him to wait because of a dying woman?"

"I asked him to wait before, and I didn't return to this country for four years. And then it was because of Papa's death and not for Liam. Now I must ask him to wait so as to save face for my mother, whom he sees as his sworn enemy. Henry, this is a situation involving class and privilege — in his heart of hearts I'm not sure he trusts me because of who I am."

When William was told the news, he collapsed and was whisked off to Philadelphia to recuperate.

"It looks like it's you and me, Henry," Beth said to him.

"I've already written to Jonty and told him why I'm staying. Now you go and see this guy, Beth. Don't put it off any longer."

"I just told him I would spend my life with him."

"Beth, you know as well as I do that if you were merely changing vacation plans, putting it off for forty-eight hours might soften the blow. Telling him at the end of the week isn't going to make the slightest difference if he's going to hate this as much as you think."

He was right, of course. Beth managed to get hold of Liam by telephone at *Facets*. She could sense that he had picked up that something was wrong from the tone of her voice. "I'll see you at the apartment," he said. Beth opened her mouth to say "I love you," but he had already hung up.

The doctor arrived soon afterward to visit her mother. After a brief meeting with him that confirmed what she had already been told, Beth left Liane with Henry and went to Greenwich Village.

She had hoped he would make love to her. She had hoped he would at least hold her in his arms and comfort her, but he did none of these things. He sat and listened while she told him what little there was to tell. When she had finished, he sat for a moment without speaking and then said, "This is exactly what Anna said would happen. She said you would come back into my life, reassert your hold over me, treat me like some goddamned stud and then make some excuse not to go through with anything."

"Some excuse? Liam, how can you call this some excuse? My mother is dying!"

"We all are, Beth." The tone of his voice was harsh, cold. "That's why I'm not prepared to hang about any longer waiting on your pleasure. Or your mother's. How do you know she's not faking this to hang on to her precious reputation?"

"I've spoken to her doctor. It's true."

"How long is it going to take?"

"They don't know — how can they know something like that? How can you *ask* something like that?"

"Well, maybe I could put a time limit on it, like, if it takes six weeks I'll be around. If it takes six months, forget it, babe. How about that?"

He was angry, angry, angry. It burned around him like a barrier of flame through which she could not penetrate, through which he was determined she should not penetrate.

"Liam, don't, please."

"I won't, don't worry. I'll not service you and stand around waiting for Ada Holman to die, only to find you're waltzing off again to Italy or Vienna or God knows where. I've got a life to live, Beth." He got up and started to pace the room, swinging around to face her, driving one fist against the other. "Maybe Anna is right, maybe I just want you because you *are* unattainable, and my vanity is tickled by having a rich countess in my bed. Trouble is, she's only willing on *her* terms. I tell you what Beth —" He was standing over her, his hands on her shoulders, massaging them hard. She could hear his breathing, quick and savage, and her body ached with the pleasure as well as the pain of his touch. "Let *me* set the terms this time. You come to me now, and you can see your mother as much as you want, look after her as long as you want. How about that?"

How easy he made it sound! "Liam, darling Liam, I know I have to do it my mother's way even if I don't know why." With difficulty Beth pulled herself away from him. "Love is different things to different people. You know that."

"Only too well! For me, love is love me now, not love me later — maybe. For you, love is love me now, then leave me, then love me again in a year or two or three, then leave me, and so on. I've too many things going on in my life to get on your particular carousel again, Countess!"

Anger replaced the physical ache when his words reminded Beth of what Liam's ex-neighbor had said to her when she was looking for him. "Are those 'things' Anna Grābez and her crowd of anarchists, by any chance?''

"What's it to you?"

"Plenty. You told me yourself she was playing a stupid game, so why are you playing it now?"

"I told you that four years ago — four years in which I don't think life was too hard on you, Countess. Am I not correct?"

He was right and that was the terrible thing. "Don't bring up the past, Liam."

"You brought it up when you mentioned Anna's stupid games. Funny, when you look into some things they often don't seem as stupid."

"Hence the articles on Emma Goldman, Alexander Berkman, and —"

"— and writers like Susan Glaspell and Neill Boyce, women who want to change a few things in this world. If they are anarchists, then I'm all for anarchy, if that's what you mean."

"I don't know what I mean anymore."

"I don't think you ever did, Beth. I think you've got a lot or sorting out to do, and until you do it I think you and I are no good to each other."

"Strange you should consider loving and leaving such a crime when I thought it was considered an ideal in your Village bohemia! Are you sure it's not you who has to sort out what you want, Liam O'Connor?"

Baffled, angry, the blue eyes stared back at her, loving her, hating her. Beth felt tired, tired of trying to understand this maddening man, tired of trying to make him understand her. "I'm going now, Liam," she heard herself saying.

"Do that, Beth. Go back to your world and leave me some peace in mine."

She couldn't help smiling. "Peace? Is this the talk of a fighting Irishman? Have all those rocks and tin cans turned into little scraps of paper? Are you frightened of me now, O'Connor? What would happen if I challenged you now, as I did seven years ago?"

He looked at her standing there in front of him, the generous mouth taunting and tempting him, the body he knew and loved so well beneath the black dress she wore for her father, the one she had been wearing when she had walked into O'Rourke's gym and back into his life.

"I'd lose, Beth. I already have, haven't I? And the confetti isn't little scraps of paper, me darlin'. It's ashes of roses, dust and ashes, Bethie. Maybe I am frightened of you, more scared of you than anything and anyone in the world, in O'Rourke's gym, anywhere at all. Go home, Beth, go home."

She did as he said, with the taste of their dead relationship as sharp as the taste of her tears on her lips.

Chapter Thirty-Seven

New York

When Beth afterward thought about the winter of her mother's dying, it seemed completely separate from any other period in her life. Life and time were happening outside the brownstone mansion on Fifth Avenue from which she rarely moved. What spare time she had, she spent with Liane, and that in itself had its own unreality, filled with careful gaiety, a self-conscious laughter, the agonizing effort to appear relaxed and calm.

Yet she could not have wished herself anywhere else, leaving her mother to face this trial alone. She had not imagined how close she would come to feel to someone she had once seen as the implacable enemy of her happiness. It seemed tragically ironic it should take this ordeal to bring it about.

During one moment of comparative calm her mother said to her, "I always only wanted the best for you, Beth, because I love you." Even if her mother's best was not hers, Beth knew it to be true. If she had not stayed, she would never have known it, and it seemed as important to Beth as any other declaration of love in her life. With it, they made their peace, and the making of that peace was crucial to her happiness.

Ada Holman died in the spring of 1908. If she had been able to say it herself, she would probably have placed her death as she had placed her life: "And I died almost two years to the day after dear Mrs. Astor." That perspective would have been the most meaningful to her, even though the glory days of the great hostesses were over. New York society was now too diffuse to be ruled by one queen, or even two.

The death of her father had made Beth a wealthy woman. She was now a *very* wealthy woman. She and Henry had made it clear they were happy with the arrangement by which their Uncle Cecil and William jointly took charge of affairs. Then William surprised them all by declaring his intention of marrying their mother's day nurse, a motherly, fair-haired woman slightly older than himself. During the course of Ada Holman's illness, the nurse had apparently taken on some night duties of which no one else in the household had been aware.

What had started off as one of William's many casual flirtations had matured into something that had taken on greater significance. It was difficult to accuse the woman of merely fortune-hunting, since she seemed totally infatuated with William, obsessed with his health and happiness. Aunt Medora assured Beth it was the best thing that could happen and admitted she had no objection to sharing the burden of policing William for the rest of his life.

"Frankly, my dears, if she *is* a fortune hunter, she's worth every penny, and we can make the marriage contract such that it won't be worth her while to leave him."

Talk of marriage contracts made Beth think of Max, something she hadn't done in a very long time. She had heard from mutual friends in Italy that he was closely associated with Gisela Valeska, who had become one of the best-known women in Vienna.

Beth brooded. A relationship of a few months, a child, and then five years of silence. It bore some resemblance to her love affair with Liam, and she wondered if Anna Grabēz had been right. Max had been an episode in her life; now it looked as if her relationship with Liam O'Connor would go the same way.

As she thought of Max, Beth felt a sudden chill. She was now even richer than she had been, and where there was money, there was Max.

She must leave. She felt it as clearly as if Gisela Valeska had spoken to her, as if this woman who was so like her had for a moment shared her mind. The thought frightened her quite as much as the premonition itself. She had been delaying a decision to return to Europe because of Liane, who had now made some friends in New York.

The delay had had nothing to do with Liam. Part

of her was still tied to her mother, whose memory stood like the barrier it had always been between her daughter and the man she had so despised. In death, Ada Holman haunted Beth's conscience quite as effectively for the moment as she had done in life.

There were ghosts to exorcize. She must leave at once, take Henry and Liane with her and go back to Italy where she had been happy, even without Liam O'Connor. There she had felt safe from the fear that Max von Schönstein would come back into her life.

In the empire of the double eagle they were celebrating the diamond jubilee of Franz-Josef and six centuries of Hapsburg rule. By October, the annexation of Bosnia-Herzegovina would come, and it looked as if the old order would go on forever.

So Beth returned to where she had once felt happiness, failing to see — as so many failed to see — the world shivering and trembling on its axis.

Chapter Thirty-Eight

Venice

In an earlier European interlude, a villa above Siena had won out over a *palazzo* on the Grand Canal. This time Beth chose Venice. Jonty and Henry were going to do some travelling together and then would join her and Liane.

Beth was not as free to move about as she once had been, because she was anxious to start Liane's formal education. Through friends in the diplomatic service she hired an English governess, who joined them at the fifteenth-century Palazzo Tiepoli, which Beth had rented as their permanent base in Italy.

Venice was well suited to Beth's mood. The city

seemed to float on air in an aura of reality suspended, which made even the five great golden domes of St. Mark's as insubstantial as part of a dream. The mists that drifted in from the Adriatic softened colour and outline, as if one glimpsed the city through a veil. Here, even decay was beautiful and part of life, not something to be feared.

Behind the mossy walls of the *palazzo* were sunny terraces, concealed and shadowy courtyards with trailing creepers, statues glimpsed among the crimson oleanders, a feeling of separation and security from ghosts of any kind. Venice was full of its own ghosts, heard in the echo of a laugh drifting over the *palazzo* wall or the swish of a gondolier's cloak at the Regatta Storica, the great water festival held in September.

The English governess, Miss Nancy Austin, rather resembled William's new wife. She plunged with brisk Anglo-Saxon gusto into Venetian life, arguing with vociferous enjoyment with servants and market sellers in fluent Italian heavily accented with English, and deploring the absence of "good long walks" in the city itself. Eventually a natural indolence lying beneath the Englishwoman's hearty surface overtook her and Miss Austin adapted to canals, boats, and a city built on mud flats amid tidal channels. She turned her energies toward exploring everything from the Palazzo Ducale to the Basilica di San Marco. She was a gifted storyteller, and her vivid re-creation of the early Veneti fleeing to the lagoon swamplands before Attila and his Huns was as gripping as a fairy tale by the brothers Grimm.

Beth often sat in on Miss Austin's lessons, receiving

an education she had not benefited from as a child. She was working on a series of articles on the churches of Venice for *Facets,* and there were more than enough of them to keep her busy. It was easier to escape reality while contemplating Tintoretto's *Last Supper* at Santo Stefano or examing Pietro Lombardo's intricate marble rosettes and crosses outside Santa Maria dei Miracoli.

She had expected Jonty and Henry to join them for the winter, but Jonty's asthma was causing him problems, so Henry invited Beth and Liane to come to the French Riviera, where they hoped the climate might be kinder. Reluctantly, she refused. She couldn't move again so soon, especially as Liane had now made a few friends of her own.

When spring returned, so did Henry and Jonty, unannounced. Beth was upstairs in her bedroom, where she liked to write, gazing up for inspiration at the painted ceiling. It was their laughter she heard first, filled with the carefree spontaneity she remembered from the past, a lightheartedness that had made her happy at a time when she had wondered if she would ever be happy again. With a cry of delight she ran from the room, her light gown of Havana muslin floating around her, her hair loose on her shoulders. "Jonty! Henry!" Leaning over the balustrade of the upper hall, she looked down on her unexpected guests.

There were three of them — Henry, Jonty, and a third, younger man. He too was smiling, but his expression remained a trifle reserved, as if he was doubtful about his reception.

He was beautiful, as breathtakingly perfect as a

Greek statue: great, candid gray eyes in the upturned face, lightly bronzed skin, a mouth any woman would die for, the face saved from effeminacy by a haughty patrician nose that blended perfectly with the rest of his features. In the shaft of light from one of the windows his hair shone, golden as the glittering mosaics on the walls of St. Mark's Basilica, hair one could imagine the deity giving to the angels themselves. The strong column of his neck rose from an open-necked blue shirt, buttons down the front of which his slender fingers were twisting.

He's a boy, thought Beth; he's only a boy. What are Henry and Jonty doing with this child? She felt angry with them for disturbing her peace. Instead of bringing contentment, they brought this young god, and now she had to worry about moral values, corruption, and all the things she had told herself didn't bother her in the least.

"Come down, Beth, and don't look so horror-struck! Come and meet Anthony!"

Henry pronounced the name in the English fashion, the "h" silent. So this god was English, apparently. Gathering her light gown around her, Beth came down the stairs, the marble of the hall floor cold under her bare feet.

Once on a level with them, she saw to her relief that the boy was not as young as he had looked from a distance. She had thought him about fifteen, but now she saw he was probably eighteen or nineteen years old. But even close up, his extraordinary beauty was undiminished. Jonty made the introductions.

"Beth, this is Anthony Rivers. We met him in

Biarritz and invited him to stay. We were sure you wouldn't mind, not in a *palazzo* large enough to accommodate the whole of the Medici family!"

"I think she does."

It was the boy who spoke. His accent was upper-class British, aristocratic, the tone musical. His expression, which a moment earlier had seemed almost pleading, was now as arrogant as his accent and the curve of his elegant nose. Beth felt her hackles rising.

"Mr. Rivers, I am not usually inhospitable, but I —" Her brave little speech faltered to a halt. How could she phrase it? Are you my brother's lover? Jonty's lover? Is this a triangle? Yes, I am shocked?

"Beth." Henry put his arm around his sister. "It's all right — it's not what you think."

"What am I thinking, Henry?"

"Come on, Beth, we all know what you're thinking and it's quite the opposite. Actually, we're Anthony's saviours."

For a moment it looked as if the boy would turn on his heel and walk out. Then he shrugged his shoulders and followed them into the salon with a not entirely convincing air of indifference. As they went through the doors Henry exclaimed, "God, Beth, it's almost as grand as one of Palladio's villas on the Brenta. Where's Liane?"

"Visiting friends on the Lido. She likes it here."

"I'm so glad. I can't wait to see her again. Come on, we'll tell you about Anthony."

The story didn't take long to tell. Anthony Rivers had been sent by his father to spend a year with an old family friend in France. From the moment of his arrival the boy had been subjected to constant and repeated advances by his host, a retired English general of ancient lineage and a taste for very young men. Things had been bad enough in the general's Paris home, but they had become worse in Biarritz, when the general had, one night, finally resorted to violence. Anthony Rivers had escaped and had literally run into the arms of Jonty and Henry, who were returning from a late-night walk. They took him to their villa, where they concealed him, and he left Biarritz with them.

Horrified, Beth looked at the boy. His expression was now such a mixture of defiance, embarrassment and misery that she was furious with herself for jumping to conclusions.

"Mr. Rivers, please forgive me — I had no idea and I should have known better than to think that Henry and Jonty —"

"No." It was Jonty who spoke, with the smile Beth had now learned to distinguish from his smile of true happiness. "You were right. Never trust a man, Beth, and we deviates least of all, because that is what we have learned to be: devious."

"What about your parents?" Beth asked the boy. "Surely you could have written and told them and they would have taken you away."

Anthony Rivers smiled. "You don't know them, so it's impossible to explain to you why they would never have believed me. Let me just say that the general has impeccable bloodlines and a distinguished record of service. I would have been accused of a vile slander and my life would have been made completely miserable."

"I see."

The boy looked straight at her, his embarrassment gone. "I think you do," he said. "Thank you."

At that moment, the double doors of the salon opened and Liane flew in, followed by Miss Austin. "Henry! Jonty! Pietro said you were here! Oh." The child stopped in her tracks and stared at the young man. "Oh my goodness," she said, "you are just as beautiful as Pietro said — like Donatello's David, wouldn't you say, Miss Austin?"

Amid the burst of laughter, Miss Austin declared, "Manners, young lady, manners! You are becoming more continental than the continentals!"

Anthony Rivers extended his hand. "My name is Anthony, and I'm delighted to meet you. May I ask your name?"

"My name is Liane von Schönstein, and I am Viennese and American, and more continental than the continentals." This with a sly glance at Miss Austin, who rewarded it with a shocked "Tut-tut!"

"May I ask how old you are?"

"I am seven. How old are you?" Miss Austin looked heavenward.

"I am nineteen, but I think you may be older than I am."

"No," replied the child, puzzled. "That's twelve years older than me and it always will be."

"Liane, you are getting far too precocious," laughed Jonty, gathering her into his arms. Delightedly hugging him, Liane asked, "Will you be staying? I do hope so, for Mamita needs the company. She sits in her room too much, everyone says so."

"Don't worry," said Henry, "now we're here we'll take her out so much that her feet won't touch the ground."

With delight and gratitude Beth heard the love in her brother's voice. It made her feel warm. She hadn't realized until that moment how very cold she had been feeling inside.

Chapter Thirty-Nine

Venice

The oleander bloomed and the nightingale sang
among the myrtles and cypresses. Bells rang out from
the campanile across the city, splintering the summer
sunlight and the early-morning mist. With the young
Englishman, Beth found herself living a girlhood she
had never had: carefree, insouciant, self-absorbed. She
understood what he had meant when he had told Liane
he was younger than she was, because there was a
quality of innocence and vulnerability about him that,
by comparison, sometimes made her feel much older
than her twenty-six years. Mostly, though, she felt
young at heart for the first time, it seemed to her,
in all of those twenty-six years

" 'Underneath Day's azure eyes
Ocean's nursling, Venice lies
A peopled labyrinth of walls.'
Know who wrote that?"

"Of course I don't. Whatever else your childhood
may have been like, Anthony, you clearly had a
marvellous education. Who, then?"

"Shelley. Come on, we'll go and buy some Shelley
— and Byron too."

" 'They sing in the squares, on the streets and on
the canals. The vendors sing as they cry their wares,
the workers sing as they leave the workplaces, the
gondoliers sing as they wait for custom.' Who said
that?"

"Goldoni — in Italian, of course."

"I can never catch you, damnit! Do you know
everything?"

The candid gray eyes looked into hers, and his blond
hair shone in the warm Italian sun. "Only in books,
Beth. I'm not good at life."

"Don't say that! You mustn't say that! Of course
you're good at life, otherwise all that's left to be good
at —" She stopped, the words catching in her throat.

"Is death, yes. Perhaps that is what I shall be good
at. Nothing will so become me as the leaving of life
— who knows?"

He laughed, head back, his wonderful clear young
laugh extending the smooth column of his throat. Beth
wanted to hold him, comfort him, she wanted —

No, she couldn't. She would not allow things to
become complicated by insidious yearnings for a boy
so much younger than herself, a boy who had already

had to escape from a situation not of his making. She was just going to relax, laugh, and enjoy herself in his company.

"Won't your parents be worried about you by now?" she asked.

"Not worried so much as outraged. But I don't think they'll cast me off when I decide to return — I'm the only son and heir, and appearances must be maintained."

Beth understood what he meant. She was content to think only of the present.

Eventually, he asked her about her marriage. She had never before put into words the sequence of the past nine years and found it difficult to do so. It all seemed unreal and insubstantial to her, and some of the elements were grotesque and fantastic. It was hard to explain Gisela Valeska and the fact that she, Beth, believed in her gift of prescience and understood the strength of Max's obsession.

As they talked they wandered in the villa garden, in a glade of foliage and grass that made it seem as if they were in the heart of the countryside. Jonty and Henry were away on a visit to Padua and Bologna, where they would be meeting friends. Anthony had asked Beth's permission to stay. Sensing an uneasiness in him which she had interpreted as a reluctance to move from the safety of the villa, she told him he was free to do whatever he wanted.

Dusk fell while they were in the garden, and above their heads the stars appeared. Beyond the walls of the garden a gondola passed; they could hear the swish of the water and the gondolier's gentle song. It was now that sweet and dangerous moment between light and dark, the time of day for talking of matters close to the heart.

"Why don't you divorce him, Beth, now that both your parents are dead? Wouldn't it be best to get him out of your life?"

"I don't think I shall be rid of Max that easily, even though I haven't seen anything of him for so long. And I'm afraid he's more likely to reappear if I do anything to disturb the way things are at the moment." She did not want to disclose to him the real reason: if Liam O'Connor would not marry her, she had no interest in changing anything. And it was true that she felt she had less cause for concern if she didn't rock the boat — as long, that is, as Max's obsession with Gisela Valeska lasted, or the clairvoyant allowed the affair to continue.

Beth turned to look at the young man beside her. In the soft light of dusk his blond hair seemed silver rather than gold, the haughty curve of his nose more dominant. She could see on his face the tension she had sensed since Henry and Jonty had announced their plans, and she wondered why he remained so ill at ease. Was he starting to worry about his parents?

"Anthony, is something wrong? Are you unhappy at being here in Venice like this? We could always contact your parents, you know. You could be misjudging them. Shouldn't you give them a chance to hear your side of the story?"

Anthony moved impatiently, his arms brushing against hers. "I'm sorry, Beth. The last thing I want is for you to think I'm unhappy here when you have been so kind to me, and I have been so happy — so very happy. You have no idea how happy!" Beth could hear both tension and passion in his voice, but not happiness.

"Then what is it? I've no wish to pry, but it might help if you talked about it."

Anthony swung around toward her on the small marble bench they had been sharing. "Why do you think I didn't want to go with Henry and Jonty, Beth?"

Beth shrugged her shoulders helplessly. "Because you were worried someone might catch up with you, because you feel safer in Venice — I don't know, Anthony."

"No, no, that's not it!"

His anger alarmed her. "I'm sorry, but I really don't understand. Let's leave it, Anthony, let's drop the subject. Let's not spoil a beautiful evening."

"Let's spoil it, Beth," he said, grasping her hands in his, the passion still in his voice, "— or let me spoil it! The reason I didn't go is because I'm not sure about myself, about how I feel about them, about men, or about women. Did I hate the general because it was a man touching me, or because he was old and fat and disgusted me? Wouldn't I have had the same reaction to a woman of my grandmother's age? When you're at a boarding school, these things go on. Was it just because there were no girls there, no girls *anywhere*, or was it because I'm really like Henry and Jonty? Oh God, Beth, I care enormously for them both, but I don't want to be like them! Oh how I don't want to be like them!"

Beth forgot the reserve she had maintained with the

young Englishman, the restraint she had deliberately cultivated because of her own response to his extraordinary physical beauty. She put her hands on his shoulders, caressing them, circumspection overcome by the desire to comfort him.

"Anthony Rivers, what an imagination you have! You may find it difficult to judge the nature of your reaction to the general, but think for a moment of Henry and Jonty. They are both still young — even Jonty's in his thirties — and they are both good-looking. Now, tell me, do you want to kiss them? Think about it hard, imagine it — do you want them to make love to you?"

"Lord, no!" His look of horror was enough to convince Beth, if she had had any doubts herself, and comic enough to start her laughing. "I'm sorry, Anthony, but if you could have seen your face when I said that, you'd have the answer to your fears — such distaste, such outrage!"

Anthony had started to laugh as well, and they sat, hands on each other's shoulders, rocking with mutual amusement in the moonlit garden.

How it moved from laughter to love-making, she would never quite remember, but laughter turned to kisses and caresses, and then to much more, to her own nakedness and his young body against hers, urgent and demanding — and to her yielding to his pleas. "*Cara* 'lizabeta, *celeste* Elizabeta, please, please, don't say no. Let me love you, love me, Beth, please love me. *Te amo*, Beth, from the moment you stood on the stairs and I saw your body through your gown and your beautiful bare feet. You give me faith in myself. Please don't refuse me!"

And when she acquiesced, it was not just for him alone or because of his entreaties. It was also for her and because there seemed no valid reason at that moment to deny to themselves what they both wanted so much. Afterward, as they lay on the mossy turf and she stroked the silken fair hair, he moved his hands gently over her body. "So beautiful, beyond imagining. No wonder Leander swam the Hellespont, no wonder Helen's beauty launched a thousand ships and burnt the topless towers of Ilium! I read you with my fingertips, like a blind man. You, Elizabeth, make me believe in immortality with a kiss!"

Drowning again in his arms, allowing the tide of feeling to pull her along, Beth thought of other words, other lines: those whom the gods love; beauty too rich for use, for earth too dear. So young, this boy, and yet, when he touched her and when he spoke to her of love, he made her think of the ephemeral nature of life, and not of immortality. Drift with the tide, she thought, forget. This is for now, for the moment — for tomorrow we die. Isn't that what the Bible says?

Afterward, as they walked back to the villa, his arm around her shoulders, she not touching him, fearing the cynosure of unseen eyes, she asked him, "If you have wanted to make love to me for so long, how is it you doubted yourself?"

The hand around her shoulders stroked her hair. "Because of earlier experiences, yes, but mostly because of the way men react to me, and not just the general. I thought there must be something wrong with me."

In the courtyard, in front of the creeper-covered Gothic structure of the Villa Tiepoli, Beth turned to look at him. Each time, she thought, one sees him afresh. His looks are so unbelievable that one thinks one had imagined the impossible and then one discovers him again. "Anthony," she said, "all your life everyone — men, women, children — everyone, will react to you, and if you look in the mirror you will see why. You have the gift of beauty."

His smile held all the sadness she feared and yet the enchantment she had been unable to resist. "Do they not call it the fatal gift?"

Beth shook her head, her thoughts shifting to another time, another man teasing her, cajoling her, laughing her into his arms and his bed. "No. Beauty is not the fatal gift. Charm is the fatal gift. My husband has it, and one day it will destroy him or someone else — I don't know, but it will destroy. Sooner or later it will prove fatal to Max, or to me, or to Gisela Valeska."

"No, never to you." Anthony held her hard against him. Still the feeling of doom circled close to her head, beating its dark wings like a great night-bird, shutting out the stars above from her view.

He slipped into her bed each night, giving her the gift of his beauty, in turn making her feel the most beautiful, the most adored woman in Venice. There was something powerfully aphrodisiac about someone so lavishly endowed by the gods finding her extraordinary and irresistible. He was discreet during the day. "I don't care about Miss Austin or Henry and Jonty, Beth, but I know you do. And, of course, there's Liane to consider."

Miss Austin, mercifully, didn't seem to have an inkling about the state of affairs between them. Beth wondered if it were Miss Austin's conventional approach to social mores that blinded her and whether she might have noticed their love affair if their ages had been reversed. As it was, she saw Beth as the mature mother of her charge, and she tended to treat Anthony almost as a schoolboy. She also seemed unaware of the nature of the relationship between Henry and Jonty, since they maintained separate bedrooms. Although in her late forties, Miss Austin was still very much an innocent.

The same could not be said of Henry and Jonty. Their antennae picked up the new vibrations at the villa within twenty-four hours of their return. All Henry said to his sister was, "Do you know what you're doing, Beth?"

"No, and I don't want to talk about it."

"Then I won't say any more. If you are aware that you don't know what you're doing, I'm less concerned than if you thought you had everything under control." With which enigmatic remark, he dropped the subject and never returned to it.

It had to end one day, and Beth knew it. There was no future possible between her and this golden boy. She imagined he might tire of her, see another pretty young face on the Lido — after all, he was experienced now, sure of himself — or decide to return to England. She even wondered if she would regain her own senses, but that seemed unlikely. His grace, wit, and intelligence continued to delight her.

She never imagined the end would be brought about

by the woman whose fate she felt was so profoundly bound to her own. But as soon as she saw the signature on the letter with the Paris postmark, she knew Gisela Valeska was about to affect the direction of her life once more.

Chapter Forty

Paris

Dear Beth,

As you can see from my address, I am in Paris. I shall be here for a few weeks while the count is on manoeuvres in Bukovina, near the Rumanian border. Then I shall be going into hiding — for how long I do not know. I have finally freed myself from Max, but he doesn't know this yet. If he did, he would kill me. Please, I beg you to come and see me as soon as possible. It is vital I speak to you. Call me here and I shall be ready to receive you at any hour of the day or night. Please use the phrase, "Send a letter to my love" if all is well and so that I know it is really you.

> *Tell no one your plans except, perhaps your brother, and leave Liane with him.*
>
> *Empress, I would not re-enter your life unless I had to.*

The letter was signed High Priestess.

The soft light of the late-afternoon sun seemed to dim, and the shadows on the terrace to lengthen. The breeze freshened, blowing the trailing vines about Beth with the sound of birds' wings. "It's finished," she thought. Whatever news Gisela Valeska had to give her, she knew that her love affair was over. The second reaction she had was surprise that Gisela knew where she was living and about the presence of her brother and child in Venice.

Then, and only then, did she feel afraid. If Gisela knew, it meant that Max knew, and he would soon discover Gisela was no longer his. The sensation of foreboding that had hung over her all that intoxicating, love-making summer now coalesced into one moment of blind panic before she calmed herself. In the distance she heard the voices of Henry, Jonty, and Anthony, who were just returning from an excursion to the island of Burano.

She could not trust herself to speak when they greeted her. Wordlessly she held out the letter to Jonty first.

He read it, handed it to Henry, and then sat down beside Beth. Gently, he took her hand in his. "I suppose I always felt it had to happen," he said. "I prayed it wouldn't, but my real fear was that he would tire of her and come back for more money, or just for malice. I never thought she would break free of him. I wonder how she did it?"

Henry looked up from the letter. "Do you know anything about all this?" he asked Anthony quietly.

It was Beth who answered. "Yes, he does, and he understands better than — " Horrified, she stopped herself. She had been about to say "Liam O'Connor." A sudden longing to have her fighting, angry Irishman with her overcame her, and she closed her eyes, gritting her teeth.

"No," said Henry, misinterpreting her half-finished thought. "I do understand, Beth. You want to see her, don't you?"

"I feel I must."

"Tell you what," said Jonty, practical as ever for all his habitually assumed air of insouciance, "I think we should pack up the household and move to Florence. Miss Austin has been talking wistfully for weeks about how she would love to see the Uffizi Gallery — and Liane can show her the Boboli Gardens and the swans. She'd like that. We shall know where you are, Beth, and you can send letters to us *poste restante*. That way, no one can trace us. In fact, we'll tell everyone here that we're moving back to the Riviera. They'd expect that of Henry and me at this time of year."

That's right, thought Beth with amazement, it's nearly fall. Where had the summer gone? She turned to look at Anthony. He was standing near the old stone fountain in the middle of the courtyard, at a little distance from them. The letter was in his hand and he was gazing at her.

"Well, Anthony," said Henry with a lightness that was only too obviously assumed. "Will you join us?"

Anthony turned his glance to Henry and smiled. "No," he replied, "I think not, thank you all the same. I think the time has come for me to go home."

Beth's vision blurred as the tears rolled slowly down her cheeks. She started to move back into the house, which seemed already to hold the darkness of evening, blinded as she was by the sunlight in the courtyard and the tears in her eyes.

"Beth." He had followed her, the light behind him like a halo, illuminating the bright hair.

"*Non angli, sed angeli,*" she murmured, smiling at him, loving him.

"Ah, *cara*, I'm no angel, but I am indeed Anglo-Saxon — stiff upper lip and all that. You have to do this thing, and I have to go back."

"You can go with Henry and Jonty, you know that."

"I know, but it will never be the same again. Not now. Oh, I brought you something." He pulled from his pocket a piece of creamy lace, beautifully worked. "They make it on Burano, stitching it, not on bobbins. Isn't it pretty? Just like you. No jewels, Beth, I'm afraid."

"Anthony Rivers, you are my jewel, and you always will be," she said.

He did not come to her room that night, and in the morning they found he had gone, leaving only a note in his room.

> *My dears — all my dears —*
> *Don't worry about how I manage for money.*
> *I shall sell a ring and a tie clip and — voilà*
> *— I shall have a ticket! I will also call ahead*
> *to warn my parents of the return of the*
> *prodigal son. There, I'm afraid, the similarity*
> *to the parable ends. So much more to say that*
> *I will not attempt to say it. I know you can*
> *read between the lines.*
>
> *Anthony*

She loved him all the more, if that were possible, for avoiding the good-bye scene she had so dreaded.

In the space of forty-eight hours Beth had made travel arrangements for Paris, started the process of moving them all from Venice to Florence, and wired Gisela Valeska.

The rue de Rivoli setting was not unlike that of the Ringstrasse. The woman, however, had changed. Gisela was wearing a softly draped garnet-red dress that closely followed the lines of her body, ending with a flurry of ruffles at the narrow hem. Beth felt it wasn't the dress alone that made her seem thinner, almost gaunt. The facial structure was even more striking, the flesh pared to the very minimum, the eyes glittering like black opals. She was leaning back on a sofa, a saluki lying at her feet, as elegant and slender as his mistress. There were orchids in the belt of her dress, fleshy and mottled against the garnet silk. Beth was struck afresh by the power of the woman's presence.

"Empress, forgive me for not rising to greet you, but today is one of my bad days, I'm afraid."

"You have been ill?"

"In a manner of speaking. Please sit down, Countess. Let me introduce you to Sultan — the best gift I was ever given."

Gisela motioned Beth to a chair near her and Beth saw that her hand shook. Gisela noticed her glance.

"Ah, you must be wondering if it is fear that makes me tremble. Not fear alone — that I could deal with — but something with which I have needed help. It doesn't really concern you, and yet it is part of the story. I took cocaine to help me through the nightmare, and it in turn became a nightmare that threatened to kill me." Gisela put up her hand to stop Beth from speaking. "No, do not be alarmed — I am over the worst now. Would you like coffee? Champagne?"

It was clear that Gisela did not want sympathy or platitudes at that moment, so Beth said simply, "Well, as a matter of fact, I'm extremely hungry. Could we go and eat, perhaps at my hotel?"

Gisela laughed and Beth was relieved to see some of the old gaiety in her expression. "We can eat right here and we'll do just that! I have a wonderful chef, and my appetite is his despair, although it is getting better now. Let me make the arrangements and we'll talk over dinner."

They were served a beautiful white wine, dry and subtle, delicately smoked trout, exquisitely cooked veal, crisp vegetables, tiny fruit tarts with a silken glaze. Over the simple perfection of the meal, the two women watched each other become more comfortable and relaxed. Gradually the story Beth had come to hear unfolded.

Max had been waiting for Gisela when she had returned to Vienna, and he had taken possession of her once more.

"When I got back to Vienna, all I could think about was Max. And there he was, in my apartment. I was in his arms and he in my bed in a matter of minutes. I'm sorry — does this hurt you?"

"No — but it shocks me. I'm more my mother's daughter than I thought I was. What happened to change your feelings?"

Gisela sighed. Her slender fingers wound around her wineglass and Beth could hear the click of her rings on the cut crystal. "There were two other men in my life — not lovers — who hated Max's power over me. One was the man who developed my psychic gift, and the other was the man who protected me from Max when you and I first met in Vienna. Do you remember how I spoke of sending a letter to someone who could arrange to have Max sent away by his regiment?''

"Send a letter to your love — Yes, I remember, and you asked me to use that phrase in my reply to you," said Beth. "But you said this man was not your lover."

"He wasn't. He is a high government official who used me to carry out certain tasks for him. I am privy to many secrets and some are useful to the state. It was this man who arranged my trip to your country and my introduction to Eddie Delaney — God, poor Eddie, I never thought — who was to know?"

"Liam was right, then!" exclaimed Beth. "You were a spy!"

"Yes, and I cannot deny it became an ever-more-fascinating part of my life. Such power it gives one, Beth. There is something wonderfully erotic about it, almost as good as making love!" Gisela laughed. "But it was neither of these men who put an end to my relationship with Max. It was Max himself."

"What did he do?"

"It was what he said, Beth, what he told me." Gisela leaned across the table, the candle flames flickering as she spoke, shifting the shadows over her face, catching the glitter of her eyes. There was a pause, and Beth could feel her gathering her strength for what she was about to say.

"He told me that he killed my mother."

Beth couldn't speak. What was there to say? What appropriate response could there be to such a revelation? Suddenly Gisela's hand trembled violently on the white damask of the tablecloth, and she curled her fingers into her palm in an effort to control them. Beth put her hands over the other woman's and felt the pulse beating violently in the slender wrist. "How? When?" she finally managed to ask.

"When I was fifteen years old. Within the year he became my lover. It was what he had planned. He had started the affair with my mother only because of his desire for me, but she planned to give me to someone else and asked Max to arrange it. That was why he had to kill her, he told me. Even then I was to belong to no one else — even then."

It was not Max's role in the story that struck Beth so much as that of the woman she remembered had been called Franzi Valeska in the letter which had opened her eyes so many years ago. She felt physically sick. "Are you saying that your mother planned to — to give you away when you were fifteen? Your mother?"

Gisela laughed. "Life is different in America, no? My mother gave me away when I was eight, but the man was more interested in my gift than in my body, and my mother's ignorance of that fact protected me for several years. He was a protector, but in a way very different from what she and most women of my background mean by that word. I remained a virgin until Max took me at the respectable age of sixteen. And I wanted to be taken, Beth — I wanted it!"

"My God," was all Beth could find to say. Gisela pulled her hands abruptly from Beth's and her voice was angry when she spoke.

"No, Countess von Schönstein, don't you judge my mother! What do you know about the life of such women as Franzi and Gisela Valeska? My mother knew I had two valuable assets — my psychic talent and my looks, and she played them both for the very highest stakes. She did it for *me!* Never, never doubt that I was loved by my mother and that she did these things for me!"

Gisela pushed her chair back and got up from the table, her gown snaking around her as she started to pace the room.

"Gisela, forgive me. I'll make no more judgements."

Gisela turned to Beth. "Pour me some brandy, Beth. There is more to come, and you'll judge me again, I promise you."

Beth handed the brandy to Gisela, who continued to pace the room as she talked. "You can never judge me as harshly as I do myself, and that is why I am shaking this way." Gisela held up her hand in front of her, and Beth thought of her brother William. "Alcohol?"

"No. The cocaine was enough — so easy, Beth, and it made me feel so good, so forgetful, so free from care. Underneath it all I think I had always known the truth, but I had hidden it from myself. When the visions started, and the fates tried to tell me, I could only stop them with cocaine. Then the desire for Max grew stronger and the images went away. I was the mistress of my mother's killer, and I didn't care!"

Gisela drained the rest of the brandy in the glass before she continued. "And you know why he told me, in the end? He told me to prove how complete a hold he had over me. He had become angered at Baron Eihrentahl's efforts to remove him from Vienna permanently, and to show me how futile it was, how absolutely I was his creature, he told me how and why he had killed my mother. He told me I had known it all along, and he was right."

There was a long pause, and Beth said, "But it was enough, wasn't it? Enough to break the spell for you. Max had finally miscalculated, hadn't he?"

"Yes." There was wonderment in Gisela's voice, as if she still found it hard to believe what had happened. "He stood there before me, laughing, as beautiful as ever, as seductive as ever, saying, 'Oh sweet girl, but we have such fun together, no? *Ein Hetz*, Gisela, such a spree,' and I felt sick. It was not just that I saw him for the first time. I also saw myself. Then — ah, then! — I had to be careful."

"You didn't show him how you felt."

"You guess right. I hid everything. He made love to me, and it was one of the worst times in my life. I was a line girl, no different from a line girl. You remember them?"

"Yes."

"I went to one of my protectors. Together we made plans. Max would go to Bukovina while I took the cure for my addiction. It was very bad, even Max could see that, and it was beginning to enrage him. I am now supposed to be in a clinic in the Swiss Alps, cut off from the rest of the world. I did spend some time there, but I came here when I was free of the addiction to cocaine and to Max." Gisela smiled and shook her head wonderingly. "And the first was the hardest! I would never have thought it possible to be more addicted to anything than I was to that one man, but I was."

"Gisela, if what you say is true about your mother and what she wanted for you, why would Max have needed to reach you through an affair with her? Surely she would have been only too happy to accept a direct proposition?"

"I asked him that myself. The answer was so perfectly in character I'm surprised I hadn't thought of it. 'Because it amused me,' he said, 'to take the mother and then take the daughter from her. Such a game!' What he had not reckoned on was the strength of my mother's passion for him and the plans she had made for me herself. He said to me, 'By then she would have fought me tooth and nail — even I had underestimated how clever I am with women.' He is, you know, Beth."

Beth nodded. She was thinking of her husband's humour, her gentle sexual awakening; she knew only too well what Gisela was saying. It was hard to remember now how she had been moved from hostility into willing acquiescence, and thence to passion. But it had happened.

"But of course you know," said Gisela. "You tried to kill me for him, and then yourself, no?"

"Thank God you came out into the street when you did! Is any man worth that much, I wonder?"

Gisela's answering smile this time was so joyous that its radiance seemed to warm the soft candlelight. "Not death, no, not killing for. But living for, Beth, yes. That's why I am alive now — not for myself, and not because of or in spite of Max, but because of one man."

Beth's smile answered Gisela's. "Tell me about him."

Gisela watched the American woman rise from the table and move over to the fire. At this moment in time, they were probably as unalike as they had ever been, for where Gisela was pared to the bone both physically and mentally, Beth von Schönstein's beauty had a lush sensuality that was new. Her pale skin had taken on a faint peach colour in the Italian sun, and her dark hair seemed more abundant than ever. Every movement, every gesture was changed. She walked with the serene confidence of a woman who has been told she is beautiful, again and again.

"You have a story, too, Beth. Why not tell me yours?"

Beth looked at her swiftly before lowering her eyes. So, there was pain too — that much Gisela had seen before Beth's gaze was averted. "But you already know my story," was the evasive reply. Quick as a flash, the image came to Gisela, taking her by surprise.

"No, no — about the golden one, the gray-eyed boy."

"Gisela!"

Beth stood, paralyzed, looking at the other woman. She had forgotten what extraordinary things this Viennese clairvoyant could do, had forgotten her true power.

"Forgive me, you owe me no stories, no revelations. Here, Sultan!" She extended her hand to the saluki, who rose with graceful indolence and came close to his mistress. "Sit by us, *mein Schatz*, while I tell the Empress about the man who gave you to me." Gisela picked up a letter that lay on a small table close to her. "This, Beth, is from Baron Rudolph Eihrentahl. It will tell you better than any words of mine about my darling Rudi, my love."

Chapter Forty-One

Vienna

"*Gisela, my darling,*
  You ask how long I have loved you. Since the first moment I saw you — but men always say that, don't they? How to find new words, new phrases, to express what I feel to you who have heard all the pretty words and phrases before from all the men who tried and failed, and from the one who had it all, the one I have hated more than I thought it was possible to hate a fellow countryman — anyone who was not an enemy to the empire.
  I have loved you since you walked through my office door. Such a young girl in her sables and her glitter,

those great eyes of yours both curious and defiant. The daughter I never had, I thought, and then I felt the ironic laughter inside me at the hypocrisy of the thought. When I kissed your hand, I felt my spine melt and I nearly made you an offer there and then. Drop the count and be mine — so romantic of me, darling Gisela, wasn't it? Thank God I didn't. Not because I have scruples now that I didn't have then — God, I'd have taken you on any terms — but because I didn't know then what I later discovered: the depths of your obsession.

Then we fenced with words. Did you realize that was what we were doing, Liebe? Heavens, I thought, the girl is bright as well as beautiful. Thus began my own obsession. And what did I do? I gave you a history lesson. You could not know that is what I do to those I most favour. I talk politics, intrigue, military history. I make love with these subjects, darling girl, and that is what I did then. Clever of me, no? And when I saw you were worried about something I said — about threats to the emperor's life, I think it was — I became rather less clever. I insulted you in my efforts to comfort you.

Yet, when I saw your response I was almost glad I had been so clumsy. What fire! What passion! I thought to myself, I may never make love to this woman, she may never take me into her bed and let me love her, but at least I have seen a shadow, had just a taste of what it would be like to share the fire.

Woman. The little girl had gone by then, and I saw you as a woman. Remarkable and beautiful, and rare. You teased me about the billets doux *— I was* getting sharper, Gisela, I actually recognized you were teasing me by this stage. Not flirting, I thought, but teasing. Of that I felt sure.

Then you saw my maps. "This is lovely," you said. "This is lovely." When you had gone, I took that map off the wall, carried it home and put it above my bed. Every time I looked at it I heard your voice, and I didn't sleep for a week. No, no, I'm not exaggerating, Liebchen, I promise you. Military men are very precise, you know. We call a spade a spade, a week a week.

And when I thanked you, how very personal I became! "The emperor is grateful to you," I said. Not even "I am grateful to you."

For what? For days and nights of such exquisite agony? Do you know what stopped me from asking you to be my mistress? That it could have been dangerous to the security of the empire! There, Gisela. But I was passionately in love with you. And as I gradually learned the depths of your obsession with von Schönstein, I realized it was hopeless for me.

I was angry then, for a while. I had come very close to compromising myself over a woman who would not have had me anyway. I told myself I was fortunate and tried to forget you, which was difficult when the scent of roses from your billets doux filled my office. "General so-and-so says this — military attaché such-and-such says that — " I used to look for personal messages, hidden meanings between each word and line. Sometimes I was lucky and you teased me; I felt pleased when I realized I could still recognize it. You had changed me a little, after all.

When the business of America came up, I thought

to myself, "She's getting over it, I have a chance!"
How vain I was, my darling. Vienna and the world
are full of handsome, amusing men and I thought,
"I have a chance"!

And yet, even so, I could compromise myself. I knew
the American colonel's reputation, and still I gave you
the introduction. Well, it was for the emperor, after
all, and I am a servant of the state.

It was hell. To console myself, I thought, "If she
can sleep with an American colonel for business
reasons, she can sleep with me." Such a romantic,
no?

You came back after von Schönstein had killed the
man. Not the first he had killed for you, as we had
learned — and you couldn't wait to throw yourself
into his arms. I hated you again.

For all of — what? — a year, perhaps. Then the
cocaine started. We had occasion to meet again about
that time — I think it was the strike in November,
or maybe the uprising in Russia, I don't remember
— see what you have done to the military precision
of my mind! I wondered what had brought about the
dependency on the drug — you already knew the count
was a murderer and sometimes unfaithful to you —
so I used my court contacts and dug around. I found
out what had happened to your mother.

His friends had lied for him, of course. There was
nothing I could do, either through personal or legal
channels; for that matter, if I had been able to do
anything, I felt sure you would never have forgiven
me. But the count did me the everlasting favour of
telling you himself. Such a miscalculation! I think
I knew you better by then than he did.

*We had been meeting more often, remember?
Through the Russo-Japanese war, the Moroccan crisis,
the Anglo-Russian convention — there was always a
political or military expedient to cover my true reasons.
I am good at concealment. It is my job, after all.*

*Gradually, we began to talk about more personal
things. You about your gift, which I believed in for
the first time, because of the fear it engendered in you.
Fear is always believable; it is much more difficult
to fabricate than ecstasy. You talked about your mother
and I held my silence. When you talked about him
it was more difficult to keep quiet.*

*Then came the day you said to me, "Max says you
are a romantic."*

*From such a man to hear such a thing! I thought
I could not possibly conceal my confused emotions
at your pronouncement. Then you added, "But I find
that hard to believe. You are always such a perfect
servant of the empire, so correct, so precise. You are
never in doubt, and romantics make mistakes. What
makes you a romantic, Baron Eihrentahl?"*

*Do you remember what I did? I gave you another
history lesson, but this time it was about my other
passion. I talked about long marches on horseback
through Lower Austria in the autumn sunshine, the
nightly billets in those beautiful little villages, or
evenings spent on lonely watches in Transylvania or
some other far-flung post of this great empire of ours.
I talked to you of an enchantment that was always
new and that I would give anything to experience
again.*

*And then I looked up at you, despairing at my own
inability to say, "I am a romantic, Gisela Valeska,*

410

because I have nursed a hopeless passion for you for the past seven years."

And I saw something in your eyes.

You left, and I thought it was my imagination.

It was then that von Schönstein made his blunder and my life changed.

Every moment is fresh in my mind, every word we said, every breath I took that day.

"Hide me," you said. "It is over. Finally for me, it is over. But he will kill me before he'll let me go. Please hide me."

And I, militarily correct as ever, said in my warm human way, "Why should I hide you, Fräulein? Why?"

I thought you would be equally clever and cold. I thought you would say, "Because I am important to your work for the emperor."

Not you. You said, "Because you are in love with me." *Remember, my darling?*

You said it with surprise, as if it were suddenly dawning on you, this thing I had concealed for so long. And you added, "In your own way you have been making love to me for years."

Your surprise attack foiled me. I crumbled — God, how I crumbled. Head in hands, feeling the tears on my fingers, I said, "Yes," *then* "yes" *again — in case I had not made myself clear.*

Then you were on your knees by me and you kissed me. Very gently, once, on the forehead, as if I were a child.

"You know, Baron," *you said,* "I think I love you. I don't know how or when it started, but I think a *part of me has known it for some time. Could it be that, do you think, that has helped me find my freedom?" See how I remember every word you said?*

I didn't care. I found out afterward he had just told you the truth about your mother, but I still didn't care. I chose to believe you.

Hiding you at my country estate was easy. My wife had died a few years before and I was betraying no one. No one would suspect me of going there to visit a woman, because I didn't do such things. Your cocaine addiction was bad enough for the count to see the necessity for immediate action, and he never suspected me of ulterior motives. I am not the type for such frivolities, the trivia of life.

But you women are, aren't you? Gisela Valeska, how is it then that you are all beginnings, all endings, everything to me? See, beloved, I must be a romantic, mustn't I? After all?

I was a lost cause before I made love to you. Once I had made love to you, the battle was over, the victory yours.

My victory too, that's the glory of it. Your breasts beneath the palms of my hands, your hair against my mouth, my manhood within you. That's how I see it now, my manhood in terms of you. Once it was the honour of the regiment, courage under fire, my seat in the saddle, the erectness of my spine.

Such trivia!

What it all comes to this: your skin against mine, your lips against mine. The sweetness of you and the wonder of you.

And you say you love me. Do you? How can you? I wonder how it is possible. I don't know the answer to that, but I know I love you and have for years, darling Gisela.

And, in the end, that's all that matters.

Rudi

Chapter Forty-Two

Paris

Beth looked up from the letter, tears in her eyes. Gisela was looking into the embers of the fire, smiling, gently stroking the saluki at her feet. Silence fell in the room as the shadows of the present began to move across her face once more. Gently, she took the letter from Beth's hands.

"You realize, Beth, what my freedom and happiness mean to you?"

"If Max cannot get you, he will probably come for me."

"Almost certainly. In a few days I shall be leaving here for a destination that even I don't know. Rudi is taking me there. Max will look for me; he will not find me, and then he will look for you. He knows you have been in Italy — he knows a great deal about your life, for as he said once to me, 'You never know when I might need to find Beth again.'"

"For money? Has he really gone through all that money?"

"No. This time it is not for money." Gisela turned away from the fire and faced Beth. The fear in her eyes was unmistakable now. "Beth, when Max comes looking for you, he will believe he is coming for me. The two of us have become confused over the years in his mind, until he is no longer sure that we are two separate people. Sometimes he would call me his wife, and at first I was elated. Then I realized he thought it was you. At other times he would know he was speaking to me, but he would address his remarks to you. I would say, 'Max, this is Gisela,' and he would reply, 'I know, but if I say it to you then Beth will know, won't she?'"

Beth's hands and feet felt numb, chilled. "Perhaps he believed you would convey his thoughts to me by psychic means."

Gisela shook her head. "I think not. I have spoken to friends in the medical profession in Vienna, particularly to those who study the human mind. They tell me it is possible that for Max the division between what is real and what is not is ceasing to exist, if it has not already done so. You met his family, I think?

Beth thought of the ruined splendours of the Bavarian estate and its two chatelaines with their staring, unseeing eyes, and she shuddered. "Yes."

Gisela rose from her chair and came over to Beth's side. Her eyes burning into Beth's, she put her hands on the hands of the woman whose fate seemed inter-woven with her own. For a moment Beth felt a kind of terror she had never experienced before: Was she Beth or was she Gisela? Had she too lost hold of her own identity? Had this woman's soul entered her? Was this part of the powers of the clairvoyant, and was it Max alone who saw the truth? Perhaps it was she and Gisela who were mad, bound by a double persona, a shared insanity from which they could never break free.

Until one of us dies, she thought. Only then both are destroyed — isn't that what I once felt?

As if reading Beth's thoughts and thus heightening Beth's feeling of dread, Gisela said, *"Doppelgängers*, Beth, is that what we are? Max believes that, only I tell him he is wrong and that we have already proved him wrong."

"I had the feeling once that if you were destroyed, then I too would —"

Gisela grasped Beth's hand so hard that her rings cut into her fingers. "Don't say it! That's what Max believes. I told him he must be wrong, for if we were *Doppelgängers*, one of us would already have ceased to exist. The true legend of the *Doppelgänger* is that if you meet one another, then one of you dies. That would have happened years ago when we faced each other on a street off the Ringstrasse. We both survived that moment, and there was a knife in your hands."

"What was Max's reaction when you told him he must be wrong?"

The saluki came over and joined his mistress, putting his head on her lap. Gisela rested her head against his silky coat and closed her eyes.

"He said he was one of the *Adeligen*, that was all. That he was one of the chosen ones."

Beth needed no translation, no interpretation. Right was might, he was saying. Mankind begins with the barons. I make my own rules.

"What shall I do? Tell me, Gisela, through the crystal or the tarot or however you can. What shall I do?"

"No tarot, no crystal, Beth, but I'll tell you what I think is best. Go back to America and take Liane with you. Go back to fresh beginnings, to hope and optimism. Leave this Europe that crumbles slowly beneath the weight of old orders, old injustices, the death of too many dreams, the birth of too many new betrayals. You are safest in America. To kill a man in a duel in Paris or Vienna is not as serious, I think, as to murder him in Chicago. In his saner moments Max will remember how he so nearly lost his freedom, if not his life, in your country. This time there will be no one to spirit him away. In America mankind does not begin and end with the barons or counts. They alone are not the chosen ones."

"And you?"

"Me? Oh, I shall be as safe as I have ever been. I have a mission now, for I have to convince a man that I truly love him, and that seems to me to be very important. This much I know, that Europe will soon destroy what is corrupt and bad, but also much of the bright and beautiful and best."

Bright and beautiful and best. Suddenly, unaccountably, Beth had a vision of Anthony Rivers standing in the darkened villa with the afternoon sunlight behind him turning the blond hair to gold.

Book Five

The Lightning-struck
Tower

Chapter Forty-Three

The House on the Hudson

"What a blessing, really, your mother didn't live to see the day," said Aunt Medora. "She would have thought the world was coming to an end."

Beth blinked. That was the trouble with the swift efficiency of Atlantic crossings, she thought. One had no time to adjust. And they were now talking of airships crossing oceans in the next twenty-five years! Maybe by then there would be even less of a contrast between the Old World and the New.

The topic of conversation was the divorce of Jack Astor, the horror of which was compounded by the rumour that he intended to marry an eighteen-year-old with what would have been considered indecent haste after a bereavement and for which there was no adequately descriptive phrase after a divorce. Beth gave a little laugh and said, "I think the world will survive, Aunt Medora. After all, it was supposed to end in May with the return of Halley's Comet."

"Oh *that*," said her aunt dismissively. "That's just a heap of superstitious nonsense from the Old World."

With an airy wave of her hand, Aunt Medora threw out centuries of superstition. It was exactly what Beth needed. Far better to feel the earth tremble because of society's pecadillos than because of the slings and arrows hurled by outraged gods or the powers of darker forces. In the heavily furnished sitting room of her aunt and uncle's newly acquired New York home, her conversation in an apartment on the rue de Rivoli with a Viennese clairvoyant seemed overwrought, a product of hysteria and fevered imaginings. The talk moved on to the subject of her brother William, who was fast becoming a carbon copy of his father and whose wife was producing almost a baby a year.

"You and Henry have a lot of catching up to do," said her aunt archly.

"Haven't we? replied Beth, suppressing a strong desire to giggle at the wild inappropriateness of the remark. Her reaction pleased her, for she took it as a sign of renewed mental vigour and health.

"William has become so practical," said Aunt Medora. "He is thinking of moving out of the brownstone, as you know, and moving farther up Fifth Avenue, but he also feels we should dispose of the Hudson property this winter. No one goes there anymore, and the upkeep is simply ridiculous now."

"Oh no!" said Beth in dismay. "He can't do that, can he, without consulting the rest of the family?"

"Well, I think he can, dear, but I'm sure he wouldn't if he knew you were still attached to it. Why? Were you thinking of opening it up again?"

"As a matter of fact, I was thinking of staying there again, though eventually I shall have to spend a good deal of my time in New York, of course, for Liane's sake. Miss Austin has agreed to come over, but only for a while, and I shall be looking for a school. Liane must have a permanent base and make friends."

"You and Liane are both welcome to stay with us as long as you like — you know that, my dear. Will you be seeing your — will Liane's father — I mean —"

Beth put her aunt out of her misery. "My marriage is over, Aunt Medora," she said firmly. "It is very unlikely I shall ever see the count again, but I am not thinking of a divorce for the time being — if ever."

Beth saw the relaxation in her aunt's body. At this moment Liane came into the room and Beth breathed a sigh of relief. She didn't want to hear the words of commiseration foreshadowed by the look on her aunt's face.

"Ah, Liane" said her aunt, "we were just talking about you, honey."

Liane gave her aunt a searching glance from her hazel eyes and went over and sat by her mother, leaning against her. Beth knew that Medora found her niece puzzling and the relationship between mother and daughter informal and unsatisfactory. Liane's ability to chatter in three languages was termed "showing off," and her extensive vocabulary "forward."

"Your mama was just talking about sending you to school, Liane. Wouldn't you like that?"

Liane transferred her gaze to her mother. "I have

Miss Austin," she said. Before Beth could reply, Medora had pressed on. "But sweetheart, just think of all the people you could meet and the new and different things you could learn! I sometimes fear the world is changing for the worse, but we must move with the times. That's what this country is all about, freedom and progress. What will you be when you grow up, I wonder?"

Liane looked at her aunt. "Something better than a rich fool, anyway," she said.

Medora's face went bright red, as though she had been slapped. Beth took her daughter by the shoulders, restraining the urge to shake her. "Liane, apologize to your Aunt Medora, and to me. Your aunt and I may have the good fortune to be rich, but we are not fools."

The child's face was set and pale. "I'm sorry, Mamita."

"And?"

"I'm sorry, Aunt Medora."

The urge to shake was now replaced by the need to comfort. Her daughter's unhappiness was only too plain in the face that looked up at her. Holding Liane close to her, she thought to herself, "Better this, better dealing with property sales and where to live, where to send Liane to school, better even to deal with a rebellious child who doesn't fit in than to drift through lotus-land in Havana muslin and bare feet, pretending to be useful when I write about Tuscan villas and fourteenth-century monasteries."

A rich fool. Liane had struck closer to home than her mother would have cared to admit, but she wasn't sure what her alternatives were. Thinking of writing made her think about *Facets*, and that only made her think about Liam O'Connor. Suddenly Beth felt as heartsick for Venice as her seven-year-old daughter.

Golden light filtered through the glass over the door of the house on the Hudson. Outside, Liane was running through the leaves with her new Labrador puppy, laughing and shrieking with happiness. How easily children heal, thought Beth, watching her daughter.

"This is beautiful, Mamita! Was I here before?"

"Yes, you were when —"

When. Leave it, leave the thought where it belonged, in the past, along with the brilliant blue eyes and curling hair and strong hands around her waist. My darlin' Bethie. So powerful was that memory that she could almost hear the playful Irish accent echoing around her on the high green plateau above the river.

To Beth's disappointment, the guesthouse was in worse shape than the main building, to which most of the caretaker's attention had rightly been given, and she was forced to move in among the gilt and the Circassian walnut and the Flemish tapestries. Miss Austin, however, was most impressed.

"A *beaux arts* country home. Absolutely charming. Good and solid. Think of what you did with the Villa Tiepoli, Countess, and what you could do with this. Start now, before all that ivy gets going in the spring, and you have the damp creeping in the windows in that shocking manner it did in Venice. Roll up your sleeves and we'll all take a hand, m'lady."

Dear Miss Austin! Practical, indispensable, and a

424

firm believer in Satan finding mischief for idle hands to do, even among adults who should know better. Carried along by Miss Austin's enthusiasm, Beth got to work on redecorating, refurnishing, simplifying, and enhancing. Liane ran wild with the village children, and Beth listened with amusement as her hybrid Italian-English accent became more American every day, as did her vocabulary, not all of which was approved of by Miss Austin.

Thoughts of Venice and Paris receded. This was now lotus-land in its own way; here too she could forget. So absorbed was Beth by the practicalities of taking out one of the twin fireplaces in the drawing room because of draughts, or removing a rare Persian rug from the reception hall because Liane's puppy relieved himself on it, that she failed to remember that forgetting held its own dangers.

Who would have believed it? she thought. I am happy.

There was a heavy snowfall at the end of November, and Beth decided it was time to return to New York. Not enough work had been done to improve the heating arrangements in the mansion, and it was extremely cold. Besides, much as she personally would have liked it, she couldn't cut Liane off from the outside world. The child's adjustment to her new life had been hard for her, and although she had now made friends with a girl from one of the country homes nearby, her friend had already returned to the city. As the children from the village had now returned to school, they were also not available for Liane to play with.

On the first day of their return to New York, Beth bumped into Gloria and Lester Baker in a book store on Union Square. They seemed delighted to see her, which in turn delighted Beth, and they urged her to get more directly involved in the running of *Facets*. "It's great to have your money, Beth, and the foundation is working very nicely, but we'd like to have you."

"That's very flattering, Gloria, but I don't really see what I could offer. Writing articles is one thing, but I've no experience in administration, running an office, or anything like that."

"It's not so much any of that we want," said Les, "as a slant, an angle, a flavour you could give the magazine. Your experience is cosmopolitan and European. Your perspective would be great on some of the movements this city is exploding with right now. Some of them feed off political and historical situations in the Old World, and some are adding fuel to the fires burning over there. We'd really like to have you along, Beth."

Gloria Baker looked Beth squarely in the eye and added, "And if it's Liam O'Connor you're worrying about, you needn't. He left the magazine in the summer. I think he wanted to get back to the rough-and-tumble of the daily newspaper world. You'll see his byline in the *Herald*, the *Times*, most of the major newspapers. He's freelancing at the moment, and quite successfully, I might add. So give it some thought, Beth, and get back to us."

"I will," said Beth, "I will."

Dizzy with delight she returned to the house she

had rented on Fifth Avenue, much higher up than her parents' brownstone, which was now up for sale. Something more than a rich fool, she thought to herself — they have given me the chance to be something more than a rich fool. Twenty-four hours later, she was in the *Facets* offices off Lafayette.

Life changed. It took on a structure new to Beth, although her role was kept relatively undefined. Under the heading "The Return of the Native" and the quotation "With diamonds in her ears, and her toes out at her boots," she covered everything from the dance schools among the synagogues of the East Side, whose owners were often tailors by day and instructors by night, to the self-made men on Wall Street, some of whom reminded her of her father. She talked to the gorgeous girls at the Jardin de Paris and the Casino, who could expect to marry millionaires. She met with the women of the Midnight Mission who worked with the cruisers and chippies along Broadway from Canal to Twenty-third or in the concert saloons. She heard the playing of the *Marseillaise* and the *Internationale* in Tomkins Square, and she met the intellectual anarchists at bohemian soirées in Greenwich Village.

It was inevitable that she would eventually run into Liam O'Connor, but she had thought it would probably be at one of the anarchists' meetings, and she had braced herself to be prepared to see his face on these occasions. She had not expected to come face to face with him at a new automobile showroom on Broadway, where he was looking at the Pierce-Arrows, Packards, and Haynes-Appersons with a striking fair-haired woman whose elegant understated clothes screamed of trips to Paris and Poiret.

It was his laugh she heard first and recognized, and then she saw his dark hair. He was leaning toward his companion, who had her arm through his and was gesticulating theatrically at the automobile in front of her.

For one dreadful moment Beth thought that, in nineteenth-century fashion, she was going to faint at the salesman's feet, and then he looked up and saw her. Frozen with shock, Beth heard the salesman beside her extolling the virtues of whatever automobile it was they were looking at as she waited to see what Liam would do. She herself felt incapable of any movement at all, whether of acknowledgement or escape. Like mirror images they stood and stared at each other across the showroom aisles while his companion continued to chatter on vivaciously.

After what seemed like the passage of hours, Liam and the woman turned and started to move toward one of the exits. As they reached the door Liam said something to her, and Beth saw her laugh, tap him on the shoulder, and go out into the street on her own. Then he turned and walked in her direction.

"Thank you," Beth said to the salesman. "Could I just think it over awhile? Let me have your card and I'll get back to you."

Liam had reached her side just as the salesman left to join another couple on the showroom floor.

"Hello, Beth."

"Liam."

What do you say, she thought, to a man you have lost three times? What she wanted to say, now, at last, was, "I love you," but that would be impossible. Impossible to say on the floor of an automobile showroom after the space of years, a love affair of her own, and the sight of the beautiful blonde woman smiling up at him, clinging possessively to his arm.

So she said nothing. Nothing at all. Just stood and stared at him as he was staring at her, then turned and walked away. Too much water under the bridge, too much pain in seeing him again to talk about the weather or the newspaper business, his rich girl friend or her own mad husband.

According to Ada Holman, there were always other women, and they were usually unimportant and often a blessing. Perhaps this one was unimportant to Liam, but she hadn't the strength to find out. She didn't want the answer. Maybe her mother had been right about something else as well. Cultivating the externals was far less painful than fretting over lost opportunities, and far more rewarding.

Outside, the snow had started to fall. Beth thought back to the time when she was sixteen years old, riding in Central Park in a scarlet sleigh with bells ringing, and Max laughing beside her. She had been thoughtlessly, utterly happy, she remembered, because she had believed she was truly in love.

Chapter Forty-Four

The House on the Hudson

Being alone was easier to bear in the house on the Hudson. How ironic, she thought, that she should remain within the framework of her childhood, now that she was free to choose! She remembered Jonty's laugh when he had said to her, "Heck, Beth, we're all trapped. Didn't you know that?"

Now that the worst of the winter was over, she had come to be by herself, to take a needed break from New York and from *Facets* for a while. With the dawning of the year 1911 a terrible restlessness had come over her, and a yearning to return to Europe, but travelling abroad was impossible because of Liane, who was now happily settled in New York. It was

430

also impossible for other reasons, but those she didn't want to think about. There had been no news from any source as to Max's whereabouts or activities, and she herself had made no enquiries. Of whom would she make them, and to what end?

Instead she had come to the house on the Hudson. Just after she arrived there had been a late ice storm, and she had seen the landscape decorated in a spectacular beauty of white on white, white on black, white on gray. No lemon or lime, no gorgeous oranges and gold. Just this exquisite monochrome of silver and silence that fed the soul in the moments before the sun melted the mists and the sea of whiteness melted from the landscape.

The crystalline beauty seemed to echo the icy detachment of her mind. Beth read all the books she had brought with her and set herself to completing the modernization of the house begun the previous fall. Outside, spring, which had held its breath, returned, and the leaves started to open.

"I wonder why my parents never gave the house a name," she said to the caretaker, who had been with the Holmans for as long as she could remember. "We always called it 'the house on the Hudson,' and in the village they say 'the Holman house,' don't they?"

"Yes, they do that, but it had a name, ma'am. Sure did — least, your father gave it a name, but your mother wouldn't hear of it. She said it was too spooky for her." The old man looked up at her over the large broom with which he was sweeping the marble steps before the great front doors. "So it never got named nothin' in the end."

"Do you know what my father wanted to call it?"

"Yup, I do. Ravenswood. That's what he chose. He'd seen them — the ravens. They came down from the mountains and forests sometimes, they did, and that's what he wanted. You all right, ma'am?"

The old man looked at his mistress with alarm. She had closed her eyes, swayed, and held on to the balustrade for support.

"Ravens? Surely there are no ravens around here, are there?"

"Well, not so as you see them every day, but up in the hills and such —" The caretaker waved his hand in a wide arc that encompassed the Adirondacks, the Catskills, and even the Berkshires. "Kind of pretty, I thought, but there you are, so it got called nothin'."

"Ravenswood," Beth repeated. The wind had freshened and was tugging at the new spring leaves, blowing the twigs and dead leaves of the previous year from under the caretaker's broom.

"Looks like we got another storm on the way," he announced cheerfully. "I'd best be getting on with me chores, or there'll be nothin' left to sweep up!" Chuckling at his little joke, he pushed his fast-scattering pile of debris down the steps in the direction of his wheelbarrow, leaving Beth standing alone.

She pushed open the front doors, and made her way back into the darkness of the oval reception hall. The cool green and white of the marble gleamed with an austere light, and she felt chilled. The hall suddenly reminded her of the catafalque in the Pantheon in Paris, where the ashes of the famous dead are kept. She hurried through to the gold salon, where there was a fire lit.

Some of her father's books were still on the shelves

of the gold salon, and among them Beth found an old field guide to the birds. She took it down, sat beside the fire, and turned up the entry she was looking for.

"Raven. *Corvus corax*. 1) Northern Raven. C.c. principalis. N. Can. to S. Minn., Mich. and Me. A few in mts. s. to Ga.; occasional on coasts of N.J. and Va."

There was also an American raven with a somewhat different distribution.

The objective, unemotional words on the yellowed page were strangely comforting, confirming the caretaker's information. How much more chilling it would have been if she had found there were no ravens here! This was part of their range, and if she saw one, that would be the only reason for its presence. It would not come as a sinister portent from another world. Such fears belonged to lands where the dead were thrown from towers or where women sat like harpies in their faded finery, staring sightless into the distance, beyond the shabby splendour of their surroundings.

Through the silk velour draperies over the long windows, Beth could hear the wind rattling and tapping the creeper against the window. Think of Miss Austin, she thought, think of practicalities. Instead, she heard other words in her mind — "a tapping, as of someone gently rapping." What a time to think of Edgar Allan Poe! "Oh for God's sake, Beth," she said out loud, getting up impatiently from her chair and bending over the comforting warmth of the fire — "deep into the darkness peering, long I stood there, wondering, fearing —"

There was a sharp rap on the door and she jumped so violently that the field guide fell from her hand onto the hearth. Beth snatched it up before it could be scorched and turned to see the caretaker's wife standing there.

"Oh, Mrs. Biemann, it's you!"

"Yes, ma'am. I came to find out if there was anything you were wanting Jacob to add to his list."

"Jacob — his list?"

Mrs. Biemann looked surprised. "Yes, ma'am, the supplies. In case we get another ice storm, though it's unlikely."

"Oh yes — I mean, no, there's nothing, Mrs. Biemann."

"Very well, ma'am, I'll tell him. We're just off." Mrs. Biemann hesitated a moment in the doorway. "Is anything wrong, ma'am? You look — well, you look pale."

"Oh no, I'm fine, Mrs. Biemann." Beth laughed and wondered if the other woman heard the hysterical quality in the sound. Apparently she hadn't, because she merely said, "Very well, ma'am. I'll let him know."

As the door closed on Mrs. Biemann, Beth came to a decision. She was becoming too introspective; she should go back to New York and get busy. She owed a great deal of hospitality, for a start — she'd been asked out so many times and had given virtually no dinner parties. In a few years I will be thirty, she thought, and I have spent a decade loving a man I seem destined not to have. It's time I got on with my life. In so many ways, I am still a rich fool.

She smiled to herself as she thought of Liane and started up the stairs to her bedroom. From a disastrous marriage had come her rebellious, loving, strong-minded daughter, without whom she could not now imagine her life. It was time to go back to her, and the next time she came to this house she would make sure Liane and Miss Austin were with her. How they would laugh at her imaginary fears. One would tell her that she read too much, and the other would say she sounded liverish and in need of a good purge.

Giggling, she swung open her bedroom door.

"Beth? Where are you, Beth?"

Somewhere, behind her, in the reception hall downstairs, someone was calling her name. Beth saw her own face reflected in the large pier glass between the bedroom windows, and was confronted by the image of her own terror: lips parted, eyes staring in a white face blasted by fear.

"I know you are here, Beth — I know you are here."

The Biemanns might not yet have left for town. She must go downstairs, confront him, get herself closer to the possibilities of help or escape. Calmly, she thought, *doucement*, Beth — sweetly and gently, as though you suspected nothing, feared nothing. She saw the knuckles of her hand white on the doorjamb just before she turned and walked back to the top of the circular staircase.

"Max — is it you?"

She heard her voice ringing out across the empty space, floating down to echo back off the green-and-white Italian marble and reach the figure below.

"Me, sweet girl. It is really me!"

He was holding out his hands to her, smiling up at her. She had forgotten how handsome he was, with his supple stance that contrasted with the military set of his shoulders, the perfectly shaped head, the even, aristocratic features. When she had tried to recall over the years how she had been so in love with Count

Maximilian von Schönstein, she had been unable to imagine it. Now that she saw him again, after all the time that had separated them, she understood.

She looked down into the sensuous glance of the velvet brown eyes that could change so instantly to a champagne sparkle, mercurial and quicksilver like his moods, which moved with fascinating, alarming ease from gaiety to the fire of anger or passion. Even now, knowing what she did, she understood. One could kill for this man, she thought. Yes, one could kill for him.

Or be killed. The fear which had for the moment been submerged by the shock of her discovery surfaced again.

"Come down, darling girl, come down! Or shall I come to you?" With the lightness of movement she remembered so well from the dance floor, and from her bed, he ran to the foot of the stairs.

"No, no — I'll come to you, Max. Wait there while I come to you."

Never had the flight of stairs seemed so long, so cold beneath her feet, and his eyes watched her face as she came toward him, every inch of the way. Other words from the past returned to her, lines read to her by another love in the magic of summer Venice: "like a wild-eyed angel, I shall come to you in the night shadows — and I shall give you kisses cold as the moon, serpent-caresses — as others rule your youth with tenderness, mine shall be a rule of fear."

Le Revenant. More than just an apparition or spectre, but the one who returns. You read too much, you are too much on your own. Think, Beth. Be practical — what would Miss Austin do?

"So beautiful — even more beautiful than the young

girl you were. Perfect and remote and cold, like an angel, like a phantom." Had he read her thoughts? Steady, Beth, think like Miss Austin.

"Max, how wonderful! Let me ring for Mrs. Bie-mann — let me order —"

"No, Beth — no Mrs. Biemann. The elderly lady, is it? She has left with the man. We are alone."

So much for her pathetic attempt at subterfuge. He must have watched them leave and let himself in. She had not heard the front door, but she herself had used the French windows in the dining room earlier in the day, and she could not recall locking them. The Biemanns themselves only checked all the doors at night.

"So romantic, Max." She kept her voice light, tried a little laugh.

"*Natürlich* — I am Viennese!" Laughing at her, he took her in his arms and whirled her around the great oval hall, their feet moving smoothly across the marble floor.

His fully cut dove-gray coat swirled around them, his teeth gleamed white as he laughed and sang to her in his creamy tenor voice: "*Wien, Wien, nur du allein, sollst stets die Stadt meiner Traüme sein.*"

When Beth made as if to move from his arms, she felt him grip her hand and waist, and fear paralyzed her so that she stumbled and fell against him.

"Beth, darling girl, sweet girl, come closer — remember, remember when we made love? I made you happy, no? I made you happy?"

"You made me happy, Max."

She saw his mouth coming toward hers, and it seemed thinner, more cruel than she remembered beneath the silky moustache. A thrill of distaste surged through her and she tried to push him away. "No, Max, no!"

She would pretend no longer. She would fight rather than let him kiss her or make love to her, and she would have to fight because the house was empty. There was no one to help her but herself. Over Max's shoulder, beyond the glass above the front doors, she could see the trees swaying and bending in the wind which had now come up strongly, adding its own keening note to the silent scream of fear inside her.

"You don't want me to make love to you?" Max was holding her away from him now, an expression of tender incredulity on his face, as if he bantered with a child. His hands, however, still gripped her hand and waist like vices.

"Max, it was over a long time ago, years ago. Leave me alone, Max. You don't need me anymore."

"Ah, sweet girl, but I do. Not to make love to, if you don't wish it. I only thought you might want to, after all these years. It is what I do best, *Liebe*, you know that. But I need you, Beth, I need you to tell me something."

She knew what he would ask, and there was nothing she could tell him. She looked desperately up at him and saw anguish in his eyes, not love or laughter, or even anger. It was the first time she had seen anything approaching suffering on her husband's face.

"They have hidden her from me, Beth. They have taken her from me — and I must have her, you see, I must. I have tried everything — drink, cocaine, other women — but I must have her. Nothing else is enough, only Gisela, my sweet girl, my sorceress — my snake-woman, my flower-woman, my butterfly-lady."

He was crooning at her, stroking the hair around

438

her face and neck, running his hands over her neck, her breasts. "Gisela, where are you? Where has he hidden you? Why have you gone from me?"

Beth put her free hand over his and held it, but his eyes looked through her, beyond her, searching blindly for the object of his obsession.

"She has gone, Max. Put her from you, learn to live without her."

"Live without her! Only if no one else has her — no one else can have you, Gisela!"

He was looking at her as he spoke, and he pinned her hand behind her back, holding her against him. Beth could feel his breath on her cheek, and it seemed to her as cold as the breath of one returned from the dead. For a moment she felt relief as she saw his expression change and the laughter come back into his eyes. When he spoke again, his voice was caressing, tender.

"So like her you are — the two of you, so alike. Was that why I chose you, I wonder, and not any of the other daughters laid with their dowries at my feet? She was already in my blood, and then I came here and saw you. Gisela, sweet girl — no one else's, you hear? Only mine, Gisela, only mine!"

Beth heard her own voice screaming, as if it were someone else who cried out. "I am Beth, Max! Look at me, I am Beth!"

"Not important, *Liebchen* — no matter, you see, for if I kill you, then I kill Gisela, hmm? Then you are both gone, and I shall be free. I don't want this pain, it is too ugly. I want to laugh and sing, Gisela — I don't want this pain any longer!"

"There will be no freedom, Max — this is not

Vienna, where your friends can protect you. I am not Franzi Valeska!"

For a moment Beth saw a flicker of sanity swim into his eyes, and then it was gone again. "Of course my friends will protect me — what are you saying? Life begins with us, the chosen ones; no one else matters. See, Franzi, I must have Gisela. No one can stop me, no one."

It seemed that there were now three women in the room with whom Max was struggling. Beth saw his hand move to an inside pocket and she screamed again, trying with her own free hand to grasp the knife before he could. Around her the room swayed dizzyingly, and there was a roaring in her ears as if he had his hands around her throat and was choking the life from her. Her vision was blurred as though darkness had fallen, and all she could see were his crazy, desperate eyes; all she could hear was the hoarse sound of his breathing as they struggled together. Her shoulders and arms felt painful and tired now; she could feel herself weakening. He was using the strength of his thighs to push her back against the wall near the front doors. Desperately Beth twisted her head around — if she could only break away from him she could run out through the doors. Perhaps she could manage to free herself at the moment when he tried to bring the knife down, when he would have to slacken the grip he now had on her hand and arm.

"Gisela — always mine — sweet girl, sorceress — you make me do this — you —"

She relaxed her grip and the light from the sconces above the doors reflected off the knife blade as it rose in the air. For a moment the flash blinded her, filling

440

the black space around her with a thousand points of light, and she could hear the roaring once more.

As the blade came toward her, Beth heard herself screaming as the points of light splintered and crashed around them both. Suddenly, there was a sharp pain in her back, and at the same time something hit the back of her head.

Before her, Beth saw Max von Schönstein staring at her. To the blackness and the glitter was added a throbbing scarlet, which seemed to be gushing and flowing from him in a great river of red across the white of his shirt front. Up above their heads great shards of glass rained down as, dazedly, Beth turned around.

It seemed to her that, somehow, there was a gaping hole where once there had been a fanlight tinted with the colours of the seasons. And as she looked up at it, across her line of vision flew a great bird, its wings motionless as it caught the currents of the upper air before it disappeared from sight.

When she turned back again, Max was at her feet, the folds of his coat spread around him like the wings of the great bird itself. The sound of a drum seemed to thunder through her head, beating out the words: "I have killed him. We have killed him. Gisela and I, we have killed him."

As the thought came to her, so did the image of one of the cards from the tarot. Not the Empress or the High Priestess or any of those who seemed to have a significance for herself or her *Doppelgänger*. Unaccountably, what Beth saw was the likeness of the Magician, juggling with spheres of gold, a magic wand in his hand.

After that came darkness.

Chapter Forty-Five

New York

Images surfacing in her mind, making her scream again; blood spouting from an open mouth — or was it his neck? — a roaring and thundering of forces beyond her control, the psychic strength of her and her *Doppelgänger*.

"I killed him — we killed him."

"It's all right, Beth, you didn't kill him. It was an accident — the storm killed him, or, rather, the glass did."

"You don't understand! We made it happen, Gisela and I. We had to, or he would have destroyed us, we had to!"

"You're right, Beth. If you had done it, it would have been out of necessity — but you didn't. You were injured yourself."

"He tried to kill me."

"Yes, but the knife didn't touch you, and it didn't touch him."

The mists started to clear at the words, her focus returning. She was in a hospital somewhere — how had she got to this starched white sanctuary? — and it was Henry who sat beside her.

"Am I in Venice?"

"No. New York. Dearest Beth, you've lost a week of your life, but you're going to be fine. You had a bad concussion."

"A week? How did you get here so fast?"

"I was already on my way. I got a wire from a Baron Eihrentahl that had me packed and gone from Venice in double-quick time, I tell you."

"He told you Max was coming to look for me."

"Yes."

"Did you find —?"

"No. The Biemanns found you. You'd been lying there for hours by the time they got back, I'm afraid."

Images again. Herself and Max — how must it have appeared to the horrified onlookers? Max, bathed in his own blood, and she beside him, the knife between them, and glass everywhere.

Glass. Why glass? Beth slipped away, into sleep this time, but it was the first thing she asked when she surfaced again and found Henry still by her side.

"Because the window broke — you know, the fanlight over the front doors."

Gold and scarlet, lemon and lime. Beth saw the trees beyond bending and swaying as they had done when she had struggled with Max. Henry leaned forward and took her hands.

"Beth, I don't know why you think that you and

a woman somewhere in Europe killed Max, but that's not what happened. It was a freak occurrence, and thank God for it, but there was nothing supernatural about it. The area was quite suddenly hit by a violent electric storm — it must have been just after the count reached the house, because the Biemanns were on the road at the time. It brought down one of the big elm trees outside the front doors, and it crashed right through the fanlight. It had already been weakened by the ice storm and Jacob was planning to get it cut down. What's more, the leading between the glass panels was weak, and could have given way anytime. When the tree came down, it smashed those heavy panels and the pieces must have been pushed into the hall with enormous force. One of them struck the count in the carotid artery and he bled to death in minutes. You yourself were hit on the head, neck, and back by one of the main branches. Beth, you had nothing to do with anything; this Gisela had nothing to do with anything. Even the knife had nothing to do with anything, as it turned out. It was a freak of nature, an act of God."

"Ravenswood — the bird!" Beth tried to sit up as something else came back to her, the memory of the great bird swooping away through the gaping hole. "A bird came through the window — a raven, I think, but it was so big. It flew over us and then went away."

"Perhaps it did, Beth," said Henry, gently pushing her back onto the pillows. "No one has mentioned seeing a bird, so it must have gone by the time the Biemanns got there. Or maybe it was the concussion, and you imagined it."

Beth didn't try to explain. Henry would only think she was hallucinating.

But she had not imagined it. It had been just as Gisela had said it would be, but it was only important to her. Only she knew the significance of the bird at that moment in her life: that a clairvoyant had seen both the moment and the raven a decade before, in another country. Beth saw Max, lying on the marble floor with the folds of his coat spread around him and thought suddenly of their daughter.

"Liane. What has she been told? How is she?"

"Better now that she has been told you're going to be all right. We had to tell her something, Beth, because it's been a week. I talked with the rest of the family and Miss Austin, and we decided to say that her father had come back to the States to try to make some sort of peace with you both, that he was killed in precisely the manner in which it happened. We didn't have to mention the knife, thank God, and we didn't have to lie about his death or your accident. I'm sorry we couldn't wait for you to decide what should be done."

"It's just what I would have said. She has been so — so uncurious about her father, so detached from any apparent need to know about him. I always felt it was because she had you and Jonty to stand in for him."

A spasm of pain crossed Henry's face and was gone. It was the first indication to Beth that Henry had any regrets at all about his way of life. She looked at her brother, at his dark good looks which were quite like her own, only gentler and softer, with his father's hazel eyes. On the surface he had none of the effeminacy of Jonty's voice and carriage.

"Henry, do you ever regret the way life has turned out for you? Do you wish you had made other choices?"

Henry smiled. "Of course I have regrets, Beth — who hasn't? But this is the way I am; nothing can change it and it has nothing to do with Jonty or anyone else. I used to wonder about it a good deal, but now I take life as it comes, and I've stopped blaming Mother, or Father, or myself. No point, is there?"

"No." Suddenly it hit her. "I'm a widow, aren't I?"

"Yes, you really are now, although you have been without a husband for years, haven't you? The funeral was yesterday — very quiet, just the family and Miss Austin. Liane cried, but we think it was as much because she was frightened of losing you as anything else. They say she can come and see you tomorrow." Henry paused. "Beth, Jonty and I know where Anthony is. He's back with his parents and is going to Oxford. Do you want —"

"No, no — oh no!" In that moment of recollection, Beth knew how enormously inappropriate it would be to rekindle what had been between them, even if it were possible. Anthony Rivers was a glorious memory, and he belonged in the golden summer of the imagination.

The marvellous boy. Where had she seen or heard that? They had read it together, she and Anthony, about a poet, she thought, who had died young.

No. Leave that thought alone and bury it deep. Keep only the aura, the essence of the affair in her heart, and be glad it happened.

She had not loved and lost Anthony Rivers, for he

was a dream, and not reality. The man she had loved
and lost was Liam O'Connor.

Beth found it impossible to think of going back to
the house on the Hudson. She had no desire to relive
the images that still came in the night, though they
had now disappeared from the daylight hours. When
Aunt Medora first mentioned the Berkshires to her
she had been reluctant to take her advice, imagining
another Newport. However, Henry had persuaded her
it was a good idea to get away somewhere new for
her convalescence and had offered to come with her
and Liane, as Miss Austin was returning to England
for the summer. They went by automobile with as
much luggage as they could pile in, the rest being
sent on by train.

As soon as they had crossed the Taconic Range and
were into the Berkshires themselves, Beth was won
over. It was an overcast day, with rain threatening,
and the towering mountains with their thickly wooded
lower slopes, the empty stretches of valley with barely
a house in sight, seemed as splendid as anything she
had seen anywhere in Europe.

Through her aunt's family connections she had
rented a house in the vicinity of Lenox and Lee, close
to the Housatonic River. It was not a huge estate with
exotic gardens, nor yet one of the imitation Italian
villas erected as country cottages by people like her
father, but a pleasant, solid brick house in a Georgian
style, with large airy rooms reassuringly free of gilding,
heavily ornate woodwork or chilly expanses of Italian
marble.

With the return of her health, Beth gradually became

aware of a new sense of freedom. It took time for her to realize that the difference was the fact of Max's death. Absent from her life though he may have been, his dark presence had always been with her, even those times she had been happy: laughing with Jonty and Henry in Venice or Rome, or in someone else's arms. In the limpid air of the Berkshires she took what seemed like the first truly deep breaths she had taken in a decade. It was a sensation so satisfying that the absence of other emotions seemed of little account.

When she returned to New York in the fall the doctors gave her a clean bill of health. There appeared to be no permanent neurological damage from the head injury, and the specialists were as pleased with her emotional recovery as she was.

Beth had not asked Henry why he and Jonty had decided to spend the whole summer apart. She knew that it was more than just Henry's decision to be with her, because they had invited Jonty to come and stay with them.

Letters arrived from him all summer, so she presumed the relationship was not over, and a week or so after their return to New York, Jonty walked into Beth's new apartment on Fifth Avenue.

"Jonty! How marvellous to see you! Henry's not here at the moment, I'm afraid. He's taken Liane to a dog show, of all things."

Jonty embraced her warmly, and Beth felt real pleasure at seeing his worldly, smiling face once more. He looked tanned and fit, and, as usual, extraordinarily elegant.

"That's fine, Beth, because I really have to talk to you, and alone is best. How are you feeling? You look wonderfully well."

"I feel it." Looking at Jonty, she saw that his eyes were serious, searching her face as if trying to see for himself the truth about her words. She knew immediately what he was going to say. "Gisela. You've seen Gisela. Is that why you went to Europe and Henry stayed with me?"

"Partly. It's a little more complicated than that, but we certainly agreed I should try to see her while I was over there."

"Where is she?"

"Back in Vienna by now, I should think, but I saw her in Paris, just before the great summer exodus."

"She knows? How was she?"

"She knows, of course. As to how she was — when I found her, she was dancing the tango in a dress that clung to her like a cloud of gray smoke, with one of those gorgeous new toques on her head, laughing at a very Prussian-looking gentleman who nevertheless danced superbly and whose eyes were almost indecently explicit when he looked at her, which was all the time."

"Rudi."

"Yes, that's what she called him." Jonty sat down opposite Beth, took out a gold cigarette case and lit up one of his favourite Turkish cigarettes. Narrowing his eyes against the fragrant smoke, he leaned back and drew deeply on it.

"Beth, Henry and I knew you would eventually want to go after the loose ends that still lay unravelled in Europe, and we decided I should do it —"

"Before I did," said Beth. "Jonty, you sound unrecognizably serious."

"Don't I? But I am, Beth, for the moment." Jonty

leaned forward and took Beth's hand in his. From Jonty, who kissed and embraced at the drop of a hat, such a gesture combined with seriousness was rare.

"Listen, Beth. I went to see Gisela Valeska at the Hotel Vendôme, where she was staying. There is more to her than meets the eye, and I feel a fool saying this now, but she gave me goosebumps."

"You don't have to explain that to me."

"And, my God, she looks like you! That gave me the shivers too." The pressure on Beth's hand intensified. "Leave her alone now, Beth, and everything to do with her and Count von Schönstein. The message she had for you says the same thing: 'Tell Beth to turn back on the past — for herself, for Liane and the Fool.' She said you would understand the last part."

Beth could feel the tears burning in the corners of her eyes. "I understand, but I'm not sure Gisela does, anymore. Not about the Fool. Jonty, did you tell her what happened?" Beth felt Jonty's hand on hers shake slightly.

"I didn't have to tell her, Beth. She already knew — everything, even things I didn't know, or understand."

Perception came to Beth, clear and unshadowed as if she too had the gift of prescience. "She saw the raven in the glass, didn't she, Jonty?"

Jonty didn't reply, but Beth could see that he was shaken. He let go of her hand and drew deeply on his cigarette.

"I don't know what she saw, Beth. I couldn't understand the half of what she was saying."

"Jonty, listen." Beth leaned urgently toward him. "I know you did this for me; I know you want me to forget all about what happened, but I cannot. I have to go, Jonty. I have to see her again. Then, I promise you, I'll be only too happy to put the past behind me and forget. Until I do this, the nightmares will stay with me. I have to see Gisela Valeska just once more."

Jonty was silent for a moment, and then he said quietly, "She warned me this might happen. She felt you would see each other again. She told me to tell you she would be in Vienna, waiting for you."

Chapter Forty-Six

Vienna

The guests in the foyer of the Ringstrasse's Grand Hotel could not help staring at the two women. At this moment in their lives the resemblance between them was more striking than it had ever been, as if the shared circumstances of their lives over the past few years had softened the differences that had once existed. They stood, smiling at each other, clasping hands. Beth spoke first.

"You are happy."

"Yes, I am happy."

This was a different Gisela from the gaunt beauty Beth had seen in Paris. She was glowing in her deep pink dress, shining as if with an inner light. She took

Beth by the arm and said, "My car is waiting outside. Let us see if we can find what you are looking for, Beth."

In the sleek, chauffeur-driven Daimler phaeton Gisela said, "I am taking you to as much of the answer as I can give you."

"Doesn't the answer lie with you?"

"Only part of it, and even I cannot explain everything he has told me."

"He? Baron Eihrentahl?"

Gisela laughed. "No, not Rudi. He would prefer me to forget about the past, about clairvoyance, about this man — everything. But I owe this man a great deal and I want you to meet him. The circle will be completed and I too shall be content."

"Why did you think I would come?"

"Arcanus told me you would."

Arcanus. Hidden. Was that not what they called the tarot — the Grand Arcane?

The Daimler stopped outside one of the more magnificent of the Ringstrasse mansions, where they were admitted by a footman as powdered and periwigged as his eighteenth-century forerunners would have been. In some of the Ringstrasse palaces, it seemed, time had stood still. He bowed to Gisela and motioned toward the stairs.

"He is waiting for you."

They started up the colossal marble staircase together and Beth heard Gisela's breath catch. "Take my hand, Beth. Here I always think of *Mutti*."

Beth too had her own memories of great marble flights leading to terror and the unknown. As the two women climbed they sensed there were other ghosts hovering somewhere in the shadows beyond the circle of light from the chandelier high in the painted ceiling overhead.

At the top of the stairs, Gisela turned and led the way to a pair of heavy doors at the end of a dimly lit corridor. When they reached them, she turned the handle and let them both in without bothering to knock first.

At the other end of the room sat a man built like a giant. He was very old, his long hair white, his shoulders stooped. But an undefinable power shone from his tawny eyes.

"Arcanus — Alexei — this is Beth."

"Empress. I am Alexei Islenyev."

The voice was as strong as the voice of a much younger man, and when he smiled at her Beth caught a glimpse in her mind's eye of a young colossus of a man, laughing, the world at his feet.

As Beth crossed the room Alexei Islenyev extended his hand to her. It was gnarled with age, the skin as white as the bones beneath. When she touched him, it was as if the blood that ran in his veins flooded into her in a continuous stream and she had become one with the currents of energy that gave him life. Behind her, Gisela put her hand on Beth's shoulder, and Beth could feel the imprint of each of her fingers as clearly as she had once seen the imprint of a deer's hoofs in fresh snow.

She must have made some involuntary movement, because she heard Gisela say, "Don't be alarmed. He needs no crystal, nor yet the tarot. He will show us, in his way, and it will be clearer to me now that you are here."

The sequence of events that followed she could never fully remember or try to explain, for suddenly the room they were in disappeared and Beth saw the Hudson Valley. She was not inside the house, but was an observer beyond the trees, above the green lawns, looking down on the fanlight above the front door.

Beyond the glass she could see two figures struggling, slowly, as if they fought in water, as though someone had choreographed for them a macabre dance of death around the central point of the knife blade that glittered in the air. Beth saw herself, and she saw Max. Or was it Gisela who struggled and she who watched beyond the elms?

"Gisela, Gisela!" She heard Max's voice, full of longing and desperation, and Beth wanted to weep for him, put out her arms and save him from the moment of destruction that had already begun in the movement of the trees that dipped and swayed beyond the glass.

And it seemed to her as she watched that a great bird came out of the heavens and that his eyes were the golden eyes of Alexei Islenyev. His claws were like the hands of the magician, and in them he carried a branch as thick as a tree trunk which he thrust through the glass, onto the dancing figures.

Then a roar like a cataract hung in the air, entering Beth's brain. Like music, pure and powerful, it filled her with sound just before she felt an impact on the back of her head, then she was inside the house, fainting again, falling again.

When she opened her eyes, or regained consciousness, or whatever it was that happened, she saw the room in the Ringstrasse mansion, the man called Arcanus before her and Gisela by her side, just as they had been before the vision. She opened her mouth to speak, but Arcanus put one gnarled finger to his lips.

"Ask me not. There is no answer. It is as you saw it, and only thus can it be answered."

"One question — there is one thing I must ask you." The magician bowed his head.

"Why? Why for me?"

Alexei Islenyev looked at Gisela, and his smile was the smile of a young man, confident and tender, as if sure of his power to charm.

"For her. For the daughter I never had, the wife I never had, the woman I loved and lost. Once in the past, when I was a young fool."

The Fool again, laughing and dancing on the edge of the abyss. It made Beth think of the world she had left behind. Arcanus seemed to have read her thoughts.

"Yes, that is what matters now. You must go. We are the past and you are the future. You and she — you are not the same and never were. That is why you survived. The link between you was your physical resemblance and the count's mad obsession. That has now gone, and there will be a new madness that will sweep his kind from the circles of power. Whether what comes after that will be any better remains to be seen."

There still remained one more question Beth had to ask. "Why did I come here? Why did it seem so necessary to me?"

"To complete one circle before starting the new. It is only because you have seen the completion that you wonder now at the need." Suddenly he seemed exhausted. He leaned back in his chair, waving his hand at Gisela.

"Take her now, Gisela. Get her out of Vienna as soon as possible. *Adieu*, Empress."

The audience was clearly over. Arcanus the Magician sat with his eyes closed, as if he had already forgotten they were with him, and Beth saw for the first time that he was far older than she had realized. The closeness of his death seemed to brush against her in the silent room like the wings of a great bird.

There were Venetian carnival masks on the wall of the café in Trieste, where Beth was awaiting a boat to take her back to America. They made her think of Italy, of happy memories and laughter and love. For Europe had not been all unhappiness, even though it had been sadness that had brought her back to Vienna to meet Gisela Valeska.

When they had said good-bye in the foyer of the Grand Hotel, Beth had noticed with surprise that there were tears in Gisela's eyes.

"Don't cry, Gisela — you are happy now, aren't you?"

"Yes. And so will you be happy, Beth, I know it. One should remember only the beautiful in life. Beautiful things are like crystal, for when you look at them you see through them to true reality, the absolute. That's why beautiful things make one happy."

"I'm not sure I know what you mean."

Gisela had laughed and said, "Neither am I, but it is Rudi's rationalization of what I do, what I see. He calls it *Reine Anschauung*, pure perception."

"Is that how you see it?"

"No. There is no rationale."

No rationale, no rhyme, no reason? What did she, Beth, believe?

Enough. Beth forced herself to turn her thoughts away from the past to the present, to this city which was the crossroads of the Austrian, Italian, and Slav cultures. Trieste seemed to sum up for her the cultural riches of Europe, a mixture as flavorful as the meal she was eating: Austro-Hungarian sausage with an Italian wine, followed by a cup of rich, aromatic Viennese coffee. Smiling at her fancy, Beth looked out at the gray evening light which was beginning to descend over the treelined promenade curving along the city's waterfront.

But as she watched the sun set, a feeling of melancholy washed over her and suddenly Trieste, with its mixture of races — Magyar, French, German, Slovene, Serbian — all of them marching to the music of their own drums — seemed inexpressibly sad. The strains of "The Blue Danube" waltz seemed to fill the air around her and the gay melody of the Saxony Dragoons' regimental march now sounded ominous and threatening.

The vision returned of herself and Max dancing their death-waltz, the knife shining in the air between them. And the sound of Max's laughter.

"Süsse Mädel." All of them, caught like flies in honey, the sweetness cloying, choking them. Beth shivered. She would never be able to explain what the three of them had seen in that room. The vision had been fit only for the baroque splendour of the Ringstrasse *Palais*, now hundreds of miles away in the decayed and fading empire of the double eagle.

Chapter Forty-Seven

New York

It was enough that her ghosts were laid to rest, Beth told herself. Now she must give her attention to her daughter and to her own career. Perhaps it was just as well that she could not share what she had experienced with anyone, she thought, since it left Arcanus and her vision permanently in the past, and her nightmares had disappeared. It was enough that she was now forever free of Max who had bound her to Gisela Valeska.

But it was not enough and she knew it. Without the nightmares there was space and time for dreams that were filled with longing and from which she awoke empty of hope. Beth told herself that they too would pass. After all, Gisela had told her she would find happiness and she had been given enough reason in the past to believe in her predictions.

Apart from Liane, her most constant companions were Henry and Jonty. They had been trying to persuade her to come to Europe with them for the winter, and although she was tempted, she felt she had to stay in New York for both Liane's sake and her own career plans.

"I cannot play the dilettante anymore, Henry, I really can't. Besides, I don't want to, not really."

Her brother gave her a long, loving look. "And yet you are still sad, Beth. Jonty and I can see it — underneath that calm exterior you are sad."

"I think it's a sadness I would take with me to Europe, Henry. I don't think Venice or Paris would provide a cure this time. It's not like hay fever, unfortunately."

"What isn't?" Henry asked. Beth turned aside his question with one of her own, directed at Jonty.

"What do you find is the best cure for when you are sad, Jonty?" she asked, her voice light and unconcerned.

Jonty, who understood only too well how to dismiss painful reality, was out of his chair in a moment. He took Beth by the elbows and pulled her to her feet.

"Hey, Beth, can you tango? Yes? Come on, we'll all go out on the town tonight. Let's dance, dance, dance!"

Suddenly the room was filled with laughter as Jonty whirled her around, talking nonstop, peppering her with questions. "Where shall it be — Bustanoby's?

Louis Martin's? *Viva la cabaret*, Beth! Where do you want to go?"

"I don't know, Jonty — oh, I don't know!"

From the doorway came the sound of Liane's laughter as she watched her mother and Jonty whirling around the room. Henry grasped Liane's hands in his and pulled her into the centre of the room. "C'mon, honey! You be my partner!" Over his shoulder he called out, "Murray's, Beth, let's go to Murray's!"

It was like being in Italy again, when love and laughter came easily and the happy ending was being with Henry, Jonty, and Liane, and no one else. This was the fairy tale, and she needed nothing more.

Murray's Roman Gardens on West Forty-second Street had been in existence for a while but had recently taken up the current craze for cabaret entertainment. As at most of the other lobster palaces, a meal now came liberally seasoned with dance and entertainment in which the customers sometimes took part. As always, champagne flowed along with the wine, the whiskey, and the songs. Murray's cabaret boasted a revolving dance floor, and the decor was a heady mix of Egyptian rooms, Roman gardens, statues, and a French exterior in the imperial classical style.

When Beth, Henry, and Jonty walked into the mirrored dining room, they were among gamblers, gangsters, actors, and socialites — the eclectic blend of Murray's clientele. On the dance floor a striking young couple was demonstrating the cakewalk to a tune that sounded dissonant and ragged to Beth's ears. She looked at the movements of the two dancers and then at her companions.

"Wow!"

"You should see how they do it in Harlem."

"No, she shouldn't, Jonty. She's quite shocked enough by this."

Although she protested at Henry's remark, he was right. There was something new and disturbing about the messages conveyed by the rhythm, the effect it had on her. She wanted to dance, dance and — yes, she wanted to make love again. She did not yet care to think about who the man might be, and she wondered, as she had wondered before in her life, if it actually mattered to her which man it was.

People were staring at her and that too gave her a good feeling. She wore a Paul Poiret-inspired dress and turban that she had had made in New York from drawings Jonty brought back from Paris; it was in shades of yellow and copper, colours she had never worn before. On the front of the turban sparkled a golden topaz holding a small white plume of feathers. She had painted her lips, coloured her cheeks, and shaded her eyelids, and she felt like a new woman, more than ready to join this world of young bloods and old roués, this new bohemia so unlike the other bohemian world she had so briefly touched what seemed like a lifetime ago.

What has love to do with anything? she wondered, laughing at Henry and Jonty over her glass of champagne. All that mattered was to feel happy, and there must surely be more than one man in the world who could make her feel that way.

"Countess?" Beth turned, surprised that anyone should recognize her. A sleek-looking gentleman was bending over their table, smiling at her. He was dressed expensively but showily, his hair slicked back with a high gloss, like a tango pirate from the Argentine. "Would you honour me with this dance?"

Panic filled her, the emancipated woman gone in an instant, replaced by the daughter of Ada Holman. "Why, I —"

"Forgive me, sir, but I had just persuaded the Countess to have this dance with me." Smiling blandly, Jonty bowed to the stranger and extended his hand to Beth. With a shrug of the shoulders, the stranger bowed and returned to a nearby table.

"Thank you, Jonty."

"Not at all. Now you're going to have to tango with me. Come on, Beth!"

What a handsome couple we make, she thought, watching herself and Jonty reflected in the mirrored walls, moving together in the seductively formal steps of the dance. His pale blond good looks were a perfect foil for her own dark vibrancy, and he was a marvellous dancer.

"You should have been a gigolo, Jonty!"

"I was, remember?"

"I didn't mean to —"

"And you didn't. I have only ever regretted the things I *haven't* done, the opportunities I've missed in life. I tell you, Beth, there's only one philosophy to live by in this life!"

The room whirled around her, the music strong and sweet, like Viennese coffee — *Kaffee mit Schlag* — cream and the bite of cinnamon. You are right, Jonty, how can I regret Max totally, when I have Liane? "And what's that, Jonty Shotover?"

"When in doubt — do!"

"No *don'ts*, none at all?"

"Very few, Beth, very few."

She heard her laughter across the sound of the music, and it sounded to her like the laugh of the very young girl she had once been, a long time ago, when Max von Schönstein had smiled at her and swept her off her feet and into his arms.

It was at the very moment she was remembering Max that she saw him. Just when she was deciding no more regrets, no more sorrowing and sighing, that there was more than one man in the world who would do for her, she saw Liam O'Connor, and he had undoubtedly seen her. "Seen" was an understatement. He was staring with all the power of those eyes that could turn her bones to water. Beth stumbled and clutched at Jonty's hand.

"You okay, Beth? Are you getting tired?"

"No, I'm fine. I've just seen a ghost, that's all."

Jonty looked at her, perturbed, and moved them both to the edge of the dance floor. As he did so, he too saw Liam O'Connor.

"Oh, I see, that ghost. I thought you had had some visitation from Vienna or Bavaria."

"Worse, Jonty, worse. Oh God, let's leave, please."

"He's coming over." Jonty grasped Beth's hand tightly in his. "What a short memory you have, Beth my dear. Only regret the things left undone, the opportunities missed." Beth saw what looked suspiciously like tears in Jonty's pale blue eyes, so unlike the eyes she was desperate to avoid. "Is he too much for you, Countess? Lost your nerve, have you?"

"Jonty, you're a bully. Take me home."

In answer Jonty took her by the arm and led her around the edge of the dance floor toward Liam